WRITTEN IN VAMPIRE'S BLOOD: THE STRANGER

By Matthew & James Dale

Acknowledgement

This book has been in the works for a long time coming. So, we would love to thankfully acknowledge those who helped make it possible for it to finally be a tangible piece of literary work.

To my wife, Lindsay Dale, my son Matthew, and my daughter Marshae, who gave me motivation, when I was stuck and out of ideas. She encouraged me to write down my dreams and get it out of my head.

To my brother, James Dale, co-writer, and editor, who found a way to make the dream come true, putting the finishing touches on the first instalment of this series of books, to get ready for print. A billion thanks!

We would like to dedicate this book to our immediate families and friends, and to the next generation of great minds, our children, and our nieces and nephews.

Table of Contents

Introduction

Written in Vampire's Blood: The Stranger is the first installment in this series. This book follows Joy Maxwell, an ambitious southern belle, who moves to the Big Apple to fulfill her lifelong dream of becoming a news reporter, but soon realizes that she bites off more than she can chew.

This coming-of-age story includes the trials and tribulations of Adeline, an NYPD detective (and a fledgling). Against all odds, she survived the process of transitioning from life to the afterlife. She came to terms with her immortality, but her greatest challenges were solving the "Sanguine Murders" case, overcoming betrayal, and finding the strength to love again.

Chapter 1

Realizing her dream of becoming a full-fledged reporter has never been this close before for Joy Maxwell. But it comes at a sacrifice. She must move away from home to the big city, and her mother is not too pleased with the idea of her leaving.

"Joy, nothing good ever happens to a country girl with dreams of making it in the big city," she said. "I am your mother, and I love you. I trust that you will be okay. I know that little Savanah can't make you successful as New York can, so I wish you all the best. Be careful, darling. There are plenty of creeps and weirdos lurking in the shadows. The news reports strange things happening to people all the time."

"Momma, I'm a big girl," Joy said. "I can take care of myself; I promise."

"I love you, Darling, be careful and come home soon as possible."

The day started like any other day before; the sound of Joy's alarm clock woke her out of her sleep. She laid there and daydreamed about her mother's home cooking back home in Georgia. "If I were home right now, I would have a plate of a good ol' southern breakfast, smothered homemade biscuits with sawmill gravy, yummy grits, chicken fried steak, eggs over easy, and some fresh-squeezed orange juice," Joy mumbled to herself. "Boy, I do miss Momma's cooking. Not that I couldn't cook that spread myself, I couldn't finish all that by my lonesome."

Joy got out of bed and walked to her bathroom. She turned on the faucet in the tub and pulled the tab for the shower. She sat down on the toilet to relieve herself of all the guilt her mom gave her for leaving home and going up north to pursue her dream job as a reporter. "If Momma could see me now, Part-time reporter and part-time cashier at a supermarket. *I'm living the dream*," Joy said to herself.

Joy got in the tub and stood under the shower to wake up. She finished up, toweled off, and put on her clothes and apron. Her shift at the supermarket started soon. Luckily, she lives right up the street from there. Joy hurried up, grabbed her purse, and locked the door to her apartment. She turned around, and her neighbor, Mrs. Meddle, said, "Good morning, Joy."

Joy rolled her eyes and mumbled under her breath, "Nosey old buzzard."

"What's that, sweetie?"

"Nothing Ma'am—have a great day."

Joy exited her apartment building and turned to walk up the street. Joy's belly growled, and she rubbed her belly. Several patrons stood around a food truck outside of her building. Joy walked over to the vendor and said, "Good morning, kind Sir."

"Good morning, my lady," the Vendor replied.

"May I have a small black coffee, two sugars, and a corn muffin."

Joy pulled out some money from the front of her apron and paid the vendor for the coffee and corn muffin.

"Thank you!"

"Please come again."

Joy got to the supermarket rather quickly. Her manager was outside smoking a cigarette by the employee entrance in the alley.

"Good morning Mr. Gillman," Joy said.

"Good morning Ms. Maxwell," Mr. Gillman replied.

"Smoking those darn cigarettes out here is going to kill you one day," Joy said.

Joy entered the building and walked toward the lady's locker room. She and her co-worker bumped into one another in the hallway.

"Good morning, Deidre, she said. "You almost knocked me over."

"Sorry, good morning, Joy, I love your handbag; I have one just like it," Deidre replied. "You better hurry up, missy, you're going to be late. I don't understand how you live up the street from here and are always the last person to punch in for your shift."

"Thanks, you're a diamond in world filled with rhinestones." Joy quickly stored her jacket and handbag in her locker and walked over to her cash register. The day dragged along slowly, but it was only a couple of hours into her shift. Joy kept checking her watch after she cashed each customer out. "Thank you for shopping at Super-C supermarket. Please come again," Joy said with a genuine smile each time she cashed out a customer. Joy thought about a possible news story with each customer that came through her lane.

Then a tall, strange man wearing a long trench coat joined her line. His hood covered his head, his sunken eyes, baby face, and a crooked smile caught Joy's attention.

"Don't look now Joy, a freakazoid just joined the line in your lane," Deidre said. "From the looks of him, you might have to spray down the conveyor belt and use hand sanitizer after you cash him out."

Joy giggled and said, "Oh hush up now, you're too much."

The mysterious man put down his items on the conveyor belt one by one and stared directly in Joy's eyes without blinking or looking away, not even for a second. From the intensity of his gaze, he appeared to hypnotize her. Joy turned her head away and said, "Sir, your total is $19.08, p-p-paper or plastic?"

The man dropped a crumpled up twenty-dollar bill on the conveyor belt. He didn't break his intense gaze upon Joy. She straightens out the bill, put it into the register, and gathered his change.

She then put the receipt into his hand, which was resting palm up on the conveyor belt. She placed the change in hand.

The ominous man grits his teeth and grabs Joy's hand, and whispered, in Latin, "Cuncti dies unus moriatur."

Joy pulled her hand away, and she said, "Oh my lord, what did you say, Sir?"

The stranger didn't reply, and the man behind in line said, "Move it along, stalker before I make you."

He walked away, and Joy continued to cash out the other customers behind him in the line. Deidre walked over to Joy and asked, "Are you alright?"

"Yes, I think so," she replied. "Just a little spooked, I guess."

Nearing the end of her shift, Joy looked a bit perturbed about the entire exchange with the man that grabbed her hand earlier.

Joy sat there in front of lockers, hunched over in the fetal position.

Deidre walked into the lady's locker room and noticed that Joy was spaced out and said, "Joy! earth to Joy, come in Joy." Deidre nudged her and waved her hand in front of Joy's face. "Hey, snap out of it."

Joy came to, "Ah, I'm alright, Deidre," she said, batting her hand at Dierdre. "I'm okay; I was just thinking about that stranger from earlier; he gave me the creeps." Joy shivered like she had gotten the chills.

"Don't worry about him. You worry too much," Deidre advised.

"That guy is long gone. That creep left hours ago; it was at the beginning of our shift."

"I don't know; I just have this funny feeling."

"Would you feel better if I walked you home?"

"No, don't you worry your pretty little head over me, you go on home. Besides, it's raining outside, and I don't want you to catch a cold for my sake." Joy said, declining Deidre's offer.

"Are you sure, Joy?" Deidre insisted. "There has been a string of rapes and murders in this area. Haven't you heard about the *'Midtown Murders'* on the news?"

Joy shook her head and said, "Yes, I've heard about it, but that usually happens at night, and it is only five o'clock now. I am a little shaken, you know, but I'll manage."

Diedre sighed, "I guess you're right, Joy, you still have some daylight left; besides, you only live like fifteen minutes away from here," Deidre stated.

"That's true; I feel a little better now, thanks,"

"No problem, girl," Deidre hugged Joy. "I'll see you tomorrow, Joy."

"Okay, later."

"Now, I got to get home and get my son before my sister has a heart attack. You know, she is going clubbing tonight and probably has a hangover as usual," Deidre divulged to Joy. Deidre turned around and walked away.

Joy looked at her watch and walked towards her apartment building. Some cats in the alley jumped out of a full garbage can. She gasped and clutched her chest. The color drained out of her face, and the hairs stood up on the back of her neck. She looked over her shoulders and picked up the pace. The pep talk she had with Diedre didn't help; she thought about that strange man with every move she made.

Paranoid and nervous, she picked up her pace to a brisk walk. She didn't want to see the stranger from earlier today. "Maybe I should catch a cab to get home faster than my little legs could carry me," she said. She scanned the street, and there weren't any taxi cabs around. Her mind was racing faster than her heartbeat and legs. With every step she took, she thought about what her mother told her before she left for New York. *'Joy, I would never wish for you to fail, but not everyone survives the Big Apple.'* Despite her mother's doubts and with little determination, Joy came to *"The Big Apple, the city so nice they named twice."*

Joy came to the city to follow her dream of becoming an investigative journalist. So far, all she has been able to get is the occasional puff piece. Not exactly what she bargained for when she moved to the big city. In between, covering ladies showcasing their Dorito chip that resembled Elvis Presley. Joy worked part-time as a cashier for Super-C supermarket to make ends meet.

Joy ran through the minutes of the day, over and over in her head. As she got closer and closer to her home, she started to believe that maybe Deidre was right. Maybe she overreacted. "I haven't considered the fact that the bastard was a lonely nerd. And who's afraid of a nerd, right?

Everything has been good so far until today. When this strange man harassed her, he gave her the impression that he was going to her hurt her or something. Normally when people come through the line to get checked out, she greets them and makes small talk. But, when this man with the crooked smile came in her line and Deidre how strange he looked.

Plus, he gave her a chilling penetrating stare. A gaze of consequence, despair, one that told a story, a long tale that Joy was in, and she didn't want to know how it ended. Joy shivered at the thought of that creep when he rubbed her hand on the conveyor belt. She put her hand on her abdomen to stop the butterflies from swirling around in her stomach.

Nimbus clouds formed and heavy rain poured down out of the blue. "I'd better hurry up before I catch the death of a cold," Joy said with a southern drawl. "Even though I am already soaked from head to toe, I need to get home and get out of these wet close."

Not paying any attention to her surroundings, Joy fell in a deep puddle in the sidewalk. It was a gaping hole filled with dirty rainwater.

"Crud muffin!" Joy screamed. Budget cuts were the cause of this. Bureaucracy was ruining the city, and commercial contractors were blamed for leaving unfinished construction jobs all over the city. "Why wouldn't they leave a sign up that there is a hole here or something shit? Somebody is going to get killed, falling in one of these holes!" she said.

"Are you alright," a tall man asked her with concern as he helped her up.

"Yes, I'll be alright, I think," Joy responded with a little disgust in her voice."

"Are you sure," he said.

"Yes, Dammit!" Joy snapped at the good Samaritan, then slapped away his hand.

"Okay, alright, lady, I was just trying to help. You don't have to be a bitch about it." he articulated in exchange. Before he moved on, he mumbled, "I should've left your ass in that hole."

Joy's mascara drained down from the sides of her eyes. She curled her upper lip, and she rang out her dress and apron.

"My day couldn't get any worse than this." She made it to her apartment building and stopped at the entrance to take a breather. Moody, emotional and overwhelmed by the day, she just busted out in tears. "Is this what I moved here for? This can't be it. I moved here to showcase my talents as an investigative reporter. Not to be a cashier at a Super C supermarket," she said. "Today was the worst day ever: First that stranger scared the bejesus out of me, then I fell into a puddle of dirty water. This is just too overwhelming. I could scream."

Joy flashed the muddy water off her hands and continued to babble to herself. "I need to call home; my mother always knows what to say to make me feel better." The walk into the building was the longest ever. She was soaked and embarrassed. She sighed, and her shoulders slumped down to her sides. Her face was longer than the famous "I have a dream speech," but not as appealing.

Joy fumbled with the keys, then opened her mailbox. She pulled her mail out of it and locked it. She shuffled through the mail with each step up to the second floor where her apartment was. She didn't realize that she was dripping water all over the floor in the passageway. "Phone bill, electricity bills, credit card bill, at least they remember me," Joy says to herself in repulsion.

Joy looked down and noticed the mess that she made on the floor. The lobby was empty, so no one else saw the mess she had made. "I should just run upstairs before anyone else notices," she thought to herself. She sighed, dropped her head and hands by her sides. "Ignoring this mess will only make it worst. Plus, it would be wrong to have somebody fall on a wet floor. "Dagnabbit!" she shouts. "I'm just going to have to go upstairs and come back and clean this mess up."

All the commotion caught the attention of some of her nosey neighbors, who opened their doors to see what the commotion was.

"This day just won't end," Joy murmurs under her breath. This was just the beginning of Joy's problems. She clamored up the stairs to her door, took out her keys to open her door. She stopped and stared at a little damage between the door jam and the door, but she shrugged it off and entered her apartment.

Joy stepped inside and closed the door behind her. She threw the mail down on the kitchen table. Usually, she is very neat and organized. Normally, she would've put the mail in the tray by the door. She hated to create a mess because eventually, she would only have more to clean up. She just wanted to strip down to her birthday suit and jump into a warm and soothing bubble bath. But she resisted, at least until she mops up the passageway, stairs, and the lobby.

After mopping, Joy went back inside her apartment and still hadn't noticed the full extent of the damage to her door. She kicked off her wet shoes and hauled off her wet clothes in the kitchen. Then she put back the mop and bucket, then made a beeline straight to her bedroom. She carried all her wet clothes with her and draped them on the radiator to dry. She then turned on the faucet in the tub, checked the temperature to make sure it was just right. Then she walked into her bedroom and looking at her naked body through her full-length wardrobe mirror.

Joy stared at herself through the strands of her hair that fell onto her face She blew the hair away from her eyes, rubbed on her stomach, and put her hands on her hips. She smiled, stood up straight and recited one of her self-affirming mantras, "No regrets, Joy Maxwell."

Joy remembered something that her father told her every morning until he passed away. "Joy, live for today, but plan for tomorrow." The words from her dad made her realize that better days were always around the corner. She closed her eyes and rummaged her fingers through her hair to check if there weren't any pebbles or bugs in it. The soothing motion of this calmed Joy enough to relax her.

Joy walked back into the bathroom and turned off the faucet in the tub. She poured a fragrant French lavender bath oil from a set that she received from her mom this past Christmas into her bathwater.

She put her hand into the water and waded it in circles to blend the oil with the settled water. I should call my mother to give her the rundown about the terrible day that I had," she said.

Joy went into her living room for her handbag to get out her I-phone. Rummaging through her muddy and soggy handbag, she discovered that everything in her handbag was wet and filthy, including her I-phone. "Dang it! If one more thing happens to me today, I am gonna scream," she cried. She remembered reading somewhere that she can save her phone if she submerges it in some uncooked rice.

Joy sat down in the kitchen and dumped out the contents of the handbag onto the table. She picked up a picture of Deidre and her family. "Oh no, this is Deidre's handbag," she said. "Now I won't be able to call my mother tonight, the only thing left to do is take a bath and go to bed."

Joy pushed herself from the table and walked through the

living room. She noticed that the place was in shambles. "I've been so busy and distracted that I hadn't the time to clean up." She looked at her coffee table and saw one her of drinking glasses. A drinking glass that no one would know about because she hardly ever used it. This is a glass that she kept in the back of her cupboard and reserved for when the super comes to fix something. She never used it herself because a roach crawled in it and died when she first moved in. She was so disgusted that she stuffed it in the far recess of her cupboard.

"Be cool, Joy," she uttered to herself in reassurance. She hurried into her bedroom to put on a robe before going next door to Mrs. Meddles' apartment. "If anyone else but me came in here, she would know. If that is so, I could use her phone to call the police," she thought while knocking on Mrs. Meddles' door. Shivering in fear, she franticly waited for the neighbor to open the door. "Mrs. Meddles, Mrs. Meddles, it is me, Joy Maxwell," Joy yelled. She could hear Mrs.

Meddles through the door, walking as fast as she could to answer it.

"Who is it," Mrs. Meddles answered with a shaky tone.

Mrs. Meddles was eighty-seven years old, and the building's watchdog. She's a little old white-haired, fair-skinned black lady who wore a black pantsuit every day like she was going to a funeral. She used a cane and had all her teeth. The elderly woman always slipped that fact into all her conversations with people, especially to the children who lived in the building.

Joy always thought that she was too nosey, so she never said anything more than hi and goodbye. She regrets not talking with her more often. If she had, she would be sure that Mrs. Meddles would have paid more attention to her apartment. Like she does for all the other occupants in the building. Legend has it that she single-handedly got rid of some drug dealers several years ago. So, she is well known, well respected, and well-loved by everyone in the community.

Joy anxiously awaited as she listened to the locks on clang together as Mrs. Meddles unlocked them one by one. Locked doors were something that she could never get used to. Growing up in a small town, everybody left their doors unlocked. They never had to worry about break-ins. The only time that anybody in the town ever locked their door was during a big storm.

Finally, Mrs. Meddles opened the door and said with a slow, shaky voice, "Are you alright, child?"

"Mrs. Meddles, Mrs. Meddles, listen to me very carefully, did-you-see-anyone-go-in-to-my-apartment-to-day," Joy said slow and loud with panic in her voice.

Before she replied, Mrs. Meddles stepped to the side and waved Joy inside her apartment. "I am old, child, but I am not dumb, deaf, or blind, so you can talk to me like you have some sense, sweetie!" she said.

"But to answer your question, yes—yes, I did see a man, not the super, enter your apartment," Mrs. Meddles informed Joy. "He was tall and slender and wore a long trench coat. His eyes were dark a sunk into his pale, hairless face. He spooked me when he turned around and looked at me through the keyhole. It was like he could see into my soul. His glare hypnotized me."

As Mrs. Meddles described the man that she saw at Joy's door, the more she knew that it was the guy from the supermarket checkout line earlier. She got the chills and shivered; the hair on the arm stood up, and she had goosebumps all over her body. Her face went blank, and tension built up in her shoulders. She tried to swallow, but a lump was in her throat the size of a piece of coal made it difficult to do. A knot formed in her stomach, and she uttered, "M...Mrs. Meddles," Joy mustered up the strength to say. "C…can I use your phone to call the police; Please!" before the old lady could answer, she picked up the receiver and dialed 9-1-1.

"Hello, 9-1-1, what's your emergency?" a voice said on the other line.

Joy didn't answer the operator; she was stuck on the possibility that there might very well be the creepy guy in her apartment. The operator repeated her greeting a couple of times before she responded. "Y…yes, Ma'am, hi," she said, then repeated. "Yes, Ma'am, I…I am Joy Maxwell." While fear shot throughout her body, Joy said, "I think there's a strange man in my apartment."

"Ms. Maxwell are you there with someone now?" the operator asked.

"Yes, Ma'am, I'm at my next-door neighbor's house,"

"Ms. Maxwell, the only thing that we could do is send a police car out to your location to fill out a report. When the officers arrive, they will advise you to go down to the precinct and see a sketch artist so that we could put out a BOLO (Be on the lookout.) About an hour and forty-five minutes went by before the police showed up to fill out the report.

In the meantime, Joy had to endure the ramblings of Mrs. Meddles. When the police finally came and knocked on the door to Mrs. Meddles apartment. Joy opened the door and said, "Nice of ya'll to show up; I've been waiting here for over an hour."

"Sorry Ma'am, we got here as soon as we could, I'm officer Brothers, and this is my partner, officer Wong," he replied.

Smitten with officer Brothers, Joy stretched out her hand and said, "Charmed, I'm sure." She escorted the officers into her apartment, and they walked into her living room. They both took off their hats and put them under their arm. They looked around the apartment and didn't see anything out of the ordinary, just the damaged door jam. "Ma'am are you missing something out of your apartment?" asked officer Brothers.

"No, I hadn't had the time to check. But this glass was left on the coffee table, and I don't remember leaving it there," Joy replied.

Officer Brothers took down notes, raised his eyebrows, looked at his partner, then he put back on his hat. "Well, Ma'am, we don't see anything or anyone out of the ordinary, so there is not much we can do now. You could go down to the precinct to look at some mug shots."

"We'll escort you down there in our squad car. Have you ever been inside a police cruiser before?" Officer Wong asked.

"Okay, hold on, officers, give me a minute while I get dressed," Joy said without hesitation. "I had no intentions of staying at her apartment by myself." She held the front of her robe closed as she passed the two officers.

"Ms. Maxwell, Ms. Maxwell," the officers tried to catch her attention, but she pretended not to hear them. "I think she may have spooked herself out, watching a scary movie or a jealous ex-boyfriend is trying to freak her out," officer Wong said.

"Even if that's the case, let's just amuse her enough just to give her peace of mind," officer Brothers replied.

Joy was dressed and ready to go in a few minutes. She said, "I'm ready!" As she sprinted from her bedroom. She walked over to the table, gathered the items scattered about and put them back into the purse.

"Okay, Ms. Maxwell, we'll escort you downtown," officer

Brothers said.

Joy locked the front door, and they walked downstairs into the lobby and exited the building. She stopped and looked up at the moon above, admiring its beauty. She couldn't help but notice the color of the moon. It was a bright red hue. The flushed effect of Lady Lunar reminded her of blood, cold and deadly. The sight drew her mind to her mortality.

"Any time you're ready, Ma'am," officer Wong said. Joy broke her concentration from gazing at the moon, then officer Wong entered the vehicle on the driver's side and closed the door. Officer Brothers remained on the passenger side of the car and opened the back door for Ms. Maxwell.

"Thank you, officer Brothers, you're such a gentleman," Joy said and batted her eyes at the officer.

"Anytime, Ma'am, I'm here to protect and serve," he said and smiled at Joy, then he closed the door after she got inside the back of the car.

Joy crossed her legs, twiddled her thumbs on her lap. Officer Wong noticed how tense she was through the rear-view mirror and said, "You can relax, Ms. Maxwell; you're in the company of the police. We won't let anything happen to you."

Joy took a deep breath and exhaled. "You're right; this whole ordeal gives me the hebbie-jeebies," she said. "Forgive me, officers."

"Officer…what's your name again?" Joy asked.

Officer Wong said, "Me ma'am, are you talking to me."

"Yes, but please don't call me ma'am, my name is Joy maxwell. But y'all can call me Joy. Ma'am makes me feel old." Joy articulated with a hint of arrogance. Before officer Wong could answer, Joy changed the subject. "How long will it take to look through mug shots, officer Brothers?"

"It depends on you," officer Brothers replied

Joy thought that if she didn't recognize anyone from the mugshots, the officers could identify the stranger from the security tape at her job. She hoped that it would take all night because she doesn't want to go back to her apartment tonight alone.

Joy made small talk until they got to the precinct. She was intimidated by big-city police officers. She lived in the big city for a couple of years now and hadn't spoken to or met a cop. Coming from a small town in Georgia, everyone knew everyone. The station in New York seemed like a military base in comparison; everyone seemed preoccupied with themselves, very distant and disconnected. Her heart rate increased as indiscriminate chatter filled the room. There were criminals in handcuffs being brought in by officers. While detectives were interrogating people inside cubicles along the perimeter of the precinct.

A sea of unfamiliar faces surrounded Joy. Some had badges, guns, and others were criminals. It was hard to differentiate who's friend or foe. She panted, and beads of sweat formed on her forehead. The color drained out of her otherwise rosy cheeks. Everyone was like a bunch of worker bees, with no personal ties to the queen, just their duties.

"Ms. Maxwell, you don't look so good, please sit down, and I'll get you a beverage. While I'm gone, my partner will show you the mug shots," said officer Brothers.

"Thank you, officer Brothers, you don't have to worry about me," Joy replied, posturing as if she was sure of herself. "I'll be fine."

Joy sat at a desk, maybe it was officer Brothers' or his

partner's, but she couldn't tell which one because it was so messy. She sat at the desk and practiced some ujjayi breathing techniques to calm herself down. She hadn't been exposed to thugs, dealers, harden criminals, and victims of all types. She was sheltered, her parents protected her from being exposed to this type of environment. Everyone in the police department looked hardened yet venerable.

Joy realized how small and insignificant she was in the grand scheme of things. It was like witnessing a rose sprout through the concrete for the first time and understanding immediately why its thorns were so sharp. She understood why people who lived in a metropolis must be so guarded and anti-social. Being a reporter, she can't help but to analyze everything for what it's worth.

"Here we go," officer Wong approached the desk with six huge binders and dropped them on the desk.

"Wow!" Joy said with her southern drawl. "I can't believe that New York's finest don't have a database of mug-shots on a computer."

Officer Brothers approached the desk and put a can of soda down. He answered Joy with a stern tone, "Ms. Maxwell, we do have a database of mugshots on the computer, but these photos that are in the binders happen to be older suspects and a possible match the suspect of your situation. So, if you want our help, here you go. Search in this binder first, then let us know if you find anyone that fit the description of who you say may have broken into your apartment."

Embarrassed and overwhelmed, Joy opened the can, took a sip, cleared her throat, and opened one of the huge binders of mugshots without another word. Joy carefully looked through the binders and didn't find anyone who'd even looked close to her ominous starker.

"I don't recognize anyone from these mugshots. What are we going to do?" She asked while raising her arms in the air then flopping them down by her sides. "I don't want to go back to that apartment knowing that somebody has been inside there without me knowing."

"Ms. Maxwell, you told us that you didn't see anyone else in your apartment, correct?" asked officer Brothers.

"Yes, but I know someone else was in there. You don't believe me; you and your partner think I'm crazy. What was it you and your partner said at the apartment…? Oh yes, *'Maybe she just spooked herself after watching a scary movie.'*

Officer Brothers stood there with one hand akimbo and scratched his head with the other one. Joy slouched in her seat and pushed the binder away from her. She looked up at the clock, put her head down, and sighed. It was just 12:36 am, a long way away from sunlight. She folded her arm across her chest and rubbed her temple. *"What could I come up for us to do for six hours?"* she thought. Then she sat up straight and asked, "Officer Brothers, what about the…?"

Before Joy could finish what she had to say; she was abruptly interrupted by a giant of a man. "Brothers," he said with a deep, authoritative voice, "Where's your partner?"

"She's around here somewhere, Captain," he said while surveying the room. "She must've stepped out for a second, Captain Constantine." Officer Brothers answered like he was a student being reprimanded by the school principal.

Joy sat there with a bewildered look on her face because officer Brothers was such a brawny specimen of a man.

"I need for you guys to go out to this address." The captain handed officer Brothers a piece of paper.

"What happened?" Officer Brothers said and looked down at the paper with a puzzled look on his face.

"I don't know. I just received an anonymous call. The caller said that someone was just murdered at that location. When you find him, whoever this wacko is, nail his ass to the wall because he asked for me specifically. So, you two check it out, get on it right away."

"I'll get right on it, Captain," officer Brothers answered like he was relieved to leave Joy behind; he didn't want to babysit her anymore. He'd seen women become paranoid from living alone. He felt in his bones that Joy was just overreacting. But to err on the side of caution, he didn't want to leave her at the apartment alone. In case there was some credence to her story. "Captain, I have a young lady here who may be in trouble," he explained. He gave Captain Constantine the run-down of Joy's situation.

"Okay, I'll handle it, go ahead and see if there's some substance to the claim," Captain Constantine said. "Get on it, officer Brothers."

Officer Brothers marched out of the precinct and bumped into his partner, holding two cups of coffee in her hands. "Hey, break time is over," he said. "Capt. wants us to head out on a call."

"Okay, it's about time we see some action. What about Ms. Prissy?" asked officer Wong.

"Capt. said he'd take care of her."

"Okay young lady, I am Captain Warrick Constantine. I will help you with your problem," he said soothingly to Joy. "Follow me to my office, so I can hear your story and possibly find a solution to your problem." Captain Constantine turned around and headed to the office at the end of the corridor, and gestures for Joy to follow him.

The precinct was split in two in a huge open bay. It had a row of desks facing each other on either side of the building, leaving a walkway in the middle. Sort of like an old police T.V drama, like "Hill Street Blues." The desks were sectioned off for criminal importance burglary, narcotics, homicide, etc.

Joy speed walked after the captain, trying to keep up with him, but he was too fast, and his legs were too long. He asked her a few questions, but Joy couldn't hear him because of the roaring crowd in the department. The precinct was swarming with policemen, victims, and thugs exchanging some expletives and pleasantries. Joy quickly understood that Captain Constantine was a no-nonsense kind of man, unlike officer Brothers, and his partner officer Wong. It was apparent that she wouldn't be able to couldn't stall him for too long.

The captain flashed into his office, never looking back. "Have a seat, Ms. Maxwell," the Capt. commanded. "I need for you to let me in on what happened to you?"

The Capt. sat back in his chair, and he pointed at another chair facing him on the other side of his desk. "Before you start, are you hungry?"

"No, thank you. I am too nervous to eat, but you can if you need to," Joy replied, crossing her arms and her legs.

"I was about to eat when I got the call. I am so hungry; I would fry my hand up and eat it if it was done right."

"Well, let me start with your guys took nearly two hours to show up to my apartment when I called. When they finally got there, the impression I got from officer Brothers and his partner, officer

Wong was that I was a neurotic lonely heart. They emphasized that I had nothing else better to do but to use up their time with my trivial circumstances." Joy put her fingers into the air as she paraphrased. "Officer Wong suggested that I watched a scary movie and spooked myself." She grits her teeth as she expressed her disgust with the police department's insensitivity.

She shouted in the captain's office. "Not to mention

I'm here with you, and all you can talk about is how hungry you are. I don't know, but that does not sound like you are performing your duties of serving and protecting my ass!"

"I understand your day has been very intrusive, and you feel vulnerable right now. The last thing I want is for you to feel like you aren't our top priority. I assure you that we are trying to get to everyone here as fast as we can," the captain said. "Also, we treat everyone that we aid the same. You must see that no cases are chosen above the rest, everybody's case is different here in New York. If you were a police officer, would you want to see to it that your case gets sorted out first, or help a child who was neglected, abused, and living in squalor?"

Joy slumped in her chair, sighed, and crossed her legs. For once in her life, she was at a loss for words.

The captain continued to drive his point home, so he stood up and planted his fists into the desk, the blood escaped his knuckles, and he said, "Or, better yet help a possible breaking and entering, or the parent, or spouse of a gunshot victim. What you should understand, Ms. Maxwell, there is a barrage of calls that we receive in this department daily. Many of these cases, the victims involved do not survive the incident.

"So, I apologize for your discomfort, but you're alive, and as far as I know, you're not hurt. As of right now, you're getting help Ms. Maxwell from not only a cop, but a damn good cop. So, let's start from the top, shall we."

Ashamed and feeling silly for exacerbating the situation more than it needed to be. Joy spoke with a southern drawl, "Well, for heaven's sake, Capt. Warrick Constantine, I am sorry for my behavior." She took a deep breath and started from the very beginning. She told the Capt. every detail, from the moment she first saw her stalker up until the point that she had to call the police. Joy did not leave out anything.

"Can you tell if this guy followed you before yesterday?" asked the Capt.

"Not as far as I can tell," Joy replied.

"I want you to think carefully, Ms. Maxwell. It is very important. It may be the difference between catching him,"

Joy couldn't help to think that she may have caught the attention of someone she didn't want to be entangled with. She had a confused look on her face and asked, "Captain, I get the feeling that I am in more trouble than I can handle." Joy paused and took a breath before she finished her statement. "Captain, should I be worried?"

"It seems like you know something more than you're letting on Ms. Maxwell."

"I am starting to get the feeling that I have a dark cloud over me."

"Please, Ms. Maxwell!" the captain said and slammed his hand on the desk. "If I had a dime for everyone that said that to me over the years, I'll be a rich man."

"Captain, I can get an image of the intruder from my job's security footage when it opens in the morning," Joy said and sighed. "Come on, Capt., you can tell me; am I in danger?" Her voice cracked, and she twiddled her thumbs on her lap.

"Look, I am not going to mince my words. From the sounds of it, you may be in danger. This seems like the same M.O (Modus operandi) as the *Midtown Murderer*, but I can't be sure. Listen to me

Ms. Maxwell, two of the seven girls that were raped and murdered in your area of Midtown Manhattan reported a similar story that you just told me. There were extenuating circumstances that didn't allow us to make this connection until recently," the Capt. discloses. All the victims had different characteristics, and there are no other connections whatsoever.

"On top of that, we had no viable leads. The Mayor and The Commissioner over at one Police Plaza have been on my neck to apprehend this guy."

Tears welled up in Joy's eyes, and Captain Constantine handed her a box of Kleenex. She sniffled and said, "Thank you."

"Now, thanks to you, with your statement, things may have changed. There are some other details that I am not at liberty to discuss the case with you, but as of right now, after listening to the information that you just gave to me and my officers. I believe that this is the same perpetrator that we've been looking for. Two victims mentioned in their statement before their untimely death that someone broke into their apartments, and someone left a half-full glass of water on their coffee table.

"So, to answer your question Ms. Maxwell, yes, you are in mortal danger."

After the Capt. revealed the truth about the connection to the Midtown Murder's, Joy's face went pale.

"So, Ms. Maxwell, it's very important; please try to remember if you saw him before. Your description of this stranger could be the break that we need to nab this maniac. He's at large, and the lives of unsuspecting poor young girls could get slaughtered in the street like cattle," Capt. Constantine reiterated. "I just want to be certain."

Ten million things went through Joy's at once, leaving her

dazed and in a state of confusion. Puzzled, because she couldn't quite figure out why she was singled out by this creep. She calculated several scenarios in her head. "First, where in the hell did I see him before the supermarket? Second, how could I help catch the culprit? Being an investigative reporter, I may have the story of my career, or I should just leave New York and go back home to Georgia. Third, is this even worth my life?

Just then in it was like a light got switched on. Joy immediately remembered seeing the bastard. "Captain," she said. "I think that I remember seeing him at a neighborhood meeting that I covered about a week or so ago."

"Wait... you're a reporter?" The Capt. asked with a surprised look upon his face.

"Yes, I am," she replied. "Does it make a difference?"

"No."

"Yes, I work for channel five. I have been there for a little over seven months. I started about a week after I moved here from Georgia. I'm a remote anchorwoman, I have only covered small puff pieces, but that's neither here nor there. I, however, did cover a neighborhood watch meeting a week or so ago, and I think I saw him there."

When she told the Capt. this, his eyes lit up. "Do you think your cameraman caught him on film?"

"I don't know; all I can do is go to the news station, recover the recording from the neighborhood watch meeting and look at it to see. Plus, I can go to the supermarket where I work part-time and possibly get the tape from there before they open at 7:00 am. His image might have been caught on camera there too. I have a feeling that was that nerdy creep that was in my checkout line.

"The only problem that we might have is that the security system is on a twenty-four-hour setting, and if we don't get there before nine o'clock this morning, the feed will automatically be stored in a database offsite. When it does, that could take a while to get a hold of," Joy said.

"Don't worry, you should have enough time to get what we need to identify this guy," the Capt. said. He immediately picked up the phone on his desk and made a call. "Sergeant, come to my office?"

The Capt. hung up the phone and said, "Ms. Maxwell, this is the break-in this case we've been looking for. I could kiss you. I'll assure that you won't be alone until we catch this culprit. I will get a policeman to accompany you wherever you need to go.

"Are you sure that I will be safe," Joy said, expressing her concerns.

Before the Capt. could respond, there was a knock on the door of his office. "Come in, Sergeant," the captain said. "Listen, Sergeant Thomas Blake; this is Joy Maxwell. I need you to take Ms. Maxwell here to a couple of places tonight and don't leave her side. Do whatever she asks and bring her back here, pronto. I can't stress that enough. She has evidence that could help close the *Midtown Murder* case.

"So, Sgt. Blake, I'm asking you to guard this woman with your life," he commanded. "Ms. Maxwell's evidence will be useful, an important break in the case that we need," Captain Constantine reiterated the importance of guarding Joy.

Capt., I assure you I'll keep her safe," Sgt. Blake said. "Are you ready, Ms. Maxwell?"

Joy gave Thomas her hand to help her out of the seat and they both walked out the Capt. office.

The minute that the door closed, Capt. Constantine got right on his phone to call his lead detective, Lt. Adeline Drakon. "Lieutenant, drop whatever you're doing and come to my office, please," he said.

"Sgt. Blake, do you have a partner that will be going with us on this outing?" Joy asked as they walked downstairs.

"I do, but he won't be joining us tonight. He's out on leave due to a family emergency," Sgt. Blake replied. "So, it will be just the two of us. Will that be a problem, Ms. Maxwell?"

"No, no problem, Sgt. Blake."

"Where are we going, Ms. Maxwell?"

"First we're going to my apartment in Midtown, then to the channel five-building, finally to my job at the Super- C supermarket," Joy replied.

"Where you want to go first?" asked Sgt. Blake.

"I have the key to the station, but we must go to my apartment first. I don't have my handbag or purse with me, and the key to the station is in it. If that's Okay with you, let's go there first."

The Sgt. Scratched his head and asked, "What is this all about?" he mushed up his face and tilted his head to the side. "Why was the Capt. so fired up about me escorting you?"

Joy took a deep breath and exhaled. "I might be the next victim of the *Midtown Murderer*, who has raped and killed at least seven women in Midtown Manhattan," Joy reluctantly replied. "I may quite possibly have his face on camera."

"I see. Well, I am highly decorated, and if it is any constellation to you, I will do my best to protect and serve you Ms. maxwell. Capt. Constantine has made you, and this case priority number one."

They walked outside the precinct, and Joy cautiously looked up and down the street. She looked up in the sky, whipped her head backward, and prayed that they could get the tapes with a clear shot of the stalker on it and get back to the station safely.

Sgt. Blake opened the car door for Joy, and she got into the car. He got inside the car and drove towards her apartment building. As they got closer, she fidgeted in her seat and looked through all the windows in the squad car. Officer Blake's erratic driving did not help matters much. He received the message from the captain, loud and clear. Sgt. Blake recognized how important the evidence Ms. Maxwell had, and he didn't want to screw it up.

Sgt. Blake approached Joy's neighborhood, and her anxiety became increasingly apparent. She was noticeably shaking; her hands were clammy, and she was sweating profusely. He looked at her, cleared his throat, and said, "You know," he said in a firm but calm tone enough to catch her attention. When she turned to him in acknowledgment, he continued.

"I grow up in the Bronx near Yankee stadium. If you don't know what I'm talking about, I grew up in one of the roughest parts of New York City. One time, I fought the toughest kid in school, his name was Mark William. I stood up to him because he bullied every kid that was smaller than he was. Don't get me wrong, I was afraid–I was extremely terrified. But before I fought him, I remembered something that my father told me–God rest his soul. *The only thing that you should be afraid of is not trying because nothing tried, nothing done.*' I always live by that because you can never lose when you're doing the right thing."

Joy nodded at Sgt. Blake and smiled. He reached in the glove compartment and gave her a box of Kleenex. The words that Sgt. Blake said, was affirming, and it strengthened her conviction. She felt empowered about what she needed to do. "What happened when you fought that bully?" she asked.

"Remind me to tell you later."

"Why?"

"Because we're here," Sgt. Blake said quickly as he swiftly pulled into a parking spot right in front of Ms. Maxwell's apartment building.

Joy took a deep breath before she exited the car. Sgt. Blake pulled the latch to his door to get out. She put her hand on his arm and said, "No, stay down here, Sgt., besides it won't take me that long." She got out of the car, sprinted to the building, and walked inside the building. She jogged up two flights of stairs to get to her apartment. When she got her front door, it had been pried open. The wood on the doorframe was splintered.

Joy didn't take any chances, so she went back downstairs and waved to Sgt. Blake from the entryway of the building and said, "Yoo-hoo! Yoo-hoo!"

Sgt. Blake looked over at Joy, then she put both of her hands around her mouth like a bullhorn said, "Someone broken the front door to my apartment." She shrieked her words not to alert the would-be intruder. "Sgt., please come quickly!" She waved her hands faster in a come-hither motion.

"What happened?" Sgt. Blake asked. "Did you see something?"

"Yes," she replied, panting and holding her chest.

Sgt. Blake rushed upstairs with his service revolver drawn. He saw that her apartment was indeed broken into. When he entered the apartment, he saw that it was rammed sacked. Before he went in any further, he signaled with his hand for Joy to stay back. He turned his head to her and whispered, "Stay here." He radioed in before going any further. "Dispatch, this is Car 1325. I am on a 10-61 in Midtown on 49th between 10th and 11th, and there's a possible 10-21.

Dispatch replied, *"10-4, stand-by."*

Sgt. Blake carefully tiptoed inside to secure the apartment with his service revolver in the air. He creped through the kitchen, the living room, and he turned into the bedroom, panning the room prudently. All of Joy's drawers were pulled out from the dressers and dashed on the ground. Her unmentionables were tossed about the room. Perfume, lotion, and powder were spilled all over the mattress and floor. "It looks like the culprit had enough. He tuckered himself out searching through all of her belongings," he whispers to himself.

Joy snuck inside behind him and observed how Sgt. Blake looked swift as he moved through the apartment like a big cat on the prowl. He leaped over furniture and peeked in every room–opening all the pantry, linen, and closet doors. After he secured her domicile; they both made a quick assessment of the apartment. He stood inside the living room then holstered his service weapon. "Blake to Dispatch–everything is secure," Sgt. Blake said on the radio.

"That's a 10-4 Sgt," dispatch replied.

"Ms. Maxwell, look around and see if there anything missing,"

Sgt. Blake said. "Make sure to write down anything that you find missing or damaged, so I can write it down in my report. Also, try to find your keys, so we could finish what we set out to do."

"How long will that take?" Joy asked, "because we don't have much time."

"Don't worry, there's a unit coming. When they arrive, they're going to dust for fingerprints. If they find one, we will have it to match the culprit responsible for this and possibly all the others as well,"

"What if it is the *Sanguine killer*."

"Who's that?" Sgt. Blake scoffs and said, "Is that what you guys in the neighborhood are calling him."

"No, that's what I'm going to call him when I report this to my boss at the station," Joy replied.

"Don't count your chickens before they hatch just yet, Ms. Maxwell. This might not be the so-called *"Sanguine Killer."*

Joy found a pen and pad to write on, and she looked around the apartment. She itemized her belongings in disbelief. "Sgt., I can't find the keys to my job!" Joy exclaimed.

"What? Please look again, Ms. Maxwell," Sgt. Blake replied.

"I did look, it was supposed to be in my handbag, but I forgot that I took my friend Diedre's purse from work home by mistake. Shit—that means her handbag is gone."

"Calm down, Ms. Maxwell. How do you know it's not your handbag?"

"Deidre has a 5x7 picture of her husband and kids that she shows everyone at work—Darn it!"

"Tough break. This guy did a good job making a mess of your apartment. It's going to be hard finding anything in here now. But I'll help you look anyway; there's got to be something here that could tie this guy to at least this breaking and entering," Sgt. Blake said.

Joy grumbled under her breath as she tiptoed over broken glass in the kitchen.

"Hey, what about the cameraman; do you think he might have

a key?" Sgt. Blake asked.

"I don't know, but I'll call to see if he does," she replied. Joy through the hallway towards her bedroom to make the call. She slapped her thigh when she remembered that her phone was in her handbag and Deidre had it. She stopped, scratched her scalp, and flubbered her lips.

Joy was on the verge of tears when she was startled by a noise coming from her bedroom. She ran back into the living room and said, "Sgt. Blake, did you hear that?"

"Yes, I did hear it—stay here, let me check it," the Sgt. said, as he pulled out his service revolver from its holster and moved toward the direction where the sound was coming from. A window was open, so you could hear everything clearly in the neighborhood. A Puerto Rican couple was arguing in Spanish two floors up. Cats were mewing and jumping in and out of garbage cans in the alley down below. And the smell of burnt rubber from screeching tires on the pavement by two cars possibly racing on the street.

"Dispatch-1325," Sgt. said on his walkie-talkie. The clicking sound from the buttons and white noise in between the exchange filled the dead air.

"Dispatch-go," the female dispatch replied.

"10-10 a possible suspect at my location and need assistance, requesting a unit to my location."

"10-4 dispatching additional unit," the female responds.

Sgt. Blake took the gun off safety, and he entered the bedroom locked and loaded. He entered the room, aimed his gun, and shouted, "Come out slowly with your hands up, so I can see them. Then turn around, step backward towards the sound of my voice slowly and interlock your fingers on the top of your head. Come out on three, or I'll shoot."

Sgt. Blake cocked the hammer on his NYPD issued Glock and stretched his arms out in front of him, preparing himself for the recoil of the gun and lining up the sights to his dominant eye, settling himself before pulling the trigger. He stood in front of the closet and said, "One, two, three."

In one seamless motion the closet doors opened, and the perp rushed out and was right in front of his gun; before Sgt. Blake applied pressure on the trigger; the assailant attacked him. He was startled and opened fire upon the ominous figure.

What emerged from the closet was a pale gothic figure with dark, dreary attire. He had on black jeans, topped with a dark fleece hoodie and long shiny jet-black hair. His claw-like fingernails were black and sharp as razor blades. The monster had a tall, slender build, like a swimmer or cyclist. His face was like that of a demon's, certainly non-human features, especially his eyes. The irises were red, surrounded by a black sclera in the place of white. What Sgt. Blake was face to face with, was chilling and cold. Its breath wreaked of rotting flesh. He was in the presence of death itself, or a manifestation of one's worst nightmare.

With Deidre's purse clutched in its fist, the demon reached for Sgt. Blake's gun. His mouth was wide open, and he was shocked and frozen stiff from the horrible sight. Chills ran down his spine. Although he was in a state of suspended animation, he managed to involuntarily empty his entire clip at the creature. The blood demon dodged almost every shot from point-blank range except one. That bullet entered the creature's temple, and the impact turned its face to the side.

Sgt. Blake continued applying pressure on the trigger until the slide stayed open and smoke floated from the barrel. The gunshot wound didn't faze the blood demon. Slowly he turned his head, forward and the bullet pushed out of the wound, and it started to close. After the wound healed, there were only remnants of blood streaming down the side of its face.

Joy mustering enough courage after hearing the melee entered the room to see the bullet spontaneously push out the demon's temple.

"It's him, it's him, that's the creep," Joy shouted, identifying her stalker.

Sgt. Blake frantically pulled out his walkie-talkie and said, "10-13, 10-13 where's my back up!"

After Sgt. Blake uttered those words; the creature effortlessly trusted its fist forward and punched a hole in his chest cavity and pull out his still-beating heart. With that one blow, the shear force blew his ribs, lungs, and muscles from his chest out his back.

"No!" Joy screamed out loud, a screeching sound, after she just witnessed Sgt. Blake died in front of her eyes.

Joy back peddled and tripped over her own feet. She fell back and hit her head on the coffee table behind her, knocking her out unconscious. Helplessly lying down there on the ground, with her body limp and lifeless, the creature slowly walked over to her and knelt over Joy, with its hand dripping of blood and Sgt. Blake's beating heart in hand. The demon placed the heart on her chest over her heart and said, "Everyone has to meet their maker one day. Unfortunately, today is Sgt. Blake's day."

The blood demon cricked its neck, and its canine teeth grew longer. He raised the still-beating heart above his head, and the blood drained into his mouth. He looked down at Joy's limp body and used the blood on his hands to trace an outline around her body. He wrote in old Akkadian language, *"Istet umu,"* (one day) in blood on the wall.

The police sirens blared in the distance, the demon twitched his ears and hastily gathered Sgt. Blake's badge as a souvenir and vanished in the shadows. Joy was awakened by the commotion of the police officers inside her apartment.

"Code blue, officer down," one officer messaged dispatch. The officers on-site covered their mouths in disbelief of seeing the dead body of their falling comrade. Another officer said, "What in god's name could have done this to Sgt. Blake.

Chapter 2

The phone rang, and Capt. Constantine picked up the receiver. He deflated into his chair after listening to the caller on the other end. He hung up the phone and put his head in his hands. Lt. Drakon leaned forward and said, "What's hap'n, Cap'n?"

The Capt. sniffled and paused for a moment, then mumbled under his breath, "Sgt. Blake." He swallowed the lump in his throat to hold back tears. "Sgt. Thomas Blake was killed in the line of duty," he said. "He was murdered by someone or something at Ms. Maxwell's apartment."

Lt. Drakon leaned back in her chair and shook her head in disbelief. "Oh my god!" she said. "How did it happen?"

I sent him out to escort a key witness in the *Midtown Murders* case, and he was ambushed by someone looking to get after the witness," the Capt. replied.

"There's nothing worse than the death of a fellow officer; I didn't know him well, but from what I heard of Sgt. Thomas Blake— he was a good guy."

There was a moment of silence; the Capt. reached for some Kleenex and blew his nose.

"Wait, Capt., what happened to the witness you said he was escorting?"

"Well, fortunately for her, she's alive as far as I know." Capt. Constantine slammed the jacket of the *Midtown Murder* case on his desk, got up from his chair, turned around, put his hands on his waist, and stared out of the window of his office.

Did you know Sgt Blake was my first trainee and my first partner before I made detective twelve years ago?" asked the Capt.

"He was my closest friend and an exemplary police officer. I trained many rookie cops fresh out of the academy, and he was the best by far. He could've made detective years ago—he passed the test with flying colors first try, but he loved being a beat cop. He loved to protect and serve the people in this city."

"Damn, Capt. I am truly sorry for the loss of your best friend," Lt. Drakon said "I won't rest until the bastard responsible for this is apprehended."

The phone rang, and the Capt. just stood there with one pressed upon the window frame and ignored it.

Lt. Drakon called out to him, "Capt., Capt., Captain Constantine!"

Finally, the Capt. turned around, walked to his desk, sat in his chair, and picked up the phone after several rings. The Capt. Held the receiver to his ear and didn't say a word. He closed his eyes, shook his head, and hung up. He sighed, pushed the folder across the desk, and said, "I need you on this one, Lieutenant."

"I'm on it," Lt. Drakon said, picked up the folder, then stood up and walked towards the door.

"Wait, that was your new partner on the phone; he is your number two on this. He is downstairs right now waiting for you."

"Partner...partner, really captain, you know I work alone," Lt. Drakon said in utter disgust.

"Yes, Lieutenant," the Capt. replied. "That was Sgt. Devin Mason on the phone; he just got transferred here from narcotics. I don't have time for your belly aching, now go downstairs and meet and greet your new partner. He is a highly decorated officer out of Philadelphia, and he was the head of the Special Crimes Unit there.

"Lt. Drakon I have faith in you. You're the best and the brightest this precinct has to offer. For the sake of your career here, I know you'll do your darnedest to get this case solved. Now, if you'd excuse me, I must locate my uniform because I have the daunting task of informing Tommy's widow of his untimely death."

The Capt. pressed the intercom button and told his receptionist to get his uniform ready. The Capt. stood up, took his overcoat off the coat rack, draped it over his arm, and ushered Lt. Drakon out of his office while walking behind her.

The captain stopped at his receptionist desk, then headed toward the locker room.

Lt. Drakon shook her head, slapped the folder on her left hand, and trotted downstairs to search for her new partner. The sheer thought of having a partner made her nauseous. When she arrived on the first floor, she surveyed the lobby for Sgt. Mason. On the other side of the lobby, she saw the most attractive man she'd ever laid eyes on in her natural life. She walked towards him, grinned like a Chester cat, and said, "Hello, I'm Lt. Adeline Drakon; how could I help you?"

Sgt. Mason smiled back at the Lt., shook her outstretch hand, and replied, "Hi, I'm Sgt. Mason, your new partner. I just transferred here from narcotics. He had a rugged, tough guy bravado, like when undercover police officers had that spent considerable time dealing with gangsters and thugs out in the mean streets. Sgt. Mason stood 6'-3" tall, with a five o'clock shadow covering his squared chin. He had green eyes and dirty blond hair flowed past his shoulders down to the front of his chest. He was dressed in a dark blue blazer, pressed tan dungarees, and looked like he just stepped out from a Ralph Lauren ad.

"Pleased to meet you, Sgt Mason."

"Same here, Lt. Drakon."

"Let me get you up to speed. There is a cop killer on the loose here in the city, dubbed the *Midtown Murderer*. His latest victim was Sgt. Thomas Blake, from this same dept. So, I don't have to tell you how important it is that we apprehend this bastard. I hope you brought with you whatever expertise you've acquired while working the mean streets of Philadelphia, PA. We need all hands are on deck for this one."

Lt. Drakon stepped past Sgt. Mason opened the door and walked out the precinct toward her unmarked Dodge Charger.

"My condolences. Did he have a family?" Sgt. Mason asked while following closely behind the Lt.

Lt. Drakon looked back at Sgt. Mason, paused for a moment, and said, "Yes, a wife of seventeen years and two kids."

"Tough break, I'll put my best foot forward on this one for sure," he replied.

The Lt. opened the driver's side door, sat down, paused for a moment, closed her eyes, and said to herself, "God protect us!" then she unlocked the passenger side door for the Sgt.

The Sgt. got into the vehicle and asked, "Where are we heading to first, Lt.?"

"We're going straight to the scene of the crime to secure the very witness Sgt. Blake was protecting. She must have seen something bad. A police officer got killed to keep her mouth shut. Let's hope she doesn't; with her testimony, this will be an open and shut case," she said, then she drove off.

"I can relate to this whole ordeal—I just helped bury my partner a month ago. This doesn't get easier. It's just a harsh reminder that our lives are on the line every day we walk out of the precinct."

Lt. Drakon pointed at the computer screen of the opened laptop and told Sgt. Mason to punch in for work. Their hands touched, and she quickly pulled it away from his. She cleared her throat and focused her eyes on the road. Sgt. Mason smirked and logged in his credentials into the computer.

The Lt. weaved in and out of traffic with sirens blaring. She made a sharp left turn and parked out in front of an apartment building. "Alright, we are here. If you don't have any gloves, there are some in the glove box you can use. In my experience, people like familiarity when there's a crisis. So, just follow my lead when we get in there."

"You're the boss," Sgt. Mason replied.

"I need you to know that Sgt. Thomas Blake was loved and respected at our precinct. Since you're the new kid on the block, some of the guys that's already here might give you shit, so don't take it too personally.

"Thanks for the heads up. I appreciate that. I don't want to step on anyone's toes here."

"I know very little about what transpired here—allow me to gather intel first before we look at the body. Don't get all *Narco* on me in there.

"Duly noted, I've been around the block a few times…I get it. I'll use discretion and show respect. I understand that it may be a bit difficult for you having to deal with a new partner and all. I surmise that you don't play well with others around here. I'm not a rookie. My badge reads detective just as your badge does. I'm more than capable of do the job, Lt."

Lt. Drakon shook her head as Sgt. Mason got out of the car, walked across the front, stepped up onto the curb, and sat on the hood of the car. She sighed and thought to herself, "This is going to be fun."

The Sgt and Lt. ran toward the building of their key witness Joy Maxwell to avoid the sudden downpour of rain. There was a bezzie of cops from her precinct gathered outside the entrance. The chatter between the officers stopped, and they all remained quiet when they noticed Lt. Drakon. They all stared at her in utter disbelief. Indiscriminate chatter erupted as she and Sgt. Mason walked through the lobby. One of the officers greeted Lt. despite the awkward silence that washed over the crowd of policemen.

Sgt. Mason raised his eyebrows and said, "This is going to be very interesting."

As the officer gave Lt. Drakon the low down of what transpired, she could hear all the chatter directed at her while entering the building. The tension was so thick you could cut it with a knife. The Lt. listened to the sorrowful whispers of the all too familiar details of how she was just raped, fatally injured, and left for dead. She had to endure all their male chauvinistic views of how vulnerable females were in the line of duty.

The fact that most women who are raped suffer psychologically and their souls are wounded indefinitely. It didn't bother her one bit though, Lt. Drakon proved daily how competent she as a police officer. Naturally, she thought nothing was different, but with her, everything has changed for the better.

"Lt. Drakon, glad to see that you're back," one officer said as everyone else continued to stare at her like a deer caught in headlights.

"Lt. what did you do?" Sgt. Mason asked. "Everyone here is behaving as if they saw a ghost."

Lt. Drakon hesitated a moment before she answered Sgt. Mason. "Trust me, you'll find out soon enough." Reflecting on what took place that fatal night, Lt. Drakon began feeling ashamed that someone had gotten the best of her. She quickly put her feelings aside as she entered Joy Maxwell apartment. She walked in promptly and abruptly commanded the attention of the entire room. "I want everyone out, except for the witness, so everyone, please leave."

Nobody hesitated; the Crime Scene Investigations Unit and the coroner excited the apartment. Lt. Drakon turned to the closest CSI to her and asked for a booty for herself and her partner. "Sgt Mason, talk with the witness while I get caught up with the medical examiner," she exclaimed.

"Sure, no problem, Lt.," replied, as he put on the booties over his shoes. After a brief conversation with Dr. German (The M. E,) they went into the room where the body of Sgt. Thomas Blake laid dead.

Upon seeing the deceased, she immediately recalled and relived that night she strolled through central park; a day she couldn't forget. She remembered taking a simple walk in the park that she routinely done dozens of times. But for some reason she took a shortcut. She usually didn't go that way because it was dark. The bushes were too overgrown and there were too many places where somebody could hide.

Lt. Drakon threw caution to the wind and walked down the path anyway. She wanted to get back home quicker. With her recent engagement to her fiancée looming over her head and the engagement party she was running late for; she was too preoccupied to be aware of her surroundings. A misguided decision that would change her life from that moment forward.

Lt. Drakon stood there in the room stunned and frozen in time. She couldn't move a muscle. She panted, clenched her cross pendant, and recalled that her ears popped after a stranger hit her in the back of the head with a metal pipe. The impact was so hard that it shattered her skull sending her to the ground.

In excruciated pain, Lt. Drakon managed to reach for her firearm, but a second man knocked the gun out of hand with a metal bat and it slid into the bushes. She held her broken hand over her head and braced for another hit.

Lt. Drakon took a few breaths, then a third man mounted her and spread her legs apart. She screamed, kicked him in the face. He fell backward and held his nose.

Another man swung a heavy metal chain he had wrapped around his hand and hit both of her knees, her hip, and her elbows as she held her guard to protect her face.

He struck her with the chain over and over as she rolled from side to side. The blows to her shoulder broke her clavicle bone, cracked side two ribs, and punctured her lung.

Two more men kicked and stomped on her head. One man kicked her in the eye with his steel toe boot and fractured her ocular bone.

After being beaten for two minutes by five men, Lt. Drakon laid there motionless.

The first man dropped his pipe, flipped her over on her stomach. He pulled down her pants, her panties, then he pulled down his trousers. He laid on top of her lifeless body and sodomized her.

All five men took turns raping her for twenty-five minutes. Afterward, they left her there to die without a shred of decency whatsoever.

A good Samaritan saw her lying there naked, bruised, battered with blood oozing out of every orifice and called 911. About fifteen minutes later, medics arrived, assessed Lt. Drakon's injuries, checked for vital signs, wrapped a neck brace around her neck, and placed her on the gurney. The EMT and Paramedic rushed her to the ambulance, hoisted her in, and raced to the nearest emergency room.

The ambulance arrived at the hospital, where surgeons were ready for her arrival. They brought her straight to the operating room and began frantically working on her to save her life. Miraculously, the doctors stabilized her, but she was in critical condition.

Her grandfather Dr. Vaughn German, rushed to her bedside after someone told him what happened to his granddaughter. When he had arrived, he saw the surgeon responsible for stabilizing her and asked, "What's the prognosis, doctor?"

"Is she an organ donor?" the doctor replied. "It would be a miracle if this woman lives through the night."

Dr. German shook the doctor's hand and thanked him for all he had done to save his granddaughter's life.

The doctor nodded and said, "I'll give you some privacy with her."

Dr. German grabbed his granddaughter's hand, and then he kissed her on the forehead. He sat down next to Lt. Drakon's bedside and couldn't believe how fragile she looked.

Tears welled up in his eyes when she flatlined. He leaned over to her dead body and sobbed on her wrist.

In a moment of desperation, Dr. German did what he vowed never to do to anyone ever again during his unnatural life. He unbuttoned his shirt cuff, rolled up his sleeve, and raised his hand in the air. Autonomously, he grew razor-sharp nails from his fingertips, used his index finger, and slit his wrist over Lt. Drakon's mouth. He held it to her lips until she began suckling on his blood.

The heart rate monitor remained unchanged for a few seconds, then her heartbeat registered on the monitor. Lt. Drakon grabbed Dr. German's hand with both of hers and sucked it until he nudged her off. He sat down in the chair next to her bed, and the wound on his wrist disappeared. He buttoned his shirt cuff and crossed his legs.

Blood drained from the side of Lt. Drakon's mouth as Dr. German stared at his undead granddaughter's body. He wiped the tears from his cheeks with a silk handkerchief. The heart rate monitors beeped as she lay there, reborn into this world again as a blood-sucking demon, a vampire.

Weakened from the exchange, Dr. German cleared his throat and walked out of the hospital room.

The door swung back open, and another figure walked inside. The ominous figure wore a silk, grey, double-breasted pinstriped suit.

Lt. Drakon opened her eyes and said, "Grandad! What are you doing here?"

The man cleared his throat and replied in a thick Austrian accent, "No, my name is Timothy Frank, and everything's going to be okay. You were involved in an accident."

Lt. Drakon looked down at her hands, caressed her body, and said, "Timothy Frank? I don't know anyone named—"

"I know, but you will soon enough," he said and snickered. "You will be fine, my Childe; your grandfather saw to it that you would."

Lt. Drakon stood there with her arms by her side, with her back turned to everyone in Joy's apartment.

Dr. German tapped her on the shoulders and asked, "Are you okay? You've been standing there for five minutes just staring at the wall."

"Yes!" she replied as if nothing had happened. "So, what is the cause of death, Doctor?"

"Blunt force trauma, the victim was either hit by a cannon shell or struck in the chest with a huge cylindrical tool. The odd thing is that his heart is gone and it's nowhere to be found in the apartment. I would have to get the body to the lab for further analysis."

"Fine, Dr. German, could you put a rush on that? This man was one of our own. I don't need to tell you how important this case is, Doc."

I understand more than you know; Lt. Sgt Thomas Blake wasn't just a colleague; he was my friend."

"Has this place been dusted for print yet?"

"Yes, the CSI unit did. They took pictures and collected shells. All of them came from the deceased; Sgt Blake must've spent his entire magazine. Whatever he was aiming at, he hit but couldn't stop it. Upon inspection, we only found one single solitary shell casing. But we must do a ballistics test to be sure the shots came from the deceased. With no signs of return fire, I could safely say that it was only him firing. Surprisingly, they accomplished all of that before you rudely kicked them all out, Lt."

The Lt. inspected the room, and she notices that there weren't any holes in the walls from the barrage of bullets hailed from the Sgt. Blake's gun. Working out all the possibilities in her head, Lt. Drakon surmised that the perpetrator must have worn a Teflon vest. That is the only way to explain why another victim isn't lying down in here next to the dearly departed.

Lt. Drakon analyzed the size of the room and said, "Our perp must be injured, he couldn't have gotten far; he should've suffered at least a broken rib and deep tissue contusions. She pulled out her radio and said, "Put out an APB (All-points bulletin.) Search all emergency rooms in a fifty-mile radius with anyone seeking treatment for a broken rib and deep tissue contusions on their torso.

The Lt. put her radio back on her hip and turned to Dr. German and said, "I've seen enough; you and your team could finish up in here. Please call me with any news regarding your findings. I'm going in the other room to see if our witness could identify this cop killer."

She stepped away from her grandfather and walked toward the room with Sgt. Mason and Joy. "Oh, Dr. German, before I forget, what is this writing on the wall mean?" she asked with a curious look on her face.

"I believe it's written in an old forgotten language, Akkadian to be exact. A language that, unfortunately, I'm regrettable out of practice. He put on his reading glasses, squinted and said, *"It says: Unum omnes dies moritur,"* (One day everyone dies) Dr. German replied.

"Who wrote this mess? I bet my badge that it is—"

"Lt. get in here, please! I think she's off her rocker," Sgt. Mason shouted as she walked into the room. He met her halfway, and said, "I think she has post-traumatic stress disorder, or she is on some potent psychedelic drugs. The paramedic said that she bumped her head but refused any medical attention."

"Sergeant, what are you talking about," Lt. Drakon replied.

"Lt. just listen to her, and you will know what I'm talking about."

The Sgt. led the Lt. into the other room. Joy sat on a recliner and held a cold pack to her head with her hand. She said, "Excuse me, Ms. Maxwell, hi, I'm Lt. Adeline Drakon, the lead detective on this murder case. I know you had a rough night, is everything okay with you?"

"Besides witnessing a man punch a hole into another man, I'm just peachy," Joy replied.

"My partner seems to believe otherwise."

Joy put down the cold pack on her leg and said, "Look, I knew nobody would ever believe me, but I know what I saw."

"Please, if you could start from the beginning and tell me what you saw," Lt. Drakon said.

"I know this might sound farfetched, but t…that thing stalked me at work. H…he must have followed me up to my apartment. I didn't notice at first, but I noticed a glass on the coffee table that I personally don't use. I was startled, then I went over to my neighbor's apartment and called the police. Soon after that, two officers escorted me down to the station. Sgt. Blake took me back here to get some of my things, and that's when—A…as soon as I unlocked the front door, the apartment was disheveled.

"It's okay, Joy, that your time," Sgt. Mason said.

"I heard a noise, and Sgt. Blake took out his gun and went to investigate what it was," she said. "While he was in my bedroom, I heard shots firing. When I walked back there, I saw It punch a hole in Sgt. Blake's chest ripped out his heart with his bare hands and drank the blood that dripped down from Sgt. Blake's still-beating heart.

"I backpaddled from the room, and he chased after me. I fell and hit my head on the edge of the coffee table in the living room, then blacked out. That's all I remember—he did smell like rotten eggs, though."

Lt. Drakon raised her eyebrows and struggled to search for the words to say.

Sgt. Mason leaned over to her with his hand covering his mouth and said, "So, what do you think? Does it sound crazy to you, Lt.?"

Joy threw down the cold pack on the ground, stood up, and said, "If you're going to continue questioning whether I'm sane or not, Sgt., I would appreciate it if you would talk loud enough, so I could hear you." She folded her arms across her chest and rolled her eyes. "Like I said, I'm telling the truth, I mean, I'm not crazy; honest to God," Joy reiterated.

"O…okay, Ms. Maxwell, please calm down, let's get back on track here, come with my partner and me downtown, so we can sort out all the details we have thus far. I know it has been a long and eventful day, to say the least. On behalf of Sgt. Mason and I, we realize how problematic and traumatic today must have been for you," Lt. Drakon said.

Joy took a deep breath, exhaled, and looked out the window. She turned to the Lt. and blurted out, "That's it! That bastard wanted my purse. That was his goal all along." She stormed out of the bedroom and said, "We should head down to the channel five news building and get that video I shot of him."

Sgt. Mason turned to Lt. Drakon and said, "What did she say?"

The detectives walked out of the bedroom and caught up to Joy in the living room rummaging through her things.

"He must've wanted the key that I kept in my purse to the news building," Joy said then snapped her fingers. "He must've wanted to get the DVD with the footage my cameraman recorded of the prime suspect in the *Midtown Murders*. Sgt. Blake took me back to my apartment to get my handbag with my purse in it. But when I remembered that the handbag and purse, I had was Deidre's, it was too late. That, that thing killed Sgt. Blake. He was doing his job. He was just trying to protect me. His death was all my fault."

Joy put her hand over her face and sobbed. "If I remembered that I didn't have my handbag, we wouldn't have come to my apartment in the first place," Joy said. "I think I'm going to be sick." Joy ran into the kitchen and threw up in the sink.

"That doesn't make any sense," Sgt. Mason said. "I mean, why would someone go these lengths to retrieve footage of themselves. Nobody looking at the video wouldn't have paid close attention to it. Unless the actual murder was recorded on the DVD in question."

"That means he kept Ms. Maxwell alive, so she can lead him to where the keys were," Lt. Drakon said and took out her notepad to refer to the phrase written on the wall in the living room. *"Cuncti dies unus moriatur."* (One day everyone dies.)

"What does that even mean, Lt.?" Joy asked.

"I don't know, Ms. Maxwell, Dr. German translated it for me. He said that the words were written in an old Akkadian language. I don't know what significance it has in this case, but I'm sure we will find out soon enough."

So, who was this message written for the police, or Ms. Maxwell?" Sgt. Mason asked.

"The only person that could answer that question is the individual who wrote the message on the wall," Lt. Drakon replied.

"He already has a huge head start, Ms. Maxwell. If your theory is correct, we need to get to the channel five news station before the perp does," Sgt. Mason said.

"I might know of another way to get a recording of this guy

from the surveillance footage from the security cameras at the supermarket where both Deidre and I work!" Joy exclaimed. "I know that creep followed me while I was on my way to work yesterday morning." She looked at the clock on the wall and said, "It's six o'clock in the morning, I could contact my manager to tell him to prep the footage at the supermarket before we get there. Hopefully, my cameraman recorded that bastard."

"What time does the store open?" Lt. Drakon asked.

"The supermarket opens at seven o'clock daily. It's not far away. We could get there before the manager opens."

"Let us get moving. Let's not waste any more time conversing, Sgt. Mason said.

Lt. Drakon, Joy, and Sgt. Mason exited the front door and the CSI's that waited in the hallway re-entered her apartment to finish securing the crime scene.

All three enter the Lieutenant's unmarked Dodge Challenger, then she drove pulled from the curb with her flashing blue and red lights illuminate from the rear window.

Meanwhile, an ominous figure across the street from the Super C supermarket dipped in the shadows when a car pulled to the curb.

The stranger lurked in shadows motionless and watched every move that the driver made. He held the purse he took from Joy's apartment in his hand. Unbeknownst to the man, his beady eyes followed every movement he made. As he idly awaited in the alley like a cat on the prowl. His patience bared fruit: the driver opened the back door to the employee entrance, and his badge read: Manager, Mr. Tom Gillman when he turned around and flicked his cigarette on the ground. He propped the door open with a brick and light up another cigarette.

As he took a long drag on the cigarette; he raised his head to exhale the smoke.

The blood demon approached the manager like an owl swooping down on its prey. Without provocation, he grabbed Mr. Gillman by the throat and lifted him eight inches off the ground and pushed him into the surveillance room ten yards from the rear doorway of the supermarket.

He gripped the manager by the neck tighter than an eagle's talon with more pressure than a boa constrictor. Mr. Gillman pulled at the blood demons' fingers to no avail. The vampire stared at the manager and squeezed his hand around his throat. With a deep raspy voice, the vampire said, "Get me the security tape now!"

Mr. Gillman shook his head up and down, with terror in his eyes, and reluctantly complied to the blood demons' demands.

The vampire released his death grip from the manager's throat, and he dropped to the ground down to his knees.

He coughed incessantly, frantically gasping for air while holding his throat.

In a blood-curdling tone, the blood demon said, "I said get me the security tape."

Mr. Gillman got up and sat down in the chair in front of the monitors, computer servers and moved nervously to meet the blood demons' demands.

"Listen to me very carefully, so I won't rip your still-beating heart from your chest. I need to see the footage from yesterday morning around 8:30 am," the vampire said.

Tears welled up in Mr. Gillman's eyes. He sniffled, trembled, and fumbled around the control board.

The blood demon grabbed him by the hair and yanked his head backward.

"Ahh...okay, alright, give me a minute to think, I'm under immense pressure here, take it easy!" exclaimed Mr. Gillman.

"Stop sniveling and get on with it!"

After locating the exact time frame that the blood demon requested, Mr. Gillman said, "Hey, listen, he said nervously.

"I've been a grocer for twenty years now, and I pride myself in knowing all my regular customers that shop at the store. Maybe if you let me know you want on the footage, I could further assist you with what you're asking of me.

The stranger leaned over Mr. Gillman's shoulder, and his canine fangs grew out.

Mr. Gillman shivered and sweat dripped down the sides of his face. He couldn't believe that a legend a myth—a secret whispered throughout time. The creature that goes bump in the night. A blood-sucking Vampire stood five inches away from his jugular vein. And whether he's cooperative with it or not, he will devour his soul.

Determined to plead for his life, the manager said, "I...I have a family that I love dearly, my grandson was born last week, and I want to be there to witness him experience all the great things life has to offer."

Mr. Gillman trembled like a leaf, and the vampire remained stoic while surveying the footage from the morning before. The vampire spotted what he was in search of and said, "Stop the tape, rewind it two minutes. The stranger noticed in the video that he touched Joy's hand; and this action denotes being submissive, something is damning for his kind. After reviewing the footage, the

58

blood demon commanded the manager to erase the footage.

The store manager complied, but he simultaneously emailed the footage to his wife in case the vampire killed him. The moment he does, the vampire stood up tall, spreads his arms, unveiling his true form and his bloodlust for captive prey. The vampire's eyes turned jet black like octopus' ink. He exposed his fangs, expressing hunger–a deep ravenous thirst, a sinful greed. He unleashed his fury onto the manager.

The blood demon grabbed his head with one hand and his shoulder with the other and pushed them apart. Mr. Gillman's jugularvein throbbed as the vampire leaned in and pierced his two-inch fangs into his neck. He yelped out with shrieking bellow as the vampire and drained the manager of his life's blood.

Mr. Gillman squirmed until his body went limp. The vampire stopped sucking, reached inside his trench coat pocket, and pulled out a few red cross blood bags. The demon plunged the butterfly needles into three of the four puncture wounds on his neck and drained the manager's blood until the bags were filled.

The stranger grabbed the three bags of blood from the desk like a doggy bag from a swanky SOHO restaurant. He hastily dragged Mr. Gillman's body out the building to the alleyway.

After he tossed the manager's carcass next to the huge store trash bin, the vampire saw Deidre in the alley in shock standing motionless.

Like a blur, the vampire attacked Deidre. He grabbed the handbag and effortlessly ripped her head off her body. The vampire ravaged through the handbag, located the key to the channel five news building, and escaped in the shadows as stealthy as he came, all before Deidre's body and head hit the ground.

The sun raised over the horizon and the stranger receded into the shadows to avoid direct contact with the sun. While he stood in a dark alleyway not yet exposed to the power of the sun, a car pulled up with Joy Maxwell in the backseat averted the vampire's attention. Instead of going to the station, the blood demon smirked and slowly submerged himself deeper in the darkness to avoid detection.

"Right here is good," Joy said, "Mr. Gillman should be in the store already and he should be opening the doors in about fifteen minutes."

Lt. Drakon parked the car in front of the supermarket. Joy and Sgt. Mason got out of the vehicle while she turned off the ignition.

Joy tried the front door to the supermarket, but it was still locked. She then walked around back to the employee entrance. The door was left open. Immediately she knew something was wrong.

"Mr. Gillman would never leave the door open. Every morning we ring the bell, and he or the security guard buzzed us in," Joy explained.

Lt. Drakon and Sgt. Mason drew their service revolvers and canvased the area for anything suspicious.

Joy scurried inside toward Mr. Gillman's office to check if he was injured or sick. Joy looked in the office and noticed that there was no sign of her manager. "This is odd! Where is he?" Ms. Maxwell asked in frustration.

"There is no sign of false entry to the entrance door and no signs of foul play. We should go inside the supermarket; maybe Mr. Gilman's in there somewhere," Lt. Drakon said and holstered her weapon.

"Before we do, let me check the security room. My manager

would normally check the monitors and survey all the areas before he opened the supermarket. Joy as they walked down the corridor toward the security room and yelled, "Mr. Gillman, Mr. Gillman?"

Joy, with Lt. Drakon by her side, opened the door to the security room, and there was blood spatter on the monitors, and a dent in the wall. A broken chair was on the ground by the gaping hole in the wall and.

"Oh my gosh…oh my gosh! I hope nothing bad happened to Mr. Gillman. He's the nicest man I've ever met before in my life," Joy exclaimed.

Sgt. Mason noticed when the wind blew that the door moved slightly and ricocheted back like it was hitting up against something. When he walked outside to investigated, he pulled back the door, and there was a lifeless body with a badge that read store manager, Mr. Gillman pinned to his shirt. With his mouth gape open, he had ligature marks and four puncture wounds on his neck. Bloodstains covered the front of his dress shirt and tie.

"Lieutenant, come out here and look at who I just found," Sgt. Mason said.

Joy and Lt. Drakon ran toward the exit door to the rear of the building, and she screamed and covered her mouth after discovering Mr. Gillman's dead body. Upon her gruesome discovery, Joy turned her head at the sight of the mutilated remains and cried out, "No—no, I can't believe this. Why would anyone do this to Mr. Gillman?"

"I'm sorry for your loss, but Ms. Maxwell, please calm down, take a few steps back, let my partner and I check the area to see what we can find," Lt. Drakon said; then she took out a pair of latex gloves and put them on her hands.

Distraught and crying hysterically, Joy remembered why she

and the detectives went there in the first place, "The footage!" Joy exclaimed. "Sgt. Mason, the video, let us go back inside and check to see if the recording is still there.

Sgt. Mason shook his head after he pulled the latex gloves down to his wrist. Joy ran back inside, and he gave chase. She entered the security room tapped on the keyboard to pull up the footage from yesterday morning.

Joy checked the files in the computers database, and she said, "Darn it, that bastard already erased the footage. There's nothing here. It all has been wiped clean."

"Will you be okay, Ms. Maxwell?" Sgt. Mason said as he touched Joy on her shoulder.

"I'll be okay. I'm used to seeing dead bodies by now," Joy replied.

"Let's go outside and get some air. The fresh air could do you some good," Sgt. Mason said to Joy as he put his arm around her and helped her up out the chair situated in front of the monitors. I promise you, Ms. Maxwell; we will get the monster who did this."

Joy leaned on Sgt. Mason for support as they both walk down the corridor towards the rear exit of the building.

Lt. Drakon radioed in for the coroner and the CSI unit to come to the scene.

Sgt. Mason noticed the severed head in a pool of blood on the ground; the glare from the sun illuminated it has rose higher in the sky. The darkness of the alley made it hard to see at first glance.

He abruptly turned around and guided Joy away from his gruesome discovery. "I could use some coffee," Sgt. Mason said. "Let us use the front entrance. There's a Starbucks across the street before we walked to the building," he said in a high-pitched tone.

"I don't know, I guess. I hadn't eaten anything since yesterday," Joy replied.

"Let me alert my partner on our wear abouts, excuse me." Sgt. Mason grabbed for his radio and said, "Lt. Drakon, we have a 10-54 in the alley. Please be advised."

"10-4, stand by," Lt. Drakon replied. The radio went silent for a minute, then she said, "I've made contact, female D.O.A, late twenties, I'll call it in."

Lt. Drakon kneeled next to the headless body and searched for clues. She picked up a name tag that read: "Deidre." She remembered that Joy mentioned that Deidre had her handbag with her purse, and the killer must have gotten the key to the channel five building. She stood up, and Deidre's head was positioned in-between dumpster and the supermarket.

Joy and Sgt. Mason walked back across the street from Starbucks; she dropped her coffee cup on the pavement when she saw Lt. Drakon next to a headless dead body of a headless female dressed in the Super C supermarket uniform. The head of her friend Diedre was out in the open by the dumpster.

Sgt. Mason tried to stop her from entering the alley, but she managed to get pass by him.

As Joy approached Deidre's dead body, Lt. Drakon said, "Ms. Maxwell, you shouldn't be back here."

"She can't be dead," Joy said with her hand over her mouth as tears streamed down the side of her face.

"Please step back, Ms. Maxwell. We can't have you contaminate the crime scene," said Lt. Drakon with no regard for her feelings.

"Are you not human–you callus bitch? Deidre was my friend and now she's lying there dead in an alley."

Lt. Drakon paused for a minute and thought to herself that as a policewoman for ten years, she has never lost her composure. Giving how close they both are to the victims of this case; she was grief-stricken and on the verge of tears. More so than when she was attacked and left for dead. Although she felt empathy for Joy, Lt. Drakon hadn't forgotten her duties as a lead detective on a murder scene. She thought to herself, "If Ms. Maxwell tramples the crime scene, we may never catch the killer."

Lt. Drakon took a deep breath and said, "Please, Ms. Maxwell, I'm going to need you to clear the area. I must protect the integrity of the crime scene; any clues here could lead my partner, and me to whoever committed these heinous murders."

Joy paused for a minute, thought about Deidre's family, and said, "Our job is to solve this case, catch the person who robbed Deidre's husband of never seeing her again and her children of not having their mother, either.

She then took a deep breath, wiped the tears from her face, and said, "I'm sorry, your right, Detective, but all of this is my fault. Oh my, the killer will be after me next. But I understand that you have a job to do. I'll get out of your way."

Lt. Drakon reached for the radio and said, "Dispatch, Double homicide at the Super-C supermarket in midtown, white male mid-fifties, Hispanic female late twenties over."

"Lt. Drakon, do you think it is the same perp who killed Sgt. Blake, or it's just a coincidence," Sgt. Mason said.

"Sgt. Mason, I don't believe in coincidences. Everything happens for a reason. It is a series of extenuating circumstances that brought us all here together for a reason. I believe in causality, and I intend on figuring out how this will play out," Lt. Drakon replied. She approached him and showed him Joy's driver's license, and whispered, "Do you think that Ms. Maxwell has anything to do with these murders?"

"I'm a good judge of character, and she doesn't fit the profile, but I've seen some shady shit while working narcotics in Philly; we can't know for sure, can we. One thing's for sure is that she's withholding key evidence from us–I would bet my badge on it."

Lt. Drakon scratched head with the inside of her arm and Sgt. Mason walked toward the sound of approaching police sirens.

Chapter 3

Joy Maxwell exited the alley and walked towards the Challenger with her arms folded and her head down. Her inherent guilt bogged her down like a damp-down comforter. The image of Sgt Thomas Blake creeping through her apartment, then his heart being ripped out of his chest by the stranger. "Damn, Mr. Gillman, I told you those damn cigarettes would kill you," she said after looking down at a cigarette butt on the ground. "Deidre, I'm sorry you got caught up in my shit. This should've been me lying dead in the alley. Your family will miss you dearly."

Joy covered her face and cried under the guise of her palms. She sniffled, trembled, then she hyperventilated uncontrollably. She crouched in between two parked cars and dry heaved while she gasped for air. She propped herself up on the Dodge Challenger and held on for dare life. A few minutes in this position, her breathing went back to normal.

Joy stood up and dried her mouth with her sleeve. She shook her head in disbelief at what has transpired over the past few hours. She couldn't wrap her mind around the reasoning of the stranger responsible for the murders. "Who's this freak of nature? Is he the person terrorizing the city? Are all these heinous acts of violence somehow connected? But, how? Why did he spare my life?" Joy thought. "I'm going to help catch this low-life, blood-sucking amoeba if it kills me too," she said.

Lt. Drakon and Sgt Mason stood face to face in the alleyway discussing whether Joy's connection to the victims can't be coincidental. But by her reaction to this ordeal rules her out as a prime suspect for the murders.

"Lieutenant, I think we need to question Ms. Maxwell about

the fact that her purse was here at the scene of the crime," Sgt. Mason said.

"I agree, Sergeant," Lt. Drakon replied. "But we still must rule her out as the prime suspect."

"But you must admit it; this might be the lead we are looking for."

"Okay, *Norco,* we will take this clue in consideration and do everything by the book to discern who or what committed these heinous crimes."

"You know what, Lt., I may be new at this being a murder detective all but two days, but I am supposed to be your partner. I thought that we were working together to try to solve cases here. Sgt. Mason said while gritting his teeth. "I know you're "The lead" here, but you think just because you're pretty, a hotshot adrenaline junkie, and slick-talking S.O.B. that you are going to run all over me. I have news for you Lt., I'm not some dim-witted bird brain looking to fly around you and expose my colorful plumage to get your attention here. I'm not some rookie cop looking to brown nose with you either."

"You know what, you're right; I am the lead here. I outrank you Sgt, that means I have more experience, and if the shit hits the fan, it's my ass in the ringer, not yours. My career is on the line here. This is not one of your sting operations where you could go all gun-ho. Furthermore, I'm your superior, and if you ever undermine my authority or my decision-making again, there will be hell to pay. You got that, Sergeant!"

Lt. Drakon turned and walked away from Sgt Mason. The loud sound of sirens blared from the approaching emergency vehicles to the crime scene was a fitting end to their little spat. Sgt Mason remained speechless but heard the Lieutenant loud and clear. He lunged forward and grabbed her arm and said, "Wait a minute, Lt. you don't think that I'm handsome?"

The lieutenant looked at Sgt. Mason's hand on her arm, and he removed it. "When I took out my frustration on you, I said that you were pretty. But when you chewed me a new asshole, you didn't comment about my good looks."

Lt. Drakon adjusted her jacket and placed her hand on the gun in the holster on her hip, and said, "Do you think this is a joke, Sgt?"

The captain walked up to them and asked, "Is there a problem here?"

"No, Captain, nothing that I can't handle myself," Lt. Drakon replied.

Sgt Mason stretched both of his arms in the sky, took a step back away from Lt. Drakon, and said, "She's right, Captain just a misunderstanding. The Lieutenant has it all covered." He stepped away from the Capt. and walked back into the alley to talk with the CSIs. The Capt. didn't press the issue any further than that. New partners have been known to bicker or quarrel a lot, sometimes even request a transfer just to get away from each other.

"Okay, then since we have that settled, Drakon, tell me what happened here? The captain asked.

"Here we have a Hispanic female, about 5'-4" mid-twenties, cause of death, decapitation," Lt. Drakon replied. "Mrs. Gaya was a co-worker of Ms. Maxwell here at this supermarket. It looked like the perpetrator grabbed Mrs. Gaya, and he used a very sharp blunt object to sever her head from her body." She looked down at the victim's identification she had in her hand earlier this morning.

The Capt. Lit up the half of stogie in his mouth then put on a pair of latex gloves.

"The manager must have heard the commotion and exited the building to investigate and risked his life trying to protect Mrs. Gaya.

His body was found a few yards past the exit door. He had ligature marks and four puncture wounds on his neck. There were no defensive wounds around his shoulders, arms, or fist. He must've been ambushed by the killer."

Suddenly, blood-curdling screams echoed in the alley from the rest of the staff in uniform as they made their way toward the employee entrance. They moved through the crowd of people that gathered on the street.

"Oh, my God, are those dead bodies?" asked the staff.

"Is that a severed head?" asked Jill, a cashier.

"Is that Mrs. Gaya?" asked Josh, the stock boy.

"Oh shit, is that Mr. Gillman?" asked Fred the butcher.

Sgt. Mason ran toward the crowd yelling, "Keep them back! No one gets past the yellow tape!" he said. "Set up a parameter, and you, officer Giovanni, canvass the area for clues."

"Yes, Sir, no problem," the uniform officer replied.

Sgt. Mason saw the Medical Examiner and Crime Scene Unit and yells, "Let them through!" The sergeant led the M. E and the CSI to the bodies. "Here, the Lieutenant and I believe the female *vic* was attacked and killed first, then the manager, Mr. Gillman, next over there by the entry door.

Lt. Drakon was inside by the manager's office, giving the captain their theory of what happened to the victims when Sgt. Mason brought the M.E back to the office. "Here we have a fifty-six-year-old

Caucasian male, 6'-4," we know the C. O. D (Cause of death) of both victims were the same; so far, we have not located the murder weapon. We will know more when the M. E and the C. S. I unit collects all the evidence," she said.

The captain saw the M. E and said, "I'm glad you're here. We need you to carefully extrapolate these two murders. I want to know if it is the same perpetrator that we've been searching for these past few weeks. The entire city of New York is on edge. We need to get this guy; the whole entire Manhattan is being held hostage. This case is a high priority for the department. We must catch whoever is responsible for these murders and prosecute him to the full extent of the law. Whoever it is doesn't seem to care about human life. It means nothing to them."

"My team and I will burn the midnight oil to gather pertinent evidence tying this maniac to these murders. You can count on us, Captain," the M.E replied earnestly with a heavy Armenian accent. Being both the supervisor down at the coroner's office and at the Crime scene investigators unit, he understands the importance and the insurmountable pressure this case now puts on him. The medical examiner lives with the heavy burden of being both a doctor and an immortal blood-thirsty demon.

He has practiced medicine throughout his life as a man and continued to practice living as the undead. Although he's a vampire, that fact has not completely diminished his respect for order in humanity. He has prided himself on protecting the balance and retaining law and order. The M.E recognized, based on the manner in how the victims were killed, that it was done by a fellow blood demon.

Understanding the subtle difference between legend and myth, he must gather the evidence in a way that doesn't oust all vampires, including himself. It may look as if his views are a bit askew; on the contrary, he does care about justice for the victims. If humanity discovered that there are blood demons roaming the earth amongst them, it would cause chaos. He's constantly faced with the dilemma of being torn between the world of mere mortals and the immortal world of his true nature.

Before he turned his granddaughter into a vampire after she succumbed to death from her fatal injuries, he solemnly swore never to create another blood demon ever again. Of course, she was the exception to the rule. She was pure of heart, and one day he hoped that she could become his ally in defending the order from those who threaten the delicate balance between man and blood demon.

Working with her many times before, he understood that she always had good intentions. He doesn't regret going back on his vow by deciding to give her the gift of immortality. This second chance of continuing a life where she could protect the city with heightened abilities, especially since such a great person. Her life was cut short. He thought that by saving her, that she could save so many innocent people from the same ordeal–giving her line of work.

While observing the bodies and surveying for possible evidence at the crime scene, he said, "Lt. Drakon may very well be my salvation, a chance to atone for all the atrocities I am guilty of doing in this world. Over the years, I taught Lt. Drakon a lot, and she know that I saved her life, but I doubt she has fully grasped the full concept of what I've done for her mortality.

"It's time now, and I need help with keeping the balance. I can't do it all by myself alone. I could see it now–if it gets out that a vampire has been the one responsible for these murders across the city. It would be a disaster. Everyone in the city would take to the streets with pitchforks, wooden stakes, and fire chasing after the monster like a Mary Shelly novel."

"What did you say?" asked an officer close enough to him and heard his ramblings.

The M. E. realized that he was thinking out loud and said, "Nothing."

Outside the yellow tape, Joy slipped away from the crowd in front of the Super-C. She took out her cellular phone and called the television station to get a meeting.

After a few rings, the receptionist answers and said, "This is live-action news where we're always on your side, how can I direct your call?"

"Becky, this is Joy Maxwell," she replied.

"Hi Ms. Maxwell, how can I help you?"

"Call me Joy, Becky. Mrs. Maxwell is my mother. Becky, could you transfer me to Mr. Richardson. I'm on the verge of getting the exclusive of the biggest story of the century. Make sure you patch me through."

"Sure, thing Joy, I'll do just that," Becky said to Joy before she transferred the call.

Joy waited patiently for her boss Mr. Richardson to answer. When he didn't pick up, Joy pushed the end call button on her cell phone and put her plan into motion.

As she stood up across the street at the bus stop, the killer lurks in the shadows surveying the crime scene admiring how his handy work has caused such a big commotion. The vampire took a deep breath in enjoying the stench of human decay and grief in his lungs. He revelled in the fact that he's the one responsible for all this death. Although the situation excited him, he's disciplined enough not to reveal himself. "Cuncti dies unus moriatur," (One day everyone dies,) he said through his devilish grin.

Joy noticed the devilish figure in the shadows and ran back across the street into the crowd to alert the police of the suspicious figure nearby. She tried her best not to make any sudden movements that would otherwise draw attention from the person in the dark to her intentions. With heightened senses, the blood demon easily noticed her movements, but he didn't react.

Joy got through the crowd and reached the yellow tape.

Lt. Drakon, Sgt. Mason, Capt. Constantine, and Dr. German stepped out of the supermarket. Deep in council, they all walked toward the body of the manager Mr. Gillman. "Lieutenant Drakon," Joy yelled over the noise of the crowd and got her attention. She nodded to the officers to let her through the yellow tape. Joy ran toward the detectives at full speed, terrified as if she saw a ghost.

Joy tripped and stumbled over her own feet and fell face-first to the ground. She put her two hands out in front of her to break the fall. She got up as quickly as she fell, determined to relay the message.

Relentless in her resolve, when Joy reached Lt. Drakon, she was out of breath and said, "L...look across the street—, the man who killed Sgt Thomas Blake in my apartment is out there right now."

"Where?" Lt. Drakon replied and whipped her head around as fast as she heard the news.

Sgt. Mason and the Captain drew for their service revolver simultaneously.

Joy led the detectives through the crowd and pointed toward the area of the bus stop where she was just standing.

Lt. Drakon made eye contact with the blood demon and asked, "Ms. Maxell, are you okay?"

"I am now!" replied Joy. "He's wearing an all-black coat with a hood."

The Lieutenant rushed past Joy and radioed in the description of the suspect. "Calling all officers close in proximity to the Super-C, be on high alert. We have eyes on the murder suspect. He's on east 38th St. standing 6'-0," wearing an all-black coat with a hood, he's standing at the 44-bus stop," said the dispatcher after Lt. Drakon gave the message.

The vampire heard Lt. Drakon radio in his description and location. His eyes shadowed each officer as they converged on him in the alley.

Sgt. Mason said, "I'll go to the left to trap him in."

"Good, I'll head him off this way, so he won't escape," Lt. Drakon said.

Capt. Constantine shouted, "This is it, people, let's not screw this up now. We got him surrounded."

The officers inched toward the blood demon as he stood there motionless at the bus stop. He took one step backward into the alleyway and disappeared.

"What the fuck? Where did he go?" asked Lt. Drakon and lowered her weapon down by her side.

The rest of the officers on the scene stood around in dismay.

"He's gone!" Sgt. Mason replied and scratched the top of his head in disbelief.

"Did anyone see the suspect!" Lt. Drakon yells in the radio.

"How could he vanish into thin air?" uttered the captain in disbelief.

Lt. Drakon put a BOLO (Be on the lookout) call through the radio for any signs of the suspect in the area. "He couldn't have gotten far, sweep the area for this bastard," she said. As panic and tension set in, the officers on the scene scurried to scan the area for the missing murder suspect.

Joy yelled out so the detectives could hear her, "I think I know where he's going to be next."

"Where, Ms. Maxwell?" Lt. Drakon asked, and the rest of the officers looked in the direction where Joy stood. "I hope you have a good idea because inquiring minds want to know."

"He must be on his way to the channel-five building. If I'm correct, he will go there to get the tape from my cameraman."

"How can you be so sure, Ms. Maxwell?" asked Sgt. Mason.

"Call it a hunch, Joy replied and shrugged her shoulders.

Lt. Drakon gave Joy the thumbs up and turned her attention back to the bus shelter. She looked closer, and there appeared to be trace evidence left behind on the plexiglass by the blood demon. She got even closer, and it was a phrase written in blood. She holstered her weapon, sighed, and said, "I can't make this out; it's written in Latin." She calmly asked the CSIs to process the bus shelter.

Lt. Drakon turned around, and Sgt Mason jogged up to her. He was out of breath and said, "I've never seen anyone move so fast before. One moment you were standing right next to me, and then I looked up, and you were across the street. Man–I must be getting old; you should be representing the US in the summer Olympics; with your speed, we would never—"

"Son, you just need to get up to speed here. This is homicide, and you're not in narcotics anymore," the captain said.

Captain Constantine noticed the phrase written in blood on the bus shelter and asked, "What do we have here? What language is this written in?"

"It's Latin, Captain," the lieutenant and a uniformed officer replied simultaneously.

"How do you know?" asked Sgt. Mason.

"I've attended parochial schools all the way through to college. I was an altar boy, and I am a devote Catholic. I recognized the writing because the bible that's read from in church is written in Latin," replied the uniformed officer in a thick Brooklyn accent.

"Well, can you translate it, officer? asked the captain.

"Yeah, sure thing Captain, give me a second." He looked closer and mumbled under his breath before reading the phrase aloud. "It says, *Cuncti dies unus moriatur*, which means one day everyone dies."

"Who is this message intended for? Is it for one of us? Lt. Drakon asked.

"I think it's for me," said Joy as she walked up behind the officers at the bus stop.

The CSI stepped by the officers and dusted the bus shelter for prints and gathered the evidence on the scene left by the perpetrator.

The captain asked, "Did anyone get a good look at the suspect besides Ms. Maxwell?"

"No, Captain," everyone replied in unison.

"Okay, first things first, let us all close in on this suspect. We need to be hot on his trail. With these bodies piling up one by one in my city, it is messing with my ulcer. The captain reached inside his pocket for his Pepto Bismol, screwed off the cap, and took a big gulp from the bottle. The captain grimaced, rubbed his stomach, and turned to Joy and said, "Ms. Maxwell, throughout all the commotion, have you noticed anything missing from your possession?"

"I don't think so. I couldn't really tell my apartment was in shambles. I haven't had the time to look through my things, given all the things that have gone wrong these past couple of days. Deidre accidentally mistook my handbag for hers, and we never got the chance to switch them back," Joy replied with a southern drawl.

Lt. Drakon recalled seeing Joy's wallet and remembered that it seemed out of place and asked, "What about your wallet, Joy?"

"What do you mean? Why are you asking me about my wallet, detective Drakon?"

"—What she meant to ask was, can you remember the contents of your purse?" said Sgt. Mason.

"Oh–okay yeah," Joy said. "The usual, money, maxed out credit cards and the keys to the channel-five building, every full-time employee has a set. My boss never wants to lose a story, so all reporters have 24-hour access to the newsroom."

"Good, Lt. Drakon and Sgt Mason, you two take her over to the channel-five building; maybe we could catch this guy there," The captain said.

"But I don't have my pocketbook," Joy replied. "Deidre had my pocketbook.'

Lt. Drakon reached in her coat pocket and handed Joy her handbag.

"Where did you find this?" asked Joy.

"I spotted it at the crime scene by the body in the alleyway,"

Lt. Drakon replied.

Joy rummaged through the handbag and said, "My purse is missing!"

"Everybody, clear the area and get back to the station before the shift changes over, the captain barked orders to the remaining officers on scene. "Scour the streets for this guy; catching this cop killer is top priority. Listen up, I just got three calls just now, one from the mayor, one from the governor, and one from the commissioner over at One PP (One police plaza.) These weren't social calls people; they're bringing in the FBI on this one. There have been six victims so far, possibly more we haven't found yet. And we have no leads whatsoever!" The officers looked on intently as Captain Constantine made his speech.

"We've gathered zero evidence other than this message written in blood at a bus stop. Ms. Maxwell is our only witness, she's the only one who can identify the perp, and if we go off that, we could be looking for a stalker and not the real murder suspect. Any criminal defense attorney worth his/her weight in salt would have a field day with this.

"We have forty-eight hours to apprehend a suspect or suspects tied to these murders. Lieutenant Drakon, you know what I need from you. Sgt. Mason, I know you're a new transfer; just follow your partner's lead. And for God's sake, try and keep up."

Lt. Drakon leaned in close to the captain and said, "Let me do this on my own–he's only going to slow me down."

"Tough shit Lt. Drakon, he's with you lieutenant, Sgt. Mason is your partner. Now deal with it!" the captain exclaimed and walked off. He got into his squad car and drove off.

Stunned by the captain's response, the lieutenant joined Sgt.

Mason and Joy, then folded her arms across her chest. "You heard the captain, let's go out and get this bastard," she said as they walk to the patrol car. "Joy, what's this guy looking for on the tape that your cameraman has?"

"I'm not certain. I don't even know this person," Joy said.

"Answer me this, who else would he go after at the station?" asked Sgt. Mason. "Considering he may have taken your keys from your purse that you said Deidre had."

Irritated at the notion that she could somehow be linked to the murderer, Joy said, "Would you want me to guess, or would you prefer that I give you all the facts that I know pertaining to this case?"

"Sgt. Mason raised his eyebrows, scratched his head, and said, "We truly appreciate the sentiment, but I can't help to wonder that you were withholding information from us."

"I hope you would want to hear the truth along with those facts– I mean, I don't want to mislead anyone here because if I lied, that mishap would send you two on a wild goose chase around the city chasing your tail," Joy continued.

"I mean, we did find your wallet at the scene of the crime. And you still hadn't given us your alibi when the murders occurred, Ms. Maxwell," Lt. Drakon said.

Joy scoffed, folded her arms across her chest, leaned forward, and said, "You got to be kidding me! What am I a murder suspect now?"

Both detectives looked at one another in the front seat of the car.

"Screw you both!" Joy exclaimed and sat back, crossed her legs, and looked out the window of the police sedan swerving in and out of traffic with the sirens blaring. After a moment of silence, Joy said, "Do you really believe that I could actually be responsible for murdering six people! I don't think that you do. If you did, I would be down at the station; you two would be playing good cop, bad cop, and not in this car following up on a lead that I've given you. If you two are the best that NYPD has to offer, then the city is going up shits' creek without a paddle."

Lt. Drakon looked at Joy through the rear-view mirror and said, "To answer your question, Ms. Maxwell, you are a suspect. Everyone connected to this case is until we've determined otherwise. So, you're going to cooperate with us and answer all the questions we ask you truthfully, or I'll arrest your ass for obstruction of justice, little miss country girl."

At that moment, they arrived at the channel-five building, the Sgt, Lt., and Joy exited the vehicle. They cautiously approached the main entrance of the building. Lt. Drakon said, "I don't like this situation one bit. We don't have no idea where the murder suspect is. It's like the blind leading the blind–no offense Ms. Maxwell."

"None was taken, Detective. We're here now, so let's just make the best out of a bad situation," Joy replied. She pulled open the front door, stepped to the side, and said, "After you, Detective."

Unsure of where to go or who to look for, Lt. Drakon devised a plan. Her cell phone rang before they reached the security desk. Startled at the sudden noise of the ringtone, she reached for the phone, and answered it. "Hello, this is Lt. Drakon speaking." There was no answer on the other end. "Who is this?" she asked. After she didn't get a response, she pressed the end button on her cell phone.

Sgt Mason said, "What was it? What happened? Was that the lab? Did they get back to you with the results from the trace evidence?"

"No, must have been a wrong number," Lt. Drakon replied while putting her cellular phone back in its case located on her hip.

Joy smiled–putting on her southern charm, and said, "Good morning, Becky, that's a nice top–is that new blouse you're wearing?"

Becky blushed at the compliment, smiled, and said, "No, this old thing."

Joy smirked and said, "Is Mr. Richardson in his office? I need to speak with him right away. This is Lt. Drakon and Sgt Mason, and they're here to investigating a murder. In fact, the suspect may be in this building as we speak."

With a frightened look on her face, Becky froze, and Joy pulled the phone towards her, turned it around, picked up the receiver, and dialed the number to Mr. Richardson's office.

Mr. Richardson picked up the phone and said, "Go, time is money, and money is time, so don't waste mine."

"Boss, this is Joy Maxwell; listen carefully; you need to evacuate the building ASAP. We have reason to believe that person responsible for the *Midtown Murders* is here in the building right now.

"You gotta be shitting me! What the hell are you talking about Ms. Maxwell?"

"Don't ask questions. Just warn everyone in the office and get them the hell out of there."

"Are you sure, Joy? I need you to be certain; I have a television/news station to run here."

"As sure as I'll ever be Boss."

The president of channel five news was apprehensive but saw a breaking story, a newsworthy opportunity to report. "Okay, Ms.

Maxwell, who is your source? Did you contact the police?"

Lt Drakon grabbed the phone from Joy, hung it up, and asked, "Ms. Maxwell, what floor is he on?"

"Eighteenth, Joy replied.

"C'mon, let's go!" said Sgt Mason.

They all got into the elevator, and Joy pressed the button for the 18th floor. When they arrive, Joy barged into Mr. Richardson's office with detectives Drakon and Mason. He turned around in his chair with the phone at his ear. Perturbated by the unannounced entry into his office, he scowled, put his hand over the microphone from his headset by his mouth, and said, "What is the meaning of this? Joy, you better have a good reason for barging into my office like you're the police."

The detectives flashed their badges at Mr. Richardson and commanded him to hang up the phone. "Hello, I am Lt. Drakon, and this is my partner Sgt Mason; we have reason to believe that the suspect responsible for the midtown murders is here in the building. So, if you don't want to be the one responsible for this guy kidnapping or killing anyone here in the building, I suggest you follow our direct orders."

Mr. Richardson said, "I'll call you back!" Then he put the microphone in the air and replied. "Detectives, I don't think it is a great idea to announce to everyone that there is a murderer on the loose in the building– it would cause pandemonium. Besides, you guys aren't even certain he's here; now are you." He leaned back in his chair and put the tips of his fingers together with his elbows on the armrest. "Now, don't get me wrong, I want to cooperate with you on this, but I must ask: do you know what or who this guy is after here at the station?"

"No, we don't, but Ms. Maxwell insists that this individual has an interest in her cameraman and some tape he has in his possession. Maybe there is some incriminating evidence he has a recording of."

Mr. Richardson rubbed his chin, spun around his chair, processed the information he just heard.

Now knowing that the *Midtown Murderer* was inside the building, he doesn't want to cause a stir with the employees already in the building. Being a clever and resourceful person, he thought of a way to use this situation to his advantage without endangering any lives.

Mr. Richardson abruptly spun back around and pressed a button on his headset.

"Security!" said the voice on the other end.

"Pull up the security feed on the monitors in my office–let's see if we could pinpoint this guy's actual location here in the building," Mr. Richardson said.

"Yes, sir, Mr. Richardson."

Lt. Drakon realized that Mr. Richardson might be on to something and moved closer toward the monitors. Lt. Drakon asked, "A corporate building such as this one should have security cameras everywhere, correct."

"Yes, it does, state of the art." Mr. Richardson waits as the security feed is transferred, and all angles could be seen on all the monitors in the newsroom.

Joy approached Lt. Drakon, tugged on her right arm, and said, "Are you crazy? We must evacuate everyone from this building."

Lt. Drakon replied to Joy without taking her eyes off the monitors, "He's right, you know if we announce to everyone that the

Midtown Murderer is in this building, it would be detrimental to everyone's safety." She looked at Joy and said, "Including mine. Furthermore, we might alert this guy that we are on to him, and he just might vanish into thin air as he did earlier. If we could get a twenty on his exact location, Sgt Mason and I could get this guy and end it once and for all."

"Mr. Richardson, what are we looking at here?" asked Sgt. Mason.

Mr. Richardson hesitated at first but allowed the detectives to access his state-of-the-art close circuit security system. "We have access to every room, on every floor in the building, even in the parking garage. It's just a matter of where to look first," Mr. Richardson replied.

"Okay then, I would like a copy of all footage from five o'clock this morning until now," commanded Lt. Drakon.

Mr. Richardson pressed the button on his headset and said, "Make a copy of all footage from five A.M to now, by request of the NYPD."

"But Mr. Richardson—"

"No questions. Give them what they want."

Mr. Richardson looked at the lieutenant and said, "Anything we could do to help officers."

Joy immediately understood his angle for an exclusive and said, "I'd like to be the lead reporter on this boss." Joy thought to herself, *"This story is the big break I've been looking for. Pulitzer Prize, here I come."*

"Hurry up, there are lives a stake," Lt. Drakon said and slammed her fist into the desk.

Mr. Richardson saw that she put a dent in his desk, so he clicked a button on his headset and said, "Mrs. Burnstrum could you come to edit room three and direct these detectives towards the security centre."

"Right away, Sir," Mrs. Burnstrum replied.

The detectives turned to the door, but they waited for Joy to accompany them to the security centre. She stared motionless at the monitors studying for a glimpse of the killer. She had no intention of leaving with the detectives.

The detectives hastily exited the newsroom and met Mrs. Burnstrum in the hallway. She escorted them to the security centre.

Joy waited until the door shut, then she pulled up the chair closest to her boss.

"Get down here right away!" Mr. Richardson said to his attorney on the phone, then hung up.

Joy waited until he ended his call, then she said, "Boss, I'm the best person for this job, I'm smart, I'm resourceful, I'm—"

"What job would that be, *my little southern belle*?" Mr. Richardson replied while fiddling through some papers on the desk.

"The lead reporter on the exclusive story about the *Midtown Murders*."

"Okay, Ms. Maxwell, tell me why I should use you for this story?" he said and put down the papers on his desk. "This should be interesting," Mr. Richardson mumbles to himself whilst gently sitting back in his chair. Mr. Richardson tapped on his watch and said, "*Downhome,* you have five minutes; Shoot!!"

"I'm the only person alive that could identify the killer," she said, then cleared her throat. "I mean, he did murder detective Blake in my apartment, my manager at the supermarket, and my best friend in the whole wide world. I am a part of this, whether you like it or not. You need my insight. Nobody encountered this guy and lived to tell the story about it, but me."

"Okay, Ms. Maxwell, I'm convinced you're my lead on this, but if you screw his one up, you're done. You'll never do journalism in this town again."

"Fair enough, you won't be disappointed, Boss, I promise."

Meanwhile, Lt. Drakon and Sgt Mason were both in the security room waiting for a copy of the security footage. One of the security guards in the room asked, "What does this guy look like?"

Sgt. Mason avoided the question and said, "The main thing I want you to look for is anyone who seems out of place or suspiciously looking for something out of the ordinary."

At that moment, Joy entered the room and said, "Has anyone seen him yet?"

"No, we have not, Ms. Maxwell. I'm glad to see that you could join us," Sgt. Mason replied.

"Joy, are you the official lead reporter on this case?" Lt. Drakon asked.

Looking perplexed, Joy said, "Y…yes, how did you know?'

"No need for the dramatics Ms. Maxwell. We know you've been strategically putting yourself in position to get that role since this all started. Besides, we could use your help," Sgt Mason replied.

"Ms. Maxwell don't jeopardize our investigation. If you do, I'll book your ass for obstruction," Lt. Drakon said.

"Consider yourself deputized," Sgt. Mason said.

"That's a ten-four, Detectives!" Joy replied.

The lieutenant looked Joy in her eyes and said, "Make sure that you run everything through me before you submit the article to your boss Mr. Richardson." She put her hands on her waist and exposed the gun on her hip. "I don't need all the facts in the newspaper before we crack this case. We normally work with other reporters this way and it usually benefits all who are involved. You scratch our backs, and I'll protect yours, *Capiche.*"

Lt. Drakon brought her attention back to the monitors when a funny feeling came over her. An overwhelming hunger from deep within gnawed at her like a trapped animal biting off its own limb to escape. The room began to spin as she stood in the middle of the room surrounded by all those television monitors. She folded her arms across her chest to hide her pain and discomfort.

Lt. Drakon kept her composure and showed no signs of distress. She focused on the images on the monitors to distract herself from the thirst. Sweat dripped down her face like condensation on a cold glass of water on a summer day. Her heart rate elevated, and she started to pant like a wolf howling at the moon. All the blood rushed from her face, and she looked flush.

Her vision was blurry, so she closed her eyes and rubbed them to regain focus. She leaned on the desk with both of her hands, and her eyes remained closed—panic set in over her like a down comforter.

Sgt Mason noticed the difference in her appearance and asked, "Lieutenant, are you Okay?"

"I'm fine, Sergeant, just pay attention to the screens, please; we need to catch this scumbag," she replied.

Now that Sgt. Mason brought attention to her appearance, everyone starred at her making her even more uncomfortable.

Joy nudged Lt. Drakon's arm and said in her soft southern accent, "Sweetie, come with me to the little girl's room–you look terrible."

The lieutenant nodded her head. But she felt embarrassed. She couldn't figure out what was going on with her, so she followed Joy to the bathroom.

Sgt. Mason turned his attention back toward the monitors as Joy and Lt. Drakon leaves the room.

The two women bumped into Mr. Richardson in the hallway, and he said, "Lt. Drakon, you don't look so good, are you okay?"

A bit irritated about her current condition and all the unwarranted attention it's getting her. Lt. Drakon's thirst has gotten worst. Her heart rate increased even more. It beat louder and faster like a locomotive barrelling down a train track. The stench of fresh blood from all the people in the hallway agitated her more. She looked at each person that stared at her walking by and noticed their pulsating heartbeat through their jugular veins.

Lt. Drakon never felt this venerable in all her natural life. She could feel her insides starting to eat away at itself. She tried to open the lady's restroom door when a man put his arms around her, pushed it open for her, and asked, "Lieutenant, are you okay?"

Lt. Drakon straightened up, reached for her service weapon, but she didn't have the strength to lift it. She said in a deep voice, "Back off–NYPD!"

"It's okay, Lieutenant," the man replied and extended his hand toward Lt. Drakon with his badge in it.

After seeing his badge, Lt. Drakon nodded her head to show her gratitude and stumbled inside the bathroom. Joy put the lieutenant's arm over her shoulders and helped the rest of the way. There were half a dozen females inside the ladies' room. She brandished her badge and said, "Everyone out!" Nobody moved an inch. They just continued doing what they were doing. The lieutenant took out her gun and said, "Out! This is official police business." The ladies cleared the bathroom. "That means you too, Ms. Maxwell."

Lt. Drakon repeated the phrase as she stumbled through the bathroom, kicked open the stalls one by one until she realized that she and Joy were the only ones inside the restroom. As her condition became more manageable, she walked over to the sink and tried to turn on the faucet, but her limbs remained cumbersome.

Lt. Drakon looked up at the mirror and was frightened at her faded reflection. She turned her head when she heard someone turn the knob on the door of the bathroom door. She quickly ducked into one of the stalls and plopped down on the toilet seat. She was perplexed at what she saw in the mirror and couldn't risk anyone seeing her this way.

The person fiddling with the knob was Timothy Frank; he poked his head inside the bathroom but didn't see anyone in sight. Timothy then stepped into the restroom and locked the door behind him. He then stopped at the mirror and adjusted his tie, and said in an Akkadian accent the phrase, *"Cuncti dies unus moriatur,* (One day everyone dies.) *Nolite ergo hoc satis erunt in principio statim,"* (Don't worry, it will all be over soon enough and then a new beginning.)

Lt. Drakon yelled out from behind the door of the stall she was in, "This is the ladies' room, you pervert." There was no reply. Still feeling weak and venerable, she asked, "Timothy, I presume." Lt. Drakon could hear his shoes click, clack on the surface of the black and white vintage subway tiles covering the floor with each step he took toward her.

Timothy walked slowly to the stall Lt. Drakon was in and stood right in front of it. She looked down and saw his shiny shoes facing her as she sat there defenseless and afraid of what was about to happen. She closed her eyes and put her head in between her knees.

Withdrawn inside her own traumatic memories, Lt. Drakon remembered the night she was attacked and left for dead. She heard the stall latch jiggle and the movement of the stall door.

Suddenly, it was as if the space-time continuum stopped and the lieutenant, at her weakest state, felt empowered. Lt. Drakon felt a strength she had never felt ever before in her natural life. Even though her energy was depleted by the extreme hunger that had her toppled over in the fetal position, she sprang into action. She felt a sense of desperation and anger that she immediately could attribute to the moment that her ex-fiancé left her.

Lt. Drakon was infuriated at her so-called brothers in blue, who despised her for achieving a higher arrest rating than any other officer since she graduated from the academy. Her sexist male counterparts couldn't come to terms with the fact that a female had more accommodations than any police officer in the tristate area.

In English, he repeated the phrase, "One day everyone dies, one day everyone dies." as he shook the door of the stall, Lt. Drakon was locked behind. The Lt. didn't pay attention and drew her service revolver from the holster and kicked the stall door off its hinges. She stood there unfurled as she looked from right to left with her gun drawn. The man was gone; he vanished into thin air. Feeling foolish, she attempted to fix the broken stall door after she holstered her firearm. She then straightened up and walked over to the sink, turned on the faucet, put both hands under the running cold water, and splashed water on her face.

The Lt. thought to herself, "I got to get a grip on reality."

Ms. Maxwell pushed open the bathroom door and saw Lt. Drakon hunched over the sink and said with a southern drawl, "Sweetie, are you feeling better?"

Lt. Drakon reached for some paper towels, wiped her face dry "I'm fine, Ms. Maxwell," she said. "Hey, did you see a man come in here with me?"

"No, Lieutenant, I only saw the man who held the bathroom door open for you before you entered the ladies' room."

Lt. Drakon thought to herself while looking at her full reflection in the mirror, "Did I just imagine him?" she said, "No, I couldn't have, I'm a highly decorated detective with the NYPD. I'm not crazy. Somebody was in here with me." She dismissed the whole ordeal to stay sane and grounded. She then stood up straight, balled up the used paper towel, and tossed it in the trash can. She adjusted her clothes and walked towards the door past Joy.

"Ms. Maxwell did you see the face of the man that held the door open for me?" asked Lt. Drakon.

"No, no, I didn't, Detective. Why? Was I supposed to, sweetie?"

When Lt. Drakon heard that, she ran out of the bathroom, hoping to catch him in the hallway. But there was nobody out there; the man was long gone. Until Joy confirmed that she indeed saw the man in the hallway, she thought she was hallucinating and that he was a figment of her imagination.

Lt. Drakon felt like what just happened was surreal and tried to make sense of it. Still confused, she tried to figure out what was the missing piece of the puzzle.

Joy walked close beside Lt. Drakon like a child begging to play outside. "Detective, why was the man so important?" she asked. "Did he do or say something to you, Sweetie?"

Lt. Drakon ignored Joy's line of questioning and continued walking to the security/surveillance room.

Joy grimaced at Lt. Drakon's swanning complexion and said, "You're so pale–a little sun could do you some good sweetie." While trying to keep up with her, she yelled, "Detective! Detective! you never answered any of my questions."

Lt. Drakon stopped walking, stared at Joy, and said, "You're right, Ms. Maxwell. I haven't answered any of your questions, nor did I respond to your insensitive remarks either."

Joy placed her hand over her heart and said in her southern drawl, "Bless your heart, I didn't mean to offend you, Detective." If looks could kill Ms. Maxwell would-be dead-on-arrival, on her way to the morgue with a toe tag.

Lt. Drakon's color began to return to her face before she and Joy entered the security/surveillance room.

"Okay, calm down detective, I apologize," Joy said. "Did you get a look at his badge?"

"Whose badge?" replied Lt. Drakon.

"The man who held the bathroom door open for you. Think Detective, he may very well be an important piece in solving this case."

The Lieutenant pondered for a moment and said, "Timothy Frank!"

"Timothy Frank?" Joy asked in disbelief. "There's no way that was him walking away from the bathroom."

"Wait, what do you mean?" asked Lt. Drakon with a puzzled look on her face.

"The person that I saw wasn't Mr. Frank," Joy reiterated.

"But I thought you said that you saw him from the back."

"If you ever seen Mr. Timothy Frank before, you would recognize him from any angle you saw him from."

Lt. Drakon slammed her hand on the wall in the hallway. "You had to have seen Mr. Frank!" she said while biting her lip, looking agitated.

Joy pushed Lt. Drakon on her shoulder and said, "Snap out of it, let us both get in this room, and maybe this is the big break in the case we all are looking for."

Lt. Drakon sighed, and they entered the security room.

Chapter 4

Captain Constantine sat in his car with a cup of cold black coffee and churned in his seat with a heavy heart. He fretted on how to break the news to his friend's wife and family. With this not being the captain's first time telling the family of a falling officer the terrible news, it is the first time doing so for somebody close to him. The captain reached in his inside suit pocket and pulled out a small flask filled with scotch. He twisted off the cover, then took a few swigs from it to boost his courage and to numb the pain he endured over the situation.

Afterward, he twists the cap back on the flask, leaned over to the glove compartment, opened the glove box, and tossed the flask inside it. The captain slammed it shut. He reached for his Bianca breath spray in the cup holder, spritzed the solution inside his mouth to mask the stench of scotch he had on his breath. He flipped down the driver's side visor, and his reflection surprised him. He adjusted his tie and attempted to wipe away the evident dejection off his face with the handkerchief he had in the front pocket of his blazer. He got out of the squad car and adjusted his overcoat, and said to himself, "Feet don't fail me now."

Everything moved in slow motion as the captain saluted a high-ranking officer from the color guard. They made their way to Thomas Blake's front door when he had flashbacks of his former trainee and first partner he had on the force. They were partners for eight years and remained close friends for seventeen more. Until last night when a killer abruptly ended their friendship.

The men reached the front door and stood shoulder to shoulder on the front porch. The captain sighed, trusted his index finger forward and pressed the doorbell. It resembled an arrow moving through the air before hitting the target. *Ding dong, ding dong…!* The doorbell echoed inside the interior of his friend's house. He could also hear movement coming from the window of the family room inside the house.

Mrs. Blake stood there after the door opened with her hands on her hips. She had her face turned away from men and said, "Really Tommy, you or your sister couldn't have answered the doorbell. You both knew I was busy doing something." She turned and saw the captain and the color guard; it took her a few seconds to realize what was going on. Her eyes welled up with tears as she focused on the two men towering over her.

Mrs. Blake said, "N...no Connie." Captain Constantine stretched out both arms toward Mrs. Blake and caught her as she fainted into his arms. He supported the weight of the collapsing widow before she could hit the ground. He and the color guard carried Mrs. Blake to the family room and sat her limp body on the couch. Both officers didn't utter another word; they stood idled by and waited for Mrs. Blake to regain consciousness.

Mrs. Blake regained consciousness moments later, and she saw the officers standing in the doorway of her living room. At that moment, her worst fear had been realized, from the expressions on the officers' faces, their ceremonial attire, and the folded American Flag they give to the families of a falling officer killed in the line of duty. The captain slowly walked toward Mrs. Blake seated on the couch in the family room while the other officer waited by the doorway.

"How did this happen?" Mrs. Blake asked while tears streamed down her face from both of her eyes.

"I am going to spare you the details," the captain replied. "All I'm going to say is—your husband died in the line of duty as a hero protecting the community he vowed to protect."

Mrs. Blake sobbed, and the captain handed her some tissues

that was in a box on an end table. Mrs. Blake said, "I knew something was peculiar when he didn't call me this morning. He usually calls me when he stayed late at work. In twenty years, my husband never forgot to call me." Mrs. Blake stood up and walked to the purse she had lying on the coffee table and searched for something inside her purse.

Mrs. Blake paused then pulled out an old picture of she and Sgt. Blake together in his uniform fresh out of the academy. She slowly walked back to the couch, sat back down on the chair, stared at the picture and shook her head from side to side in disbelief. "I can't believe he's gone," Mrs. Blake said as she raised the picture to her bosom and sobbed uncontrollably.

Mrs. Blake looked at the captain and asked, "How am I going to break the bad news to the kids? How am I going to say that their father is gone? Our son Thomas Jr. was close with his father; he's going to be devastated when he finds out." Mrs. Blake stopped sobbing and wiped the tears from her cheeks, looked the captain directly in his eyes, and said, "Connie, please tell me you're going to get the bastard responsible for killing my husband!"

Mrs. Blake stood up and pointed her index finger into the captain's chest and raised her voice, "Promise me, Connie, that when you do catch him, that you don't bring that son of a bitch in. You promise me that you're going to kill that mother fucker the same way that he did my husband."

The captain grabbed Mrs. Blake's wrist with his right hand and then used his left arm and put it around her shoulders. He got choked up and fought back the tears that welled up in his eyes. He regained his composure and whispered in Mrs. Blake's ears, "I promise you; we will do everything humanly possible to apprehend the person responsible for this." The captain then kissed Mrs. Blake on her forehead.

At that moment, the captain noticed Detective Blake's children at the top of the stairs. The color guard ushered them both down to the family room, where the captain and Mrs. Blake stood hugging each other, grieving about the events that took place. The captain said, "Don't look now your kids coming this way." The captain wiped away the single tear that slowly streamed down his cheek with his hand, grabbed his hat and straightened himself up in preparation for the children to enter the family room.

Mrs. Blake said, "I can't—I can't do this! Why? Why me? Why us? Why now?"

The captain relied on all his strength to fight back the tears that were on the brink of coming out. He said, "Leslie if you want to get dress now, I'll take you downtown, so that you could identify the body."

Mrs. Blake nodded to the captain acknowledging the fact that this is protocol. She reached for some new tissue papers to wipe the tears from her cheeks. She placed her open hand onto his shoulder to comfort him before walking past him. After all, her husband was his friend too.

Mrs. Blake hugged her kids and stared at them both. Thomas Jr. said, "Mom, why are you crying? What happened to dad? Why are these policemen in our house?"

Mrs. Blake sighed and said, "Well, Tommy, your father was hurt last night, and the captain and I must go downtown, so that I could see him. This officer will stay here with you both until I return."

"Dad is dead, isn't he!" Thomas said, lowered his head and sobbed.

Mrs. Blake and the kids embraced. She let the kids go and headed to her bedroom to get dressed. Thomas Jr. looked at the captain while his arm was draped around his sister Katie's shoulders and asked, "Did you catch the person that killed my father?"

The captain looked Tommy right in his eyes and said, "No, not yet, but we will. I promise you; we will." He handed him the folded American Flag.

Mrs. Blake hurried downstairs and headed directly out of the house to the captain's car. He dispatched two officers to look after the kids. They saluted him until he drove off.

The ride downtown to the morgue was a quiet one. Mrs. Blake clutched her purse on her lap with both of her hands the entire ride there. She wore a pair of red leather gloves—the last gift Detective Thomas Blake bought for her.

As the squad car pulled up to the entrance of the city morgue, the captain turned to Leslie and said, "Are you ready?"

"As ready as I'll ever be," Mrs. Blake replied.

The captain opened his car door, walked around to the passenger side door, and opened it for Mrs. Blake. Leslie took the captain's hand as she exited the car. She looked at the captain and said, "Thanks, Connie! Thanks for everything you've done for my husband and my family over the years."

"I'm sorry it had to end this way Leslie," The captain replied, then he escorted Mrs. Blake into the building. They both headed towards the area where they keep the dead bodies.

The medical examiner stood over a body covered by a white sheet.

The captain nodded at him and pulled back the sheet.

Mrs. Blake saw her dead husband laying there, cold, stiff, expressionless, and void of color. She put her hand over her mouth, touched his forehead, and cried. She leaned on the captain's arm. He nodded to the medical examiner, and he covered detective Thomas Blake's body with the sheet.

Meanwhile, back at the channel five building in the newsroom, Mr. Richardson saw Lt. Drakon and yelled at her, "You need to leave this room right now, you little bitch!"

Lt. Drakon put her finger in the air and said, "Shh!"

Mr. Richardson was for a moment, his face turned bright red, then he continued his tirade, "I permitted you to view the security tapes, you frigid little bitch; now leave, I said. My lawyer is on his way here right now!"

"That's fine, I'll tell him that you gave us permission to view the surveillance tapes, and if anything happens, you'll be just as liable."

Sgt. Mason put his hand on Mr. Richardson and said, "That's right, Boss, my partner thinks he's impersonating someone named Timothy Frank. If that's the case, then the real one could be in danger."

"We need more information," Mr. Richardson asked. "Let's all put our heads together and figure this thing out," Joy said.

"I could give you some information, but what I tell you should be off the record!" Lt. Drakon said and had her arms folded across her chest. She focused her attention on one of the monitors in front of them.

"Lt. Drakon, you could trust me–my lips are sealed. Whatever you need to share with me won't leave this room," Joy replied.

"This guy is vile, callus, and heartless. He's killed three people earlier this morning just before the sun came up over the horizon. One of his victims was a fellow police officer," Lt. Drakon then said, then paused for a moment while she held back tears. "He was a good detective. That bastard tore his heart right from his chest with his bare hands while it was still beating.

"The other two victims were civilians: a young mother of two and a store clerk; and a middle-aged man who was the manager of the

Super C supermarket. Someone told me that he just became a grandfather before his untimely death by the hands of this—this monster."

Lt. Drakon turned and faced Mr. Richardson. She looked him directly in his eyes and said, "With this maniac on the loose, everybody in this entire building is in danger. So, if you excuse me, I can't sit here and continue to exchange pleasantries with you any longer. I have a dangerous murder suspect to apprehend." Lt. Drakon pushed herself away from the table where the monitors were.

Mr. Richardson pointed at the monitor and said, "Look! I think that's the guy that you're looking for."

Lt. Drakon rushed back toward the monitor and asked, "Could you tell me what floor he's currently on?"

Joy tapped on the screen and said, "I think that's eighteen, but are you sure that's him? It doesn't appear to look like the man you said you saw in the bathroom—does it, Detective?"

Everyone leaned in closer to the monitors. But nobody couldn't make out his face because the suspect held his head down away from the view of the camera.

Mr. Richardson blurted out, "Damn, we can't see his face! Could we get a better angle, so that we could get a closer look at this guy's face?"

"Just zoom in on the badge," Sgt Mason said.

Mr. Richardson does, and everyone leaned in closer to the monitors.

"Is that him? Is that our guy?" said Sgt. Mason, and he looked at Joy.

"Yes, that's the creep from the supermarket and in my apartment," Joy said, with her finger pressed against the monitor.

Lt. Drakon slipped out of the room before anybody noticed.

Sgt. Mason drew his service revolver after the door shut behind her. "I hope that's him; I don't feel like filing a report explaining why I shot the wrong guy," he said and shook his head as he followed the lieutenants lead out of the room. "She's like Houdini; I hate when she does that."

"Yeah, that's him," Joy said. "Your killing spree is over, you son of a bitch!"

Sgt. Mason was out of breath when he caught up to the lieutenant. He took a few deep breaths and geared himself up to catch the prime suspect of last night's brutal murders. He mentally prepared himself that he's going to grapple with him. He turned to the lieutenant, nodded to her, and put his gun in the air by his face.

Before Sgt. Mason could react, Lt. Drakon ran off without him. She moved as swift as a racehorse. Even though she wasn't one hundred percent herself, she wasn't deterred at all.

Lt. Drakon quickly pushed open the door from the twenty-first floor into the staircase, and then she darted down three flights of steps after the wretched murder suspect. She felt the heavy flow of blood through her veins. With the increased adrenaline, she heard her heartbeat louder—harder and faster than ever before.

Lt. Drakon took her left hand and clutched her chest to make sure that she wasn't having a heart attack. Determined to apprehend the suspect, she continued the pursuit of the murder suspect. She said to herself, "Come on, girl, you can do it. You can have the heart attack after we handcuff this guy."

Before Lt. Drakon pushed open the swinging door to the eighteenth floor, she could hear heavy painting and the elevated heart rate of someone approaching her twenty. She raised her nose in the air and inhaled; she could smell that it was Sgt Mason.

Sgt. Mason radioed in to dispatch: "The suspect is on eighteen, and we are in pursuit."

Lt. Drakon went through the door, and her senses went into maximum overdrive. Her sense of smell, hearing, and sight went far beyond their normal functions. She stumbled onto the wall, closed her eyes, and put her fingers on her temple.

Lt. Drakon thought to herself, "I may have an unbalanced equilibrium because I can't tell which way is up." She closed her eyes tighter and clutched her chest. In a normal state, the hallway would've been silent, but in her state, she heard every single conversation from each room on the eighteenth floor simultaneously. The indiscriminate chatter echoed in off the walls like white noise through the television set. She leaned on the wall and steadied her breathing to stop herself from hyperventilating.

Sgt. Mason pushed through the door and asked Lt. Drakon, "Did you see which way he went?"

Lt. Drakon calmed herself down. Her breathing and heartbeat return to normal; she regained control over all her senses. The voices in her head stopped as well. She opened her eyes then replied, "No, no, I didn't."

"Oh shit, there he is!" Sgt. Mason yelled.

Both officers gave chase. As Lt. Drakon ran by each room, she could hear everyone's heartbeat loud and clear, like her feet hitting the ground. She remained focus only on the pursuit of the suspect. "Stop or I'll shoot!" she said, and people suddenly erupted into the hallway. "Excuse me! Get out of the way! Somebody, please stop him!"

Lt. Drakon maneuvered through the crowd like a shark in open water. She scrambled through the channel five employees like a running back juking through the defensive line. She busted through the entrance doors and yelled at the crowd of people on the sidewalk. Her swift movements through the crowd shadowed the suspect like a cheetah chasing its prey through tall grass in the Savanna.

As Lt. Drakon gets closer, the undaunted suspect quickened his pace right into the path of Sgt. Mason, who shouted, "Stop, or I'll shoot!" Sgt. Mason gripped his service revolver and pointed it directly at the suspect. "Get down on the ground now, or I'll blow your fucking head off!"

Lt. Drakon ran top speed and emerged through the crowd transformed as a vampire. "Get down on the ground now!" she exclaimed in an ominous supernatural voice.

Everyone closes to her noticed Lt. Drakon's transformation and scurried out of the way. Lt. Drakon's loud, demonic, and mighty roar shocked the crowd as they ran for cover. Still unstable, her transformation reversed, and she subdued him when her heart rate slowed down.

The vampire snarled, then noticed her transformed state and snickered, exposing his fangs.

Sergeant Mason drew his weapon and said, "Listen to me, surrender; you can't escape; you're surrounded." Imploring that the dubious, soulless beast won't hurt any more innocent people.

The vampire's smile widened, he turned to Lt. Drakon, raised his hands in the air, and sang a soulless rendition of a gospel song "One day at a time," written by Marijohn Wilkin and Kris Kristofferson: "I'm not human/ I'm more than a man/let me help you to believe what I am/then I can show you what you have become/I could teach you to be all that you are/I'll show you the stairway that I've climbed centuries ago/I'm your Lord/For your own sake let me teach you to/Take one day at a time/One day at a time sweet Adeline that's all I'm asking from you/You will have the strength to feed every day/this is what you have to do from this day forward/ Yesterday's gone sweet Adeline/tomorrow and eternity is yours/So for your sake let me teach you to take/ one day at a time/walking amongst men in human form will only be a memory/Well Adeline you know if you're beginning to transform now/the voices and inner thoughts of others are starting to crowd your mind/So for your own sake let me teach you to take/ one day at a time/One day at a time sweet Adeline that's all I'm asking from you."

Unimpressed with the vampire's butchery of a perfect ode to the lord, Lt. Drakon and Sgt. Mason looked at each other perplexed by the vampire's serenade. They both said, "I hope this exhibition wasn't a diversion by this maniac, distracting us from his true sinister plot to harm more innocent people."

At that moment, two armed guards exited the building through two metal doors that led to a stairwell and approached the suspect from behind. Both security guards stood on opposite sides of the perp and closed in on the vampire with their service revolvers pointed directly at him. Before the security guards could react, the suspect disarmed them both.

Like a master of martial arts, the vampire moved in ways

words alone could not describe. With a double aerial kick, the vampire's foot reached one of the security guard's head and smashed it like watermelon–killing him instantly. He grabbed the other guard from behind with one hand and picked him up off the ground by his jaw like a ragdoll. The vampire then put the security guard in front of him in one swift motion, using him as a human shield. with his hostage in hand, the vampire inched closer toward the doorway, which led to the stairwell and his escape.

Lieutenant Drakon and Sergeant Mason both said simultaneously to the vampire, "Don't you dare go through that door!"

The vampire smiled and darted through the doorway up the staircase like a lightning strike with the security guard in hand no less.

Lt. Drakon and Sgt. Mason ran toward the doorway and cautiously looked in and then up only to see that the vampire reached the eleventh floor, pulled the door off the hinges, and entered the hallway like a blur. Sgt. Mason ran to use the elevator in the lobby, and Lt. Drakon gave chase up the stairs moving faster than humanly possible.

He pressed the elevator button repeatedly and looked up as the numbers descended to the lobby. When the elevator reached downstairs the door to the elevator opened, Sgt. Mason said to himself, "I hope this elevator will move faster than my legs could ever run."

Lt. Drakon radioed in to Sgt. Mason and said, *"I'm on eleven; where are you?"*

"I'm still in the elevator on seven over," Sgt. Mason replied. He held up the walkie-talkie and thought to himself, "How the fuck she got to the eleventh floor so fast? I got to get back in the gym.'

Lt. Drakon said over the radio, *"Hurry up. We can't let him escape."*

Sgt. Mason also heard her as she commanded, "Stop, or I'll shoot.

Lt. Drakon caught up to the suspect and stopped before she sprang into action. She panned the hallway and listened for the suspect's exact location. "I know where you are, you dirty bastard!" she exclaimed.

Lt. Drakon radioed into Sgt. Mason and said: *I got eyes on the suspect, make your way to eleven; but be very careful.*

Meanwhile, in the surveillance room, a few security guards,

Mr. Richardson, and Joy's eyes were glued to the monitors awaiting the climax to unfurl.

Joy got an eerie feeling and said, "Where is Mr. Frank?" she turned to one of the security guards and asked, "Hey, could you do an independent search on the monitors for Timothy Frank? He's wearing a grey pinstripe suit."

"Yes, I can," the security guard replied, then he checked the monitors for any sign of Mr. Frank in the building.

"There aren't any monitors in the stairwells though," Mr. Richardson said. "Oh shit, we're going to search for Timothy too! We don't know if he's caught up in all this."

Mr. Richards comments, "Good thinking," Mr. Richardson picked up the phone and asked, "Has anybody heard anything from Timothy?"

Nobody answered him; Mr. Richardson then said, "Okay, I'm going to try and get him on the phone—hopefully he'll answer. I pray that he's not hurt, tide up in a storage closet or something like that. On second thought, make it known to all security and all housekeepers to keep a lookout for him."

With the adrenaline raging through her body, Lt. Drakon fully transformed again.

As soon as she does, the stranger stopped dead in his tracks as she completed her full metamorphosis. Vampires' sensory perception is sharper than a dolphin, and they can also communicate telepathically. He waited for the right moment to get Lt. Drakon alone. He had sensed who she was earlier at the bus stop across the street from the Super C supermarket.

Sgt. Mason approached Lt. Drakon with his service revolver in hand.

"Nice of you to join us," Lt. Drakon said. "I hope he didn't notice me in my different form," she thought to herself.

"Please, you know I couldn't miss an old fashionstandoff between you the suspect," Sgt. Mason replied.

"What a joy to witness the birth of a newbie, A beauty to witness, it's amazing, welcome to this new world. Now, once you feed, the last part of your humanity will disappear, and you will be eternally altered for the rest of your days on earth," the vampire said with his arms open wide. "Join me. I'm so ecstatic that I witnessed your transformation."

The vampire snickered aloud, basking in its hubristic grandeur. He raised his palms in the air, and with a delightful grin, said, "Everyone will die one day, but living as the undead is the only way, going on and on without needing a name. I remember when death was taken from me, and I still remain the same, this curse condemned me and now I take death for what it's worth, To roam aimlessly on earth, as a succubus creating parasites, a legion of zombies with one bite, contracting an incurable disease that's virtually unknown, Feeding on the living, clinging onto immortally in this existential form."

After the vampire noticed that Lt. Drakon was unmoved–he was disappointed. He adjusted his posture, fixed his tie, and tucked his shirt in his pants.

Lt. Drakon didn't have an inkling about her transformation. Being unable to see herself, she didn't realize what he meant. Her heart rate stabilized, then she transformed back to her usual human form.

"Damn, I expected something different, someone more intriguing and interesting than this," Lt. Drakon said to herself. "Jesus! he's pathetic. His spirit is broken." She leaned in slowly, close enough to tell him, take it easy. She extended her hand towards him to comfort him. He took it, and she felt while how cold it was to the touch.

Lt. Drakon got even closer to him, and she heard him mumbling something under his breath. She couldn't make out what

he was mumbling, so she carefully leaned in even closer. He said, "Death is a dream. Life is fantasy, Death is a dream. Life is a fantasy."

Lt. Drakon let go of his ice-cold hand and stepped back away from him. He had this crazy look in his eyes. He repeated the phrase louder and louder, "Death is a dream! Life is a fantasy!"

"Take two steps back, put your hands in the air, and get down on your knees," the lieutenant said and took out her service revolver.

The vampire stopped singing for a moment, then he screamed, "Death is a dream..."

Lt. Drakon pointed her service revolver at the suspect and took the gun off safety, and said, "I'm not going to keep repeating myself. I said, take two steps back, put both of your hands into the air, slowly get down onto your knees, lay on your stomach, put your face down on the ground, and fold your fingers behind your head."

The suspect complied, but he continued to whisper his ramblings: "Death is a dream. Life is a fantasy."

Lt. Drakon pointed her gun directly at the perp. She took out her handcuffs, mounted him, and put one knee firmly on his back in between his shoulder blades. With her planted other foot on the ground, put her service revolver back on safety and holstered it on her hip. She quickly put the handcuffs on his wrist one after the other, securing them both together behind his back.

"Going for the insanity plea, I see. Well, it's not going to work," she said. "You deserve to get prosecuted at the full extent of

The law. I hope you get the death penalty. You deserve to die a slow, painful death, in front of the families of the victims that you butchered." She grabbed him by the collar and pulled him up closer to her.

"I'm going to be in the courtroom to witness the trial and when the judge reads off a guilty verdict. I will attend your execution. You've destroyed the lives of good people; one was a fellow police officer, Detective Blake. He was a husband and a father of two. He was a seasoned veteran, a true professional, and a role model. The model citizen and the type of police officer that children dreamed about becoming when they got older.

"Now get your crazy ass up off the floor." Lt. Drakon yanked the perp by his collar and the chain connecting the handcuffs and pulled him up onto his feet. She announced on her two-way radio: *"We bagged the suspect. We're on the eleventh floor."*

"Good, we will be right down," Sgt. Mason said over the radio. *"I'm pleased we could bring a cop killer in for the captain. A somewhat promising end to a shitty day."*

Sgt. Mason met Lt. Drakon on the eleventh floor. They both smirk at each other and looked away when their gaze lingered.

When Lt. Drakon's heartbeat and adrenaline returned to normal, so did her transformation. "Hell of a first day," she said.

"I've seen better days," he replied.

The two looked up at the floor indicator on the elevator and Sgt. Mason pressed the button for the elevator. "After completing the paperwork, would you like to go out for a drink later?" Sergeant Sgt. Mason asked.

Although intrigued by the notion, but her code of ethics forbade her from acting on impulse. She would have to subdue attraction towards Sgt. Mason.

"I…I can't. I have a million things to do. Besides, I'm tired, I need a shower, and I'm going to need a good night's sleep," Lt. Drakon replied.

"Come-on, lieutenant, just a few cocktails, I promise, I'll get you home before midnight, scouts honour. I am running off coffee alone myself. I haven't slept for two days now, and you don't hear me complaining."

"Okay, okay, I can use a drink. Maybe it'll help me relax. I've been on edge for the past couple of days now."

"Maybe I'll join you two, especially after being stalked by this piece of shit!" Joy Maxwell replied. Joy got right up in the suspect's face and said, "You fucking low life! You don't intimidate me. You thought you were going to kill me. Well, here I am, mother fucker."

Joy mushed the suspects cheeks together with her right palm under his chin, and her fingers pressed tightly on his cheeks.

Without interrupting Joy, Lt. Drakon asked, "Ms. Maxwell, is

111

this the man who attacked you and sergeant Blake in your apartment?"

"Yes, this is the shit shake drinking bastard," Joy replied.

At that moment, the light in the hallway flickered, and the suspect transformed to his true form in the dark, then changed back when the light returned to normal.

Joy screamed, released her grip from his face, jumped backward and put her hand on her chest.

The vampire grinned at Joy when the light in the hallway stopped flickering.

The elevator chimed to indicate it had reached their floor. The elevator doors opened, and Detectives Lt. Drakon and Sgt. Mason pushed the suspect into the elevator. They all turned around in the elevator, and Sgt. Mason reached to press the button for the lobby.

Joy didn't move one inch. She was momentarily paralyzed as the doors to the elevator closed. Sgt. Mason said. "What's the matter—cat got your tongue?"

The elevator doors closed, and Joy was at a loss for words. She didn't even get to mention to the detectives that Timothy Frank and her cameraman were missing.

"What happened to her?" Lt. Drakon asked.

Sgt. Mason shrugged his shoulders and raised his palms skyward.

The suspect shifted his body and growled at Joy, and Lt. Drakon elbowed him in the solar plexus, pushed him backward slammed him on the hard metal bar in the back of the elevator. "Be easy," Lt. Drakon said. "You'll have plenty of time be tough with the other inmates at the maximum-security prison–presumable on death row."

The stranger coughed and shouts, "Death is a dream. Life is a fantasy! Death is a dream; life is a fantasy!"

Without hesitating Sgt. Mason punched the perp in the jaw, knocking him out cold. He slid down to the ground on his ass. "That should shut him up!" Sgt. Mason exclaimed and shook his hand in the air.

"I don't know what happened to Ms. Maxwell; I wonder if she still wants to go out for drinks later?" asked Sgt. Mason without skipping a beat.

"Really!" Lt. Drakon said while glaring angrily at Sgt. Mason. "You just assaulted the perp. When he lawyers up, our whole case against him could be dismissed on a technicality. Great police work." She gave him that look that every annoyed woman does that warrants them to be labeled a bitch.

"Press the button for the first floor, will you. And don't punch it either," Lt. Drakon said. "We don't want the building's owner to sue the dept."

"Copy that, Lieutenant," Sgt. Mason replied.

The elevator door closed, and they quickly reach the first-floor lobby. As the doors to the elevator opened, they were greeted with jeers walking through the crowd of fellow police officers. Both Lt. Drakon and Sgt. Mason felt proud and a sense of accomplishment for capturing a suspected cop killer.

"This feels nice," Lt. Drakon whispers to herself.

"I wonder how long this will last," Sgt. Mason said and whispered to Lt. Drakon.

As they approach the unmarked police car, sergeant Mason opened the rear passenger side door and shoved the assailant into the car while pushing down on the back of his neck. But he still managed to bang the perp's head on the frame of the Dodge Charger.

The perp yelps, and Sgt. Mason said, "Settle down you're moving too much, you're going to scuff the paint on the car, we're going to have to add that to the list of charges."

Sgt. Mason slammed the car door on the perp's elbow. Sgt. Mason turned around, and Joy pushed her microphone forward and said, "Lieutenant Drakon, Sergeant Mason, any statements about the capture of the *Sanguine killer*?"

The detectives were speechless, but Joy continued, "Please give the city the closure it deserves." Joy switched the microphone from Lt. Drakon Sgt. Mason awaiting a response.

Sgt. Mason opened his mouth to speak, but the lieutenant pulled back on her partner's arm and said, "I don't want to talk about this guy on camera." She got inside the car and slammed the door.

Sgt. Mason, with a bewildered look on his face, got in the car and said, "Why not? We caught the man who has been terrorizing midtown Manhattan. Not to mention that he killed a fellow police officer, a cop who was respected and loved. So, what the hell is the problem?".

Lt. Drakon sighed, and she slumped her shoulders, then replied, "I know, I know, but I am not entirely certain that this is the guy that is solely responsible for all three murders. He fits the M.O, but could he have killed those three people alone last night?" Lt. Drakon looked intently into detective Mason's eyes.

Sgt. Mason opened his mouth, and Lt. Drakon said frantically, "We weren't there at the scenes of those heinous crimes. You weren't there in the hallway with him; he looked like a broken whimpering shell of his former self, whoever that was.'

"You think he was working with someone else?" Sgt. Mason asked.

"I do. He can't be the mastermind behind those murders. That would make him a serial killer, for Pete's sake. The evidence shows that he was sloppy, not concise, opportunistic, and driven by a purpose. If he did do it alone, he had to be under a hex or something.'

"A hex. What the hell do you mean a hex?"

Sgt. Mason was puzzled by her take of the motivation of this scum they had handcuffed and sitting in the back seat of their cruiser.

"Look, Lieutenant, it was as if he was after something specific," Sgt. Mason said. "I wonder if he got it. That's why he's playing possum."

Lt. Drakon raised her eyebrows and looked in the rear-view mirror at the man they just apprehended.

"Lieutenant, it looks random at first glance, but what if he methodically chose his victims?" asked Sgt. Mason. "Plus, as far as we knew, the killer only picked on a defenseless women for his victims. It still doesn't make any sense the lack of blood inside each victim's body. What is the motive?"

"I believe that is the only similarity here," said Lt. Drakon. "So, when we go over there, leave the interview to me, don't say a single solitary word. I'm going to give Joy just what she and these vultures need for an exclusive. But of course, I will leave most of the key factors in the case out, that the victims are all killed by one man."

Sgt. Mason nodded his head in agreement, and they got out of the car to address the media.

"We use the media to aid us in this murder cases, but to do that, we must play a game of chess," Lt. Drakon instructs Sgt. Mason. "The suppression of key evidence allows us to remain one step ahead in this case. Being able to neither confirm nor deny whatever questions thrown at you in front of the camera is paramount."

As soon as they reached Joy, a policeman continued with the search of the two guys that were missing, came out of the building.

"Detectives, detectives!" he said, beckoning to get their attention.

Without hesitation, Lt. Drakon and Sgt. Mason turned toward him to address his hails. "What is it officer, both detectives spoke almost simultaneously.

The policeman whispered to hide what he was about to reveal to the detectives.

"Where are they?" the lieutenant asked and leaned closer to him with expectations of having two more witnesses. Those witnesses could add another nail in the coffin of this bastard. But the officer didn't answer. The lack of response to the lieutenant's inquiries ironically communicated the contrary. "Okay, then, where are the bodies?"

"They're on two separate floors, Lieutenant. From what I gathered, one victim is in a rather peculiar place, and the other is in an office sitting behind a desk." The officer pulled out his notepad and flipped to the page where he jotted down the notes he had.

Detective Mason jotted down the information that was given by the officer. As he looked up from the notepad looking at the officer divulge the information about the locations of yet two more stolen lives.

"The executive Timothy Frank was in a chair facing the window. The cleaning lady said she tended to the room and didn't notice that he was dead. The cameraman was found stuffed in an equipment closet." When the officer was done, he closed his notepad and put it away.

"Let me guess his neck had puncture wounds and only a small amount of blood was present on his body," Lt. Drakon said and shook her head in dismay.

"What's your name, officer?" Sgt. Mason asked.

Before the uniformed officer could answer, Sgt. Mason read his name off his badge along with his number and said, "Come with me, officer Stevens. Did you come in a squad car?"

"Yes, my partner and I responded to the 10-13," answered Stevens. "Detective Mason, what are you getting at?"

"What? I need from you is to guard my prisoner, while I go upstairs to observe the crime scene, Copy?'

"That's a 10-4, Sgt. Mason."

"I got something else to do other than babysit this guy. I don't trust myself alone with him. Things might get violent in front of the channel-five building," Sgt. Mason leaned in and whispered to the beat cop. "I think you should put your knight stick deep in his ass, better you than me. Besides, I'll be completely on your side.

"Go ahead lump him up, beat him down in front of the cameras. Sgt. Blake's family would be grateful for the gesture."

Officer Stevens turned towards the right-wing conservatively dressed reporters waiting like a congregation of alligators ready to chomp down on their unsuspecting prey. They were all waiting for the career-boosting story from anyone with the gruesome details.

"You see them out there salivating. They don't give a shit about the victims' families. They can't wait to get an exclusive on this story; it makes me sick," Sgt. Mason said and slapped officer Stevens on the shoulder. "Watch this scum bucket, will ya! And control any impulse you may have; show a little professionalism."

Officer Stevens stood there with a blank look on his face.

"Thanks a lot, officer Stevens. I owe you one."

Before he could object, Officer Stevens was on a shit detail. Sgt. Mason's fast-talking got him to watch a suspected cop-killer. He was stuck watching the deranged blood-sucking demon in the car. He could almost make out what the reporters were chattering about.

Meanwhile, Lt. Drakon and Sgt. Mason were in the elevator on the way up to the crime scene back inside the channel five building. They mulled over all the possible scenarios in their heads respectfully. Although there are some similarities from each killing, they had to figure out what the fuck was going on?

"Do you think he has an accomplice?" asked Sgt. Mason. All the while he thought the total opposite in his head. But he wasn't exactly familiar with the entire case. Plus, Lt. Drakon was more experienced as a detective and at solving murders. He didn't have to investigate any further. He had already decided who committed the murders.

Lt. Drakon didn't answer his question. She held her hands in front of her and looked up at the digital numbers in the elevator ascended.

"So, you're still going out for drinks later?" Sgt. Mason asked.

Shocked, Lt. Drakon looked at Sgt. Mason and shook her head.

"Come on, have some fun."

"Yeah, I might, only if we don't run into any more surprises," she said to herself. Before Lt. Drakon could answer, the elevator doors opened., "Go ahead upstairs and secure the crime scene. I'll stay down here and gather all the evidence I can for now before the M.E and CSIs get here," Lt. Drakon said. "We both know who to blame for this, so hurry up and wrap it up. The quicker you do, the faster we could bring him in for interrogation.

"I want to tie this one up with a pretty bow for the captain and the victims' families; alright, now go."

Lt. Drakon smiled when the doors to the elevator closed. She flashed her shield as she passed the buildings security guards in front of Timothy Frank's office. She walked inside, and the air was thick with death. She could smell the foul stench of rotting flesh.

"Has he been moved? Has anyone touched anything in here?" Lt. Drakon asked in a stern tone.

"No, Ma'am," one security guard replied.

"No, Detective," the other guard said.

"Good," Lt. Drakon replied. She walked closer to the body, but it was dark inside the room. The Venetian blinds were fully drawn down to cover up the gruesome shit that was done to the executive. The office was dimly lit; only a small amount of sun beamed through the slits in between the blind's vanes.

The chair faced the window, so Lt. Drakon walked around the desk to observe the dead body. She saw that Timothy Frank's throat was cut from ear to ear, both his arms and legs were severely broken. The bones from his femur protruded through the skin and his pant legs. His humerus bone tore his shirt sleeves.

There was very little blood spatter on or near the body; not nearly enough was present around the area of each wound. Lt. Drakon notices each artery was clearly cut, yet there were no stains anywhere from arterial spray. She thought to herself, "So, you were the guy that bastard was impersonating. I don't know what your involvement was in all of this, but from where I stand, the facts are getting stranger than fiction."

Lt. Drakon crouched next to the body and said, "This was just like the other crime scenes and victims. Nothing is adding up. The evidence suggests that he was killed somewhere else and then placed here. I don't believe that it is possible for the killer to have done this here." She looked closely at what he wore around his neck after glaring for a few seconds she recognized what it was.

She stood up and said, "Is that the victim's esophagus fashioned around his neck like a bowtie?" The sight of his exposed organs gave Lt. Drakon an aroused fascination, a curiosity that otherwise had been non-existent. At that very moment, while deeply focused on the victim's exposed flesh, her ringtone sounded off on her I-phone.

"Hello!" she quickly answered, then she put the call on speaker and placed the phone on the desk so she could continue doing her work.

"Lieutenant, I need for you to come and check out what I've discovered," Sgt. Mason said.

"What did you find, Sergeant?" she asked reluctantly. She didn't want to be pulled away from the body she was examining. Being alone examining a crime scene has always been sort of cathartic for the lieutenant, without the CSI's and other policemen trampling all over the evidence. It gave her a chance to work seemingly uninterrupted.

"I need for you to come here now, please," Sgt. Mason insisted.

"Yes, Okay," Lt. Drakon replied. She stepped away from the mutilated body and went to where Sgt. Mason was to see what he wanted to show her. Walking through the doors of the office, she closed it behind her and said, "Don't let anyone in here unless it's by my authority."

While waiting for Lt. Drakon, Sgt. Mason received a call and stepped away from everyone in the editing room. He spoke into the phone softly and covered his mouth so no one could hear his conversation.

Lt. Drakon entered the room while he was on the phone, but she didn't give it a second thought. Something unusual caught her attention after making a quick assessment. "Detective, please, if your done pitching woos," she said with her hands akimbo.

Sgt. Mason hung up his phone and moved closer to Lt. Drakon. She briefly checked out his chiseled body and his inhaled his pleasant aroma. Sgt. Mason bent down to point out that the cameraman's body was peculiarly bent in half.

"In a manner that would suggest that he was killed somewhere else," Lt. Drakon said.

"This obviously took a lot of work— a level of work that couldn't be done in the time he had. Especially since he couldn't have had enough time for the staging," Sgt. Mason replied.

"I agree. When I saw the mutilated body of Mr. frank, I had the same assumption. There's no way he could have done this alone." Lt. Drakon paused momentarily, then folded her arms across her chest. She paced back and forth and placed her right hand under her chin. After deep concentration, she expressed her theory, "We know that the suspect killed Sargent Blake, right. At least by the account of Ms. Maxwell."

Lt. Drakon put her index finger in the air and said, "But the murders that were committed here couldn't have been him. Unless—"

"What do you mean unless!" Sgt. Mason exclaimed.

"What if he killed them at their homes then brought the dead bodies here and staged them?"

"There are several problems with your theory," Sgt. Mason replied. "It would be virtually impossible for him to transport two lifeless bodies through the building without being detected. But we could check the footage off the security cameras. That would reinforce my theory that he has an accomplice."

Sgt. Mason walked over and peered outside the window. "How does this sadistic bastard know where his victims live?" he asked.

"That's a good question. Unfortunately, I don't knowthe answer to," Lt. Drakon replied.

"Well, he's downstairs; let's go and ask him." Sgt. Mason jotted down notes onto his notepad. He stopped then read what he just wrote down. "Is there a pattern of the way he killed his victims?"

"Okay, let's take him in," Lt. Drakon said over the radio. "The M.E is with the other body, and the rest of the CSIs will be up shortly. With this being such a high-profile case, I'm sure the whole laboratory is going to have all hands-on deck. They're going to go over this crime scene with a fine-toothed comb."

After both detectives looked for evidence and didn't find any. Both Sgt. Mason and Lt. Drakon sighed and spokein unison, "I hope the CSIs have better luck."

"With the three different locations, maybe it's because he's new to the homicide game and is a notice at it," Lt. Drakon said. Her cell phone rang. She pulled it out and glared at the screen to see if as someone important. She recognized the number; it was the captain.

"Lieutenant, there has been a change in plan, an intrusive turnaround for every police officer at the local level," the captain said. "Sorry to inform you that the Feds are involved, and you're off the case. I'll give you more info when you bring the perp in."

The captain hung up, and Lt. Drakon took the phone away from her face and stared at it in disbelief. She put the phone back onto her hip and said, "That's going to throw a wrench into the whole investigation." She sighed, turned around, and rubbed her nose.

"Sergeant, that was the captain. He said that there have been impending extenuating circumstances."

"What happened?" Sgt. Mason exclaimed and raised his hands above his head and leaned in close to Lt. Drakon.

"It's the Feds; they took over the case."

Sgt. Mason put his hand on top of his head, intertwined his fingers, and shook his head in disbelief.

The detectives met with the CSI on their way out of the office. Lt. Drakon quickly addressed the agents and said, "We've found very little blood on the scene, so pay very close attention while cleaning up the crime scene. Also, check if the body has been moved because it looks like there is very little trace evidence here."

"When you discover anything, send it to us ASAP!"

Sgt. Mason exclaimed.

At that moment, a voice over the radio said, *"We got specific orders from high up to turn over all findings to the FBI."*

"Who are you?" Lt. Drakon replied"

"Lt. Drakon, I presume! I am Dr. Remy Perish."

"I have never heard of you before."

"I know!" Dr. Perish exclaimed. "I just started this morning."

Lt. Drakon didn't respond. She slumped her shoulders, put the walkie-talkie down by her side, and put her hand on her forehead. She retreated to a mental place that was all too familiar – a state of mind where she felt protected from all threats. She hardly ever exposes herself to anyone. No one knows how vulnerable she is. She kept to herself, impenetrable and stern, set apart from her feelings, even as a little girl. She has always been rigid, especially with boyfriends, which wasn't very many, and even her fiancée. That's why he eventually left her at a time when she needed his emotional support the most.

So, she felt safer guarding her emotions, protecting her venerability from harm. But in this zombie-like state, she's centered, and it keeps people at bay—the way she prefers. Lieutenant Drakon has never been good with change. Experiencing anything different frightens her. She always has been and probably always will be just a scared little girl at heart.

Sergeant Mason has been to hell and back on many occasions. Not 24 hours on the job, and he is already on the brink of one of the biggest murder cases of the new millennium. But this situation is no different from being a rough street thug. The only difference is a badge and the policeman's oath to protect and serve. After tonight, both detectives will reflect on everything that transpired on the scene of the crime of the century.

After they made their way downstairs in the elevator, the two detectives headed straight to the squad car, where the suspect remained in handcuffs in the back of the cruiser.

"Thanks, officer Stevenson," she exclaimed.

"That's officer Stevens," he replied.

"I apologize–thanks again, officer Stevens. We appreciate your support.

Sgt. Mason bent down and tapped on the window and said, "Hey, Numbnuts, you have the right to remain silent; anything you say or do, can be held against you in the court of law. You have a right to an attorney, and if you can't afford one, you will be appointed one. Do you understand these rights that I've given to you?"

The stranger smirked, looked at the sergeant, and slowly tilted his head up and down.

Chapter 5

As the detective pulled up in front of the police station, they were met by a crowd of jeering police officers – a welcome fit for a hero. It might as well have been a parade. The men in blue were grateful. Happy that the murder suspect was in custody, especially this fast.

"Tonight, at least for the moment, the city can rest a little easier that piece of shit will go down what he had done," an officer said in the crowd.

"Too bad we won't get to put a little hurting on him!" another officer replied.

"Don't worry, I'm on transport this week, so I'll arrange it so we can get our hands on him before he goes to the tombs."

Lt. Drakon heard the conversation the two officers had through the roars of all the cheers. She looked the one in the eye who talked about pulling transport duty. That officer realized she had overheard their conversation and stopped talking until she walked past the vengeful sea of officers.

The two detectives made their way to the top of the stairs and felt the intense pressure weighing heavily on their shoulders. The total weight of the whole precinct was bearing down on them. At the same time, everyone cheered them on for arresting *"The Sangre Killer,"* the person responsible for killing the admired and respected Sgt. Blake. He may not be the one behind *"The Murders Midtown."*

Lt. Drakon sat at her desk and said, "Put him in room one."

"Wait, what?" Sgt. Mason looked around and asked. "I don't know where that is, Lieutenant." He shook the suspect's arm to stop him from struggling.

"Oh shoot, I'm sorry, I forgot this is your first collar here. I'll go with you. I could give a mini-tour at the same time." Lt. Drakon got up from behind her desk and walked toward Sgt. Mason and their murder suspect.

The captain came out of his office to see what's all the commotion about. Having been occupied for the better part of the morning with Mrs. Blake, he hadn't been aware of their arrival. He saw them on their way to the interrogation room with the suspect for the first time. "I have some good news and some bad news," Capt. Constantine said. "Which one do you want first?"

Lt. Drakon and Sgt. Mason looked back at the Capt. with despair and anguish written all over their body language. "I'd rather the good news first, Captain, then the bad news after," she said.

"But Capt., can it wait?" he asked. "We sort of have our hands preoccupied, Sir."

Capt. Constantine gave them both the death stare.

"But if you insist, I would like to listen to some good news for a change," Lt. Drakon said.

"I second that Capt., I've been on an insane rollercoaster ride for a considerable amount of my orientation," Sgt. Mason replied.

"I just got off the phone with the mayor, and he has seen the news coverage of you two detectives. You know the one about the impressive capture of the low-down dirty cop killer and the suspected *"Midtown Murderer,"* The captain said and faced the man in handcuffs and anchored to his emotions somewhat rationally. He got right in the face of the man who killed his long-time close friend and first partner Thomas Blake.

Sgt. Mason and Lt. Drakon could see the ferocity in his face, even the sweltering heat rising from his head. Still, the Capt. reveals nothing of his true feelings to the perp and said, "You destroyed the lives of not only the victims but also the lives of their loved ones."

The man inhaled deeply and ran his tongue over the teeth in his mouth, leaned closer to the Capt. and licked the beaded sweat off the forehead of Captain Constantine. Although disgusted and humiliated, The Capt. instantly stepped back to act, but surprisingly remained calm and jolted back away from the blood demon and wiped off his forehead with a handkerchief.

Captain Constantine, a man of many words, was so angry that he struggled to find anything to express his anger. The blood demon surprised the captain before he could finish his statement, then the murderer began to speak. When the words started to stream out his mouth, his voice had a supernatural tone. Almost like what you'd expect a demon would sound like— a very eerie, deep, raspy, and scratchy, nothing like what Lt. Drakon heard at the channel five building.

He mumbled at first, then he said, "Today, your hearts will be tested. Your will and souls are going to bear witness to something very few ever get to see. When you do, it will be a personal revelation. The implosion of life that flows." The pale-faced demon then flexed the muscles in his neck. Everyone could visibly see the blue subcutaneous veins protrude from his face. He emitted out a strange, surly screech, and then the demon continued his rant. "A sacrifice that feeds an immortal toll. Tempest wind makes way to that sorrowful deathly day."

The entire precinct stopped what they were doing, and a ring of police surrounded them and listened to the ramblings of the murderous scum. The barrier formed out of fear, curiosity, and insecurity. Some poor souls even had their guns drawn, waiting for an outburst so that they could plug this guy full of bullets. But the commotion left a couple of federal agents in attendance, unnoticed.

"The deathly sorrow day!"

"Was this the fate of Sgt. Blake?" asked the captain. He was a great police officer, shift commander, a good guy, and my best friend. What did he do to you? What had any of the innocent people done that you killed? Does the insane agenda that you psychopaths have, justify your killing of innocent people? Or is it the need for absolution and to satisfy the bloodthirst of the evil voices in your demented little minds."

"Your assumptions are miss directed, Captain. Those people were not killed for their sins or to atone for my own. I killed them simply because they were in my way." he celebrated in his devious actions in full view of the audience of police.

"Did you all hear his confession?" The captain replied. "I did. I hope somebody else did because I'm going to use it to make sure he gets the chair and not an insanity plea. Now get him to lock up and write this shit up."

The stunned crowd couldn't believe the event that unfolded before their eyes, but the two men in suits remained anonymous. Until Lt. Drakon discovered who they were and asked, "Hey Captain, what's the FBI doing in here?"

"You have a good eye, Lt. Drakon. That's why I chose you to lead this case," the captain replied.

"There is always one watchdog in each precinct," one of the well-dressed men cynically stated.

"Go ahead with whatever it is your about to do," Lt. Drakon

said.

"Very well, this is agent Gooseberg, and I'm agent Henning.

We're from the FBI," he replied. Both men brandished their badges like they were weapons.

"Captain, what is this?" Lt. Drakon asked.

"The FBI has an interest in this case. They have presented new with evidence of—"

"Hold on, Captain. Let's talk about this further in your office," agent Henning interrupted.

"Wait, wait, no, Captain, does this mean that the FBI is going to take him?" Lt. Drakon asked, then pointed at the two agents. "They can't. This is our collar!"

I'll let you know what I find out once I get further information from these gentlemen," the captain replied, then ushered the detectives and the two federal agents into his office.

Capt. Constantine caught the disappointment, disappear, and confusion on the faces of Mr. Blake's family before closing the door. He pulled the door shut to the office tightly, walked behind his desk sat in his chair.

"Allow me to introduce myself—"

"What is this, Captain? I didn't know that we consorted with the likes of these men," Lt. Drakon blurted out.

The captain took out his bottle of Pepto Bismol and guzzled it. He stood up at his desk and hung his head hung low, ready for the ensuing verbal onslaught to begin.

"The FBI and local law enforcement very rarely get along for some reason," Sgt. Mason said.

"Listen, we are all on the same side here. So, don't make this exchange difficult for either side. Just allow this encounter to be a melding of great investigative minds," said The Capt.

"How so? what do you mean?" Lt. Drakon asked.

"These federal agents here have some information that is contradictory to your recent capture. It seems like they have a long history with the details of the *Midtown Murderer*," the captain replied.

"Shit! Come on, Capt. Constantine, all the FBI ever does is just run around and swipe huge criminal cases from local hard-working law enforcement and take all the credit for getting the scum off the street. Leaving us with our di—"

"That's enough, Lt. Drakon!" the captain said, slammed his hand on the desk, and leaned all his body weight on his fingers. He stared directly at his vocal lieutenant., and the veins bulged from his forehead. He leaned forward underneath the hanging light fixture. His knuckles were as white as snow. A little embarrassed by her outburst, he wanted to tear her a new one. Although a proud and humble captain, the captain tends to hold those of authority in high regard but doesn't care to brown-nose either.

To not prolong nonsense when there are more important matters at hand, he just bit his tongue. "Continue, agent Henning." The captain straightened up, tugged on his vest, and completely looked away from Lt. Drakon.

"Mm feisty, Capt. Constantine, you should put leach on this one," Agent Gooseberg snapped.

"Wait a minute, did you just insinuate that I am a bitch?" asked Lt. Drakon.

Agent Gooseberg was about six foot and three inches tall,

unusually stout for a federal agent. So, Lt. Drakon chose her words carefully. But that did not deter her from speaking her mind. She was never afraid of anyone, and especially not while there's demon's blood and the soullessness of the damned coursing through her veins.

Nobody had a clue of what she's capable of; heck, she doesn't even know. But whatever it is, it started to seethe to the top, and blood started coming out of her nose.

"Hey, Lieutenant, your nose is bleeding. Here tilt your head back."

"Ooh, she bleeds. For a moment there, I would've sworn that you weren't human," agent Henning quipped.

"Bite me, you yellow-belly sapsucker!"

Having recognized the stages of Lt. Drakon's changes, Sgt. Mason spoke up after standing idle while tempers flared. "Wait, calm down, Lt. Drakon. The main thing here is to seek justice for the victims and a fallen fellow officer. At the end of the day, we are all on the same team," Sgt. Mason said. "So, put a halt to the bickering, and let's get to the bottom of this and do everything possible to solve this case. Lt. Drakon, believe me, I know all too well what happens when the FBI jumps in on a case. But you have a suspicion and a theory about the case, and they have something that may back up that fact. So, come, let's just see what they have to say."

Everyone in the room calmed down as they realized the stupidity in their arguing.

"Continue agent Gooseberry and Henning," Constantine said as he looked across the room at Lt. Drakon. He didn't like how outspoken she was or how she doesn't care about how many toes she stepped on.

Agent Henning opened a file and started to flip through the pages inside. "Adding the recent murders of the store manager, Mr. Gillman, and the cashier Deidre Gaya; this is what we have per the autopsies from the medical examiner on the recent Midtown Murders. There are similarities to all the murders."

"Yeah, so," Lt. Drakon said.

"So, that's it. There are similarities."

"We have already figured out."

"What did you figure out?" agent Gooseberg asked and looked directly at Lt. Drakon.

Sgt. Mason stepped up to cut the tension between to two and said, "We discovered all the same things through our investigation also. All though I'm new to the case, Lt. Drakon brought to speed on everything, and all the findings on all the past cases,"

"My partner and I noticed during our investigation that all of the bodies had been drained of all their blood," Lt. Drakon added. "That is also the same with all of the previous murders. So, are you going to tell us that's what you got in that file of yours, hmm?" Lt. Drakon said, seemingly looking more interested in what the FBI has in their file.

Agent Henning opened the file in front of the captain and sat on his desk. "Here, I am going do you guys a favor. I am about to reveal everything we have on your "Sanguine Killer," agent Henning said, licked his finger, and turned the first page. He paused for a moment to deeply consider what he was about to do.

"Sir, are you sure you want to tell them what we know?" agent Gooseberg said.

Agent Henning continued without addressing his partner's

134

concerns. "The FBI has compiled decades of evidence and found that this brand of murders goes back three hundred years," he said. "Not just here in the United States, but apparently, all over the world."

"Are you saying that these murders are some sort of ritualistic killing," Capt. Constantine asked in his heavy Brooklyn accent.

"As far as we can tell, it can be some type of occult maybe, or at the very least a fraternity of some kind. We can't connect the victims or the murderers, but the murders do have a definite pattern."

"What do you mean?" Lt. Drakon asked. "What do you mean there's a definite pattern?" she repeated, gesturing with air quotes.

"Okay, from our search, we have gathered that the killings happen during the year in sequence on March 20, June 21, September 22, and December 21," agent Henning replied.

"In other words, on the northward equinox, summer solstice, southern equinox, and winter solstice," the Capt. added.

"What is the significance of those dates? How do they correlate with the murders?" Sgt. Mason asks with a puzzled expression on his face.

"We don't know, but the experts have several different theories on the subject," said agent Gooseberg. "In many cultures, these specific dates hold significance throughout history. They can't pinpoint a viable theory yet. So, your guess is as good as mine.

"If you look back to the recent killings in your precinct, you will see the correlation between those dates." Agent Gooseberg handed a sheet of paper to Capt. Constantine. He managed to get a quick glimpse at the document before Lt. Drakon snatched the folder out of his hand.

"Let me see that," Lt. Drakon said and took the folder from the captain but stood close enough so that he could see it too.

Agent Goosebuerg folded his arms across his chest and said, "As you see, the dates match up."

"How can you say that this is part of your theory?" Sgt. Mason asked.

"I'm too keen on theories," Lt. Drakon replied before the agent could answer.

Agent Gooseberg pulled out another sheet. "On this one, you can see that other murders were being committed almost simultaneously at the same time in all five boroughs," he said. "Six people all together with the victims of indiscriminate types and no visible connections. The only thing that we could figure was that each killing was exactly one year apart from each other."

As he spoke, the lights in the precinct began to flicker then quickly went black. Loud claps of thunder and bright flashes of lightning illuminated the captain's office.

It was pitch black and quiet for a minute. Then gunshots went off like firecrackers on the fourth of July.

The captain said, "Did you hear that? is that in house, in my precinct?"

"I don't know, but it sounds close," agent Henning replied as he drew his weapon just in case.

Lt. Drakon and Sgt. Mason moved up to the entrance of the door. They armed themselves before leaving the captain's office to move about the department in the dark. They were flanked together like a S.W.A.T team about to raid a house. Agent Henning lined up behind the Lt. Drakon, and Gooseberg went behind Sgt. Mason. They tactically moved along the wall with weapons drawn and took out their radios to communicate with the other officers outside the captain's office.

The sounds of the gunshots, screams, radio chatter, and the thunderstorm resembled a scene out of a war-torn country during civil unrest. This made it difficult to discern what was happening, but they persisted.

"Captain, we need back up out here. Everyone's dead," an officer responded over the radio.

"Who is this? What's going on in my station?" asked the captain.

"Officer Green, Sir, we are being attacked," he replied.

"Attacked? By whom?"

"I can't tell, but we are getting slaughtered."

Lt. Drakon couldn't wait for confirmation before she heroically ran to defend the precinct. The department she has served since she left the academy. Everyone else followed suit, including the captain. The bay was dark with no visibility, but the hail of gunfire was directed at the entrance towards the stairs. With each shot, the bright flash illuminated the frantic chaos that took place.

"Can anybody see what we are shooting at?" Captain Constantine shouted.

"No," an officer shouted in response.

"Then let us cease-fire until we know for sure who or what we are shooting at."

After the shooting ceased, and shell casing dropped on the tile. There was dead silence and the stench of gun powder in the precinct. A loud roar sounded over the dead silence, like the squeal of wheels that precipitates a car accident.

"What-the-fuck was that?" more than one officer said simultaneously.

Click! Clock! Click! The sounds of the hammers on several 9mm Glocks reloaded by the surviving police officers who were cocked and ready to shoot echoed in the bay. Scared and afraid from the unfamiliar screeches, each officer was still committed to their duties, and all were ready to die if they must, against the ominous threat of the precinct.

Although she doesn't accept it yet, Lt. Drakon is like one of those threats attacking the precinct. The screeches and all other inaudible vocal noises sound like a form of communication that she can now inexplicably understand. So, she used her newfound abilities to try and defuse the situation. She stood up on a desk and began to vocalize.

With trepidations, Sgt. Mason whispered to Lt. Drakon, "Hey, what are you doing?"

The captain set up a cover. "We need to get eyes on these things. We have no idea what they are, how many we are up against, or what kind of weapons they have." He signaled the FBI agents and Sgt. Mason with a penlight where he wanted them to move. He guided Sgt. Mason and Henning, and they moved slowly into view of the danger. They scurried out by the bay wall closer to the impending threat.

The darkness blackened the bay, which made it hard to see anything. When Sgt. Mason and agent Henning moved towards the bay, they signaled two other officers already out there to cover them and keep a line on Lt. Drakon.

The captain thought to call to get back up from other precincts and tried to figure out why the backup generator wasn't on yet. "Here, Lt., dial this number for another precinct to give us a helping hand. I'm going to need help to turn the fucking lights back on," he excitingly whispered. First things first, we need a bus for my injured officers. I know of at least one of them are dead."

Lt. Drakon got an answer and handed her phone to the captain, and he said, "This is Captain Constantine. I need several buses to my location."

"Officer down, officer down," a voice bellowed in the darkness.

Lt. Drakon was in the middle, alone out in the open, she went through a total transformation, but she didn't realize it. The only thing on her mind was to get the drop on the blood demons. Loud moans from wounded cops fill the space like cattle corralled to be slaughtered. Despite the darkness, Lt. Drakon saw six ominous figures on the other end of the precinct. She turned to the right, and Sgt. Mason and agent Gooseberg were creeping along the wall to her position.

Lt Drakon panned left and right between the two factions and said, "Sgt. Mason, stop, stay right where you are."

"What? You got to be kidding me," agent Henning said.

"Don't move, trust me! Don't move a muscle," she beckons aloud.

They were both puzzled but reluctantly complied. With inaudible sounds to humans, Lt. Drakon cried out, "What do you want?" In the darkness, no one else saw them except for her. She spotted two more blood demons crawling on the wall above Sgt. Mason and the unsuspecting agent, other than the ones she already counted. "Please Stop! Please wait," she begged in the language of the

139

vampires.

"You have something that belongs to me," the vampire spoke.

He wasn't the one that she expected to speak. He wasn't the largest, he was average height and build, but his nails and fangs were longer and thicker than the other vampires.

"What the fuck is she saying?" an impatient officer said while gazing upon her silhouette bouncing off the wall. "Lt. Drakon, are you communicating with those things?" the officer repeated himself aloud.

Overzealous and confused, he hastily stood up and fired his gun. Before Lt. Drakon could figure out what the vampires wanted, a battle in the dark ensued right in the close quarters of the bay in the precinct. Those police officers didn't understand what they were up against. They were fighting a losing battle.

The other officers followed suit and opened fire blindly in fear for their lives. The blood demons avoided the onslaught of precipitous bullets. Agile and acrobatic, the evil creatures flipped through the air like superhuman gymnasts. They jumped off and on walls dodging flying bullets. They used live and dead police officers as human shields as they soared through the air.

As the bullets flew, many officers were wounded and even killed in the crossfire. Lt. Drakon couldn't move fast enough. Her reflexes weren't up to par with the other vampires. It all happened so fast, too fast for an average human to do anything. She stood there frozen in time, panting and thought to herself, "I'm still human, I'm still human." She repeated the phrase as they came closer and closer to her.

The leader dropped down right in front of her and growled. He pointed to the two other blood demons covering agent Gooseberg and Sgt. Mason and dragged them out like rag dolls undetected past the captain. That's when it dawned on her figured out that they were after the murder suspect they apprehended earlier for the killings.

The leader leaped on the ceiling and followed his comrades out of the bay. Lt. Drakon trailed them downstairs to the lockup area.

Captain Constantine saw Lt. Drakon past him like a blur while he was still on the phone trying to get someone to check the reason why the generator didn't turn on yet. "Wait, wasn't that Lt. Drakon?

"Where is she going?" agent Henning asked with fear in their eyes.

"I don't know what she's doing, but I am going to find out surely," the Capt. responded.

"Why would she be deserting her post? She was so bad in the office a minute ago, it figures, that's always the case with big mouths. It's all lip service; that's where the action starts and stops."

"Look, agent Henning, I know you and Lt. Drakon didn't get off on the right foot, but she's a stand-up officer. Remember, she brought that psycho in. Lt. Drakon is one of my best officers."

One of the blood demons turned to Sgt. Mason and said, "Young one open the cell," while he hung upside down in the corridor. With one hand around the neck of agent Gooseberg, he stretched, then pulled his body off the ground. His tippy toes balanced him.

"Look, don't hurt him," Sgt. Mason pleaded."

"You don't have a choice." He looked over and saw the second vampire beside him. He reached out and grabbed Sgt. Mason by the neck and slightly lifted him off the ground to motivate him, then plunged his sharp talons in his neck just enough to puncture the skin and draw blood.

Lt. Drakon saw the pain on her partner's face and a stream of blood running from the wound caused by the hard grasp of the vampire.

A third vampire whisked by the lieutenant and said, "I don't have time for this," and pulled the metal bars apart. The stranger caught his eye and shook his head back and forth. His shoulders slumped, and he closed back the bars.

The sound of the metal bending caught the attention of the men upstairs. "That couldn't possibly be what I think it is," agent Henning pondered. "They couldn't be releasing the prisoner, my prisoner. He is under federal jurisdiction."

"No, that can't be what they're doing," the captain said.

Both men looked at each other and took off running. The captain and agent Henning ran as fast as possible down the two flights of steps down to the holding cells. The captain and the federal agent did not see nor hear anyone else pass them. So, they could only assume that whoever was down there wasn't acting alone.

The sight of her partner's blood running down the side of his neck gave Lt. Drakon some mixed feelings. On the one hand, the policeman's code has an unwritten rule. That all who wears the uniform *bleed blue bleeds true*. So, when his blood ran, her blood did too.

On the other hand, as a new vampire, the sight of Sgt. Mason's blood excited her. The presence of it cascading down the side of his neck over his throbbing veins, pulsating tempting nectar, filled Lt. Drakon with a thirst that couldn't be quenched by anything else but blood. Torn by the lure of her thirst and the Call of the duty, she took an oath to protect and serve. The internal fight was overwhelming.

"I know that it's hard for you, but there's the day when we all gave in to the thirst," the main vampire said. "Succumb, stop it—stop fighting it, embrace it, it's the unnatural aspect of your death. Your one of us now, face it, pardon my French, but taste it."

He snatched agent Gooseberg away from the other vampire holding him. He pulled the agent in close, wrapped his long hands around his head, and sunk his teeth into his neck. Agent Gooseberg screamed and struggled to resist, but to no avail. He was trapped like prey caught in the vicious jaws of a predator in the wild.

Lt. Drakon moved towards the demon and pulled out her weapon but stopped suddenly. Without provocation, the blood demon that held Sgt. Mason inflicted even more pain when he sensed Lt. her movements. Sgt. Mason groaned and grabbed at the vampire's wrists to relieve the tension on his throat as he gasped for air.

The precinct was still in complete darkness when captain and agent Henning made it downstairs. They heard Sgt. Mason moan in pain.

"Sgt. is that you?" The Capt. asked as he slowly crept through the pitch-black corridor. "Lt. Drakon! Are you there? Are you hurt?" There was no answer. Capt. Constantine called for Lt. Drakon a second time with no response. The leader of the vampire coven dropped the agent's dead body and slowly pulled away from him.

Lt. Drakon raised her weapon, carefully aimed, and had the head blood demon's head zeroed in her sight.

The blood demon snickers and said, "You have no moves, and now there are two more people I will use as leverage to get what I want. Do what I say, open the cell and let out my friend, or you could be a hero. Make the correct choice. If you don't, someone else dies."

Having witnessed the FBI agent get the life sucked out of him, Lt. Drakon understood how dire the situation was.

"Lt Drakon, answer me! What's going on? I can't see anything down here," the captain said.

"Stay where you are, Captain," Sgt. Mason murmured in a feeble attempt to warn the Capt., but the tight grip of his capture muffled his words.

"What are you going to do detective," The blood demon's leader screamed in frustration.

Lt. Drakon sighed and dropped her weapon to her side and holstered it. She decided to comply to protect her mentor, Captain Constantine and her partner Sgt. Mason.

She pulled out the keys to the holding cell and inched towards the holding cell. The cell wasn't more than several feet away from her, but the walk seemed like several miles away.

No human could navigate in the dark, but being nocturnal, Lt. Drakon saw the whole picture without skipping a beat. She reached for the bars and proceeded to open the cell door. The prisoner sat on the floor meditating with his legs crossed out in front of him. With everything going on around him, he did not make a sound during the whole ordeal.

Lt. Drakon opened the cell, and it dawned on her that the vampire she captured was the coven leader. He opened his eyes, changed from his human form, and let out a cry. He levitated out of the holding cell and hovered in the center of the hallway. The other blood demons let go of Sgt. Mason moved away from the Capt. and the federal agent Henning. They all then formed a circle around their leader like a halo. Some of them clung to the walls from the floor to the ceiling. "One day, you must come to me. I don't expect you to come now, but, one day, my Childe, one day," the stranger said.

"One day! What does that mean?" Lt. Drakon asked

"Ask your beloved doctor."

"Doctor!"

The demon raised his hand, and his minions cried out in response to the command. Then all the vampires left out of the back exit like a blur. Lt. Drakon could only see streaks of black and white.

"You will soon meet mother," the blood demon said, turned around, and flew outside.

The lights came back on after the last blood demons departed the precinct.

The lights turned on in the precinct, and all the police officers were upstairs making complete assessments of the damages and licking their wounds. Everything was in disarray. Those who weren't hurt died during the invasion. The police officers who survived were severely wounded and in need of medical assistance.

Lt. Drakon stood in the middle of the corridor with the cell key in her hand.

"Lt. Drakon, are you alright?" Sgt. Mason asked as he nursed his wounds. With the hand on the opposite side of the gash on his neck, he reached for the bars on the cell to hoist himself up off the ground. The wound was deep, and he grimaced from the pain as he applied pressure on it to stop the bleeding. Surprisingly, it didn't sever his carotid artery.

Lt. Drakon looked over at agent Gooseberg's body and bent down to check for vital signs.

The captain and agent Henning were awe-struck as they walked in silence through the corridor. They passed by all the other cells and looked for the suspected serial killer. The Capt. reached the empty holding cell he entered and said, "Words cannot express my anger. Tell me that he wasn't in here. Tell me he's in another holding cell?" Captain Constantine thrashed about the cell like a mad man.

Agent Henning knelt next to the body of agent Gooseberg and laid his hand on his chest.

Lt. Drakon shook her head and stood up.

"Why did you let him go?" he said, and his voice cracked. "You know that we don't ever under any circumstances make deals with terrorists."

Lt. Drakon didn't answer. She remained silent. She walked over to the wall, slide down to her knees, and buried her head in her lap.

"How could you?" the captain asked as he flung a pair of broken handcuffs against the cell wall.

"Hey, come on, Sir, can't you see she's been through a lot! We all have," Sgt. Mason said, holding the side of his bloody neck with a handkerchief. He sniffled then squatted over his partner. "With all due respect, Captain, that's a pretty damaging accusation. How do you know that she let him out?"

Hit by the question, the captain snapped out of his spell, stood up straight, tugged on his vest, and fixed his silk pastel-colored tie. Captain Constantine walked out of the cell when he heard the commotion going on inside the precinct.

Chaos and unrest arose like the cold air blowing in from the open door used in the escape. The lights swirled on the corridor, the walls with red and blue flashes like strobe lights at a disco. You could smell the acrid stench of urine emanating from the jail cells like the last car on the D train.

"Lt. Adeline Drakon, you are on modified suspension until

146

further notice," the captain said. He extended his hand palm side up. "Hand over your gun and badge."

Lt. Drakon didn't protest. She just got up on her feet and gave her gun and badge to the captain.

"Help me out here," Sgt. Mason reached out for someone to pull him up on his feet. "How do you know that she opened the cell door?"

The captain turned, walked away, and flashed his penlight up against the stairs. Agent Henning and Sgt. Mason turned their heads around and looked at Lt. Drakon in disappointment.

Chapter 6

Lt. Drakon was depressed and hurt because of the exorbitant amount of fellow policeman that lost their lives during the melee. The aftermath affected her dearly. It etched an indelible stain into her ever-waking consciousness, and an alarming dread seeped into her dreams that will haunt her for the rest of her career as a police officer.

She was unable to escape the guilt that loomed over her head like a tumid nimbus cloud, at least her part in it. Lt. Drakon woke up from the third leg of a drunken stupa, disorientated, a bad case of cottonmouth, and her throat was void of moisture like a barren land, much like her soul. Her lips were dry, chapped, and bound tightly like the narrow mind of captain Constantine.

The vapors emanated out her pores like CO_2 gas from the exhaust of a semi-tracker trailer. The foul odor filled the room with the foul stench of vomit and cheap booze from empty liquor bottles. She consumed liquor to drown out her thoughts and realize her unnatural transformation that she can't understand. A condition that hasn't been explained to her by Dr. German.

Lt. Drakon was awakened by Joy Maxwell reporting the news on location, talking about the events that transpired several days ago at the precinct. She sat up, put her feet into her slippers, and continued with her morning routine, seemingly trying to ignore the reports of what she and other officers had to suffer through.

The anchorman said, "We are going live on location with Joy Maxwell, who's out in front of the Midtown police department. She will be keeping us updated periodically on the siege that took place there, last week, Joy."

"Yes, I am here in front of the precinct that was the scene of an apparent invasion resulting in a prison break of the prime suspect in the *Midtown Murder* case," Joy said. "Witnesses say that last week Tuesday, this department was hit hard and fast; it looked like a scene at a bank robbery.

"Another witness said it was unreal, like something out of an old western or gangster film. This attack on the police station by unknown assailants left seven officers, three civilians, one FBI agent dead, and countless other civilians injured, including five in critical condition.

"It's odd when those who swear an oath to protect and serve the public now are the ones who need to be protected. This incident puts fear in the hearts of the residents in this community here in Midtown."

While passing the television heading to the bathroom, Lt. Drakon turned up the volume located on the side of the television, turning it up loud enough so she could hear it in the bathroom over running water. She walked into the bathroom, turned the faucet on, and splashed water on her face.

"Do the police have any suspects?" The anchorman asked.

"No, so far, the police don't have any leads." Joy replied. "The group that attacked this Midtown department were organized, powerful, and swift; they did so with great impunity. They," Joy walked past several officers coming out of the precinct going on duty and stopped one. She tugged on the coat of one who happened by close enough in the shot for her to grab. "My condolences go out to you and to all of the fellow brothers-in-arms that died in the attack. The city truly mourns their fallen heroes," Joy lends some kind words to the policeman.

The officer took his hat off and stuck it under his arm, and his bottom lip quivered. With a glint in his eye and an unmistakable grit in his teeth. He spoke, holding back his tears on air. "Ahem, there were many great men who died here last week," he said and put his thumb and index finger over his eyes. "Ahem, excuse me; my brothers who lost their lives last week will not be without justice for too long."

Lt. Drakon paused when she heard Joy interviewing a fellow police officer. She turned off the water and listened to the news while the toothbrush was still in her mouth. She heard something that worried her. He spoke with a delicate mixture of anger and anguish.

Joy pulled the microphone away from the choked-up policeman. After giving him a moment to gather his composure, she imposed another question, "Was the person freed out of jail on that dreadful day the *Sanguine killer*?"

"Yes, yes, he was," he replied with a sudden bode of confidence.

"Did he get processed? If so, wouldn't law enforcement have a better lead on who rushed their department last week?"

The young policeman didn't have the level of understanding it took to tangle with an ambitious reporter like Joy Maxwell. He didn't know what hit him, and he revealed information that shouldn't be shared outside the confines of the precinct. "It doesn't matter that they broke out the *Sanguine killer* before he was processed," he angrily said, grabbing the microphone back from Joy. Then he pushed it into her chest then walked away.

Joy raised her eyebrows, flipped her hair, and smiled. "There you have it, folks, disparaging feelings of the police, the community, and the whole city in a nutshell," she said. "This is where the temperament of the city is, and it's turned up on high. The heat has risen, and the people were fed up, especially the police."

Joy stepped down off the precinct stairs onto the sidewalk.

She positioned herself then instructed her cameraman to capture the city landscape behind her. She stood still as he panned from side to side in front of the police department. Family members and friends of the departed gathered to put up a memorial to the fallen. Hundreds of concerned citizens paid their respects to the slain victims with candles, flowers, and pictures drawn by children from the neighborhood.

"I have interviewed some of the people in the area. Some of whom gathered here to mourn and pay their respects. Other people that I've spoken with all have one feeling in common; that is anger," Joy said while the cameraman captured the disposition from the scene. "I am Joy Maxwell signing off, back to you at the studio."

Lt. Drakon heard that the suspect hadn't been processed. She shook her head, hastily turned back on the water, and finished her morning ritual. She exhaled, dropped her shoulders, and continued brushing her teeth. The volume of the television was turned up and echoed in her dreary apartment. She gargled, spit in the sink, turned off the faucet then walked back into her bedroom to get dressed.

After Lt. Drakon pulled her outfit out of the closet, her I-phone rang. She set the garments on the bed, and then she answered the phone. That was on the nightstand. "Hello, Detective Adeline Drakon," she said.

"Good afternoon, Detective, it's me!" Joy exclaimed.

"Oh, hey Joy, how can I help you, Ms. Maxwell?"

"Sweetie—it's me. We can forego the formalities."

"O...okay," Lt. Drakon said, sighed, and rolled her eyes. "Joy, what do you need?"

"Well, I don't know if you caught the news," Joy asked.

"I caught it."

"You've seen it! So, how did I do...?"

"Ms. Maxwell—?"

"Okay, okay, I have a good idea that could help you get your badge back."

"Help me! How are you going to help me?" Lt. Drakon asked and raised her eyebrows. "Ms. Maxwell, the case has been given to the FBI. So, even if I weren't under suspension, I wouldn't even be on the case." There was an uncomfortable silence on the other end of the receiver. "Joy, I have to go." She hung up the phone and continued to get dressed.

At the precinct, Capt. Constantine just received the results from the lab, which reaped no evidence left behind by the sanguine killer.

"Captain, there was no DNA from hair fibers, spittle, skin, nothing to connect this monster to the crime," the CSI said.

Daunted by the CSI results, he called agent Henning and Sgt. Mason into his office, who became partners of circumstance.

Impatient, the captain flung open his door in frustration and stood in the doorway. The door hit him in the back after bouncing back off the wall. "Agent Henning, Sergeant Mason, can I see you in my office! Now please!" The captain commanded.

They both walk into the office as requested.

"Did we get lucky?" agent Henning and Sgt. Mason asked simultaneously.

"What do you mean?" Capt. Constantine asked.

"Well, I've seen who I believe to be someone from the crime lab. It looked like some documents were dropped off in your office. So, I can only assume in the light of everything going on that it was the result of the recent attack on the precinct," agent Henning said as he walked in, sat down in the chair, and crossed his legs. "Besides, I wouldn't like to think that you're withholding any information from the Federal Bureau of Investigations."

The captain threw the file on the edge of his huge wooden desk toward the agent. "No, the result from the lab was inconclusive," he replied. Then he stood up and paced behind his desk. "What do you have?"

"Nothing yet; we've looked at every surveillance recording inside and outside the building. We have not been able to find any footage of our attackers. It's like they were just invisible," Sgt. Mason explained. "We have looked at everything with a fine-toothed comb and used every top-ranked technology available to us, and some that weren't."

"We even used the newest facial recognition software and pulled no positive findings," agent Henning added.

The Capt. stopped pacing, banged on his desk, and asked. "What if they used some type of hi-tech scrambler that would make them invisible to the cameras?"

"Sure, sure, maybe some type of composite, or like you said, Captain a substance like a... bio-chemical, that would interfere with the camera," Sgt. Mason said.

"As an FBI agent, I am exposed to all types of new technology, gadgets, and such. As far as I know, I haven't heard anything remotely close to this. I mean, the cameras didn't capture a thing, Inside or outside the precinct, or by any other camera in the surrounding area," agent Henning argued. "Not to mention, the swiftness to which they attacked us. It was like they knew where everything—"

"First of all, can you truthfully say that you know about every single inventory being worked on right now?" the captain asked. "In this country alone, there are homegrown basement scientists and inventors that pop up all the time. We have no idea about it until we see their invention on an infomercial. That's assuming it's not from overseas. Secondly, I trust my people. They're all good and loyal officers."

Henning eased back into his chair and uncrossed his legs planting both feet firmly on the freshly polished solid cherry wood floor, and said, "You're right, and I believe most of them are too, except for a couple."

"Who?" the captain asked.

"If you are this oblivious to what happened, you need not keep this position?" agent Henning leaned on the edge of the captain's desk. "How about the police officer who leaked vital information to the press, hmm? Or the incompetence of the officer, who just so happened to put the accused in a cell without processing him: No fingerprints, no mug shot, no interrogation, no nothing. I don't have enough fingers to point at all the fuck ups in this department. It's a cesspool. Internal Affairs would have a field day in here."

The captain and Sgt. Mason stood there in silence.

Agent Henning paused for a moment and backed away from the captain's desk. There was an awkward silence in the room. "What about Lt. Drakon?" he asked

"What about her?" the Capt. exclaimed. "She's already on suspension and under investigation by internal affairs for her actions. Let's deal with the facts at hand, agent Henning. I lost some good officers, including my best friend, Sgt. Blake."

"Captain, I lost a partner as well, or did you forget."

"I know all too well that lives were lost to her too," agent Henning walked behind the desk and stood toe to toe with the captain. Both men were in an old fashion face-off and two insults away from a fistfight.

"I think you have a good idea, Sir!" Sgt. Mason exclaimed.

Both men looked at Sgt. Mason with their eyebrows knitted up as he leaned up against one of the file cabinets in the office.

"As I see it, the people that came in here and attacked us will get away if we can't work together," he said. "We could be putting our heads together in here and then follow up on leads out in the street. What we don't have time for is fighting each other. Come on, you guys; we are better than this."

Agent Henning and Capt. Constantine's faces relaxed, and they unclenched their fists.

"Things just got a little intense, and in the wake of everything that's has been happening in this city, we have an important connection with each other," the captain replied.

"You are right," agent Henning said, and he put his hand out in front of him.

Both men shook hands, displaying a truce, at least for now.

The captain tugged on his vest and straightened his clothing, and said, "Many are called to take on tasks, but very few can meet the challenge."

Agent Henning curled up his lip and tilted his head up and down.

"I have always had one thing that I lived by, in all the years on the job. I used it to help me navigate through my career. Do you know what that is?" captain Constantine asked as he stood up, looking out of his colossal bay window in his office. No one answered.

Both men looked at each other, closed their eyes, and sighed.

"A code, a couple, really," the captain said. He turned, faced agent Henning, and stood behind his desk as he continued. "First, a man mustn't have any regrets because life is about experiences and moments. So, you should learn from them not to harbor bad feelings. Second, never dwell on the past; life is a progression forge ahead to the future. Keep your past experiences close, learn from them, but never dwell there.

"A man should always know; he should never ponder. He should always be assertive and confident with his action before he does anything. Without that, the world would not have witnessed greatness in men like Winston Churchill, Mahatma Gandhi, or Dr. Martin Luther King Jr. Men set examples but carried the torch of their predecessors. We forged a path where they could lead by shedding light through the darkness when society needed guidance."

The Capt. paused for a moment after his speech, then he grabbed his favorite coffee mug with the police captain's insignia on it and took a sip.

"What do you want me to do?" agent Henning asked.

"For us not to have any further regrets, we need to work together," the captain replied.

"Come on, I know you have the means to research what I suggested," said Sgt. Mason.

Agent Henning got up out of his seat without saying a word. He walked to the door and opened it.

"So, you are not going to help?" Detective Mason asked.

Agent Henning paused in the doorway, then he replied. "Wait

for my call." Without turning around, he stepped out and closed the door behind him.

"While he's doing, whatever that is, I have a lead for you," the captain said.

"Yeah, what's that, Sir?" Sgt. Mason replied.

"I just received a tip from the wife of the supermarket owner. Her grandson said that he might have discovered something, but he doesn't know what he is looking at."

"So, I need for you to go to their house and check it out. It might be what we need to crack this case wide open."

"Sure, I'll get right on it, Captain," Sgt. Mason said and took the paper out of Capt. Constantine's hands. "Before I go, Captain, how's my partner doing?"

"Her hearing is later today. Hopefully, we will hear something positive," the captain replied. "Now go, come back with some good news. I need some good news, especially after today." He sat down in his chair and sighed. "My best friend, Sgt. Blake's funeral is tonight, and I want to tell his family that we got something. So, hurry up, Sergeant, we don't have a lot of time, and the suspense is unbearable." The captain reached in his desk, pulled out his Pepto Bismol, and grimaced as he drank it to soothe his ulcer.

Lt. Drakon sat in her room alone, mulling over all the questions in her head about the events that Internal Affairs might ask. She walked into the kitchen and made a pot of coffee. She took out two Tylenol, popped them in her mouth, and down it with a mouth full of water from the kitchen faucet.

As the pot percolated, the lieutenant thought about her actions at the precinct. She put her arm across her chest and rubbed her temple with the other hand. "What could I have done differently? I know the protocol: Don't ever make deals with terrorists!" she exclaimed. "As hopeless as a situation might seem, there are always avenues that one must consider before making critical decisions." Lt. Drakon believed all this time that she made the right decision under the circumstances.

Lt. Drakon poured a cup of coffee a took a sip and exhaled. She checked her watch, then put down the coffee mug on the counter. She's running late for her appointment with Internal Affairs. She dreaded going in front of a committee that would determine whether she could keep her detective shield. She began to question her resolve more and more. With this one being the third of line questioning of her inquest, her apprehension has increased the closer it got to the time of the meeting.

All the events circled through her head, her encounter with the stranger, her grandfather, and Timothy Frank. All of them alluded to the changes in her life.

Lt. Drakon remembered angrily bursting into the M.E.'s office. "Dr. German, what did you do to me?" she demanded.

"I'm so sorry, doctor, she just barged in here, and I wasn't able to stop her," the secretary said after she ran in behind her.

"It's fine, Laura; please, give us some time and no interruptions," Dr. German said in a heavy Austrian accent. "Please, sit Lt. Drakon; calm down. I knew that this time would come one day."

Lt. Drakon was startled by how calm the doctor was. "I wonder if he knows what I'm up against?" She held back her anger and took a seat. "I want to see how this plays out," she said to herself.

Before doctor German could get a word out, Lt. Drakon's anger overcame her. She stood up, slapped both hands on the desk, leaned forward, invading the doctor's space, and said, "Are you a vampire?"

she asked while tears welled up in her eyes.

"What? Who told you that?" Doctor German exclaimed as his face remained expressionless.

"Don't play koi with me. Did you turn me into a vampire?" Lt. Drakon anxiously awaited his response. "I want to know–I need to know."

The medical examiner's face went entirely pale. All the blood he recently replenished his body with, flushed away from his face.

"I thought you loved me, Grandfather! You're like the closes thing I've ever had to a father." The tears cascaded down her face. "What did you do to me?" she asked and wiped the tears from her chin. "That's not even the worst part. How could lie to me!"

"Calm down, my dear granddaughter," Dr. German said and put his hands out in front of him. "I assure you I did not lie to you. I just hadn't enough time alone to tell you what happened—"

"Don't patronize me," she said, turned her face away, and waved the Medical Examiner off. "I can't listen to your bull shit, Doctor. "Spare me your-sordid-pitiful-attempt-at-somewhat of a-competent-explanation."

"Look, my dear; I have always had your best interest at heart. I have, ever since I took you in when you were fourteen." He got up and extended his hand towards her. "Granted, I should've told you sooner, but I will not apologize for not saving your life." Dr. German put his head down and took a deep breath. "My Dear, to answer your question honestly, yes, I am a vampire! And yes, I turned you into one. But it's more complicated than that."

"What am I going to do now?" Lt. Drakon said and flailed her arms in the air. "Am I some sort of monster now?" She kept repeating the question to herself and paced back and forth in Doctor German's office. She was conflicted with the sordid truth and her reality that she's a vampire.

The doctor slowly approached Lt. Drakon and put his arm around her. She melted into his arms and intensely cried.

"What am I going to do now?" she asked.

"Don't fret, granddaughter, I will explain everything to you," he replied.

There was a knock on the door. "Detective! Lieutenant? Lt. Drakon," someone yelled and pounded on the front door.

"Joy Maxwell? What is she doing here? How does she know where I live?" Lt. Drakon said to herself. She hurried to stop Joy's annoying rapping on the front door. She cracked open the door just enough so that she could attempt to brush off the nosy reporter's brash and pushy attitude. When she did, anyone could see that Joy's recent promotion has paid off well. She wore high-end designer clothing from head to toe, accompanied by the latest Birkin bag. "I hate reporters," she mumbled.

"What was that Sweetie?" Joy replied with a huge smile on her face.

"I told you, Ms. Maxwell. I do not have enough time to mess around today. My day is full; I have a meeting with I.A.B. regarding getting back my shield, plus Sgt. Blake's funeral is later this evening. You know the one who died in the line of duty to save your life."

"I know. I will be speaking at the service today." Joy pushed her way past Lt. Drakon into her apartment. "I have something that you would seriously be interested in, Sweetie." The conceited reporter strolled through the apartment, perusing the decor.

Lt. Drakon slammed the front door and followed Joy into the living room. "You look like you're ready to drop it like it's hot on the dance floor Ms. Maxwell," Lt. Drakon comments.

"Thank you, I guess."

"I can see your recent promotion was good to you." The new clothes, the new shoes, the new attitude, you look fabulous. Some might say–different," she said and looked her up and down. "I guess the saying is true—"

"What saying is that?" Joy asked.

"Only that you can see the true character of a person when they have more money."

Joy ignored Lt. Drakon's slights, sat down on the couch, crossed her legs, and changed the subject. "I have just received a call from the wife of my boss; that may be the key to getting you your shield back."

"So, what is it, don't waste my time, Ms. Maxwell!" Lt. Drakon stood a few feet away from Joy, and she could hear the reporter's heartbeat. The rhythm sent the young blood demon into a hypnotic trance. The network of arteries and veins was suddenly visible through her fair skin. She swallowed her saliva, covered her eyes, and turned her face away from Joy. "Come on, snap out of this," she said to herself.

Lt. Drakon's refusal to take blood made the hunger overwhelming. The turmoil of her humanity and being a vampire were at odds. With her strong willpower, she managed to suppress her unnatural urges. But that inner contention between good and evil lurking within the depths of her soul has subsided.

"Are you alright?" Joy asked. "Do you need to go to the

doctor? Because you don't look so good."

"I am alright. I don't need you fussing over me," Lt. Drakon replied.

"Are you sure because you look like you did when you were at the channel-five station?"

Lt. Drakon wiped the sweat from her head, walked over to Joy, and sat next to her. "Okay, Ms. Maxwell, tell me more about how I can get my shield back."

Joy sneered at Lt. Drakon's disregard for her wellbeing.

"Listen, I might seem callous and selfish at times, but I am not."

Joy furrowed her eyebrows, tilted her head back, crossed her arms, and said," I know something is wrong with you, you look weak, pale, and your eyes are practically sunken into your head."

It's becoming increasingly difficult to lie to her. I'm not sure how long I can defer feeding because it's the lack of blood in my system that has accelerated my body's decay," she thought to herself. "I have to think of something quick–to throw her off my trail."

Joy stared at Lt. Drakon with eyebrows and ears raised in the air.

"I…I haven't been able to sleep lately. That's all; you don't have to worry about me. I'm fine," she quickly blurted out. "Just tell me what you got, Ms. Maxwell."

"Detective, please call me Joy. All my friends call me by my first name. I would like to think that we're at least becoming close."

"Joy, could you please get on with it already! The suspense is killing me.

"Okay, so, the wife told me that she received an email from my boss before he died. She watched it and said that the contents of the recording disturbed her. Her son opened it for her. He described it as, and I quote: *"There's governmental hi-tech black-ops area 51 type shit on it,"* Joy said and put her hand on Lt. Drakon's knee. "He didn't know what his father gotten himself into, but he's not entirely certain that he should turn the only copy over to the authorities. So, he gave me the copy."

"So, what are we waiting for, Joy? Let's go!" Lt. Drakon asked and got up out of her seat too fast, and she stumbled a little.

Joy aided her to her feet and said, "You don't look so good, Detective. Stay here; I can go alone. I will keep you updated."

"No, let me go to the little lady's room. I'll splash some water on my face and maybe grab a bite on the way." Lt. Drakon sauntered into the bathroom to freshen up. After she got herself together, both ladies head outside.

Joy was left with conjecture in the car, looking over at the ostracized detective in the passenger seat. "What's going on with the detective? I mean, I know she's going through something other than her recent troubles, but what is it?" she thought to herself. "Is it love, money, or drugs?"

Lt. Drakon panted and licked her lips. Beads of sweat collected on her forehead. She closed her eyes, shook her head, and said, "What are you getting from helping me, Ms. Maxwell?" Lt. Drakon asked to humanize the young reporter so that she won't view Joy as breakfast. "Ahem, I mean, I know that you are a reporter, but why are you helping me?"

"As I told you before, Detective, you saved my life; now it is my time to save yours."

Lt. Drakon was like a turtle, hard on the outside but soft inside and willing to stick her neck out for law and order. She wanted to let her guard down, but past experiences with people prevented her from doing so. "I think this is the address. Pullover here," she instructed Ms. Maxwell.

Joy slide into the first parking spot she saw. "Lucky, we were able to find a free parking spot in the city–what are the chances," Joy said as she put the car in park and turned off the engine.

She opened the car door, and Lt. Drakon stopped her. She tugged on her arm, barring Joy from leaving.

"What's the matter?" Joy asked as she stared in the rear-view mirror. "Wait, isn't that your hot partner?" Joy primped her hair and checked her make-up.

"What are you doing?" Lt. Drakon inquired.

"Your partner, Sgt. Mason, is just my type, tall, dark with rugged good looks and an athletic body to boot. He's attractive, and I just want to get to know him."

"I mean, yeah, if you like that sort of qualities in a man," Lt. Drakon replied and rolled her eyes.

"My mother always said: *'Inevitably, it is the little things that a man eventually notices.'* Catch his eyes, and the rest must follow."

"What about being yourself? Being yourself is relative. You're never yourself when you're in crosshairs of love."

"Detective, when you're conducting a life-changing interview or when your mother nags and nags about numerous things: from getting married and giving her some grandchildren. You're always yourself, just different facets of the same person."

"I guess you're right."

165

"Most guys are like puppies; they go with whoever is feeding them."

"You're very insightful, Ms. Maxwell."

"Was that a compliment, Detective?" Joy asked, teaming with glee.

"I guess," Lt. Drakon replied.

"Good to know; let's go and see if we can do something about your situation."

Both ladies exited the car, and they walked towards detective Sgt. Mason exchanged banter, and headed toward the widow's residence. After ringing the doorbell and knocking on the front door several times, Joy said, "I guess no one's home. We have been here waiting and knocking for fifteen minutes now."

"Wait, what are you ladies doing here anyway?" Sgt. Mason asked as he treaded down off the porch stairs.

The smell of fresh human blood hit Lt. Drakon's nose. It caused a slight elevation of her senses – for her, the smell was like the aroma of bacon sizzling in a frying pan. She held her mouth closed so she wouldn't expose her extended vampire fangs—the young blood demon answers with indeterminate hums and responsive executed head nods.

"Have you spoken to the wife yet?" Joy inquired.

"No, it seems like no one's home. The captain just told me that she had a tape that he would be interested in–that's what you guys are here for, correct." Sgt. Mason said, put one foot up on the step, and placed his hand on his knee. "I wonder what they have on this tape of theirs. I wonder where they are?" He trotted off the stoop, walked to the back of the house, and peered through the windows of the house.

"You don't think anything happened to them?" Joy yelled and walked off the porch. "I mean my boss, that nice old man, was murdered. Maybe the tape is evidence of his senseless killing."

Lt. Drakon peeked in the house through the window on the front porch. She could see anything of consequence. Her instinct to feed was getting stronger. The unmistakable scent of blood urged the fledgling to go inside. "I think we should go in the house, somethings wrong, I can feel it," she said as she peered through the window hiding her teeth from the others.

Joy followed behind Sgt. Mason like a smitten schoolgirl and laid her old southern charm on him. "How can a modern girl–a modern working girl, find someone to share her time with?" Joy asked and batted her eyes at him and puckered up her lips. "Being alone in this big *ol'* city is a *lil'* too much for a small-town gal like myself."

Sgt. Mason crouched down and picked up shards of glass that were on the ground. He looked up at the windows, and there were no signs of false entry into the house.

"Ms. Maxwell, for the little time that I've known you—you don't strike me as vulnerable," Sgt. Mason replied while his focus never wavered from Lt. Drakon's curvaceous body. "I get the impression that you can handle yourself just fine."

Sgt. Mason walked past Joy up the drive to where Lt. Drakon was.

"Hmm–well, I be darned!" Joy exclaimed.

"You got a raw deal!" Sgt. Mason yelled toward Lt. Drakon as he returned to the front porch from the side of the house and stood at the bottom of the stairs.

Lt. Drakon was so focused that she couldn't hear him. He

realized her preoccupation and screamed, "I think you were rail-roaded in this situation!"

Lt. Drakon remained unresponsive. Sgt. Mason stepped up on the stairs and got closer to her. "There's broken glass back there, but no one's home. I didn't see any broken windows, though."

"Hmm, that's interesting. Be more proactive and kick in the door, so we could be certain that the family's okay. They could be tied up in a backroom or even worst." Lt. Drakon ordered Sgt. Mason.

"I can't do that. There's no reason to suspect foul play. Maybe they just stepped out for a second," Sgt. Mason replied as he walked up to the door and peeked inside. "Besides, you are not even supposed to be here anyway. Your presence could compromise everything if there's evidence of foul play."

Joy felt slightly overlooked. Her concerns for her slain boss's family covered her feelings. "Ahem! Do you think something is awry, Detective?" Joy asked.

"I don't know, but something smells fishy," Lt. Drakon replied and turned faced Joy and Sgt. Mason. She gasped and quickly covered her mouth with her hand. She felt for her fangs with her tongue, and it already retracted. "I know something is wrong; I can feel it in my bones."

"I believe her, Detective Mason, let's check it out," Joy said. "You never want to second a woman's intuition—especially when that woman is a detective."

"You guys may be right, but I am the only one with authority here," Sgt. Mason replied. "I'm not the one to state the obvious, but we only just met Ms. Maxwell. Sorry for being abrupt; I have no idea who you are and how you work. It doesn't matter how beautiful you ladies are."

Both women looked at each other when Sgt. Mason complimented them.

"By the way don't you have an internal affairs interview?" he asked. "Let's do this one by the book. Don't jeopardize your possible reinstatement by making poor decisions."

Lt. Drakon walked down the stairs towards Sgt. Mason and said, "I assure you that any choice I make, save lives, including yours, Sergeant. I haven't made it this far by making brainless decisions. Remember this the next time you insinuate that I've made bad decisions.

"Lt. Drakon shoulder bumped Sgt. Mason when she stepped away from him and said, "Come on, Ms. Maxwell!"

Sgt. Mason chased down Lt. Drakon, grabbed her arm, and spun her around. "I am sorry, and I don't know who attacked the precinct last week, but you did save me. You may have saved all of us," he said. "For your sake and the integrity of this entire department, I have to do this one, by the book." Sgt. Mason put his hand on her shoulder.

Lt. Drakon brushed his hand off her shoulder and stepped past the sergeant void of emotion.

Regretful for his brazen macho man ego, Sgt. Mason realized that he hurt Lt. Drakon's feelings. He grabbed her arm to prevent her from walking away from him. Before he could utter an apology, Lt. Drakon pulled away from his clutches. She opened the passenger side door of her car, got inside, and slammed it.

Joy shook her head at the Sgt. Mason's awful chauvinistic action and entered the car.

Sgt. Mason glared at the lieutenant and said, "Good luck on

your interview. I told them how you saved my life; hopefully, my account helped."

Joy pulled away from the curb and drove Lt. Drakon downtown to the Internal Affair's office. The two women barely said three words to one another the whole trip.

Joy parked in front of the building, and her mobile phone rang. She answered the phone while Lt. Drakon was still in the car.

"Joy Maxwell, this is the producer at channel five," a female voice on the other end said. "Get yourself ready. You're scheduled to cover the Sgt. Blake's funeral. You will also follow the precession of the fallen police officers and the civilians from last week's massacre."

"What, wait, I can't," Joy replied.

"I know that you were friends with two of the victims. There's no one I can think of that could put the right emotions into this coverage."

"Hold on," Joy excused herself and took off her Bluetooth as Lt. Drakon left the car. "Detective, after you get your badge—"

"You mean shield," Lt. Drakon said.

"Oh, you know what I mean. Are you coming back?"

Lt. Drakon nodded and said, "Thanks for the lift, Joy. I'll see you shortly." She turned around and walked into the building.

She walked down the corridor and saw a man standing outside of the office where they were conducting her hearing. "They're ready," she whispers to herself. "The system can't wait to slap its heavy iron hand on my chest, knocking all of the air out of my lungs while crushing my lifelong dreams of serving as a police officer."

Lt. Drakon saw four males, including the one at the door.

"Look at the good old boys—if I were a man, I wouldn't have to go through this shit. I can't believe it, not one female on the panel," she whispered to herself. All her trepidations began to transform into anger and resentment. Her anger swelled up inside her like the good year blimp when she sat down.

Lt. Drakon took a deep breath to calm down her emotions. She didn't want to jeopardize the one thing that she loves the most. She poured herself some water and took a sip.

"Good morning, Lt. Adeline Drakon," the officer said.

"Good morning—sorry, I don't know what your name is," she replied.

"Sorry, where are my manners. My name is Lt. Desmond McClymont. The man seated to the left of me is Sgt. Jenkins. On my right is Sgt. Glennville Dale and the cheerful guy who greeted you at the entrance was IAB officer Collins. I know you would like to get on with this preceding," he said and poured out a cup of water. "Before we begin, I have to inform you that this preceding will be recorded."

"Unless you have a confession to make off the record," Sgt. Jenkins said and covered the microphone.

"No, no, I don't, proceed," Lt. Drakon replied.

"Okay, let's begin," Sgt. Dale remarked.

"Today's date is February 24, 2012, time 1:31 in the p.m. I am lieutenant Desmond McClymont. We are here at the top of the investigative interview with Lieutenant Adeline Penelope Drakon," he said. "We have the statements of your colleagues. Their statements will be considered in our decision to lift your suspension. Integrating all accounts culminating with yours. With that being said, I will tell you what an Internal Affairs agent once told me: *'I am not here to destroy careers.'* We try to pluck the lowest scum of the streets, and that's corrupted policeman. The worst thing is to have people who should be trusted in a position of authority which completely abuse their power. So, tell me what happened."

Lt. Drakon's fear was quashed with the tone of his speech. The way that Lt. McClymont conveyed his plan of this investigation was calming and reassuring that she wouldn't be railroaded. She told her side of the story. With the events of that tragic day still fresh in her mind, it rolled off her tongue like water off a duck.

"Alright, lieutenant, we heard enough. Based on our query and facts on your situation, it is difficult to make a quick judgment now.

So, we will look over the facts and cooperating statements and contact Captain Constantine of our decision."

The previously nearly broken female detective left the room with a renewed vigor, a brand-new sense of service.

Meanwhile, it was a bit melancholy in the halls and offices at the precinct because it was the day of the funeral of those who lost their lives during the siege on the precinct. Every single policeman and woman were in their dress uniform adorned with all their metals. An air of strife and discord filled those walls. There's a significant impasse between those who agree with Lt. Drakon letting the prisoner go and those who don't.

The phone has been ringing off the hook in the captain's office for the entire day. Especially since the rest of the building's calls have been rerouted to surrounding departments just for the day. Mainly for the coordination of the ceremony. Other calls were from departments that will be on loan to pick up the slack in the respectful areas, people lending their condolences, and about other affairs about the day's memorial services.

The captain answered the phone when detective Mason knocked on his door. With a glance, he waved for the sergeant to come inside.

Seconds later, agent Henning stepped inside him with information about the new technology that can make one invisible on camera.

Capt. Constantine hung up the phone.

Sgt. Mason said, "Captain, the family was gone before I got there. After waiting outside for what seemed like an hour. I examined the parameter, I found glass shards outside of the back entrance, but there were no broken windows on the premises."

"Do you think there's foul play?" the captain inquired.

"I can't say for sure, Captain, but my gut tells me, yes."

"Are you certain? Because I don't want to put out an alert based on a gut feeling, especially on this day. I don't want to do that, and they just went to the mall or something."

The captain hunched over behind his desk because his ulcer started to act up. He quickly went into his desk and took out a bottle of Pepto Bismol. He opened the cap, chugged down the pink elixir like a marathon runner guzzling water during a big race. The cause of the low throbbing pain twisting the captain's gut isn't only his judgment call not to consider the Super C supermarket manager's wife and son's mysterious disappearance. But the memorial service and a myriad of different things. He's a trooper, and he always found a way to suppress the stress deep in his core before.

"One thing at a time, Detective," the captain mumbled. "We will not pursue the disappearance just yet; I mean, there could be multiple reasons for them to have left before you got there. In any case, let's deal with what we have at hand." The captain's words were as much to convince himself as it was for the sergeant not to worry.

Sergeant Mason left after the captain shot him down. He went, sat down at his desk, and put his head in his hands. He looked up at the evidence board across from his desk. He took a closer look at the board and examined the method he's been using for this case to draw up all his conclusions. "The connections may be all wrong," he thought to himself while writing on the board. "A family whose patriarch had been murdered, probably would not trust the police department that gave up the only person suspected of killing him, with important information?"

The sergeant felt in his bones that something wasn't right, but his wings had been clipped. "Why would they leave? Were they expecting us?" Sgt. Mason thought to himself. "What doesn't fit here?"

He stood up, folded his arms across his chest, and scratched the top of his head.

Chapter 7

Joy Maxwell was set up outside the channel-five news van and started her coverage of the funeral. "This ceremony's as authentic and traditional as it could get. There are bagpipers, one hundred and fifty police officers dressed in their uniforms, and approximately one hundred family members and friends are in attendance today. Everyone is here to pay their last respects to their loved ones who lost their lives on that tragic day in this LODD (Line of duty death.)

"Most New Yorkers are filled with angst, as we here in midtown Manhattan say goodbye to the servicemen and women who gave their lives on that tragic day. Those who dedicated themselves protecting and serving the great city of New York. Today is a somber day, tears cascade down the faces of thousands of citizens who cared about those who served in law enforcement and toured this great city.

"All the businesses in Mid-town Manhattan have displayed many symbols to show their respect, solidarity for those slain police officers, and civilians who died in that horrible assault in the Midtown Precinct North last week. Some have blacked out their windows in the office buildings, and others hung up blue curtains or ribbons.

"What's interesting is, many of the storefronts have put up NYPD uniforms in their display windows. Demonstrating empathy for relatives and loved ones who lost someone near and dear to them.

Joy put her hand to her ear and paused for a moment. "Chuck just told me in the studio that all five Burroughs are rallying in solidarity as well. This city has not seen this brand of camaraderie since the terrorist attacks on 9/11/2001."

"Yes, Joy, I have heard that many people have taken to the streets," Chuck the head anchor added. "They're all on foot and converging together as one."

"Chuck, there is a substantial swell of people outside; it's an outpour of friends and family members of the fallen and fellow New Yorkers, who are now marching hand in hand. It's a sizable following that has grown exponentially. People are peacefully pouring out in the streets, and it's amazing how this city comes together, setting aside their differences in the wake of a tragedy. New York City is the greatest city on planet earth."

"Does it look like the crowd might turn violent?" Krystal, the Co-anchor, asked Joy. "I know that you work with two of the victims that were murdered by the suspect of the Midtown Murders, who was in custody and at the center of last week's brutal slaughter in Midtown Precinct North."

Joy stood there motionless on camera. Her throat closed, and she got a cottonmouth as if she'd been drinking all night. As a consummate professional, she swiftly collected herself, demonstrating pure composure and poise.

Joy adjusted her clothes; her cameraman handed her a Kleenex and a bottle of water. She took a sip and said, "It is taking everything inside me not to just burst into tears right now live on camera. Yes, Krystal, that is correct. I was friends with two of the victims buried today. They will be greatly missed." She put down the microphone by her side and wiped the tears away from her face with a Kleenex. The cameraman turned away from her and captured a wide shot of the landscape behind her.

"We are now entering the cemetery," she said off-camera. "You can see the Police Color guard are in perfect formation. You could see them on top of the rolling plush green hill in the middle of the rows of headstones and carefully manicured grass. The honor guards stood at attention, awaiting orders for the twenty-one-gun salute.

The lead barked commands loudly from the gut like a drill sergeant, "Company! The NYPD honor guard raised their ceremonial rifles in unison, like an Olympic synchronized swim team. "Ready!" They put their rifles on their shoulders. "Steady!" With the rifles locked and loaded, they cocked back the pin. "Aim!" Stoic in their stance, the honor guard awaited the final command. "Fire!" he bellowed. "Fire 1! Fire 2…," the lead guard screamed out after every shot. The line of vehicles advanced to the area of the final resting place.

Joy Maxwell and a bevy of other reporters from various news media outlets in the tri-state area reported the event from the sideline.

Everyone kept the flashes and correspondence to a minimum, out of respect to the family and friends. When all the attendees started piled out of their cars in succession, Lt. Drakon's appearance didn't go unnoticed. There were murmurs in the crowd from many people that disagreed with her decision to let go of the *Sangre Killer*. And those who didn't make sure she understood that her presence was not welcomed.

"She has her nerve showing her face here," one woman said.

"It should've been her in one of those coffins?" a man said.

The lieutenant did not cower from their judgmental glares, scowls, or unkind gestures. She was confident that her choice wasn't made light on that faithful night. She alone had to make a difficult choice, and many would've made the same one under the circumstances. Hindsight is always twenty-twenty. "People always talk about what they might've done if faced with the same situation," She thought to herself.

"Don't pay them any attention. I, for one, am thankful that you were there then and now," Sgt. Mason said. "By the way, I apologize for my actions—I...I was way out of line, and it won't happen again; scouts honor!" he put up the Boy Scout sign and smiled.

Lt. Drakon looked at Sgt. Mason square in the eyes but didn't say a word. There was an awkward silence, then he leaned in and said, "Also, I think you were right."

"Right? Right about what?" she solemnly asked.

"I used a favor to get a warrant signed to enter the home. I followed your instincts against the captain's orders. The house was in shambles like someone was desperately looking for something."

"Yeah! Did the search bear fruit?"

"Yes, we collected several items from inside the house, including a computer; I believe it belonged to the son. I sent them all to the lab to be processed. So, if there's anything they discover, I'll keep you in the loop." Sgt. Mason gave her a look and winked. "By the way, Lt. Drakon, partners must stick together."

"Wait, what about the family" Lt. Drakon asked. "Do you think they were kidnapped?"

"No way to know for sure until we get a call from them or the people responsible for their disappearance," Sgt. Mason replied.

There's was nothing that anyone could say that would pull Lt. Drakon out of her funk. She just couldn't shake the cold emotional veil of loneliness. She had been alone all her life, but now the darkness has taken over. While wallowing in her crapulence and self-pity, she fell into a vision of blood and gore even with Sergeant Mason's full support. The hunger and thirst filled her every thought.

Before she could snap out of it, Captain Constantine tapped her on the shoulder and said, "You do know that you don't have to be here." His words have never cut so deep before. If a poll was conducted asking everyone's opinion who blamed her for releasing the *Sanguine Killer*, she would have to commit seppuku to cut deeper than the captain's words.

Lt. Drakon put her head down to hide the fact that her eyes were filled with tears. She sniffled and put her index finger and thumb in the corner of her eyes. The stress of the situation compounded her thirst exponentially. But she perfected a way to subdue the thirst before she fully transformed into a blood demon before it became visible to all.

Captain Constantine noticed that Lt. Drakon was upset by his statement and said, "Lieutenant, you misunderstood what I meant. So, let me rephrase what I said. This is a delicate situation, you do belong here, and if there's anyone who deserves to be here and pay their respect besides the family, it's you. You are solely responsible for saving the lives of all who survived the massacre at the Midtown Precinct North, including mine. But not everyone in attendance doesn't feel the same way about the situation."

"Captain, I am not here to cause any trouble, but I feel that I owe it to all those who died by the hands of the "Sangre Killer." Lt. Drakon replied. "I won't be long; I just needed to say something. I need to do something; I owe them that much. I don't much care about everyone else's opinions of me. As a homicide detective with the NYPD, I have made a promise: I took an oath, and I promised myself and to those who died in the line duty that I will get this guy again. If this doesn't appeal to anyone else, I must mourn with my brothers and sisters in the uniform," she expressed.

"I understand that, but we all know the risks of putting on this uniform that we may die in service while protecting this city. Living with that burden having full understanding and expectation is not all up to you alone, Lieutenant. Knowing that we may not make home every night is a sacrifice we pride ourselves on, and it's done with the same promise you made. We all took the same oath." The captain put his hand on the upper part of Lt. Drakon's arm.

Sergeant Blake's wife approached and said, "Right now, some of the family members and friends are just not warming up to the idea of you being here, Lt. Drakon," she said through her clenched teeth. To muffle her voice and not cause a commotion about Lt. Drakon's presence at the ceremony.

"Wait, aren't those dead bodies?" Lt. Drakon asked and looked beyond the surrounding memorial service and saw what appeared to be the store manager's widow and their son in the clearing.

"Excuse me! What did you just ask me?"

"I'm truly sorry for your lost," she said and excused herself.

"Do you think they're dead?" Sgt. Mason asked, and he, the captain, and Lt. Drakon walked stealthily across the cemetery.

"Yes, I believe they are," she said.

The smell of their blood was unmistakable. It riled her up outside of their home earlier that morning. The more she fought, the easier it got easier to repel her vampire urges. They got closer to see that the bodies are propped up on a bench in front of an open grave. They were strung up like a suspension bridge. Whoever put them there used what appeared to be a heavy-duty fish line. They connected it from their heads to their hips to prop up the bodies.

"Why would they toy with us like this?" asked Lt. Drakon.

"What do you mean, Lieutenant?" captain Constantine asked.

"It is a sign from the culprits that did this," Sgt. Mason said.

"Let's not speculate, don't assume anything, Sergeant. Let the

CSIs process the evidence first," the captain replied, then he took out his phone from inside his jacket pocket.

"It's not an assumption, Captain. If anything, they're sending us a message," Lt. Drakon replied.

Lt. Drakon stooped behind the bench and looked over the shoulders of the victims. "There's writing on top of those headstones. You can only see it when you're in this position, Captain. It's a sign, and it was placed here like this, to show us the way," she said. "Come here, Captain, kneel here and look." She pulled the captain down juxtapose to her position.

"Dr. German, be discreet when you…" Before he could finish his statement to the Medical Examiner, the phone hung up.

Sgt. Mason knelt behind the young teenager to see too. "Damn it, it is written in blood," he said, turned his face away, put his hand over his mouth to stop himself from throwing up.

He bent over with his hands on his knees and turned his head over to Lt. Drakon. "Is it written in Latin? Can you figure out what it means?" Sgt. Mason asked.

"No, not yet, but with good homicide detectives on the case, we will soon enough," Lt. Drakon replied and stepped away from the bodies. "A Forensic team is on their way, so it won't be too long before it's deciphered."

"What the fuck," The Captain shouted. "In all my years, I have never seen anything like this. Not only were the two bodies sewed to the bench, but this sick sadistic bastard also did other terrible things to them."

Capt. Constantine accidentally knocked over the teenager's hat. For a second, he lost total composure when he saw that the boy's skull was empty after the cap fell off. He could see the back of the skull had been cut off. It had been cut from the cranium to the nape. It was then tacked at the top of the opening, which permitted it to swing back and forth like a pendulum.

The captain used a pen to move the dangling piece of bone and hair out the way. When he did, he discovered the brain was scooped out, and everything else except the eyes had been removed. The eyes were glued in its sockets. Sunlight beamed through the nostrils and the small gap from his mouth with the sun's rays on his face.

The captain swiftly rose to his feet and moving away from the mutilated remains of the son of Mr. Gilman. He dusted off his hands and uniform adorned with medals, then tugged down on his vest and smoothed out his sleeves. He reached for his handkerchief and wiped off beads of sweat from his face.

Lt. Drakon looked on as the captain got himself together. The hairs on the back of her neck stood up, so she spun her head around to survey their surroundings. "I am certain that someone else is out there watching our every move. This feeling is so strange," she said to herself. With all the other people at the funeral, she could still tell that someone was watching her. By someone like her, she could sense the difference. "I bet you it's *The Sanguine Killer*, no doubt." She can't let go of her humanity, although she's not human anymore and does not realize that her transformation heightened her instincts. There was a spy in their midst, a vampire, a fellow blood demon lurking in the shadows hiding in plain sight.

Lt. Drakon doesn't trust her vampire awareness enough to react as she should. How would she explain that to everyone else? She would have to rely solely on her own woman's intuition. "That's it!" she screamed aloud, then covered her mouth after her sudden outburst. She looked around to see if anyone heard her. "Maybe I could translate it on a translator app on my cellphone," she thought, then she copied the characters from the headstones on her cellphone. It read: *"One-day eyes shall look upon darkness and kneel before him."*

"Eureka!" she exclaimed when she deciphered the message. "Captain, I found something." The young blood demon detective stood up and handed captain Constantine her cellphone. She stood there waiting for his approval of her findings.

"Here, IAB reinstated you, Lieutenant! Glad to see you back on the job," the captain said.

"Good detective work, Lieutenant, but there's no need for you to be here. We can take it from here. We got everything under control," a deep male voice said in her hear from behind.

Lt. Drakon knew it was agent Henning before she turned around. With all the things that have gone on in her life. She decided to let go of her pity bitterness with the FBI; besides, she realized that agent Henning hadn't personally offended her. "Bickering with him will not help solve this murder," she thought to herself. She showed the cynical agent her pearly white teeth, then brandished her recently acquired detective shield.

"Do we have a problem here, agent Henning?"

"No, no, we don't have a problem," he answered and chuckled through a stone-cold rigid stare. "Do you think that this was the work of the *Sanguine Killer*?"

"Since his mindless followers freed him, we can only speculate that this is his handy work or one of his minions tying up loose ends."

Everyone in the cemetery had left the officers and the agent in the graveyard. Dr. German and the rest of the forensics team crime approached the crime scene.

"I figured that the killings were not just the endeavors of one person. I am not entirely certain that one man ever committed the Midtown Murders," Lt. Drakon said.

"How can you be certain?" asked the captain.

"Look at the message, Sir." Lt. Drakon pointed at the phone.

She explained what the numbers and symbols were. Nimbus clouds accumulated in the sky, lightning struck, and thunder roared afterward.

"Oh no, the evidence will be washed away by the coming rain. CSI team haven't collected the samples yet," Lt. Drakon said and rushed to her feet. "Come with me! Let us collect samples of blood from off those headstones before the rain washes it away."

Agent Henning, Sgt. Mason, and the CSI team hastened their steps behind the quick-thinking detective. They put on gloves, pulled out some cotton swabs, evidence bags, and quickly made their collections.

Lt. Drakon's mentor Dr. German approached her while worked frantically to salvage the evidence from the headstones. This was the first time that she saw her estranged foster grandfather since her outburst at his office. She felt a huge lump growing in her throat. If she still had a heartbeat, it would be racing through her chest. Her face was flush, and she tried to avoid direct eye contact with him.

Agent Henning picked up on the weird body language and made a statement to draw her focus. "I thought you to be tougher than that," he said.

"Yeah, what do you mean?" Lt. Drakon asked and turned to the meddling FBI agent.

"I mean, I didn't peg you as the type of person that allowed anyone to distract them or let anything throw them off their game."

Lt. Drakon sighed and rubbed her forehead with the back of her hand. "Don't attempt your FBI mind tricks on me, agent Henning. You don't know anything about me. I'm not as simple as you may think. Besides, we just met a few days ago, so don't try to crack this code with your psychological profiling, Big Brother, special agent babble bullshit on me because it won't work."

Lt. Drakon wrapped the evidence into bags, and agent Henning opened his mouth to respond. She held up her hand out in front of her and said with her eyebrows knitted, "Believe me, I am more complex than a mere quest and behavioral observations that you can string together, resulting in a match of patterns from some personality analysis. Listen, you can't fold me up and put me in a box."

"I don't doubt that Lieutenant; I wasn't insinuating that you were simple. I believe you are not, but I saw something in your eyes and written on your face bothering you. I just need to know if you can be trusted."

"Trusted, trusted with what?" Lt. Drakon asked and approached agent, Henning.

They stopped talking and snarled at each other intently. By this time, the rain started pouring down hard and heavy. The agent scoffed and looked away; he then rubbed his chin roughly with his hands, which made a scratchy sound against his stubbly five o'clock shadow. He rubbed his face so hard you could hear it despite the pitter pats of the rain droplets all around them.

"He's right, Lieutenant," the captain responded. "The FBI's going to take over and head of this investigation. They were waiting until after the memorial services."

"When?" asked Lt. Drakon.

"Today, captain Constantine will get the call any minute now," agent Henning replied.

"So, you're telling me this because?"

"Because lieutenant, this whole situation is not ideal for catching a serial killer or killers. The Midtown Precinct North–your precinct, has already been compromised. The fact is, we're not certain if the local police are equipped to handle this case."

"How can we be certain about anything."

"I know our stance may be misconstrued as difficult—"

"Hey! Are you two love birds ready to rejoin this case?" asked the captain. "Do you have something more important to do other than solving this case?"

Lt. Drakon stared the agent up and down, stepped past him, and said, "We'd better get back." As she walked away, she shouted, "Captain, if I can pick a team with anyone I want, I think I want agent Henning on my team of investigators."

"Wait, what? Hold on—I'm confused—weren't you just— Okay, I'll play along–I need to know everything about you–more than what's written in some file. I need not be concerned for my safety when push comes to shove. I need to know that you will not shy away from the hard, unpopular decisions. You have yet to prove that you're more than just another pretty face or opinionative," agent Henning replied.

Lt. Drakon paused and smiled. "He thinks I'm just another pretty face?" she said to herself and continued toward the crime scene.

"Everything's alright, partner?" Sgt. Mason asked.

Lt. Drakon and agent Henning approached and just handed over their bags to a CSI without saying a word at first. Sgt. Mason asked again, pressing the issue.

"I am fine," she looked into her partner's eyes and replied under her breath.

Sgt. Mason raised his hands in the air and stepped out of Lt. Drakon's way.

"I can't tell you until I get them back to the—"

"Excuse me, is there anything else, Captain?" she asked, interrupting his conversation with Dr. German.

"Is there going to be a problem with you working your grandfather, Lieutenant?"

She gritted her teeth and quickly replied, "No, not at all. I am impressed with his expertise; everyone knows that."

"Let's clean this up! We are now on twenty-four-hour shifts. We have to catch this son-of-bitch," the captain addressed everyone before tugging on his vest, then walked to his vehicle and drove off.

Agent Henning turned to the Medical Examiner and said, "You have been on this case from the beginning. You know more about the victims than anyone else. Because of this fact, I have no choice but to keep you. There's no denying the fact that you're the best forensics scientist on the east coast, maybe even in the country."

"You won't get anywhere with flattery. Just spit it out," Dr. German retorted.

"Please, excuse my grandfather. He's a genius but has been known to butcher the English language and American sayings," Lt. Drakon explained.

"There will be changes made when those changes happen, and I want to make sure that we have a complete understanding, that you will answer to me and only me. The captain is not in the chain of command as it pertains to this case anymore. I will need all the files on every person you believe murdered by the *Sanguine Killer* or killers. Can you handle this, Doctor?"

"Yes!" Dr. German replied.

Agent Henning took out his card and held on to it as he handed it to Dr. German. "Doctor, you do know it's a federal offense to go against my orders, right. From here on out, I'm in charge until this case is closed and these monsters are detained."

The doctor nodded and said, "Yes, I understand completely."

Everyone, including the CSI unit and coroner office, was packed up and ready to leave the cemetery. They all started to pull away.

Sgt. Mason approached his partner and asked, "Are you ready to go?"

"I'll meet you at the station," Lt. Drakon said, then she followed behind agent Henning. "It looks like we're going the same way. So, tell me, how did you know the M.E was my grandfather?"

"I'm an agent with the FBI, and we have our ways. Plus, it was written all over your face earlier."

"It's impossible for you to guess that, are you some type of magician?" Lt. Drakon asked as they reached the agent's car.

"No, but if you want to learn how, I know little magic, we can discuss it tonight over dinner tonight."

"Are you asking me out on a date, agent Henning?"

'No, I figured since we will be working together, we might as well have dinner together. Everyone gets hungry sometime or another.

I agree with the captain about one thing—"

"And what's that?" asked Lt. Drakon.

"We do need to spend more time on this case and catch this killer. So, the people of the city can rest easy when we do. I just need to collaborate with the best detective in this city," agent Henning replied while getting into his car and rolled down his window. He started the engine and put it in drive and said, "Not to worry, I'm not asking you out on a date. It's just dinner. Watch your feet, Lieutenant." He smiled, pulled away from the curb, and tooted his horn.

"I never said that I would accept your offer, agent Henning," Lt. Drakon shouted as he pulled away. She stood there alone in the rain, soggy, drenched, and contemplating everything that transpired. She noticed that her life was rapidly getting complicated.

Captain Constantine and Sgt. Mason arrived at the Midtown Precinct North at the same time. The captain got out of his vehicle with his cellphone at his ear and said, "Yes, Mr. Mayor, I was already briefed from agent Henning that the FBI would be taking over the case. Yes, I'm fully... I understand." He slammed his car door hard after hanging up the phone. He then marched up the parking lot slope to the stairs that lead straight into the precinct through a side door. He stopped at the top of the steps and yelled loud enough to be heard above the cars' screeching and all the other clicking, chattering, and clanking going on in the covered parking garage. "Sergeant! Where's your partner and agent Henning?"

"I have no idea, Sir. I left them both at the cemetery!" Sergeant Mason explained.

"Good! Hurry up, come with me."

Sgt. Mason slammed his car door and walked briskly behind the captain into the elevator.

The captain put his hands in front of the door and held it open until he got in. He released the door and pressed the close door button before pressing the third floor. "After changing out of your uniform, come straight to my office. I need to talk to you, before agent Henning gets back."

"What happened, Sir?"

"The Midtown Murder case has been hijacked from us by the FBI." the elevator stopped, and the doors opened. "I'll talk to more about it later," he grabbed the right shoulder with his left hand as they exited the elevator car.

Meanwhile, Joy Maxwell was distraught, exhausted, and beside herself emotionally from the past few weeks. She was relieved all the coverage of the siege on Midtown Precinct North was over, and the victims were laid to rest. She went to her new apartment, a loaner from the station she requested to use after hers.

It was a lavish, fully furnished condo, in a forty-floor high rise, with a great view of the city. Joy stepped off the elevator on the thirty-second floor into the corridor. She slumped her shoulders and leaned on the wall where the events of the past few weeks hit her like a ton of bricks. Memories that laid dormant in the back of her mind buddled to the resurface like heavy oil in the La Brea Tar Pits. The tears welled up in her eyes as she slid against the wall to her door. She couldn't take the keys out of her pocketbook fast enough. When she unlocked the door, she got in and locked the door behind her. She leaned her back up against the door after entering her apartment.

Tired, Joy slid to the floor and wailed. She didn't have the time to mourned or shed a tear for anyone; it all happened so fast. She knew six people that were buried today and hadn't cried a drop until now. "They died over a week ago, and I haven't cried once. What kind of monster am I? What's wrong with me?" she bawled. She pulled her knees up to her chest and continued wailing. She was so busy covering the attacks to advance her career she hasn't had time to grieve.

Joy got up, sauntered into her bathroom, and looked at herself in the mirror. "Who am I?" she blurted out loud. She walked to the living room past a cup that was placed on her coffee table. But with her eyes, all swelled up with tears, she sniffled, reached for a Kleenex, and blew her nose. With her eyes closed, she didn't notice the ominous figure sitting on the couch perfectly camouflaged in the shadow of the night.

"Joy Maxwell, pull yourself together! Come on, girl, you're on the verge of presenting your talents to the world. You're going to surprise those small-minded people back home with a Pulitzer one day soon," she said to herself in the mirror.

Joy wiped her tears from her cheeks, disrobed, and stepped into the shower. The water cascaded over her body like a force field, an imaginary shield she has always used to escape from the world whenever things got too hard. She let her mind wander. For her taking a shower has always been her sanctuary. It's not only therapeutic but cathartic. As a little girl, she would take a shower and pretend it was protective armor, and all the badness and trappings of the world would wash away.

Chapter 8

Back at the department, the captain was in deep talks with Sgt. Mason in his office. He stood there and faced his huge bay window looking out into the street at the rat race. Sgt. Mason unsuspectingly awaited the words from his boss. "Look at them; they're like hamsters on a wheel, running without an end. This is how life is summed up. From the time we enter this world, our existence is always questioned. What's the purpose of it all?"

Sgt. Mason knitted up his eyebrows and said, "What's wrong, Sir? I don't understand—"

"The meaning of life is simple survival, from the metaphysical down to the molecular level. It's the force that drives life is to exist."

"Sir, I understand that Sgt. Blake was your best friend, and I could only imagine how much his passing has affected you. But you're not making any sense right now. What are you trying to tell me?"

The captain pulled on his vest, turned around, and said, "The night will come when blood shall run, and the streets will be painted red. One day, eyes shall look upon darkness and kneel before him."

Sgt. Mason snickered, exhaled sharply, stood up, and put his hand out. Both men embraced and gave each other handshake. A gesture is only known by a specific fraternity, *The Order of the Blood,* which was formed by humans who want to become vampires.

"You're in the order?" asked Sgt. Mason. "I knew you were in the order. That's why I accepted your transfer from Philadelphia. Since we know that the two of us are in the *Order of the Blood,* we need to establish a hierarchy. I am the seventh day for rebirth."

The captain cocked his head over his right shoulder, lifted his tongue, and displayed his mark first. This mark showed the other what degree they held in the order. Sgt. Mason crossed his right arm across his chest with a closed fist, dropped down to one knee, then snapped to attention.

"Let your blood run through mine. May we drink death and live immortal," they said in unison.

"Brother, time is of the essence. I got the call from the mayor that the FBI will take over the case. Agent Henning will be the lead on the team. I am not certain who he will keep on his investigative team," captain Constantine scoffs and shakes his head. "We must be careful; we have a great secret to protect. You know as well as I do that we are on the edge of a new dawn—*A New World Order*, a time when the world will be ruled by the *Blood God*."

"Do you think it's wise to help the vampires take over the world?" Sgt. Mason asked. "I don't think we should just give them everything. They already have their hands in everything, and they are everywhere. They have reached every major capital in the world."

"We're insignificant; change is going to come. It is inevitable. So, the only thing left is whether you want to stay on the ship or jump down the razor blade and slide into the alcohol river," the captain replied.

Sgt. Mason grinned, tilted his head up and down, and said, "What do you need me to do?"

"Agent Henning is on his way, and I need you to be on his investigative team."

"How do you know that he's going to use the NYPD?"

"Don't worry about that. I know his type; he will pick someone he thinks is the best person with the worst character for the case. He will pick Lt. Drakon. He will keep that person around, one who he deems an Ally or an Albatross."

"So, he's going to use her regardless."

"Have you heard the saying, keep your friend close and your enemies even closer."

"I get it. What does that have to do with me, Brother?"

"We have orders to watch over her, and she's important to the cause."

There was loud chatter outside his office, then a loud knock at the captain's office door. The captain moved to the side and said, "Come in."

Agent Henning opened the door and stepped halfway inside with an entitled look on his face, and said, "Knock, knock! Good, Captain, you're in. Can you come out here for a sec? I would like to address the whole precinct; thanks." He punctuated his request with a cheesy two-finger salute.

The captain exhaled through his nose like a prized Spanish bull who was just side-stepped by an elusive Matador. He fixed his vest and walked out of his office with Sgt. Mason behind him. He gave the sergeant a signal, signaling him not to forget their talk and its importance.

Agent Henning called everyone to join him in the conference room. He placed a leather messenger bag on a table in front of the room and paced back and forth in front of the room. He waited for everyone to settle down and said, "Come in, there's room, squeeze in here. I want every single officer to hear what I have to say."

The policemen and women stuffed themselves into the room; most officers were still dressed in their uniforms.

"Hey, Captain!" he said, "Do you think everyone's here?"

Capt. Constantine looked around the room and shrugged his shoulders. "It looked like everyone is here, except for four officers," he replied. "Two of them are still in ICU, I have another undercover officer, out on assignment, and my lieutenant is just coming off a suspension–whom you already know, agent Henning. The floor is yours, please proceed."

"Okay, thank you, Captain. I understand that today is one of great sorrow. I would like it also to be a day of remembrance—a day when we shall begin to move forward down the path toward justice. Justice is met when law enforcement encounter and defeat the offensive criminal entity," he said and took a sip of water.

"I know exactly how you feel because I also lost my partner," the agent articulates. "With that said, if you don't already know, my name is Special Agent Marcus Henning. I'm with the Federal Bureau of Investigations, and as of right now, the FBI has taken the lead on this case. Does anyone have any questions?" he asked, paused, and waited if anyone would object.

"Okay, both factions must work together on this one if we want to catch these bastards—"

"How are we going to do that?" a policewoman asked.

"So far, there's no leads, no evidence, and no suspects."

"That's not true, you must know something, or the FBI wouldn't be here in the first place."

"You do; what is it?" asked a rookie police officer.

"If you do, we all have a right to know what it is!" she replied.

"She right, let us all in on it," an African American police officer shouted from the right side of the room.

"Yeah, right," another officer shouted.

Soon after the initial outburst, all the police officers in there were riled up. The frustrated officers fussing filled the department like smoke in a dive joint or a seedy bar uptown.

The captain stood up and said, "Hold on! Hold on! Let's give agent Henning a chance. The most important thing is that we find the people responsible and bring them to justice. Let's just see what he has to say."

Everyone quieted down after the motivational words from their captain.

"Agent! Please proceed," Captain Constantine said and stepped away from the podium.

"I know it's hard, I realize this, but maybe we can all work together. My purpose is to set up a task force comprised of police officers and federal agents. Here, I have a list of candidates that I want on my team. I have found law enforcement personnel from your precinct. So, that you can get a crack at the bastards who came into your own home," he said and looked every officer in their eyes. "I selected people who I believe can contribute the most to bringing these bastards to justice."

Agent Henning reached into his messenger bag and took out a couple of files. He placed the bag and the files on the desk, then yanked out a sheet of paper from in between the stack of files. The paper crackled in his hands as he reads the list of names. There was a grumble from the ranks when he read off Lt. Drakon Mason.

"Quiet! She's one of us and a damn good detective," the captain exclaimed.

Lt. Drakon walked in at the tail end of the conversation. In just enough time to hear the captains bode of confidence.

"Thanks, sir!" Lt. Drakon exclaimed, and the room went silent, so quiet, you could hear a pin drop. Because no matter what they thought or how they felt about the way she handled the situation. She was still their ranking officer.

"I shudder to think what was said about me before I walked through that door."

"We all think that you're a traitor," a few officers mumbled under their breath.

The Capt. heard their ramblings and said, "Hey, that's enough, your dismissed, go back on duty. Officer Brooks, the squad sergeant, has already taken the liberty to post assignments. I suggest you get to work," he ordered, and the officers cleared the room.

"Ah, I don't have to mention to keep your eyes peeled. Anything you find goes through me first," agent Henning said.

All the police officers piled out of the room with no objections. Of course, except for the ones who were on the task force. Sgt. Mason stayed behind, and when all the other policemen and women left, he stuck out like a sore thumb.

"Sergeant…Question?" agent Henning asked.

"Sergeant Mason is a great police officer. He would be a perfect addition to your team," captain Constantine petitioned.

"I'm sure he is, but I didn't select him for my task force. Besides, sergeant Sgt. Mason is a new transfer, so I am trying to wrap my head around why you want him on my team? I have his file I know who and what kind of—"

"Here's something that'll guide your decision."

"Guide my decision!" agent Henning grumbled. "Captain, I think you're becoming a little too forward. Federal trumps local every time; you're overstepping your bounds here. Your help is not needed, my—"

"Let's not raise your blood pressure, agent Henning. All I'm saying is that Sgt. Mason is a highly decorate undercover detective, with experience in narcotics and major crimes from Philly—"

"Capt., Capt., I know this, all of that is in his service jacket, tell me something new. Stop wasting precious time, please," the agent lamented.

"His jacket doesn't mention his dealings with a criminal organization with a similar M.O. As the ones who stormed my precinct last week," Constantine disclosed. "I recognize you're the show master of this big top, but these bastards invaded my home, and those were my brothers and sisters we buried today." The captain got up in the agent's face asserting dominance.

Sgt. Mason put his hands in between the two men and said, "Come on, Captain, he isn't worth the energy."

"Am I wrong for wanting to recruit an experienced eye on this case? I align with Lt. Drakon's apprehension of the Midtown murder case after I saw those two people in the cemetery strung up like Maestro Geppetto did Pinocchio," agent Henning said, then he rubbed the palm of his hand across his chin. The stubble on his face crackled and snapped against his hand. He took a deep breath then sighed with equal force.

The disapproval of the captain's request weighed heavy on the agent. But out of respect, but his admiration for him has grown since their dealings outside this case. They have history, so he does what he asked. "Alright, now we shall begin," agent Henning said as he flipped a bulletin board behind him. "Here's an outline of suspects and victims, including Joy Maxwell.

Agent Henning flipped his blazer behind and stood there with his arms akimbo. "Look at the board–come on, tell me what you see, Sgt. Mason," he asked.

"First thing I see, out of all the people who tangled with *The Sanguine Killer*. I noticed that besides myself and my partner Lt. Drakon, Joy Maxwell was the only person to survive an encounter with him."

"Ah! Okay, right, I see that," he said and marked a check on the board, then continued. "Besides that, what else is there? Can anyone make another connection?"

"The Sanguine Killer" must be an important leader. His minions attacked Mid-town Precinct North to get him out. They must have some sort of tactical training because according to different accounts, they moved like they were special forces," agent Howard added, who was an FBI agent from the bureau for this mixed team.

"What else? I am looking for a link between them all!" agent Henning exclaimed. Several officers' hands in the room rose. He put his hand up, and they lowered them. "Why? If he's the *Sanguine killer*, which we now know that he was not alone. Before last Friday, he or they killed without any assumed intention. Then suddenly, their focus changed from a specific serial killer type to Joy Maxwell," agent Henning said, slapping the back of his left hand into right. He pointed at a policewoman seated in the back of the conference room.

"Why did they change gears?" she replied.

"Yes, this is what I want, everyone to turn their attentions on her, said agent Henning.

"Why is Joy Maxwell so important, agent Henning?" the vocal policewoman exclaimed. "Shouldn't she have an escort and a twenty-four-hour detail on her if she so important?"

200

"Yes, we should. Are you volunteering your services officer?" agent Henning retorted the officers' line of questioning.

She slid back on her chair and shook her head.

"No, moving on!"

"From what we've seen at the cemetery, the killers, whatever the reason, are not done," Lt. Drakon said. "They're after something—until we find out what it is, we're at a disadvantage."

"You're right, hold on," agent Henning said and motioned to the captain. "I think you need to put a unit on Joy Maxwell, scratch that. I want to bring her in and recap the events that happened."

"I don't think that's a good idea, agent Henning. She's been through enough as it is. Bringing her in could stalemate this entire investigation," the captain replied.

"I understand that Captain, but I need a fresh ear on this and all the help I can get," agent Henning said.

Both men went back and forth with each other until the captain conceded before the exchange got heated. Their conversation only revealed that the captain's stubbornness made it difficult for the agent—who wanted nothing more than to ensure the transition was less invasive as possible. Always being on the intruding end as a FED, he could never comprehend how Captain Constantine felt.

When the call ended, the captain scoffed then stuffed his phone into his inside coat pocket. "Now, officer Hubbert and agent Williamson, I want you two to talk to the witness when she gets here, as a matter of fact—"

"Ahem, pardon my interruption, but she recently moved to a new apartment. I wasn't sure if the captain knew that she's moved," Sgt. Mason revealed.

"Thanks, but I wish that you would've said something while I was arguing with the captain about including her with our investigation," agent Henning replied. He was the consummate professional, intelligent but built like a stone wall. He never buckled under pressure. He kept his cool without busting a sweat.

Meanwhile, at Joy's new luxury apartment, she was submerged chin deep in an oversized claw foot bathtub soaking her troubles away in a warm bubble bath. She had an exfoliating mask on her face and two cucumbers over her eyes–enjoying the perks of the recent promotion courtesy of the news station. She was sitting with her back to the door listening to her calming sounds of neo-soul and alternative rock with her oversized headphones on.

A routine she started since the whole murder spree of her near and dear friends. The soothing tunes, along with a warm bubble bath and scented candles, centered her. She was completely isolated from the world, the hustle and bustle of the never-ending rat race that everybody entered upon reaching adulthood and departed with an untimely demise. We all try to find comfort in a vice of sorts, from religion to liquid spirits, from companionship to solitude. Joy was no different.

While Joy found serenity, the stranger lurked in the shadows. He has invaded her whole life; he discovered intimate details about her that no one else knew. He has studied her every move, lurking in wait. A woman should be so lucky to have a suitor be so attentive. If only he were her knight in shining armor, it would be a dream come true. Too bad this stalker—however attentive; may not be returned in kind. The stranger's intentions were nothing short of pure evil in nature. He aimed to destroy anything in his path. His very existence was like a black hole, shrouded in darkness, not nearly as vast but just as capable of sucking the life out of everything he touched. His twisted and demented mind worked like a time bomb; once it's set off, that's all she wrote.

The stranger perched on the window like a bald eagle on a cliff surveying the city and thought to himself, "The time has come for those who live in the underbelly, greasing the wheels for these mindless cattle; forced to hide in the shadows. Soon we shall reveal the truth to the whole world. Our presence will threaten the status quo, with which they are all too familiar. Their ignorance fuels the eminent change that will be the dawn of a new day." He looked down and noticed two unmistakable police figures entering Joy's apartment. "How could I miss them," he said to himself.

The blood demon surged through the apartment like a blur and burst through the bathroom door. He emerged from the hallway armed with the strength of an army of the undead. In a flash, he swooped over Joy and lifted her out of the tub by her jaw. She wiggled and thrashed about, but it happened so fast she didn't have time to scream. Although in shock, she scratched and clawed at his arm with all her might to escape his death grip, she couldn't. He applied slight pressure to her carotid artery with his thumb, and her body went limp.

Joy's eyes widened. She sniffled and trembled like a leaf. The headphones and cucumbers dropped in the water as tears streamed down her face. The blood demon pulled Joy close and said, "Keep quiet, my child, remain still, or I'll crush your face with my bare hands." He held her up with one hand, and soapy water dripped from her naked body. He took out a phone and made a call with the other. She let out a cry, and he said with his raspy voice, "Quiet, I'm on the phone."

Although he looked young, he sounded like a seventy-year-old chain smoker. He side-eyed her and replied when he heard a voice on the other end of the call. "Rahm, I need your help. I am in a bit of a jam!" Rahm spoke on the other end, and he nodded his head.

"Rahm, we're close to completing our plans. Everything has been set in motion, and so far, it's going as planned. We have gathered enough blood to raise, *The Elder*. The only thing left is to harvest the blood straight from his lineage," he replied and looked at Joy." Vampires all over the world await the rise of the *Blood Demon King*."

He hung up the phone, shoved it into his pants pocket, then turned to Joy.

"Wait, please...please don't bite me. I don't want to live as an immortal blood-sucking vampire," Joy begged.

He looked at her like she was a specimen. Like an experiment in a petri dish as Joy squirmed in his hand.

When the detectives got to the thirty-second floor, the doors open on Joy's floor, and the two federal agents got out of the elevator. A chilling feeling came over them.

"Do you feel that?" agent Williamson said.

"Yes, I just got a cold chill up my spine. It feels like death," she replied.

Officer Hubbert and agent Williamson saw their breath vapors in front of them. Both drew their service weapons; the sound of the dull snapped as the metal whipped against the material of their holsters. Stealthy, they maneuvered towards Joy's door.

"3202 this is Ms. Maxwell's apartment, right?" agent Williamson asked.

Agent Hubbert nods her head slowly. She noticed that the locks had scratches on them, and the door was ajar. "Look at this; someone pried open the door and damaged the lock with a single swipe," she whispered.

"Shh!" agent Williamson replied. He pushed the door open, and it creaked. He gestured for his partner to cover his six, then entered the apartment.

Like a graceful big cat stalking its prey, the stranger moved swiftly to the source of the sound with Joy in tow. Still palming her head like a basketball, her feet dangled about two inches from the floor. Her nude body dripped a trail of water and soap suds behind them.

He got right up on the door and pressed his ear and foot against it as the door moved slightly inward and stopped. He keenly listened for any changes in heart rate.

Officer Hubbert pushed in the door further and yelled, "Ms. Maxwell!" Still being careful not to stand in the way from the door. "Joy Maxwell!" she called a second time, anticipating a response.

The blood demon slowly placed Joy on the ground. He spun his head around and got close to her face like a serpent—a slithering snake, would on an unsuspecting rodent. He was close enough; that she felt the chill of his breath roll off his tongue. In a snap, he grinned and exposed his fangs to her. She was so petrified; the fear suppressed her screams. With a cold, screeching, raspy voice, he said, "Do what you must to make them leave. Your life and there's depend on this, now, Move!" He thrust her forward to open the door. The shifty vampire scampered in the corner behind the door and waited to pounce on the unwanted guests if need be.

Joy looked in the hallway closet and retrieved an oversized dress shirt and covered her naked body with it. She opened the door slightly and said, "H...hello, officers."

Agent Williamson and officer Hubbert dropped their guns momentarily, showed their badges, and asked, "Are you Okay, Ms.

Maxwell?"

"We have a feeling that something is going on here," officer Hubbert said. "It's just a feeling, a strong one," she said slightly, letting her guard down.

"N...no, everything's o...okay. I'm just f...fine, why do you ask?" she replied.

The blood demon patiently waited behind the door and listened to their heartbeats for a slight elevation, a sign of excitement.

The agent looked past Joy into her apartment through the slight opening, motioning his head around to see as much as he could.

"Wait a minute, why are you here?" Joy asked.

"We are here because we were asked to come to retrieve you and take you back with us to the Midtown Police Station North," officer Hubbert replied.

"What? Why? I wonder what they want with me down at the station?"

The lights in the hallway flickered, then they turned off in sequence. First, the farthest away from them until the hallway was pitch black.

"What the hell?" agent Williamson said, looking around a bit, perplexed on what's going on. The temperature dropped, and a deathly chill filled the halls. As quick as a blink of an eye, he was snatched up and disappeared into the darkness.

Joy jumped back in shock by how fast the FBI agent was snatched.

Officer Hubbert was present when the assault on the precinct occurred. So, this was all too familiar to her— she wasn't jarred at all.

Joy yelped, covered her mouth, and tears cascaded down over her cheeks. Her eyes wandered back and forth from the offer to the stranger.

"Show yourself, NYPD! Agent Williamson, where are you? Are you okay?" officer Hubbert repeatedly yelled with her gun drawn, pointing it indiscriminately into the darkness of the hallway. Beads of sweat collected over her eyebrows. Her palms were clammy, and she held on to the gun for dear life as she stepped into the darkness.

A gush of wind blew, whipping Joy's hair across her face. In a flash, the female officer was gone right before her eyes. Now both law enforcement officers were gone.

"What the fuck just happened to them?" Joy snarled at her capture and bravely said. "What in the hell are you people? What in the world do you want with me?".

The blood demon eased away from the wall and stepped towards her. He could hear her heart speed up and slow down with fear and anger. "You needn't worry about them, my child," he replied. "What you should be afraid of is what's going to happen to you," He pulled her into him and whisked her out of her apartment. They moved so fast, faster than the blink of an eye.

At the precinct, captain Constantine paced in his office, checked his watch, and thought, "If officer Hubbert and agent Williamson don't bring back Joy soon, my metamorphosis will be delayed." He stared at the phone on his desk, anticipating the call that may change his life—literally forever. He looked up and saw an officer pass his office. "Officer Davis! Come in here, please," he said and waved him to come into his office.

"Yes, Captain," officer Davis replied after he popped his head inside the office.

"Do you know where Lt. Drakon is?"

"No, sir!"

"Carry on," captain Constantine dismissed him, walked from around his desk, then stood in the doorway and screamed. "If anyone knows where the lieutenant is, or if you see her, send her to me!" He turned around and put his hands on his waist. "She's still under my command. Who does she think she is, a FED or something?" he grumbled to himself.

Meanwhile, at an upscale Caribbean restaurant across town, agent Henning and Lt. Drakon sat at a dim-lit table eating their food. "You know when we first met, I didn't think in a million years that we would be here," said agent Henning.

"Where is here?" Lt. Drakon replied nonchalantly, right before shoveled a mouth full of her favorite Jamaican dish (Oxtail with butterbeans, rice, and red kidney peas.)

Agent Henning put his hand over his mouth and coughed after she posed the rhetorical question. His eyes welled up with water. He took up his napkin, wiped his mouth, and raised his eyebrows. "Ahem! Hmm, that's spicy." He grabbed his glass of Guinness punch and took a big gulp to quash the burning sensation in his mouth; after he bit into a scotch bonnet pepper that was in his brown stew chicken dish.

"Excuse me! Ahem, that was spicy!" agent Henning cleared his throat, picked up a glass of water from the table, and took a sip.

"I just want to know if this is turning into something?" Lt. Drakon asked.

"In other words, are there feelings involved?" agent Henning responded as he put his cup down and gazed into lieutenant Drakon's eyes—past her tough exterior, deep in her soul.

"You know my past, Richard, "she replied softly. "You should have an idea of how hard this is for me. I don't want you in my head, but here you are."

"I understand," he said. Agent Henning moved his food back and forth on his plate with his fork. "I'll have to admit, you've gotten under my skin, Adeline. The way we've been able to get along like we've known each other for a long time. I can't even come close to how what went wrong with your previous relationship. How did he let you go?"

"Before I divulge anything else about me, let me know more about you. Why are you single?" she asked.

"Okay, fair enough. I've had a failed marriage and a string of failed relationships. So, embarking on a new relationship with you might not be feasible right now, especially with this killer on the loose. All I have time for is my career," he explained.

"So, you're going to ignore what we both have been feeling," Lt. Drakon replied.

"Let's not look at it like that. Let's just take our time and allow whatever this is to evolve. The last thing we want is to rush into something that we aren't ready for."

His words cut through Lt. Drakon like a sharp knife through butter. Her shoulders slumped; she sat back in her chair and put the napkin in her plate. "I can't believe that I put myself out there—only to be brushed off like a lovesick schoolgirl. That's what you get for assuming that he would be different. Nice job, Adeline!" she said to herself.

Lt. Drakon didn't get the opportunity to get too deep into her shame of feeling rejected before she received a text from her grandfather. A perfect distraction from this horrible date she desperately needed to escape the steady rigmarole of being a detective. She read the text, excused herself, and walked out of the restaurant.

"Wait...what just happened?" agent Henning asked himself after she walked out. He called her back, and her phone began to vibrate on the table. He sighed, picked it up, and said, "Dammit, she forgot her phone." He smirked when he noticed that she put it on silent to minimize interruptions for her the date. "Nice job at putting your foot in your mouth Richard. I'm such an idiot!"

Agent Henning's phone rang twice, and he quickly put it at his ear and said, "Hello, this is agent Henning."

"Agent Henning, this is Dr. German. You and Lt. Drakon need to get down here!" he ordered and hung up.

Being so wrapped up in what transpired between him and Lt. Drakon that it didn't dawn on agent Henning of the male's voice on the other end. He put the phone in his coat pocket, paid the check, then got into his car. He started his car and said, "That was Dr. German. I thought I made it crystal clear that he took orders from me. He seemed a bit perturbed on the phone. Maybe it's because he thinks that I'm getting too close to his granddaughter."

Agent Henning pulled into traffic, then he. put Lt. Drakon's phone inside the cupholder in the center console. "I hope Dr. German knows that Adeline and I are partners and nothing else," he said to himself. He contemplated driving to the lab. Maybe he could clear some things up with the M.E, especially since she just made a big deal about being together, and her grandfather disapproves of that possibility.

"It's a good thing I didn't give in to temptation because how serious could she think this is? I mean, if it were important, she would've mentioned me to her grandfather. Why else would he sound so pissed over the phone? I'm heading for the lab; I assume that's where she's heading."

He stopped at a red light, and he heard captain Constantine's ringtone on his phone. He pressed the talk button, put it on speaker, and drove through the intersection after the light turned green. "Agent Henning here," he answered.

"You two need to get down here, now!" captain Constantine bellowed into the receiver.

"Watch your tone Captain, need I remind you of the chain of command."

"Please, spare me the semantics, agent Henning."

"What is so pressing; what happened?"

"You sent my guys out for Ms. Maxwell, and they're not back yet."

Agent Henning jerked his head back, knitted up his brows, and said, "How is that my fault? Maybe they stopped for a bite to eat, or they're stuck in traffic. There could be many reasons why."

"Okay, your right, except none of that happened. I know this because I'm at Ms. Maxwell's apartment, all her belongings are here, there's evidence of a struggle, but the walls are saturated with blood. I didn't just fall off the turnip truck, so I need for you and my lieutenant to come down here and take the lead," the captain replied, took the phone from his ear, and pointed at it. "You're supposed to be in charge, so act like it!"

The captain hung up the phone and put his phone in his trench coat pocket. "What the hell happened here.

Agent Henning put on his siren and made a sharp left turn heading in the direction of Joy's apartment. "I can't put my finger on it, but the captain is acting strange since the FBI took over this case. I hope he's not entangled in this mess somehow," he thought to himself.

He sped up to the crime scene and redialed the captain's number. For now, his curiosity of Lt. Drakon and her grandfather's secrecy must wait. "Captain, I am on my way. Secure the crime scene. I want forensic to analyze everything and call the station. Maybe they can give insight as to what happened to Ms. Maxwell."

"I told you that I am not new to this agent Henning. I'm not some rookie who doesn't know his head from his asshole. Remember, it was my precinct that they hit."

"Don't get flippant with me; just do it!"

Meanwhile, at the forensics lab, Lt. Drakon walked down a brightly lit corridor. The soft natural fluorescent lights illuminated the hall, almost complimenting her pale skin. No one paid any real attention to her; the lack of feeding made her face look grey and colorless. The still of her heart ceased to pump life-sustaining blood that added pigment to her skin. "What do you have for me, doc?" Lt. Drakon asked.

"Well, I have bad news and worst news," Dr. German replied.

"How thrilling! You're like Santa Claus; you always come baring gifts every time I'm in your presence."

"You're just a barrel of fun, Adeline," he replied, smiled and the motion accentuated the crow's feet on the side of his eyes and the wrinkles on his forehead. "I wish Santa Claus would have paid for your college tuition."

"You took me in. I didn't ask you to take care of me."

"You were my kin; how could I just—Ahem, you know what,

let's get back to work," Dr. German said and touched the corners of his eyes underneath his glasses.

"Let's do that!" Lt. Drakon replied and sniffled.

"CSI Madrigal came in and said, "Dr. German, here's-the-results-of-the—sorry, is this the best time; I can come back if you want me to."

"No, it's all right. You're not interrupting anything. What do you have for me, Tommy?"

"Here, Boss, these are the results from the hemoglobin test." CSI Thomas Madrigal was the highest-ranking CSI on the forensics team, second to the CME. He specialized in bio-fluids and DNA testing. He's Dr. German's best friend. And his professional opinion is respected amongst his peers. Plus, he's known Lt. Drakon since her grandfather took her into his home.

"Que pasa mija," CSI Madrigal said.

"Nada tio Thomas," she replied.

"Estas bien, Chica? You're not looking so good."

"I'm fine, Tio, I promise. I just need some rest."

"Okay, what do you have for me?" asked Dr. German.

"Yes, okay, I almost forgot, the mother and son are just like the others. They all have the same condition," CSI Madrigal explained. "I found traces of PCT in every single case, including those women who were killed in midtown."

"The murderer has porphyria. I was afraid of that," Dr. German expressed.

"Wait, what do you mean? Does this mean that we are close to a suspect? Are we able to narrow it down to a suspect, and this could all be over soon? I mean, how many people could have this condition? What is it called again, por*phyria*?" Lt. Drakon rambled.

Dr. German walked over to the bodies of the mother and son found at the cemetery. "I think I must show you something. This is not people with porphyria. This is about vampires," he said.

"Hold on, grandpa, Tio Tommy's right here! Wait, does he know about us?" Lt. Drakon asked.

Dr. German reluctantly nodded his head.

"Oh, really, grandfather, who else knows?" She threw her hands down to her sides in disbelief.

"Adeline, bear with me; Tommy had known about me long before I adopted you—that's a story for another day, heh."

He non-nonchalantly pointed at the neck of the female laying on the slab. He pushed his finger inside the two puncture wounds. "Do you see this mark here," Dr. German said, shining a penlight on the corpse.

"Yes, I see but, what am I supposed to see? What do you want me to see here?"

"What I want you to see is that these puncture wounds weren't caused by tool marks."

"Don't say it; these are teeth marks, am I right?"

"The blood test revealed two things to me that someone without the knowledge of the existence of vampires would not know," Dr. German said.

"What's that?" Lt. Drakon replied.

"Let me explain, unlike, in the fairytales and stories about vampires, the teeth are not used just as tools by which to puncture its victims' throat for sustenance. Realistically speaking, they are also used to inject a serum—a venomous latrotoxin, which is a paralytic mixture, used to subdue the victim (prey.) It's a compound of a hemotoxin that thins the blood and prevents it from clotting. "This venomous cocktail is secreted inside the subjects before feeding."

"I am confused. Why haven't you told me this before, grandfather? Do all vampires possess this poison?"

"Yes, but it's not what you think we vampires—"

"We Vampires! You say it like you're a different species of man. So, I'm supposed to hunt prey like I'm some sort of arachnid, huh?" Lt. Drakon caused such a commotion that the ruckus caught the attention of the entire Medical Examiner's office.

"Please calm down!" Dr. German exclaimed and grabbed his granddaughter to silence her anxiety. Seeing how much the curse that he has bestowed on her burdened her so. But he couldn't just let her die. It was hard for him to let her go, nor did he want to. He swore a long time ago that he wouldn't ever hurt his love ones again. Especially not with the blood demon's curse. Knowing how long it took for him to come to grips with the bite himself.

"I am sorry, my Dear. I never meant to bring you any sorrow. I saw you in so much pain. You're the only one left, I thought to myself," he explained.

Lt. Drakon saw the sincerity and the remorse written all over his face. She snapped her arm from his clutches and said, "You did this based on pure selfishness. You never once stopped to think about how I would feel about this sickness. You have condemned me to hell," she replied and pointed her finger in the doctor's face. "So, this means if I finally succumb to the thirst, I will kill whoever I bite? Do you know what that means for me? No, you don't, do you?" She turned her back on her grandfather and folded her arms across her chest.

Her eyes welled up with tears. She calmly said, "It may be easy for you to deal in death all day. I chose not to. That's why I became a police officer–to preserve life, but not like this." Lt. Drakon sniffled and wiped away the snot from her upper lip. "I understand now why you never let me get too close to you. I found out you were my grandfather a long time ago–long before you ever told me that you were my great-great-great-grandfather. I could never figure out why."

Lt. Drakon was in shock by the revelation down to her moral fibers. "Will I always do the right thing?" she asked herself and shook her head. She scowled and gritted her teeth. She turned back around and faced both men that raised her. "I am a cop; I have sworn to uphold the law. Right now, I need to know, will I have to kill to survive?"

"That's a complicated question to answer. If you feed on someone–the venom is always present in our saliva—"

"Wait, so why doesn't it kill us?"

"All vampires who have gone through the change have done so, on a molecular level. My understanding of the whole event still boggles my mind. One thing that is for certain, vampires are not biologically human anymore," CSI Madrigal said. "The physical appearances are not that different, except for the fangs, of course, but here's the thing, immortality happens gradually."

"What do you mean immortality happens gradually?" Lt. Drakon asked.

"Here look, come let me show you, it's ab-so-lute-ly fascinating. It's like looking at an accelerated evolutionary scale," he exclaimed. CSI Madrigal walked over to a huge white dry erase board.

While there, he began to demonstrate with a scale what he had figured out. "Charles Darwin would be turning over in his grave right now if he could just see this," CSI Madrigal muttered. He drew on the board a graduating graph. On the chart, he disclosed how long it would take before someone lost their humanity and wholly evolved into a full-fledged vampire. "The vampire infection attacks the immune system and the body's natural antibodies," he explained.

"But how does all of this help us catch these demonic blood-sucking vampires?" Lt. Drakon exclaimed.

"I'm glad you asked. Over the years, we have collected samples from many victims, and with these samples, I believe that I may pinpoint where exactly the vampire's den is located."

"How many vampires are here in the city?"

"Well, we don't now really know at this moment," Dr. German replied. "But in this city alone, with a population of approximately eight point six million, I can estimate a least twenty-six thousand in the five boroughs."

CSI Madrigal rummaged through a file cabinet in the corner of the lab. Then he searched through the rest of the cabinets along the wall. "Eureka!" he exclaimed. "Here it is." He pulled out a massive binder from out of an old army footlocker. "I thought that I lost this book during the big renovation. What I'm about to share with you I have never revealed to anyone before today." CSI Madrigal slapped through the pages like a little boy perusing a new comic book. The binder's pages were crumpled, and some other unidentifiable objects were spilling out from the edges.

"Over the years, I've accumulated enough data to pinpoint where these perpetrators are located," he said.

"That would be a much-needed break, in this case; this city

needs it," Lt. Drakon replied.

"You see, everyone has their habits, certain ritual that separates us from everyone else," Dr. German explained.

"We've kept an unofficial record of every single vampire encounter we know of," CSI Madrigal said.

"Every single one Tio?" asked Lt. Drakon.

"Yes, from victims in different parts of the city–which I might add, was highly difficult to wrangle information from other districts."

"Some medical examiners feel encroachment from us," Dr. German said.

"So, you have enough data in here we could use to find our suspect?" Lt. Drakon stepped closer to the table and replied. "Because I need something, anything here, they are winning right now."

CSI Madrigal took the file from the new incidents and began his analysis. "I don't know, let's see, using what I have, and cross-referencing it with the new cases here, I could help you get as close as possible to the vicinity of the suspect. Unfortunately, I wouldn't be able to get a positive ID, sorry, *Mija*." He rubbed his chin covered with stubble. "Ah, here we go, *Mija*, all of the clues point to right here in mid-town."

"What? That's great!" Lt. Drakon said.

"Adeline, you don't want to entangle yourself with the likes of these vampires," Dr. German implored.

"What? Why?" She replied.

"They're an elite group, comprised of some the most powerful people, excuse me, *Vampires*, in the city, possibly in the entire country," CSI Madrigal said.

"Promise me, Adeline, that you won't get too close to these vampires," Dr. German said.

"What are you talking about, Grandfather? I am a police officer, an elite one, I might add. This is my job, and I'm more than capable handle myself with those–those creatures. So, just tell me who you're talking about," she replied.

"You see, it's not just one person that I would be worried about. It's a group of people: Judges, stock market whales, and powerful real estate developers," Dr. German said in his Austrian accent.

"The saying is, stock market sharks," Lt. Drakon corrects him. "Where have you been, Grandfather?"

Everyone's attention was broken when agent Henning burst through the doors. His voice reverberated through the office. "I've been looking all over the city for you! Here, you left me and your phone at the restaurant," he said.

"Why are you shouting? You knew my whereabouts were," Lt. Drakon replied calmly.

"Now, tell me, what's wrong?" Agent Henning moved out the way while two men in white coats rolled in two dead bodies. "These are bodies of the police officer and federal agent who were killed last night that was sent to retrieve Ms. Maxwell and Joy's missing. She was undoubtedly taken by the same ones who attacked Mid-Town Police Station North."

"What are these guys after?" Dr. German asked.

"I don't know, but one thing for damn sure, they are wiping us out," agent Henning replied and shook his head. "This task force is not enough. We must pull out the big guns. Whoever this mysterious scourge is, they're unscrupulous and have no respect for the law."

"You're right," Lt. Drakon retorts. "We are the enforcers of the law in this city, not only to protects its citizens but one of the major pillars of justice. The peacekeepers of civility and the overseers of order. If the barrier ever breaks, we've lost one of the main cornerstones of our great society."

"I believe it's time to flip over every stone. I see that all that I have been done so far has not worked. I know now that we are looking for suspects. The evidence we have so far has turned up nothing. I think I found a new approach, insider knowledge, that edge that we need. With insight from my grandfather and CSI Madrigal expert analysis. We can finally get closer to these mysterious villains."

"Bull shit! How is that possible; where were they when cops were being hunted down like gazelles on the Serengeti?" agent Henning asked.

Lt. Drakon just ignored his rude outburst. "These guys are meticulous, cunning, and have been adroit thus far," Lt. Drakon rants. "So, at this point, I am conscious that our failures have resulted in nothing more than death and carnage."

"We have no other choice but to go by the book."

"Look, that's what you have to do because you're a "Federal agent."

"But we can't stand idly by and do nothing while more cops die. So, from now on, I am on a mission in the name of justice."

"Don't you mean vengeful mission?" agent Henning said, with his cynical sense of humor.

"Yeah, maybe I am vengeful. But I would bet my shield that you want revenge too." The lieutenant paused, giving agent Henning the evil eye. "I suggest that we let loose on this city, go out to every criminal organization and apply pressure to all informants 'til we get the information we need. By any means necessary, we must shake down everyone. Somebody knows something, and when we find them, make 'em spill the beans," Lt. Drakon replied.

While they talked, it took everything inside her not to reveal what she knows and who is really behind all the attacks in the city. At least not yet anyway, after learning that the people responsible for the recent horrific events are major contributors to the city's success. "I know that we do need to expose their corruption, but what can we do about this. These people are the most powerful and influential factions out here. We need cold hard facts. We better have proof, solid evidence of that fact," Lt. Drakon thought to herself and took a deep breath.

She directed agent Henning to look at some of the insurmountable proof that her grandfather and CSI Madrigal had collected over the years. Although she doesn't feel she could trust him with the complete truth. She knew she had to tell him something.

Lt. Drakon thought to herself, "I'll tell him about the existence of vampires when and if we cross that bridge. Right now, trawl out all the whales involved and rip them out of this intricate network of corruption, crime, and blood demonic vampire web that they've spun throughout the city–may be the tri-state area."

To get a leg up on the investigation, Lt. Drakon needs agent Henning on the same program. She didn't let agent Henning in on everything. She omitted the facts about the existence of vampires because it won't be detrimental in the grand scheme of this investigation.

Agent Henning approached the desk and scanned through what they had. Of course, he didn't believe all the corruption from all these influential people in the city. After scrutinizing what they had in disbelief, he came to terms with the overwhelming evidence against the big wigs of the city.

"Why haven't you said anything before now?" agent Henning asked.

Dr. German said, "We haven't said anything so far for two reasons: one, we wouldn't know where to begin—"

"What do you mean?"

"Let me finish, Agent Henning. As you can see, all the people we have collected evidence on over these many years are the ones who control the city. Two, it seems like there is a leader who we have not been able to identify yet. Someone on top of the pyramid, if you will," Dr. German said and scratched his chin.

Agent Henning stared deeply into a scrap of CSI Madrigal's file, lost in thought, puzzled by the mystery.

With his heavy Austrian accent, he said, "These people aren't just local; only a federal agent would have the jurisdiction to bring them all down."

Agent Henning raised his head from the binder, rubbed his hands together, and grinned at the notion that they had to use other ways to bring down this elusive crime syndicate.

Chapter 9

"Hey, Captain! Come and look at this!" An officer shouted into captain Constantine's office.

The stressed-out older man bounced from his desk to see about the breaking news. "Son of a bitch, another one of my officer's been murdered," the captain thought to him himself. He slowly exited his office into the bay still filled with grief; he reluctantly looked at the news. Good at hiding his emotions, he stationed himself behind the crowd gathered in front of the television screen. A replacement for Joy Maxwell covered the story. The reporter recounted her kidnapping, the brutal murders of a female police officer and a federal agent.

The captain's heart sank, troubled about the recent developments from his contrived position. He sighed and shook his head in disbelief, but inside he felt guilty for his role in sacrificing so many people to achieve his goal of becoming immortal. He didn't realize that many of his men were going to be the ones to lose their lives.

"Earlier this evening, right behind me here inside this building, a horrific double murder occurred of a police officer and a federal agent. I regretfully report that Joy Maxwell, one our stations own, is missing. I know that I speak for the news station when I say that our hearts and prayers go out to the families of the victims of yet another senseless killing of our beloved *Boys in blue*," she commented. "The carnage that happened here is eerily indistinguishable, to the attack on Midtown Police Precinct North, a short time ago, that claimed the lives of several law enforcement officers and civilians.

"Local authorities have yet to release the names of our very own *Now York's Finest* who lost their lives protecting and serving the community that we all love. They have declined to comment about the latest victims of the alleged, *Sanguine Killer*. This person, or persons, are still at large and extremely dangerous. The crime scene investigators are working tirelessly inside the apartment building (Owned by our station's CEO,) combing through the evidence. We will keep you updated as soon as the pieces come together. This is Stacy Armstrong signing off— back to you at the studio."

The reporter's report cut through the captain like a sharp sword. He stood there motionless with his mouth open like a striped bass on the end of a fishing hook.

"Captain! We're getting wiped out! We might as well be living in Afghanistan," an officer expressed. "It's time for us to take action. We gave the FEDs their opportunity to head this murder investigation. The mayor, the governor, and the district attorney of New York seem to think that we are not worth the uniforms we adorn daily. I don't know about you, Captain, but we have always handled situations like this on our own."

Called to the emotions of guilt sided by loyal duty, the captain considered his sense of morality. He stretched inside his pocket and pulled out his cell to call a contact–a connection within the circle of the vampire network. He held the receiver to his ear, then pulled cell away from his mouth to command his uniformed officers and detectives to get back to work.

The captain withdrew himself away from the crowd, receding to his berth, behind the desk. The phone rang several times before an automated voice prompted him to leave a message after the beep. Frustrated, he hung up and spun around in his chair. With his head buried in his hands, he pondered his decisions thus far. He decided to call again. Someone answered the call on the second ring. A screechy monotone voice on the other end said, "The day is young."

"The sun illuminates the darkness and one day the mourning will soon be ours," captain Constantine replied.

"So, said the man of the city," they recall in unison.

"I need to ask a question—"

"That's not possible," the voice replied over the phone.

"Listen, it's getting hard to stand idly by and watch all of the people that I have known for years die," captain Constantine said. "I realize there must be sacrifices, but it seems like many of these people are close to me. So, I need to ask why? Give me an answer, or else!"

"I must warn you that you're not in the position to make demands. You knew the risks."

Captain Constantine looked at the phone and knitted up his brows.

"If you'd like, I will pass along your feelings on the matter." A soft click in his ear ended the conversation.

Lt Drakon and special agent Henning entered the bay coming face to face with whispers and cross attitudes. The two most unlikely candidates paired up together to solve the case of the century. A weak, broken, and bitchy female detective–who can hardly see past her troubles commissioned to solve someone else's. She is paired with an old FBI field agent just coasting along, waiting for retirement.

Captain Constantine thought to himself stood outside his office looking at his officer's buzz about like worker bees. "These murders were never meant to be solved," he thought to himself. He's on the verge of spilling his guts to them, but he couldn't. The knowledge of what they're facing was a deterrent. Although doubtful of their sleuthing, he felt he would be protecting them if he'd stashed away that little tidbit.

Groggy and confused, Joy woke up from her slumber. Her eyes not yet focused, she rubbed them instinctively to adjust them to the bright sunshine. The sun rays beamed through the massive floor-to-ceiling windows–the kind you'd see in an office building. She scanned the whole room before she got out of bed; trying to make heads or tails of what happened to her, Joy slowly crawled out of the extra-large bed. She almost felt like a young child, how big it was.

"Where am I?" Joy asked herself. She touched herself, running her hands all over her body slowly, checking to make sure she still had all her limbs. She didn't feel any pain, but she did it anyway to reassure herself that she was fine, and those despicable creatures hadn't done anything unmentionable to her.

Joy searched her neck carefully for puncture wounds while looking at her reflection in the big vanity mirror. Satisfied with her findings, she turned around and explored the rest of her prison. She crept toward the door to the bedroom and opened it, slowly peeking outside the room, and stepped into an impressive penthouse. Her eyes grew big at the luxury of it all. The antique furniture, the sconces, the fixtures, and the figurines were far from anything she had seen before.

"Did you sleep well," the pale stranger asked as he stepped out of the shadows into the sunlight. His colorless deathlike skin instantly darkened from the sun.

His sheer presence and voice, raspy and cold, sent chills down Joy's spine. She quivered with absolute fear as she responded to his question. "Yes, I did! Who are you, stranger? What do you want from me?" she asked a barrage of queries. Carefully keeping a comfortable distance away from the creature. "More importantly, what are you?" Joy's curiosity swelled bigger than her stirring dread. She hoped that the mystery would finally reveal itself.

"There will be time for that, but for now, you must eat to keep up your strength," the blood demon replied. "I have prepared food for you in the kitchen on the wet bar."

Joy made short footed steps towards the kitchen.

He hastened her movements with the sound of his voice.

"How do I know that you haven't poisoned my food?" Joy asked, mindful not to have her eyes meet with his.

The stranger edged closer to Joy, invading her space. He gently ran his cold ghastly hand through her hair. He inhaled deeply, taking in her essence. He peered into her eyes like a snake rearing up for a strike. He exposed his fangs, and saliva dripped from top to bottom in his open mouth. He got close as possible without touching her. "I've been watching you for a long time, Ms. Maxwell," he whispered in her ear.

His raspy voice lingered; the passing of breath was nonexistent. Goosebumps swelled over her body as his cold nose brushed against her earlobe.

As he invaded her personal space, his intrusion sent chills up and down her spine. "There are certain things in life that are definite. Do you know what that is?" he asked.

"No," Joy replied, and her voice cracked.

"Love and death are as sure as the air you inhale into your lungs. The funny thing about the two is that you'll never know how and when death will hit you. Anytime you force nature's hand, perversions happen. You need not worry, my Childe. Eat without fretting, Ms. Maxwell, before your food gets cold. I know your hungry I can hear your stomach growling." He moved like a ghost out of the kitchen and across the penthouse in a matter of seconds. Before exiting, he punched a passcode on a large keypad on the wall and slammed the door behind him.

"Great, I still don't have any answers. Why am I here? What does this man want with me? Damn girl!" she said and smacked her palm on the wet bar. "You should've listened to your mother, Joy

227

Maxwell, and stayed in Georgia. What the hell did you get yourself into?"

Sgt. Mason entered a building on the upper Westside on a hunch. He and his assigned partner, special agent Harry Woo.

"What makes you think that the woman's tip will pan out," agent Woos asked. He slammed the door to the squad car and adjusted his blazer over his tie. He buttoned the top button.

"You can never be too sure—don't you know this agent Woo? I thought you federal agents had the inside track on everything," the sergeant said. "Don't you know that the streets always know more than law enforcement? I learned this firsthand by doing narcotics. That's the reason why "The boys," or however civilians label us." We must work extra hard and canvas the area. Wherever the evidence and clues lead us."

The two entered the bar, full of ex-cons and gangsters. Special agent Woo took stock of all the faces in the joint. His newly learned FBI training kicked in immediately. He spotted the patrons with bulges, which usually meant that they had firearms, at the very least, simple possessions charges. At the most, maybe the weapons may have a body or two attached. This was of no consequence to special agent Woo because he was here to apprehend the *Sanguine killer*(s)

"Where's your contact?" agent Woo asked.

"I don't know, and I don't see him yet. Just relax and take a seat, for now. It might be minute," Sgt. Mason replied.

Agent Woo sat on a stool at the bar at a spot where he could see everything around him. This was agent Woo's first time out in the field, but every move he made comprised of basic instincts and his FBI training.

Sgt. Mason noticed his partner's naivety. "Stay right here.

Okay, I see my connect," Sgt. Mason said.

"Not Okay, we are working together, remember."

"Yes, you are right, but this is my Confidential Informant. He's not going to talk to me freely if I go to him with a stiff." Sgt. Mason pushed the agent back into his seat. "I already know every single one involved—alright, I will grant you a little leeway, only because you're lost."

"I just need you to know something," agent Woo said as he picked up his glass of soda to his mouth and took a sip.

"What's that?" Sgt. Mason said.

"I may be a little wet behind the ears, but I'm not stupid." Special agent Woo put the glass down and stared at Sgt. Mason. He couldn't quite put his finger on it, but he sensed something strange.

Sgt. Mason stepped away from agent Woo and moved toward his contact. All he could think about was what he said. "The last thing I need is anyone here finding out what I did," he thought to himself. Disguising his trepidations, he continued with his encounter with his CI, calm as a cucumber. At least, so he thought, straight through all his screens wouldn't help against this contact.

Playing it cool, Sgt. Mason slid right into the booth in the back of the bar. He sat across from a blood demon lieutenant. He set his mouth to speak, but Mr. Night beat him to the punch.

"What are you doing here cop, you're out of your jurisdiction," the blood demon said.

"I got a transfer across the water to the NYPD," Sgt. Mason replied and flashed his badge.

The blood demon laughed deep from his diaphragm at the sergeant. Camouflaged conveniently by the shadows, the figure leaned forward over the table underneath the hanging light.

Agent Woo recognized who he was immediately and took the booth behind Sgt. Mason. Hoping his suspicions might be wrong, but he couldn't go against his gut feeling that the sergeant may be on the take. Now he's with a shifty character—Alphonse, "Mr. Night" Belan.

"Word on the streets is that you have something that I want," Sgt. Mason asked.

"Yeah, what's that?" Mr. Night retorts.

"I know from a very reliable source that you have information for me."

"You know, Detective, the funny thing about when the street talks, you never really know if you're getting the truth or heir say. So, watch what you say to me."

"Is that a threat, Mr. Night?"

The blood demon's minions converged on the table, and Mr. Night put up his hand, and they stopped awaited further instructions.

Agent Woo flipped his sport coat to the side and revealed his service revolver.

Sgt. Mason put his hand on the overzealous agent and said, "Wait, I didn't come here to get into a fight. Can you help me, or not?"

"Who's that?" Mr. Night asked and displayed his fangs.

"Who him, don't worry about him. He's green."

"Interesting, your superiors put you on the street with unripe fruit. They must really like you."

"What do you have for me?" asked Sgt. Mason.

"You know, Detective, information is a commodity. What I have has value, and it's worth a lot," Mr. Night replied and leaned back in the shadow.

Mr. Night had the upper hand on Sgt Mason. So, anything that he wanted now would be impossible to get without giving up more than he anticipated. So, obliging words flew out of his beak before he could help it. Without collateral, back it up with, he sold the blood demon a "Wolf ticket."

The blood demon quickly sensed that he was being played; he peeped game when the detective brought in the tag-along-wannabe into the bar. He was from the streets compounded with his gifts of heightened senses permitted him to sniff out the charade. He snickered and let things go on anyway.

"Okay, Detective, I will tell you what I know," he said and smiled from ear to ear like a Cheshire cat. "But before I give you what you want, I have a favor of my own."

As the New York detective listened to his list of favors in delight, Sgt. Mason realized that if he took part in this criminal's plans, it would only aid in the furtherance of his goal of becoming a vampire. It would secure a place in the vampire's design of world domination.

Sgt. Mason listened while Mr. Night gushed about briberies, back door deals, and a heads up when he needs to maneuver contraband. Favors would help secure his criminal empire, which encompasses drugs, illegal gambling, human trafficking, and smuggling weapons.

"Everything I have done so far has been for this moment," Sgt. Mason said to himself. "This is my second chance to become a vampire. The first time I attacked, raped, and nearly killed Lt. Drakon didn't go as planned. That mission didn't turn out so well because she survived the assault. So, this is my opportunity to fix my failures," he whispered.

"What did you say?" Mr. Night inquired. "I thought I heard you say something."

"No, nothing, go ahead," Sgt. Mason replied.

"Hear me out, Cop, you fucked up the last task. If you hadn't, you would be one of us now. So, I swear to whatever holy being you believe in, you better be listening. Sgt. Mason, if you fail this time—let's just say, God wouldn't know where to put you because he won't recognize you."

The threat shook detective Mason straight out of his daydream and back into reality. "I still don't know how that iron bird's still alive, let alone back on the force or as my partner. After I learned that she didn't die, I put in for a transfer here. I came here to rectify the issue."

He'd forgotten that federal agent Woo was in earshot of the conversation. Even though it was the middle of the day, very little daylight entered the bar. It was a hangout for the undead, after all. So, the darkness laid over the patrons like grandma's quilt on a cold night. The Shadows had life all on its own. So, it was easy to forget and hard to pay attention to whom was around. When he blurted out his involvement in Lt. Drakon's attack, the possibility that Agent Woo would overhear him; didn't enter his mind at all.

Agent Woo couldn't concentrate on the conversation. He was distracted, drawn from the task. His stratagem switched from eves dropping to fearing for his mortality. The scene was unbelievable; to fresh eyes, it would be enough to rile goosebumps on a turtle's shell. It appeared that he and Sgt. Mason has struck and burst a centuries-old bubble by coming into this bar during happy hour. On the surface, everyone seemed to be satisfied.

Agent Woo couldn't believe his eyes; he witnessed the feeding frenzy of a vampire den filled with blood demons. The dim-lit bar didn't help him focus on anyone's face. What he could make out was figures biting the necks of willing participants. Blood oozed from the victims' necks and from around the vampires' mouths.

The scene froze every single muscle in agent Woo's body. All his senses told him to move, but he was overwhelmed by the appalling visions of sheer carnage filled with unimaginable death. His eyes widened, and he gasped for air as he witnessed people having their life force sucked right out of them.

"I can't just sit here. I can't just stand idly by—Woo, get up off your ass unless you want to wait for your turn to die," he said to himself.

He hoisted himself from the booth, swiped a drink from a nearby table, and guzzled down a bit of bravery juice. With a dose of courage, he hopped into action. Agent Woo whipped out his FBI badge, clipped on his blazer. He drew and brandished his weapon. "Everyone, stop what you're doing and put your hands up!" he shouted at the top of his lungs. "I'm special agent Poppy Woo with FBI."

Sweat dripped from Agent Woo's forehead. His heart raced in his chest like he just ran a five-mile race. Short of breath, he panted, waved his gun around, and pointed it at every violator. He hoped to drive home his authority. He hoped they would see that he meant business. "Oh my God… this can't be real," he said and wiped the sweat from his forehead with his tie. "Is this the reason why the *Sanguine killer* is so hard to capture? He has a full team of sickos at his beck and call."

Almost simultaneously without remorse, showing not one iota of emotion. The blood demons released their tight death grips on their meals–loud thuds resonated throughout the "Bone Dry Bar." All their focus shifted primarily on him.

All the hair on his body stood on end. He widened his stance, clenched his jaw, waiting for the first freak to make a move. The chances of making it out of the club alive seemed bleak.

"Wait, hold on... don't shoot, lower your weapon, agent

233

Woo!" exclaimed Sgt. Mason. "Calm down, let everyone relax. He got to his feet and stood back-to-back with his FBI partner.

"I don't need your help—as a matter of fact; I will be reporting you to internal affairs. I overheard you making deals with Alphonse Belan," agent Woo said.

"What are you talking about? You're not talking about Mr. Night, are you, friend? He is my CI," Sgt. Mason explained.

Although in a tense situation in every way possible, they still managed to keep their weapons pointed at their would-be attackers.

"I know about that guy. He's in the FBI Database as the head of a human trafficking ring and a myriad of other criminal activities. Do not confuse my inexperience of fieldwork with the lack of knowledge of the streets. I'm privy to the who's who of organized crime syndicates. I've been with the bureau several years as a junior information analyst and a criminal profiler."

"Yes, but—"

"He's on the FBI's radar."

The two barely controlling the situation. Maintain the delicate tempo of this infernal dance of life and death.

"You think you know, but you don't, friend," Sgt. Mason said. "The streets isn't as simple as a profile indicates. Think about it, is it legally possible for that to be on the streets or my CI, for that matter, if he didn't already have a deal in place. Think about it, friend."

"So, you're trying to make a side deal with me, huh! You're not going to weasel your way out of this, Sgt. Mason. I am not going to change my mind."

"Well, first things first, let's survive this ordeal, then we can talk about it a little more."

"Hear me and hear me clearly if we happen to die tonight. I am going to kick your ass before God's judgment sends you to Hell."

"I think that you may have wait in line."

The snarling blood demons edged closer and closer to their position. They waited patiently for an opening to attack. At the same time, they were being mindful not to make the wrong move that may result in impeding gunfire, which would result in unwanted attention from passersby.

Meanwhile, the rest of the task force was on the tail end of a triple shift at the precinct. It was a Tuesday afternoon, thirteen days after the *Sanguine killer's* minions attacked the Midtown Police Precinct North, and they managed to bust him out. It has been twenty-one hours since Joy Maxwell's kidnapping. It has been ten hours since a female police officer, and an FBI agent were murdered. The remaining members of the task force met up to minimize fatalities moving forward by carefully disclosing their Intel. Matching wits, following up on viable leads, hoping that something pans out in this case.

Lt. Drakon rolled in, looking a little disheveled. It has been increasingly difficult for her to deal with her desires for human blood. Doing detective work is her only distraction.

The team corralled in an office in front of the evidence board.

"What are we not seeing here?" a detective questioned. "I can't make the connection between the *Midtown Murders*, the murder of the supermarket manager, the cashier, the attack on the Midtown Police Precinct North, the murder of the cameraman and the executive at the channel five news station. We can't forget the disturbing discovery of the bodies of the widow and son of the manager of the Super-c supermarket—in the same cemetery where we buried most of the other victims. Let's not forget Joy Maxwell's kidnapping."

Lt. Drakon re-arranged the suspects on the two sides of the board and left a space in the middle where she wrote a big question mark with a red marker.

"Well, Lieutenant, you might not want to see this or face it, but Joy looks like the most viable suspect," an agent on the team pointed out.

"She can't be when she's the victim," Lt. Drakon responded.

"All the evidence shows that she's the center of this case somehow. I haven't figured out why just yet."

"We all may be looking at this all wrong. We must ask the question, what do all the victims have in common?" Agent Henning asked. "In addition to all the death surrounding us, we have to find Ms. Maxwell before it's too late. History has shown us that the *Sanguine killer,* scratch that killers, almost everyone who become entangled with those people, end up dead."

"Based on the pattern of these recent murders, she may still be alive, or we would've found her remains already," Lt. Drakon said.

"What! Wait a minute, are you saying that we are looking for a team and not a single killer with just a few henchmen?" Captain Constantine asked.

Agent Henning walked across the room to Lt. Drakon to cover her because she looked flush and faint. He showed a little compassion by saving her the embarrassment without compromising his strict demeanor and, at the same time, watering their budding relationship, which didn't go unnoticed by Lt. Drakon.

Suppressing her pain, the lieutenant stood up straight and addressed the room. "With all our technological advancements with joint efforts of two agencies, the FBI, and the NYPD, we have uncovered nothing, zip, zilch, zero, not one single piece of evidence or DNA linking any perp to any of the crime scenes. This can only mean that they worked together and practiced their skills before."

"That right, Lieutenant, thank you," agent Henning replied. "So, we need to broaden our search nationally. I want the NYPD to reach out to all city and state law enforcement agencies. When they hear the news about the attack on the department, they would be eager to assist. Captain, can you make a few phone calls to get the ball rolling?"

"Sure, no problem. How about let's go international? Maybe you FBI guys could call Interpol and other federal agencies," Captain replied.

Lt. Drakon excused herself, then shuffled to the bathroom. The pain was getting stronger. She reached inside doing and make a quick check of all the stalls, then locked the door. "Good, no one else is in here," she said and made her way to the sink. She splashed water on her face to collect her composure then she left the restroom.

Agent Henning waited outside the women's bathroom for her to exit. "I don't think you want to go in there right now," he said. "We need to talk." Agent Henning stepped closer to Lt. Drakon. "I worried about you!" He explained with a concerning look on his face.

"Well, there's no need." The lieutenant replied, then walked off. "I have to get back to work."

Agent Henning continued talking, and then she stopped to listen. "What are we doing here? I know you've been hurt, but I'm not going anywhere. Just stop pulling away from me. I realize this is what every call is still new. I thought we were having fun. But I care. I can see that you're in some sort of trouble. Tell me, did I do something wrong?"

She turned, faced Agent Henning, and said, "Yes, I have

been pulling away, but it's not me."

"Oh, you're not going to hit me with that bull…." He stepped up to Lt. Drakon within arm's reach and pulled her close. He pressed his body to hers and kissed her softly on her nose. His warm moist lips and his strong arms felt comforting.

Everything that Lt. Drakon has gone through in the past year swirled in her mind: the brutal attack and rape by five strange men who left her for dead, her pregnancy loss, her fiancé leaving her, and being hospitalized for five months hit her like a ton of bricks. If it weren't for her foster grandfather, she would be dead and not the undead. She found out that he's her living ancestor. She hasn't come to grips with the fact that she's a blood-sucking vampire, especially the drinking blood part. A gift that will keep on giving– for eternity.

Agent Henning was one thing out of all this that made her feel safe. "Don't fight this? You can be happy," she said to herself.

Agent Henning kissed Lt. Drakon a second time, she moaned in ecstasy, and a tingling feeling went up down her spine as he slid his wide tongue into her mouth. He massaged her lower back, then smoothly pulled her into the bathroom and locked the door behind him.

"We're going to get in trouble," she said.

"Stop worrying. I'm here right now be in the moment," he replied, then he unbuttoned her pants.

"Can't believe that I'm going to do this—this soon."

Agent Henning grabbed Lt. Drakon in the back of her neck and pulled her face to meet his. In a full embrace, their lips locked, then he picked her up in the air.

"Ooh," Lt. Drakon couldn't hold back her excitement any longer. She threw caution–along with any inhibition to the wind. She wrapped her legs around his torso and caressed his chiseled pecs and bulging biceps. "He's been hiding this body underneath his suit this whole time!" she thought to herself.

Agent Henning was aroused.

Lt. Drakon eagerly awaited him to penetrate her.

He thrust his member inside her; with every inch, he left her eager for more. Her body became sensitive to every single touch, every single kiss around her erogenous zones.

The lieutenant fell into his arms after she climaxed and laid her head on his shoulder. With all the excitement and heighten sensitivity, her thirst overwhelmed her. She listened to his heartbeat and began to transform, extending her fangs. She turned and stared into the mirror and explored her fangs with her tongue. She snapped out of it, and her body tensed up, and she said, "Please, put me down?"

"Wait, what's wrong?" agent Henning asked with a disappointed look.

Afraid of what she's capable of doing if she doesn't get away from him, Lt. Drakon hastily jumped out of agent Henning's arms, rushed into a stall, and locked it. Although it's evident that he cared for her, she felt the same way about him. "I hope he didn't notice me change," she thought. "If he did, he wouldn't understand this—I mean, how could he?"

Agent Henning received a call as he was getting dressed. He picked up the phone and saw that it was an FBI agent. "Special agent Woo, you got something for me?" he asked.

"Yes, I do, Sir. Too bad, I'm unable to give it to you now," agent Woo replied.

"What happened? Are you ok?"

"No sir, Sgt. Mason and I are in a bit of a jam."

"What type of jam agent Woo?"

"That's the million-dollar question, Sir."

"Where are you, Agent?"

"Sir, we're in some dive bar called the *Bone Dry*. Have you heard of it?"

"Yes, it's only a few blocks away. Sit tight; cavalry is on its way." Agent Henning hung up the phone with the field agent and said, "You heard that, Adeline, we got to move. Hurry up. Sgt. Mason and agent Woo are in trouble."

The lieutenant tried as best as she could to retract her fangs. Agent Henning grabbed his blazer, draped it over his forearm, unlocked the door, and paused to relish in the moment of awkwardness. He wanted to tell Lt. Drakon how she made him feel, but he ran out of words to say.

Meanwhile, back at the *Bone-Dry Bar*, Mr. Night sat back and watched the standoff between the federal agents and his minions. He got off on the excitement of chaos. "Too bad, the fun must end early," he thought to himself. "With the impending arrival of New York City's finest, this bloodbath won't be good for business. On the other hand, how many chances does a man in my position get to see two FBI agents get killed in front of you? Once, maybe twice in a lifetime. Shit, this is going to be good because you guys are so fucking resourceful."

Mr. Night emerged from darkness through the haze of smoke. His fully retracted fangs protruded through his lips. He hovered toward the center of the action, placed two fingers on the barrel of Sgt. Mason's gun, and gently, he pushed down his standard police-issued Glock.

Sgt. Mason stood motionless as Mr. Night guided his gun and his hand inside the holster.

"This is an unfortunate turn of events," Mr. Night whispered into his ear. "Look what you brought into my house, Sgt. Mason. You're such a disappointment. I should kill you right now, but you're such a vile and sorry excuse for a human being—sucking your blood will probably make me sick."

Even with all his bravado was at a loss for words as the blood demon invaded his personal space. "I hope calvary comes soon. I don't think we're going to survive through this without it," Sgt. Mason said to himself.

Lt. Drakon swerved in and out of traffic with flashing lights and sirens blaring. Every police cruiser in the city followed close behind steadfast to save a fellow brother in blue.

As a blood demon, Lt. Drakon had gifts bestowed to her by her predecessor like superhuman powers, sharp sense of hearing, keen eyesight, and super speed. But with these abilities combined do not compare to their cunning wit or powers of persuasion. Mr. Night was a prime example of that.

Agent Woo stood up, waved his gun, and blew his whistle at one vampire in what looked like assisted suicide.

Agitated, Mr. Night understood how bad this was for his business. He made money from his underling's movements throughout the city, and his minion's actions fed his lust for opulence. Greed is a human trait, but it's an original sin that he indulges in. The Bone-Dry bar was his headquarters for his operation. The last thing he needed was the police shutting down his operation.

A genius in his own right, Mr. Night knew that with the authorities approaching, he must use his powers and inveigle Agent Poppy Woo to let everything go. "Remain calm," he said peacefully with his hands out. "I will not pretend like we're friends–I know things look bad, but I have an explanation for all of this." He squatted down in between the people laid out on the ground and out of the sights of agent Woo's gun.

When Mr. Night barricaded himself behind the motionless bodies, he continued to explain. "Things are not exactly as it seems here."

"Ok, I bet you're going tell me that what I saw, I didn't see, Mr. Night," agent Woo said.

"I don't know what you saw, Field agent, but I'm going to give you some valuable information because the more informed a man is, the better equipped he is making decisions," he replied. "First, every single person here are all consenting adults. It's nothing more than a sexual fetish for them. Yes, it's masochistic, but I assure you it is just harmonious pleasure—"

"I bet, until their very own demise Mr. Night."

"Look again, Field agent!" Mr. Night tapped and nudged the bodies lying on the floor one by one. Groggy and disorientated, they arouse from their induced comatose state. As their eyes opened, they gasped drastically for life-giving air.

At that moment, the abrupt sound of screeching tires averted Mr. night's attempt to negotiate with the agent. Blue and red lights swirled around the walls of the bar. A single patrol car pulled up outside the insidious *Bone-Dry Bar* and blocked the way of oncoming traffic. Not soon after, another cruiser stopped alongside it, then another, until a dozen squad cars congested the streets.

Agent Woo heard police chatter outside as they cleared the pedestrians off the streets.

"Stand back. There's a hostage situation here," one officer said.

Fear instantly shook agent Woo's body when he saw everyone gasping for air. "No! that's impossible; they were all dead a minute ago. T…there was no signs of them breathing," he yelled. His hands shook uncontrollably as cold sweat washed over the field agent.

Lt. Drakon and Agent Henning arrived on the scene in tandem. They out of the car and immediately took control of the situation. "First thing first, let's try to get audio and visual setup in there before too late," lieutenant Drakon ordered.

"I agree, come on, let's make that happen," agent Henning ordered his team to retrieve the camera robot. He winked at the lieutenant and said, "Great minds think alike."

Lt. Drakon didn't react to his comment, showing any emotion. She considered their last interaction nearly resulted in her almost tearing out his jugular vein to drink his blood for sustenance. The lack of her drinking blood or even eating solid foods weakened her severely. Foods have not been appealing to Lt. Drakon for some time now. In addition, all the pressure of her life started to take a toll on her. Her health diminished, and her body deteriorated soon after. The color vacated her face—she was translucent and resembled a walking corpse.

Even though Lt. Drakon had a moment of weakness with agent Henning. A romance was the last thing on her mind. Even though she opened her heart to the possibility of love, she didn't feel human, thought of herself as alluring or even sexy, for that matter.

It's been touch and go for Lt. Drakon. Her fiancé called off the wedding and left her while she was still recovering in the hospital. He couldn't cope with the thought of losing his future wife to the inevitable dangers of being a police officer. After he left, he was never to be heard of again. She didn't blame him because she was in the middle of a complex case, and her life was at stake at several points during her investigation. Ironically, she was given a second chance at life due to her attack, and the side effects of that chance have saved her life while in the line of duty.

243

She had to come to grips with the reality and admit to herself that if she were a mere mortal, she would have met her demise. She shut her eyes tight and whispered to herself, "Concentrate with every fiber of your being. So much of the evidence and clues aren't adding up. Come on, pull yourself together, try hard to suppress the urge to feed, and don't dwell on your tumultuous past; lives are at stake."

Lt. Drakon grimaced, put her hand on the side of her head, and whimpered aloud, "I'm so hungry."

The stranger slipped by all the police officers outside the bar and walked up on her, disguised in a policeman's uniform. While she struggled to open a bottle of aspirin to ease her pain, he said, "Those pills can't help you anymore. Stop fighting your unnatural gift, my Childe. Just give in."

The stranger leaned in closer and softly whispered, "What you need to do now, Fledgling, is feed! Drinking blood will give you strength beyond your wildest dreams. Make today the day every vampire must feed to survive, my Childe. Whether you want to, you must feed, or you're going to die soon. I can smell the death creeping up on you." The stranger slapped the bottle of aspirins out of her hands and onto the ground. As quick as he appeared, he was gone.

No matter how sick Lt. Drakon felt, her mind remained on those held up in the bar.

Agent Henning led the hostage negotiations. Agent Woo. wasn't clear over the phone about what was going on. So, the assumption was that he and Sgt. Mason was being held hostage inside.

A command center was set up in under forty-five minutes by the FBI.

Captain Constantine arrived a little after the FEDs setup. He got out of his unit and approached Lt. Drakon while she gave orders to her team, including S. W. A. T.

"You three cover all entry points," she ordered.

Sgt Don Wyatt said, "Lieutenant Drakon, I heard there's an FBI agent and one of our own in there. So, whatever you need–my team and I are here to lend a helping hand and give anything you need."

"Outstanding Sgt. Wyatt, I'm glad to hear that. We'll need shooters on the roof as soon as possible. So, you can set up your team in this store here for now across the street from the bar," she replied.

The captain asked the heavily perspiring detective. "Are you alright, Lieutenant Drakon?"

She tilted her head slightly, leaned up against the door frame of the store, panting like a dehydrated dog.

"Are you sure, Lieutenant? Because you don't look so good.

"I'm fine, Captain. I just had a long night. I'll perk up after a cup of coffee; a java juice will put me back on track."

He looked at her, exhaled, and shook his head.

"Come on, Capt., trust me, I'm alright, I promise, Sir."

"Look at you. You're sweating like a stuck pig when it's only sixty-five degrees today. I think you should go home and get some rest. Better yet, I'm changing it to an order to rid you of all the reasons that may pop up in your slick brain of yours that you must stay and ignore my suggestion. I mean it, Lieutenant, now go!"

The captain took his hands out of the pockets of his trench coat and gestured to Lt. Drakon. "Please, listen to me, you can't stay Adeline, you say you're fine, but I know you better than you know yourself," the Capt. said.

"Captain–don't do this to me now. We're so close to closing

245

this case," she replied.

He put his hand on her shoulders and exhaled. "Come on, that's a direct order–if you disobey a direct order, I'll be forced to reprimand you for insubordination. I'm going to call a uniform to take you home. You've been working nonstop for days, with no rest. It's okay, Lieutenant; we could take it from here."

"Okay, okay, you got me. I'll go." Adeline knows how much of a bulldog the captain can be and gave in.

"Good, I'm glad." The captain smirked and walked into the command center.

An officer in uniform approached Lt. Drakon, and she waved her off. "It's okay, Officer, stay. I'll take a cab home," she said. "One of ours is in distress. Your services are needed here."

"Are you sure, Lieutenant, I have direct orders!" exclaimed the officer. "I should at least wait here until you are safely inside the cab. Captain will have my ass if something happens to you, Lieutenant."

"No, I'm fine. I got this. I'm a big girl." The pain got more intense when she started to walk away. The further she walked, the harder the pain got to bear.

In the crowds of onlookers, she disappeared in the busy jammed New York streets. No one noticed as she stumbled and tripped over herself either. Most people just figured her for a junkie. One man cursed at her when she grabbed onto his jacket for support. No one else cared when she fell on the sidewalk. For her, time stood still as she went through another metamorphosis.

Her eyes went completely black, except for a brilliant red dot which now was the color of her pupils. She saw her reflection through the paint of a parked car fade. The intense hunger pain, subsided culminating with a strange yet familiar sound. All but the beautiful sounds of beating hearts had been silenced. She listened to the flushing and pumping of blood, entering, and leaving all four chambers of the heart.

Her hunger grew stronger and stronger, deeper and deeper, with each passing second. Lt. Drakon remained steadfast, resisting the urge to feed. She decided that this disease will just have to kill her before she gave in to it. She was hanging on to the last remanence of her humanity, her mortality.

The blood demon curse squeezed every single drop of life from the stark detective. It took its final blow; the shadow sucked the natural warmth from her body. Exhaling her last breath, she fell victim, consumed by pain right in the middle of the chaos. As Lt. Drakon laid on the sidewalk, vulnerable and dying of thirst, the negotiations began with the first call.

Agent Henning, a trained hostage negotiator—made the call to the *Bone Dry*. Inside the bar, the phone rang several times before someone picked up. "Hello," the very human bartender of the Bone Dry answered.

"May I speak to whoever's in charge?" agent Henning asked.

The bartender handed the phone over to Mr. Night. "Here, Boss," he said with a smirk.

"Yo! I'm the owner of the club Alphonse Balen," Mr. Night said.

"Can you tell us what's happening in there and why you're holding two of my people hostages?" agent Henning asked.

"Hear me out, Officer, all of this is a misunderstanding. All of it can be explained. If you tell your men to stand down, all of this can be over, and your men can walk out of here in one piece."

"If that's true, give the phone to my agent so that we can end this now."

Mr. Night attempted to give the phone to agent Woo, but he brandished another weapon from under his blazer instead. He pointed his gun in Mr. Nights' face and cocked the hammer. "I have two bullets for everyone in here: The first one who moves will be the first to get two," agent Woo said. "Sir, if you can hear me, I am telling you there's some weird crap going on in here!"

Mr. Night held the phone up to his ear and said, "This whole situation is not on me, Officer."

"Hey, do me a favor and put the phone on speaker," agent Henning asked.

Mr. Night put the phone on the bar and obliged the federal agent.

"Can you tell me how many people are in there?"

"There are thirteen loyal customers, two of your guys, the bartender, and me–seventeen in all."

"Good, how about injuries?"

"Nobody is hurt; everyone is okay. Apart from agent Woo, he might be sick. But that's a different matter that the bureau will have to contend with."

"Agent Woo, Sgt. Mason, I am going to come in there—So, Mr. Night, go ahead and let the customers go." Agent Henning put down the phone, stood up, and put on a bulletproof vest. He put a .38 special in the small of his back, took a deep breath, and exited the command center.

Slowly Lt. Drakon began to come back to life. Feeling strangely powerful, she awakened with new abilities like sharp hearing. She heard entire conversations. "Wow, I feel so much better." she thought to herself. She scanned her body and looked at her reflection through a store window. The reborn blood demon sprung up off the ground and made her way through the crowd.

The fledgling blood demon barged through the onlookers. Lt. Drakon carved a path to the front door of the Bone-Dry bar before agent Henning did. Before stepping out in plain sight, she handed her gun and badge to a patrolman. "Here, take my gun and shield. I'm probably going to be suspended after coming back and going in there," she said.

"What the hell is she doing?" agent Henning asked and nudged Capt. Constantine.

He ran up to the young officer he told to take Lt. Drakon home and said, "I thought I gave you a direct order?"

The fear on the face of the officer was apparent. She took off her cap, looked down, and stood at attention. "You did, Captain, but she—"

The Capt. put his hand up and said, "Save it, it's not your fault–it figures, that's just the way she is, always got to be the hero." He walked away before the patrolwoman had a chance to explain herself.

That was a stupid and foolhardy move, but she did it without a second thought. "Members of my team wouldn't hurt me, would they? I feel amazing! I'm a vampire now!" she exclaimed. "I won't feel any more pain, but if I do, I'll heal fast."

Despite all the prior knowledge that she gained from watching movies and reading books, Lt. Drakon researched everything on the subject she could get her hands on–since she found out about this gift. It was all misinformation, though because she hadn't been talking to her grandfather or CSI Madrigal.

Lt. Drakon pounded on the door and entered the bar. Confident that her vampire superpowers would give her a slight advantage. After the door closed behind, it was dark and cold. She could see her breath coming from her mouth when she exhaled. Her eyes refocused to the darkness, and she moved forward cautiously.

"Adeline spotted agent Woo and ran up to him. "Hey, weren't you supposed to let some people go, field agent?" she asked and scanned her surroundings.

"Sorry, I'm not going to let anyone out of here, Lieutenant," agent Woo replied.

"Then, what are you going to do?"

"Look, I made a decision. I can't allow these people to just roam free in the city, and whatever these things are. What I witnessed them do in here—this freak show belongs in the X-files. We need to put a stop to them, right here, right now!"

"Get the heck out of here, Field agent! Pull yourself together; your mind was playing tricks on you. They were innocent people in here!"

"No, they're not, Lieutenant! You should've seen them; it was lots and lots of blood."

"Blood! What do you mean?"

Seeing how uptight and wound-up Agent Woo was drawn, cocked, and fully loaded with his gun. He panned the room and aimed it at everyone, including sergeant Mason. He had another sidearm, undrawn under his coat. Lt. Drakon realized how unraveled at the seams he became. "He may be too unpredictable and too volatile to handle directly. I may have to create a diversion so that I could get these people out of here," she thought to herself.

Before she turned her questions to Sergeant Mason, she noticed that agent Woo's gun was especially pointed at him too. "Sgt. Mason!" she called out. "Tell me what happened here?" Lt. Drakon slipped directly in front of agent Woo's line of fire.

"Well, we came here for a meeting with my C.I., Alphonse Balen."

"What was the meeting about, Sergeant?"

"Well, Lieutenant, usually, that is confidential—"

"Spare me, were you talking about the case with your C.I?"

"No! I was—"

"T…they were discussing details of bribery and coconspirators, from local politicians, judge, and other influential people in the city and Washington," agent Woo said.

"Zip it, field agent! the lieutenant asked me—listen, Lieutenant, there's no way we were saying the things that he's accusing us of," replied Sgt. Mason.

"You got to level with me, that may be true, but something went down here," Lt. Drakon said. "Give it to me straight. Agent Woo has no intentions of allowing any of these patrons out of this bar alive, including you."

"I came here because Mr. Night knows the streets better than anyone I know. I wanted to find out if he heard anything—you know how most perps love to brag about their recent exploits. Especially if they attacked a police department and got the drop on them."

"I highly doubt those guys would brag about what they did. We already established that the suspects that hit us were professionals. But go ahead continue."

Sergeant Mason continued to explain. Lt. Drakon sniffed out the lies from the truth. The new gifts that the vampire disease has granted her. A subtle distortion that the human heart could not detect. Despite being a new reborn vampire, she quickly adapted to her unique abilities. She didn't let on that she knew he was lying to her.

She wiggled her ear, focused on the speed of his heartbeat and the change of inflection in his voice when he lied. "Agent Woo is right. There's more to this story that he is not revealing," she thought to herself.

Pressed for time, she decided to stir the pot a little. She yelled, "Hey field agent, seems like he's the only one in here that wants to spill his guts but is too afraid to do so. Listen to me, forget about everyone else and talk to me. I'm the only one in here who can help you!"

The screaming put Agent Woo over the edge. He bent over and threw up from all the weird shit he witnessed. "T…these people are blood-sucking vampires, Lieutenant," he responded and wiped his mouth with his tie. "I see you're giving me that look. I know how that must sound to you but believe me, if there was anyone in the world that would say how insane that sounded, it's me.

"If it didn't play out right in front of me, I would be in disbelief. It took me some time to come to terms with all this, this— even hearing it aloud doesn't make it easier to process." He recapped what happened from the sergeant, and he entered the Bone-Dry bar to the standoff with the vampires. Leaving no detail out, agent Woos colorfully chronicled the events.

Lt. Drakon used her skills to distinguish between virtues of truth and sins of lies; she believed everything he said. She was recently becoming aware of her immortality. She couldn't tell what was harder to come to terms with, her inner turmoil of being conflicted with her new life as a blood demon or agent Woo's story about the events that played out in this bar. No matter how relieved she may be to be alive–well, sort of, she still had reservations about the changes.

"This guy's screaming for a 51/50 evaluation. You're nuts if you believe this man," Mr. Night declared.

The lieutenant was sure that agent Woo told her the truth. As much as she hated it, the slime ball thug was right. If he left the bar, people would undoubtedly say he's crazy, and corroborating his story isn't going to help any.

She told everyone to sit down in the hopes of keeping them all out of harm's way. Moving them out of agent Woo's direct line of sight surprisingly relaxed this situation. Her main goal was to get him to give up his weapon. She slowly moved closer to Agent Woo with her hands raised, textbook negotiation tactic basics: gain trust, give up your position, then surrender.

Agent Woo caught on to her; he swiftly turned and pointed the gun in Lt. Drakon's face. "You couldn't possibly think that I wouldn't notice the technique. I don't want to shoot anybody, but I will," he said, licked his lips, and wiped the sweat from his face.

Sgt. Mason placed his jacket behind his gun on his hip, preparing to draw on agent Woo.

Lt. Drakon saw him and waved him off, signally him the stand down. She crept closer to agent Woo with her arms out and her palms facing the floor. "I know that your afraid field agent, but I believe that you witnessed something here today that I won't make light of," she said. "You said that you don't want to shoot anybody. I want to believe you, so just give me your gun, and we can all walk out of here safely. I am only here to help. I'm on your side, Field agent."

"Look, Lieutenant, I can't trust you or them. Nothing makes sense. I know what I saw; these monsters were in here feeding off human flesh. Above all, I know what I heard from him." He replied and aimed at Sgt. Mason.

"Agent Woo, I'm doling out some advice here. It would behoove you to follow it."

"Lieutenant Drakon, Sergeant Devin Mason Is in league with them. I know he's your partner and all, but don't trust him as far as you can throw him; he's scum!"

"You know what, agent Woo; I'm not going to stand here and allow you to defame my name!" Sgt. Mason exclaimed. "Lieutenant,

253

I am going shoot him myself if he bad mouths me one more time. I came here to talk to my C. I." He pulled out his service revolver and pointed it at the agent.

"Stand down, Detective, that's an order!" she exclaimed and put her palm out toward her partner. "Yes, you've said that many times already, Sergeant, you know what doesn't make any sense at all. How does an officer who just transferred from Philadelphia have an established informant in New York, hmm? I understand the game; law enforcement sometimes mixes with criminals in the hopes to nab the bigger catch. I get it. Sometimes that just comes with the territory, but explain to me how, Devin? I have wondered that lately actually, I was going to wait until we got out of here to ask, but since we are already here, go ahead explain."

"I'm beyond hurt, Partner; I'm not going to entertain that request, Lieutenant."

"Come on, Devin, indulge us," agent Woo said. "We would like to hear how a Philly police detective got involved with a notable criminal here in New York. Not just any two-bit one, one whose name carries weight in the streets, no doubt."

"Ok, look, to make a long story short, I have no obligation to reveal my sources or disclose our relationships. But since I have a gun to my head, I'll tell you this much without compromising an ongoing investigation," Sgt. Mason replied. "Mr. Night and I met when I went under on a drug trafficking case years ago. He was a big influential piece of the puzzle that helped us bring down Russian Mobster Katya Ugroza, the biggest drug czar in three continents. He aided law enforcement from Interpol, the FBI, the FSKN (Russian Federal Narcotics Control of Narcotics), the Royal Canadian Mounted Police, and several other agencies, In an international joint task force. We worked together in a collaborative effort to bring the ice lady down.

"In any case, Mr. Night is not your worry here today; agent

Woos is the one with his gun out, holding us all hostage. So, you should redirect your focus on him."

Lt. Drakon listened to Sgt. Mason speak, and she didn't hear any irregularities in his heartbeat. Even though she was new at this, there was no crack in his voice or a change in his breathing. Which meant he was telling the truth.

"Agent Woo, we are all good guys here, so how about we walk out here and sort this out downtown?" Lt. Drakon asked.

"I can't believe that you would believe his bullshit, Lieutenant!" agent Woo exclaimed. "I am telling you he is not a good guy, and those patrons were not here for some hedonistic sexual encounter involving a little blood-sucking either. I am telling you, if I weren't here, they would undoubtedly have died in this bar today."

Sweating and shaking nervously, agent Woo scratched his head with the tip of his gun, then pointed it back at Sgt. Mason.

The detective anticipated the agent's move and pressed his weapon at his temple. "Do you play chess?" Sgt. Mason asked with a smirk on his face. "It doesn't matter because I know everybody's heard the term checkmate, and this is what it looks like." His face became flush and is smirk turn to a devilish look.

Lt. Drakon threw her hands out and said, "What the fuck—wait, don't shoot."

A deceitful peace took over the vibe of the *Bone-Dry Bar*, much like a calm before a big storm.

In a fit of rage, absent of mercy, Sgt. Mason shot agent Poppy Woo in the side of his head, aimed, and shot at his partner.

"You should have died at the park; you freakin' cockroach. You're a crazy iron bird, why-won't-you-die!" he yelled and reeled off rapid gunfire in the chest of his intended target. He didn't stop until he emptied an entire clip into the lieutenant's body.

Lt. Drakon never stood a chance, not even to pull out her gun to defend herself. All fifteen rounds from his Glock twenty-two bore deep in her chest, yet the shots didn't kill her. As a matter of fact, the gunshots barely moved her. She staggered a little, but her stubbornness and shock kept the detective from dropping.

Lt. Drakon was in tremendous pain, confused because she was shot by her partner, by one of her own. In absolute disbelief, she stuck two fingers in the bullet holes in her breast. She raised her bloody hands to her face to see for herself what Sgt. Mason had just done to her.

"Die bitch, why won't you die!" the sergeant screamed.

Since Mr. Night and the others knew about Lt. Drakon, they started to make their way to an escape.

"Whoop, time for me to go," Mr. Night declared.

Mr. night waved his hand for everyone to leave the bar. He moved like a ghost, swiftly strutting to the maimed lieutenant. There were minute amounts of blood streaming from her wounds; scores of bullets riddled the torso leaving it resembling a sifter.

"Sorry about this; I kind of admire your resolve. I wouldn't have allowed this if it were left up to me, but it is out of my hands. The elders want you dead; I don't know why. Maybe you can ask Dr. German," he whispers in her ear. "Too bad you must die today. I hate to see you go, my Childe. You would've been a great vampire." He used his handkerchief and wiped the sweat from her face. "Hurry up and finish this, then you can finally be with us tonight." Then like a flash, he was gone.

From the sounds made by all the gunfire, the police got into position to raid the bar.

"The door's blocked by something, Sir!" a police officer

256

explains.

"Use the larger breaching tool; we have to get in there, now. There were shots fired, and our people could be seriously hurt," agent Henning bellowed at the top of his lungs. He shifted frantically, fearing the worst. He ran around back to see if the team had better luck getting inside the bar.

Sgt. Mason tiptoed over agent Woo's body making sure not to leave footprints in his blood. He stood over his injured partner and pointed his gun at her head, and said, "This isn't business. It's personal, bitch! I must redeem myself from failing to kill you in Central Park."

The weakened lieutenant peered up at her partner as the worthless low-life treacherous traitor reloaded his gun. Everything went dark, and her body went limp.

Standing over his partner's body, Sgt. Mason let out a vile laugh; just before he fired the last two fatal shots in her head. "That should do it. Finally, I can be rid of this witch; this righteous kill should earn me the right to become a vampire," he said and scurried toward a secret exit. He narrowly escaped before the police knocked down the front and back doors simultaneously. He weaseled away out a side exit, shutting the panel behind him.

Both slugs penetrated her skull. Lieutenant Adeline Drakon was left for dead, yet again. With very little hope of survival. She realized that she had to do the unthinkable and drink blood. She was at a crossroads, and she had to decide between her true convictions or her demise. A decision that most people would never have to make. Burdened with a revelation of truth, she prayed, *"God forgive me, I have not always prayed, and you have not always answered. I beg you, Lord, do not forsake me for the choice I am about to make."*

In excruciating pain, she maneuvered her limp body close as

best as she could to agent Woo's corpse. "It's a shame how I just became immortal, only to die so young and on the ground of a seedy den for vampires." Enraged and filled with hate and revenge, she said, "When I die, it will be on my terms. I will be at peace surrounded by family. Not today, not by the hands of my backstabbing partner."

Lt. Drakon turned over and crawled on the slippery floor of her blood. She clawed closer to agent Woo's vital fluid. When she got close enough to use her hand to scoop her third chance at life, she collected Woo's blood and put it into her mouth. She stretched her palm again, scrapping as much plasma as she could. As the life nectar went down her throat, the energy she got from it revitalized her. Her wounds began to heal. Her fangs grew, and she chomped down on his neck. The more blood she drank, the stronger she became. She didn't take enough to become entirely well, though; she didn't overindulge this being her first feeding.

Lt. Drakon got up on her feet and began to feel alive again. She shuffled her feet in the direction where her would-be murderer escaped. She barreled through the bar and then headed in the direction where she saw the rest of Mr. Night's Clan go. She picked up the scent of her partner and followed his trail. She searched the wall for an opening, perusing with her fingers along the wall. A cool breeze blew on the back of her hand from a tight crack in the wall perfectly placed in a crease next to a trophy shelf. She pushed on the shelf hard until it popped open. The panel swung open, and she entered a stairwell that ran straight to a subterranean tunnel.

Not a moment too soon, officers led by agent Henning stormed the bar just as the spring-loaded door slammed closed behind the lieutenant.

The tunnel looked like it had been constructed in the turn of the century; cobblestones paved the ground and lined the wall and ceiling, much like the building materials used on cathedrals all over the city. There were puddles of water that had settled on the floor, no doubt from a water pipe that ran along the wall.

Lt. Drakon navigated the tunnel to an archway to a building across the street from the bar. Then she heard a boom, a crash, and a bang, one right after another, coming from the front and the back door. First, S.W.A.T entered, and then the police unit secured the area. "Clear, clear, clear, clear," a member of the breach team shouted out when they secured the bar.

Captain Constantine entered, immediately surveying the area until he spotted the body of agent Woo on the floor lying in a pool of blood.

"These wounds look like they were made from a Glock twenty-two, and from the stippling, he was shot at point-blank range," agent Henning said as he examined the body. "Captain, there has been something on my mind."

"I'm listening," the captain replied as he reviewed the crime scene.

"From the start of this investigation, the more I look, the less I see. Nothing, absolutely nothing makes any sense. I think that you have been holding out on me, Captain."

"Let's not get too crazy here, watch what you say, agent, before this situation gets way out of hand. Agent Henning, are you insinuating that I have something to do with this? How could you possibly think that I had something to do with any of this."

"No, not this, but I feel that you're holding back, you know something. I believe you are withholding important evidence and tanking this investigation, keeping this case from being solved." Agent Henning stepped up in the captain's face and said, "If I find out that you are involved with this in any way, I will make it my agenda to bring you down, Captain."

"Who in the world do you think you're talking to, agent Henning? Is that a threat? Because I don't take too kindly to threats. I don't give two flying fucks if you're an FBI agent. You can't just throw around accusations without any proof. Who the hell do you think you are?"

"Well, I am noting a pattern here, and certain things are just not adding up.

But you are the only one that makes sense, Captain. You have access to everything. First thing, why are people in your precinct getting hit? Secondly, why did you send out your best, brightest, and the one detective who not only has rank but is your oldest friend? Now, I have another federal agent dead, when he was only just supposed to accompany Sgt. Mason meet with his C.I." Agent Henning stood in front of the captain with his hands akimbo.

"I pulled some strings at the bureau before I got here. Your sergeant was meeting up with Alphonse Balen, aka Mister Night; A compliant ex-criminal turned informant. So, I am confused as to why another one of my agents is dead on the floor of a crappy bar, and your lieutenant and sergeant is missing, possibly at large."

Unfazed by the federal agent's rant, Captain Constantine stepped closer to agent Henning's face. "First, what happened here today does not seem to be connected to me in any way," he replied. "Let's get the medical examiner in here to release the body so that the crime scene unit can investigate. Hopefully, they can make heads or tails of what happened here, especially since there's no one here who could tell us what happened.

"Second, we should send out an APB to find our missing comrades and try to figure out how everyone escaped when all exits from the bar were blocked." Capt. Constantine backpedaled away from agent Henning and ordered a full search for a secret escape route. His cellphone rang in his pocket, and he quickly silenced it. He cleared his throat and held the vibrating phone in his hand. Once it stopped, "Seven missed calls" from Sgt. Mason was displayed on the screen. His head spun around before he deleted the recent call list and voicemails, then he tiptoed over the body of the slain agent.

Lt. Drakon got to the end of the tunnel then came up in an abandoned grocery store. She checked it thoroughly but couldn't find anyone there; disappointed, she back peddled through the tunnel to the *Bone-Dry Bar*. The cobblestone began to turn upside down. Her head started spinning, and she experiences shortness of breath. "Agent Woo's blood helped heal my gunshot wounds, especially the ones in her skull because he was so healthy. But I should've had my fill; feeding could have allowed me to recover completely," she said to herself. Her voice echoed off the walls in the corridor. "Do I sound like that—no wonder my partner hated me so much."

Lt. Drakon struggled to stay upright; the wall held her up, but it wasn't enough. She was too weary to transverse the rest of the way on her own. Her legs wobbled like jello until they gave out on her. She fell face-first in a puddle of sewage water. "Will I ever get the hang of this vampire thing!" she said as she gasped for air.

The stress of the case has cracked a rift between the two different factions of the law, especially after Henning's accusations. Even though the NYPD has already taken exception to the FBI's presence on this case. Most police officers felt that the stranger and his crew should only be apprehended by no one else but local law enforcement. The captain wanted the collar so bad he can taste it. But the Mayor and Commissioner expressed their concerns about the department's ability to capture the perpetrator. The last thing the city needed was a bunch of emotionally charged police officers running around half-cocked, bashing people in the head in the name of revenge. The city couldn't take a fallout of that magnitude.

"Listen, agent Henning; I know how you feel about the Lieutenant. There is no need for us to argue," the captain bumped agent Henning with his shoulder as he stepped away and walked to the back of the bar. "So, I'm going find my officers, with or without your consent."

Dr. German walked in the middle of the heated discussion between agent Henning and Captain Constantine.

"Doctor!" agent Henning exclaimed, followed by a head nod.

The crime scene unit entered closely behind the M.E. and immediately got into action.

"Everybody, stop, don't move!" agent Henning said and held his hands out in front of him. "Don't anyone touch nothing? Sorry folks, I want everyone out right now. The bureau is going handle this one."

"Shh! Did you hear that?" an agent and police officer said in unison. When the bar was silent, a low, dull ringing emanated from the wall behind the bar.

"Yes, I hear it too!" Dr. German said using his superior hearing. "I know that ring from anywhere– it's Adeline's ring tone."

The two closest to the trophy case worked together on opening the door. At the same time, everyone else in the bar listened to the lieutenant's ringtone.

"Is that the intro for "Hill Street Blues?" Two officers asked as they hurried to figure out the mechanism to open the panel.

One of them pushed against the trophy self until they heard a click. The panel opened when he released the trophy. Everyone within arm's reach rushed behind the bar and pushed the heavy door open. The officers gave way for Captain Constantine, agent Henning, and Dr. German to enter the tunnel.

Only a few yards away from the archway to the tunnel was Lt. Drakon lying face down. The three clambered to her aide. The sight of her positioned face down in a murky puddle made everyone fear the worst. Dr. German checked her vital signs–even though he knew there wouldn't be one, but he played it off as if he found a pulse. "Thank God she's still alive. Hurry, let me get something. I need to stop the bleeding," he said.

"Hurry, call a bus. Her vitals are faint, officer down," the captain shouted up the stairs.

The lieutenant's phone continued ringing, and agent Henning said, "Give me the phone."

"Here," Dr. German said as he handed him the phone drenched with blood and mud.

He wiped off the screen and pressed the talk button. A barely audible female voice on the other end said, "Hello Lieutenant—"

"Who's this?" agent Henning replied, then turned up the volume to hear the person.

"Where's the lieutenant? This is Joy Maxwell. I don't have time to waste. He's coming back; please send help!"

The call dropped, and the agent looked down at the cellphone as the screen went black.

By this time, the Paramedic and EMT had arrived and pushed their way through to Lt. Drakon. They hoisted her up on the gurney and strapped her in without bothering to check her vital signs. "One, two, three," the paramedics counted as they raised the stretcher to waist height. The medics struggled to maneuver the stretcher out of the tunnel and up the stairs.

"I am Captain Constantine, the lieutenant's commanding officer, so any information you may have regarding her condition, you can direct them to me!" he yelled at the backs of the men pushing Lt. Drakon to safety.

The captain turned to Dr. German and said, "I think you

should go with her; Adeline is going to need you by her side."

Dr. German nodded his head, gathered his things, and followed the medics to the ambulance.

Chapter 10

The ambulance that carried Lt. Drakon sped down the Henry Hudson (Westside highway) as fast as possible to make it to Mount Sanai Hospital, the best trauma facility in the nation. The EMT gave her all to the dying lieutenant, an unremitting effort of chest compression, her experience, and medical know-how. The Paramedic attempted to revive the detective because she had no vital signs. He tried his darndest to get the fatally wounded femme fatale breathing again. But they were fighting an uphill battle, and unbeknownst to them, she was already dead.

Lt. Drakon is an immortal being whose soul has no home, and her soul isn't bound to a body. It has been freed to a different plain of entropy. Her spirit can never have a place in heaven, hell, or purgatory. The angel of death has passed over her and others of her kind, cursed by God and forgotten by Lucifer, the morning star himself. Ignorant of the fact, they continued to work on the forsaken. Dr. German even aided in the effort of stopping the bleeding.

The ambulance pulled up to the emergency room entrance of Mt. Sinai Hospital. "We have a detective with multiple gunshots to the chest and abdomen, low temp., she is cold to touch, her vital signs are faint. She's non-responsive to regular procedures, get a crash cart stat!" exclaimed the paramedic. "Sorry, Sir, you can't come in here."

"But I am a doctor! She's my granddaughter," Dr. German replied.

"Doctor, you of all people should know that by law, you can't be in here. I know who you are, Dr. German; she is in good hands, I promise."

Dr. German nodded his head and backed away from the door. He sat down on a nearby bench buried in a fret, concerned if the hospital staff discovered that she was a vampire.

"Clear…," the ER doctor shouted every time he charged her with the defibrillator paddles. "You can do it, Detective. Show me a sign you want live. You can do it. Give me a heartbeat." The doctor tried a fourth and fifth time, and the operating room team did their best. Lt. Drakon was non-responsive to their efforts. She flatlined, and the doctor looked up at the clock on the wall and called it. "DOA 4:30 pm. God Dammit, this shit never gets old. One more of our officers killed in the line of duty," he said and pulled his gloves off. "Where's the next of kin?"

A nurse in the room pointed in the direction of the waiting room. The doctor washed his hands, pulled down his face mask, and pushed open the double doors to the operating room. Dr. German waited patiently when the doctor walked out of the ER to break the bad news.

Dr. German stood up abruptly, met the doctor halfway with his hands held out in front of him, and said, "I know you don't have to tell me; she's gone, isn't she. It would've been a miracle she made it—she lost way too much blood. Although she was the only family I had in this world, a parent should never bury their child. But I'm a realist logically, I didn't expect her to survive, and I don't believe in miracles either, Doctor."

"Well… I guess there's nothing left for me to say," the doctor replied. "You can go and see her now if you'd like."

"Thank you. I think I will say my goodbyes. Do you have all her personal effects? I'd like to arrange for her body to go with me to the medical examiner's office. And could you please take all the bullets out of her as well?"

"Right away, Dr. German, I will personally write up all the necessary paperwork for the transfer. And all your daughter's personal belongings have already been bagged; everything is in the room. Rest assured, the transfer will be expedited, considering that she was a police officer who died in the line of duty. We understand how much you want to catch the bastard who killed her, so that is not a problem." The ER doctor sighed, put his hand on the grieving grandfather's shoulder, and said, "I'd like to say that we did everything medically possible to save her."

Dr. German clenched his lips together, tilted his head down, and brushed past him. He walked toward the room to see his granddaughter and didn't say a word. The doctor shook his head and walked in the opposite direction.

The thought crossed his mind about how he would feel if he was in the same situation. Especially since he's aware that Lt. Drakon is going to be alright. He walked away and didn't respond. He called from his office and arranged for the transfer of his granddaughter's body. When he walked into the room, he wasted no time. He took out a small jar of blood from his briefcase, looked around and made sure that the room was empty, and said, "There you are." He admired the jar and walked over to her, laid out motionless on the operating table. In a sort of dubious manner, afraid of how she might react with him trying to save her life again, he hesitated to revive her momentarily.

Dr. German has clung to his humanity and sense of decency despite being without a soul. He's been a blood demon for 465 years; he's rare in nature: an ultimate predator, a cold-blooded killer who's heartless, but he respects the laws that govern nature. He cares about order; everyone and everything has its place in the grand scheme of things.

The doctor is an exception because he managed to tether between his existence as an immortal being and integrate with people that he feeds on to stay alive. He has solidified his place in society throughout the centuries by continuously working in the medical field. His granddaughter is the last known family he has in the world. His decision to change her; may seem selfish, but the intentions, however self-serving, comes from a good place.

Dr. German slowly poured the contents of the jar into Lt. Drakon's mouth. He rubbed her neck to coax the blood down her throat. The more blood her body absorbed, the more she'd heal. He continued slowly, pouring all the blood in her mouth until the entire container was empty. Not soon after she swallowed the last drop of blood, she opened her eyes.

"There you go, my little princess," Dr. German said.

"Ahem! Come on, Grandfather, I haven't been a princess or little for a very long time," she replied in a hoarse monotone voice.

As expected, Lt. Drakon tried to get up off the table, so he put his hand on her shoulder and said, "Stay down, Adeline; you're not strong enough yet. Just conserve your energy for now until I can get you out of here." Dr. German gingerly placed her head back down on the table, kissed her forehead, and ran his fingers through her hair. "You're in the ER, on an operating table. After trying their hardest to revive you with no response or vital signs, you were pronounced dead. As we speak, I am waiting for the paper to take you with me to the morgue.

"How am I supposed to explain being alive after this, Grandfather?"

"Shh! Not to worry, I have a plan. Just lay down motionless for a while and rest. Close your eyes, and I'll take care of everything. Someone is coming, be still. It's the nurse with the paperwork for your transfer."

A beautiful curvy black nurse walked in and handed him the paperwork. "Here's the authorization of release from Dr. German. I'd like to give my condolences to you and your family. Lt. Drakon was the nicest, most delightful person I ever met; she had one of the better personalities as an officer that I had the pleasure of meeting. You did a good job raising her, and I, for one, am sorry to see her go."

"Thank you, nurse, hah…," Doctor German paused and tried to look at the nurse's name tag.

"Mavis Parnell," she said with a heavy Jamaican accent.

"Thank you, nurse Parnell."

The nurse turned and stepped out of the doorway to the operating room. Shortly after, two guys from his office came to pick up the body. They hoisted Lt. Drakon off the operating table, placed her in a body bag with all her belongings, and then zipped it up. The men walk through the hallway of the hospital to the M. E's van.

Her death took a toll on most people in the hospital. It was a somber one for everyone close to the situation. Some had mixed feelings; the rest were afraid. Some were sad because of having the tremendous pleasure of dealing with her.

A terrible fright ran rampant throughout the city; fear crept in and festered like cancer. The news of Lieutenant Drakon's death exacerbated the already fragile sense of security, not only for the people of Midtown Manhattan but for everyone in New York City. Everyone was on edge; police officers were dying left and right.

As two men rolled the stretcher out the hospital doors and put her body in the coroner van, the news of her death immediately spread out of the building.

Nurse Parnell snuck away and slipped into an empty room where she made a call.

A raspy, gruff male's voice answered on the other end. "Do you have something to tell me?"

"Lieutenant Drakon is dead; her body is going to the M. E's office as we speak," she replied.

"Good," the voice replied before he hung up.

Back at the Bone-Dry bar, Captain Constantine and agent Henning exited the bar immediately after the dropped call from Joy Maxwell. In hopes that they could get a trace on the call as a lead to find her location, but outside the bar, they were greeted by flashing lights and media questioning.

"Captain!" "Captain!" exclaimed a reporter. "Is this incident somehow related to the attack made on your precinct?"

"No, why would you make that distinction?" the captain asked. "Do you know something I don't?"

"Now, if you excuse us, no further questions," agent Henning calmly replied.

The two men walked across the street to the police hub as the reporters continued to shout at them with a barrage of questions.

"How many victims were there?" a reporter from channel five asked.

"Was this the work of the *Sanguine killer*?" asked the channel seven news reporter.

"When do the people of the city have to worry about their safety?" asked a reporter from the local newspaper.

"Do you have any suspects yet?" asked the channel two news reporter.

While inside the police hub, the captain wasted no time getting a trace on the call from Joy. "Agent Henning here; take the lieutenant's phone and see if you can put a trace on the last call. I'll handle the reporters," captain Constantine said and walked back outside and made a statement with the reporters.

"Let's get this straight, fear is something that we all have to deal with, no matter what side of the law you fall on. Fear is an

270

emotion you can't escape, whether in law enforcement, civilian, or criminal. You can rest assured that we're charging the streets hard, leaving no rock unturned. I promise the citizens of Midtown Manhattan that we will apprehend all perpetrators involved in these heinous crimes."

"Captain, are all these crimes somehow connected?" One reporter asked.

"This is an ongoing investigation, but as of right now, there is no evidence so far to say that they are connected," replied the captain.

"The confidence that you exude is not the same confidence that the people of midtown have, I'm sorry, but how can you say that the murders aren't connected, Captain. I mean, let's be honest, cops are the ones being slaughtered here in Midtown, mostly victims out of your precinct. How can you make such an assurance that you will put an end to these heinous crimes against the citizens here in Midtown when you can't even keep the police safe?" a male reporter asked.

"To answer your question, yes, the murder rate is unusually high in addition to the usual murders we have been experiencing. And yes, what everyone is speculating is correct; there's a serial killer out there whose work is not exclusive to civilians—"

"Captain...Captain! Are the Midtown Murders somehow tied to the Sanguine Killer's?" screamed several reporters and raised their tape recorders in the air.

"Listen, we have not differentiated these attacks with the known *Sanguine Killer's* attacks or just isolated incidents. Anybody with any information, I urge you to come forward. Next question!"

"Well, what are you doing differently to catch this menace?" a reporter for the Village Gleaner asked.

The captain put his head down, scratched his forehead, chuckled, and said, "Well, we have formed a joint task force consisting of local police and the FBI; as of today, we're all victims, law enforcement and civilians alike. I am not at liberty to discuss our tactics at this present time—no more questions. I must get back to the case."

The captain stepped away from the media, and his cell phone buzzed in the left pocket of his trench coat. He took it out to read the text, and everyone else's cell phone buzzed, chimed, and clicked simultaneously. Much to their chagrined, a chain text (spam) was sent out to everyone in a six-block radius of the Bone-Dry bar, and it read: *"One day, all have to answer for their sins. My mission is accomplished; another one fell victim, the law zero, and I eleven. Don't forget that I have the newswoman aloft in a tower."*

The reporters outside went into a frenzy over the anonymous message.

"Did anyone else receive a text message?" asked the captain as he marched inside the police hub.

"Yes, Captain, we all received the same text," the S.W.A.T sergeant replied.

"Can we put a trace on it?"

"I'm already on it, Captain," a police officer from the tech department answered.

"Good! What about the search on the call that came from Joy Maxwell?"

"We traced it and didn't find anything viable that we can use, Captain. The call was made using an internet app, which is harder to pinpoint than a direct phone call. I need some more time Capt., there's one thing that I can tell you that the call came from a closed network."

"What does that mean?" he asked and raised his hands.

"Captain, it means that he found out that the call is not on a shared public network. It's not like the one we use every day," agent Henning commented.

"So, that's great, isn't it? So, you can trace it back to the main server?" the captain asked.

"One would think so, but the signal is encrypted purposefully and bounces all over the place. If I can get beyond the scrambled signal, I would be able to break through the firewall. With this equipment here, it would be virtually impossible. I need my computer back at the station and some time," the tech guy replied.

"Good work, officer, whatever you need–just hurry up and keep in mind Ms. Maxwell is running out of time," the captain replied and opened the door. "Okay, people, let's wrap everything up here. The crime scene unit is processing the evidence at Bone Dry Bar.

"Agent Henning, come with me. Joy Maxwell is high above the city in solitude. She is a prisoner, locked away in some plush penthouse. We must get to her before they kill her too."

The captain rushed through the door, and before it closed, agent Henning was right behind him.

"Damn, stupid wi-fi," Joy said and put the phone on the nightstand. "I bet someone's watching my every move–Why don't you just kill me already!" She put her hands on her head and shuffled them back and forth rapidly through her hair.

"What are you doing, Joy Maxwell? If they have cameras in here, they won't be equipped with audio," She thought to herself, plopped on the bed, and screamed into the pillow.

On her in another part of the building, there's a minion from the brood, watching the closed-circuit feed from the surveillance of the penthouse.

The stranger opened the door of the room, where he positioned someone to watch Joy. "How is she?" he asked.

His footmen's voice cracked under pressure, and he nervously said, "She made a call, Sir."

"What do you mean she made a call?" asked the stranger, then he slapped the messenger across the face. "Can you tell me who she called? Don't answer that. How was she able to make a call in the first place?"

"She downloaded a browser on the television using the Wi-Fi and made a called via the internet," the messenger replied and rubbed his cheek. "I can't hear anything in the penthouse, and the camera is situated in a spot where I was unable to see the television screen. This wasn't my fault, Sir. There's no way that I could help it, but what I did was turn off the wi-fi and disconnected the call the moment I discovered what she'd done."

"Ok good, is there any way that you could find out whom she made the call to?"

"No, sir!"

"That's fine, and I'll take care of the blind spots tonight. Just calm down and relax. If you had a heart, I would've heard it pounding through your chest," the stranger said as he squeezed his shoulder. "You told the truth, so I don't have to kill you."

Meanwhile, at the M. E's office, Dr. German and Adeline were in an autopsy room alone talking. "I'm sorry, Adaline, I've come to terms with the idea that you'll hate me forever due to your sudden transformation," he said. "I made a choice, and I decided to save your life again by giving you blood to drink. I recognize how adamant your concerns are about ingesting blood from another human—"

"It's okay Grandfather, I had to take a little of agent Woo's blood for sustenance before you gave me more blood, so I forgive you," she said. Lt. Drakon attempted to sit up, but she grimaced and moaned from the agonizing pain. "I thought that drinking agent Woo's blood would heal me? Do we need to take only human blood?"

"Yes, and no. Feeding does help you heal quickly, though. There are a couple of things you need to be aware of for the next time you feed. This may not make sense to you now, but what I'm going to reveal to you will make sense in due time." Dr. German took her hand and put it right to his chest. "Adeline, if you do decide to drink blood, first things first, you're technically dead. All vampires are."

Lt. Drakon spread her fingers on his bare chest, then she hastily pulled her hand away when she didn't feel anything. She put her hands on her chest and felt the emptiness beneath her bosom.

The experience was bone-chilling. "I don't have a heartbeat! Then, how are we— how do we—"

"My dear Childe, I will explain the reason why the undead walk the earth–most stories about the supernatural are based on reality—"

"Wait a minute, do you mean all the monsters in books are real?"

"Yes, some are real. Why else do you think the stories are called legends. I will explain later in due time, my Childe. Everything will reveal itself soon what I will say that the reason we exist is supernatural and is a bit harder to explain to you here and now.

"There are so many legends swirling around out there about the origins of vampires: from the curse of Lilith, Judas Iscariot, to the Egyptian God of chaos Set. There's even the fable of Ponce

Deleon and the fountain of youth causing our virtue of immortality," he detailed. "One could argue about how this began, but the only thing that's for sure is we no longer possess a soul.

"Vampires doesn't have a spirit to speak of anymore, that puts us out of God's favour, and apparently out of the devil's eye as well. Vampires are immortal because there is no one to redeem our souls."

"But you raised me as Christian!" Lt. Drakon giggled and raised her hands in the air. "So, what now, Grandfather, should I just toss everything I ever believed in out the window?"

"That won't be necessary, I have a theory about how we can become mortal again, but we can talk about that later. Although vampires can't die of old age, we need to drink blood to remain animated, or we can shrivel up like a dry plant. The amount of blood that we drink does make a difference. The more we consume, the better we are.

Adeline, you found that out first-hand. The rule of thumb is to consume blood from someone who's still alive. That is where the life force flows."

"Therefore, we have no heartbeat; when we ingest someone's blood, we take in a piece of some else's soul for a short time. It's starting to make sense now. That's why I didn't heal; agent Woo was already dead."

"Correct, from what I have seen, you did not get enough to help you–here take some of this."

Dr. German gave her some more blood from an IV bag that he squeezed in a coffee mug for Lt. Drakon.

"I have a few more questions. why are our entire eyes black when we change?" she asked and took a sip from the mug. "Why do we have superhuman abilities, like hypersensitive hearing?"

"Simple, you're a predator now, the eyes are not black so much as your pupils are more dilated, and the hearing developed to hear the strongest heart. The stronger the heartbeat, the stronger the life force. We're surviving off borrowed time. The more blood we drink, the longer we live."

"Now, Adeline, are you going to tell me what happened in the bar?" Dr. German asked.

"Yes, the situation was not exactly what I expected; it was agent Woo who held up the bar. I don't know; what he described was kind of odd, though. Then again, nothing in this world surprises me anymore, not since learning about the world of undead vampires and such," she said and drained the mug. "What agent Woo told me makes a little more sense now that I think about it."

"What did he tell you?"

"He said that the people in the bar were drinking blood from one another."

"He witnessed *Pity party*."

"A what?"

"It's when vampires aid in an assisted suicide. It's a prevalent and lucrative business in the vampire community."

"Who's policing the vampires and the rest of the undead?"

Dr. German smiled and said, "That's a good question. The answers you seek will be revealed to you in due time."

"So, answer this question, Grandfather, so mean to tell me that people who are suicidal or terminally ill take out ads in some vampire circular requesting aide to commit suicide or does vampires take out one offering their services?"

"I don't understand the question," Dr. German said.

"Come on, Grandfather, you know what I am talking about,"

Lt. Drakon replied.

"Oh, humans answer an ad in the newspapers promoting vampire covens. Nowadays, an invitation is probably sent through Craigslist or a website that somebody's set up, and people terminally ill or considering suicide answer the ad. They then show up at a predetermined location, where the vampires—you know."

Dr. German's expression changed as he daydreamed about the days when he attended those parties himself. He reminisced about sucking out all the warm blood from his victims and how their heat made him feel like a new person. He cleared his throat and said, "Once drained, the corpses would be sold illegally to various universities for science at a high cost. Sometimes we made thousands on one deal.

"With these kinds of parties, there must have been a facilitator."

"Yes, there was."

Adeline guzzled the rest of the IV bag. The bullet wounds finally healed on their own, right before her eyes. As soon as they got better, Dr. German dressed the area to show people something; evidence that she had been shot.

"With all the talking, I've noticed that you failed to tell me what happened in there."

"We don't have time for a long story right now. I have to get back in the streets."

"Come on; we have time for a short one."

Back to full strength, she jumped off the autopsy table. "Do you have anything for me to wear, grandfather?" she asked.

"Yes, I do; look over there in my desk. I think I have something in there for you," he replied.

"Good, these clothes are tattered, to say the least!" Lt. Drakon moved toward her grandfather's desk. She opened the draw and took out a shirt to wear. "Do you know what the main issue that I have with this whole situation?"

"What's that, my Childe," Dr. German asked and anticipated that she would blame him for saving her life.

"All this time vampires existed in the world, I have never seen or heard of one until my change. Now, I find myself in the middle of all this, and I don't know why for the life of me. Mr. Night at the bar mentioned to me that you'd know the reason."

Adeline distended with mixed emotions, being careful not to let it be known that she knew answers to many of her questions, at least not before he gave her something she can use to solve this puzzle. She attempted to wrangle the story without leading her down this rabbit hole. Details that may have nothing to do with her.

"I feel as though a war had been brewing for centuries, a rift between vampires, the undead, blood demons that had nothing to do with mankind," she expressed. Lt. Drakon straightened out the shirt and approached her grandfather closely. "I've known you for a good portion of my life, grandfather, I know you, and I know that everything you come from a good place. You have a good heart, even if it hasn't pumped once in centuries."

The doctor remained silent as she spoke candidly.

"Come on, tell me something, you can give me something, help me to make sense of all of this. Time for secrets is over. You must tell me what you know about the theme and their planning because I have the strange feeling something big will happen. If you know what it is, tell me, please."

Dr. German starred into his granddaughter's eyes and remained stoic.

"Five men attacked me, you could've let me die, but you didn't. You infected me with this dark disease. It must've been for a special reason," she said.

"When I saved you, I did it to protect you," he replied.

"Right, but why did you do it? Why did you save me?"

"I never meant to cause you no pain, Adeline..."

"But you did because the curse coursing through my veins is the source for all my pain."

Lt. Drakon pinched the skin on her forearm. "Wait a minute, and you said that you saved me; this is a death sentence."

"J...just hear me out—" Doctor German stammered, then his phone rang. "Saved by the bell," he thought to himself. "Hello, Captain, how can I help you?"

"No, no, Doctor, I'm calling to give my condolences," the captain replied.

"There is no need, Captain."

Lt. Drakon snuggled up next to him and listened in on the conversation between her mentor and her grandfather. Doctor German put Captain Constantine on speaker. "How so, I got some disparaging news about your granddaughter. I heard from a reporter that Adeline had succumbed to her bullet wounds and passed away. So, I am calling to lend my condolences at your time of loss." The captain paused and momentarily fought back his emotions.

"I've known Adeline for over twenty years now; I remember when she was fresh out of the academy. She was the best cadet on the force. She was dedicated and honorable. She was a good friend; even more so, she was like family to me."

"Thanks, Captain. I will remember that the next time you call me into your office," Lt. Drakon said.

"You're alive! B...but I heard—" the captain stammered. "I'll explain later."

"She stepped away from the phone and searched through the bag of her belongings. "Where's my phone?" she said, rummaging through the bag.

"I'll meet you at the station, Lieutenant."

"Yeah, Captain, don't tell anyone yet."

"Well, I think there might be a revision to the request because agent Henning is right here."

"That's fine, I was looking for my phone to call him next, but I can't seem to find it."

"That's because I have it here with me, we got a call from Joy Maxwell, and we've been trying to trace the call ever since," the captain said.

"Perfect! I'm on my way, and you can fill me in when I get there," Lt. Drakon replied. "Oh, and Captain, I didn't know you cared so much about me. It's a shame how people have to die before you find out how much people care about you."

She smiled mumbles aloud. "How beautiful is the simplicity of expression. Captain, I'm on my way." She pressed the end button and disconnected the call.

Embarrassed, the captain laughed and looked at the phone. He turned to agent Henning, who overheard the exchange. He looked close to see if the agent noticed his discomfort. Not just that, but also if he may have sensed the slight change in Lt. Drakon's voice.

Agent Henning stood there with a mini smirk on his face, gitty like a love-sick teenager. He didn't seem perturbed about the news of Lt. Drakon's miraculous survival. If he did, he played it off quite well.

The captain sensed the difference in her voice. The death tone of a blood demon, he'd recognized that tone anywhere.

The stress she used resonated a spirit he heard with his former affiliates—the ones from which he desperately tried to keep his distance. "I wonder if I could continue to trust her. I guess I'll find out when she gets here," he thought to himself.

Lt. Drakon rushed to leave out the door. She stopped at the doorway and said, "Can we be hurt or killed by the sun, silver, holy water, or any of the other myriad of sorts, said to be useful in taking down a vampire?" She swallowed hard, choking on her words.

"No, we're immortal," Dr. German replied. "My dear Childe, most of that stuff would never work, of course, except for the obvious ones: A stake through the heart may be, getting your head chopped off possibly. I for sure can't come back from a beheading," he said and raised his eyebrows. "But garlic is a lot more complicated; that does something to us."

"Garlic, why garlic?"

"The blood demon curse is why. Garlic burns us, but not on contact like in the movies. It somehow chemically reacts on contact with bodily fluids."

The older man walked closer to Lt. Drakon, the last of his bloodline, to emphasize the importance of his words. He drew near to her and spoke in a stern tone, balled up with care and concern in his voice. "Vampires are allergic to garlic; it slows down our healing process. If garlic enters your body somehow, you will die a slow, painful death, so, be careful."

She sighed and said, "We all have to go someday. Even immortals can't live forever. As soon as I get back, I want to talk more about what you know because you still haven't answered my question." Then she exited the examiner's room, walked down the hall to the elevator.

"Did you hear what I said, Adeline!" Dr. German raised his voice down the corridor.

Lt. Drakon jumped on the elevator and thought about what her grandfather did for her. "He did what any parent would do. He played the cards that he was dealt with." Knowing that Dr. German would genuinely do anything for her actions gave her solace. She felt relieved; the burden that she once felt about being a vampire slowly went away. She excepted her fate and decided to forgive him even though he's not forthcoming. She couldn't put a finger on it, but she felt he had a secret or two. Secretive and dysfunctional as he may be, her grandfather loves her more than immortality itself.

As the elevator door closed, Lt. Drakon whimpered, "I'll be fine, Grandfather."

Chapter 11

Locked away in a luxury cell, Joy Maxwell sat down on the edge of the bed, wondering how she got into this mess. Deep in her thoughts, she pondered on what she could have done to get this negative attention. "Maybe it was a piece I did," she said to herself.

While she was going through every little detail in her head, Joy started to come up with something that would get her out of this plush tower of confinement. She devised a plan of how to escape her jail, high aloft a New York skyscraper. She made several failed attempts to contact the outside world– she decided that it would get out, she must go lo-tech.

Joy stood in front of the enormous windows overlooking the city. A drone flew high above the city landscape. She saw her opportunity to ask for help. She remembered from one of her stories that many drones have cameras attached to them. She rushed to search through her penthouse prison for things she could use to make a sign. "I hope this works; there's a chance that thing may be recording," she said.

Joy checked every square inch for items she could use. She checked every draw, cabinet, and crevice of the penthouse; her search turned up nothing.

The minion kept a watchful eye over Joy; he monitored her every move. Her strange behavior prompted him to make a call.

Joy couldn't find anything, not a pen, a pencil, or a crayon. She thought to herself, "I did have condiments and toothpaste." She checked the bathroom. "Colgate, perfect!" she said to herself.

Joy faced the full-length body mirror, being extremely careful not to expose her hand. During her search for something to write with, she found a few of their hidden cameras. She worked out the plan in her head; she opened her robe and then wrote, help me on her naked body, which would grab some attention quickly.

"Joy Maxwell, let's hope all of those Tae-Bo classes paid off!"

Joy tried to hide her actions from the man watching her, but he jotted down documented her suspicious behavior for his boss, The stranger.

"It's now or never," she said to herself.

Joy tiptoed towards the penthouse office window in the living room to display her S.O.S scribbled all over her chest.

The stranger entered the security room, where he kept tabs on the young reporter.

"What was so important?" asked the stranger. "I was in the middle of an important business matter." The stranger came in while Joy stood in front of the mirror.

"I believe she is going to try something else, Sir," the messenger replied. "I believe that she's trying another escape. I am not entirely sure, but I didn't want to take the chance. I was wrong before, so I'd rather err on the side of caution."

The stranger looked over the scratch paper where the messenger documented Joy's movements and erratic behavior.

The guard pointed to the monitor and said, "See, look at her now!"

Even though the stranger couldn't make out what Joy was doing, nor what she had in her hand, it looked suspicious.

Joy heard the buzzing and whirling of the drone's propellers outside of the window. She stood in the living room in her birthday suit, bare as the day she was born. She didn't get the attention that she had hoped to receive. Peering out at the building across the street, she caught a glimpse of the man flying the drone. What she saw crushed all hopes that her plan would work; when her would-be hero embraced and kissed another man.

The stranger couldn't figure out precisely what Joy was doing, so he quickly made his way up the stairs to the penthouse. Even with superhuman speed, he couldn't get to her before she exposed herself.

The stranger burst in the door directly in his line of sight was her bare ass. The reflection of her nude body through the window didn't arouse him like he may have thought. He wrapped his arms around Joy and shielded the view of her starkness from prying eyes.

"By the grace of the Blood Demon King, what are you doing?" he said and yanked her away from the window.

Joy deflated like a flat tire as her last-ditch attempt to be freed slipped through her fingers.

The stranger admired Joy's angelic face, being extra careful not to disturb his tender morsel. He approached her like she was the delicate petals on a flower. Observing how broken and distraught she was, tugged on what's left of his heartstrings. If he had an ounce of humanity left in his damned husk of a vessel, it went out for her.

Joy's natural allure strengthened his unnatural infatuations for her tenfold since she's been in the penthouse. As an elder, he warrants complete obedience from his followers, so he must lead by example. "Show some discipline. You can't show any sign of weakness–keep your distance from her," he thought to himself. "Here, put this on," he said, and he raised the robe bunched up around her ankles. "Ahem, being cursed, I have no curiosity about death, no war with morality to steer my actions nor conscience to sway my decisions. I am free from the bonds of fear that plagues all complex beings." He escorted Joy into the room then sat her on the bed.

Joy lifted her head and decided to engage the dark soul.

"You're not free as you say, everyone has a drive or a purpose, and you're not so different, stranger," she said.

"Yes, but every decision I make, I choose Childe– with a clear head, I do what I want. While I may follow instructions, now it is not guided by fear or some sense of obligation.

"A higher power or instinct controls all beings. What makes you so different?"

The stranger exhaled and turned away from Joy. He walked toward the window and closed the blinds so he could focus.

"What guides you then?" Joy asked, feeling an irresistible need to fill the silence between them.

The stranger remained silent for a moment then starred upon her face. Her eyes beckoned him like the allure of kindling embers from moths. His words rolled off his tongue like the water of the back of a mallard in a shallow pond. "What am I guided by?" he replied as he stood abreast with his hands folded behind his back. "If you must know, happiness guides me. You, humans, spend too much time worrying about everything else in life, except for the most important."

"Oh yeah, what makes you happy?"

Joy slightly let her guard down. For a moment, she forgot that the brut kidnapped her. She couldn't pinpoint what it was about him, but one thing was for sure– she's drawn in by his magnetism; his drab exterior was a farce. She didn't see a beast or the soul-sucking demon as he stood before her, but a small measure of the man he once was many years ago.

"It's inconsequential at this point of what makes me happy," he said. "What's more important is the essentials. What's significant is the inherent need for survival–everything else was gratuitous nonsense. Every day we rise from our slumber, searching for shiny trinkets, riches, and fame. But for most people, it eludes them.

So, what you should be worried about is your life and the

length of time you must live it, Ms. Maxwell."

"Then why won't you let me go, huh? That would make me happy." Joy smiled and batted her eyes.

The sight of her smile angered him. The blood demon's attitude changed as he flipped his claws out like a switchblade. He suddenly reverted into his gruffness; he viewed his actions as a sign of weakness because he wasn't in control of the situation. Joy had a spell on him, and he couldn't risk exposing his attraction for her. Embarrassed by his momentary lapse of judgment, he quickly changed the subject. "Nothing would make me more elated than to sink my teeth into your soft flesh," he replied. "I've held back my desire to drain every drop of blood out of your body because you have something I need!"

The stranger used his supernatural powers on the young reporter. His vampire charm put Joy in a trance and kept her there well after his mood changed from warm to cold. He interrogated and probed the poor woman's mind for the answers he desperately needed. He showed her kindness then exposed his fangs like a serpent. His action reinforced the notion that vampires can't be trusted.

Joy aimlessly sought to appease her captor, "What is it you want?" she asked with a blank stare.

The stranger couldn't bear to see Joy in a zombie-like state, so he snapped his fingers to release her from the trance. She rubbed her eyes and refocused her glare upon him. She was totally under his control, even without being hypnotized. She was smitten, and no matter what he did, she saw the goodness and kindness in him. He inched in closer and gently wrapped all five fingers around her face with the tips of his fingernails. "I have been looking for a tape," he replied.

Joy shrugged her shoulders and said, "What tape, my king?"

She had lost all sense of reality. She sincerely had no idea of what he was asking of her. It dawned on him that she hadn't looked at the recording of his father at the dog show.

"Do you remember the piece you did on the dog show?"

Joy tried hard to think back on what she may have seen–if anything, the day of the dog show. Not in her right mind, she was under the spell of the blood demon's powers; a warm attraction, a feeling filled her up inside. She took off her robe, stood up, jumped, and wrapped her legs around his torso.

Although the stranger wanted Joy, he didn't want her while she was under the influence of his charms. He had underestimated his power of persuasion, which was out of his control.

Across town, Lt. Drakon rode down the elevator to the lobby of the medical examiner's office, armed with knowledge about herself and her new abilities. She thought about her transition, her relationship with agent Henning and the calculated decisions that she had to make. "I won't tell him about what I've become," she whispered to herself. "Life is not fair."

The elevator door opened, and Lt. Drakon spotted agent Henning walking to the car. Her heart sank because she cared for him. But she must make a difficult decision – a choice that would break not only his heart but hers as well. Only if her heart hadn't already stopped–it would've indeed broken. She took a shallow breath into her shrunken dead lungs, opened the door, and get inside the car. "We need to talk," she uttered the words every man dreaded hearing. His smile immediately turned upside down.

"W…what do we need to talk about, Adaline?" agent Henning asked.

"Something strange happened to me at the Bone-Dry-Bar. I'm not at liberty to divulge anything further-just know that if we continue seeing each other… one of us will get hurt." She looked at him and put her hand over his.

Agent Henning motioned his mouth to respond to the devastating news, but he sat there and quietly held her hand.

An FBI agent on the task force knocked on captain Constantine's office door.

"Hold on a minute," he said, covering the mouthpiece on the phone, "I'm on the phone!" He squinted and peered over his reading glasses. Who is it?"

"It's special agent Marlon Waite, Sir—just give me five minutes of your time," he replied. "Captain, you might want to hear this. It is a possible break in the case."

The captain put his mouth over the receiver and said, "Mayor, I'll call you back." He waved agent Waite to come inside.

After agent Waite entered, he handed the captain a cup of coffee.

"Thanks, please take a seat. It had better be good; I just hung up on the mayor." the captain said and tugged on his vest as he stood up to greet the approaching agent.

The federal agent stepped into the office, looking like a typical FBI analyst. He stood in front of the captain's desk and handed a file to him.

"Have a seat, agent Waite."

"That's okay Captain, I'll stand, but you need to peek at this."

"What am I looking at here?" The captain opened the file scanning the content.

"That Captain is the results of agent Gooseburg's inquiry before he passed."

"Is there solid proof?"

"Yes, it's airtight. My men double-checked their findings before they filed them. Those items listed were purchased from a secret account in the Cayman Islands under a dummy company. Agent Gooseberg was the only one who had access."

"Why did this take so long to come back?" The captain said while perused through the file. He saw the name Bobby Richard and raised his eyebrows.

"Well, the investigation took a lot of twists and turns. The culprits involved tried to hide those transactions. Plus, I had to tread lightly because of his status."

"We anticipated that this investigation was going be tricky; after all, we're going after one of the biggest media moguls in the country."

"Your investigation has yielded fruit good enough to pick from the tree but not ripe enough to eat," The captain said. "What you have here is purely circumstantial evidence. We'll need more solid proof to lock him up. He's running for mayor of the city, for God's sake."

He slammed the file shut and pointed his finger at the federal agent. "He has high-powered attorneys, who are going help him weasel his way out of anything. We need sufficient incriminating evidence that could put him in a barrel and seal the lid. The rich have resources, which affords them options, they normally get away with anything, the filthy rich are like gods amongst men."

Agent Waite loosened his tie and took a sip from his cup of coffee and inched forward on the edge of his seat. "You're correct in your sentiments, but the basis of a conviction is in the interior of that file," agent Waite replied, reached over, and pointed his finger at the file on the captain's desk. "As far-fetched as it may sound, Captain, I want to find the ones responsible for the attack on your precinct as much as anyone. My colleague lost his life there too!"

"Who have you told about your findings?"

"No one yet."

"Good, don't tell anyone. I will bring the Chief, the DA, the Lt. Drakon, and agent Henning, up to speed. And if you don't mind, I'll hold on to the file." Constantine dragged the file into his draw.

"Yeah, sure, no problem, you can have that one, that's a copy. Discretion is paramount on this one, I know."

On his way out of Captain Constantine's office, special agent Waite passed agent Henning and Lt. Drakon. He pulled agent Henning aside and put his hand over his mouth, and said, "Sir, I know I was supposed to report to you first, but—"

"What is it, Marlon?" agent Henning asked and shook his hands out in front of him.

"You ordered us to keep local law enforcement abreast with all discoveries on this case, so that is what I did."

"Spit it out. What are you talking about?"

"I...it's nothing I can't handle. No worries, Sir, if there are any details difficult to ascertain during the colloquy with the captain—I'll check back with you with any concerns I may have."

Both agent Henning and Lt Drakon walked away from the exchange with agent Waite bewildered, not any more informed than before their encounter with the pudgy man.

"That guy's intelligence is off the charts, but he's incredibly strange," agent Henning said. He opened the door for Lt. Drakon, and she walked past him and stood in front of the captain's desk.

"I am glad you're ok Lieutenant, but you didn't have to come to work so soon. Take some time and take care of yourself first," the captain said.

"I am fine, Sir, no cause for concern. Besides, this case isn't going to solve itself," Lt. Drakon replied. She was confused as to how he didn't inquire about her miraculous recovery. She noticed the confusion in the eyes of everyone else, but he wasn't surprised at all.

"With sergeant Mason at large and Joy Maxwell still missing, I'd rather not. I am totally committed and fully in the game."

"You're really dedicated, Detective; I'll give you that—"

"The Lieutenant and past agent Waite outside your office, and he said that you have something for me–I'm sorry for us. Although he broke protocol going to you first—"

"Yes, he did, and I do," the captain replied and opened the draw to his big wooden desk. "Here, take a look." He slid the file to agent Henning and walked around to the front of his desk. He straightened out his vest and leaned up against it. "You see, it's the results of the investigation, on what the attacker may have used to avoid the cameras recording their face during the assault on the precinct."

"This is good news, Captain," agent Henning replied as he flipped through the file.

"Why don't you sound happy, Capt.?" Lt. Drakon asked.

"I should be but, look who's the suspect," the captain replied.

"Man! Isn't he running for mayor?" agent Henning remarked while flipping through the papers of the file.

"Wait, I've seen this symbol before," she said and snatched the paper out of the folder and ran out to her desk.

Lt. Drakon scrambled through her mess in search of the connection. "Where is it? Where is it?" she mumbled to herself.

"I know; I've seen this symbol someplace before," she said as she rummaged through everything on her desk. "Wish I could use my abilities to find what I'm looking for."

Agent Henning approached the frantic lieutenant and folded his arms across his chest.

"I know it's here somewhere!" she exclaimed.

"What are you looking for, Lieutenant? Maybe I can help?" asked agent Henning.

Lt. Drakon didn't respond to agent Henning. She ignored him and continued her search. She researched an open investigation before she was attacked, raped, and left for dead in Central Park. "I know that I'm on to something here; maybe I got too close before, and that's why Sgt. Mason and his cronies tried to silence her," she thought to herself.

"It has to be the same criminal entity which not only attacked me but also assaulted the precinct, killing several police officers, an FBI agent and freed a callous murderous killer from police custody," she thought to herself. "Whomever these monsters are, they have no boundaries and no limitations. If they have a billionaire media giant behind all this, what chance do we as law enforcement have at bringing them to justice?"

In a perfect world, justice is blind, and nobody's above the law, no matter how connected one may be. But being in law enforcement for almost twenty years, Lt. Drakon knew better and seen worst. "Got it! I found it," she exclaimed and pulled out a manila folder from the back of her bottom drawer. She scrolled through the folder, stopped, took out a sheet of paper then compared the symbols between her file and the document she ripped out of the other one.

"See, I knew I saw this symbol before," she said and handed the file over to the agent Henning. "The dummy company was the same too."

They both looked at each other and rushed into the captain's office.

"Captain, these people have been hiding in plain sight for a very long time," Lt. Drakon said and showed him her findings.

"What was this investigation on?" asked the captain. "Can you tell me who's—?"

"Was this the last case you were working on before… you were assaulted?" agent Henning asked.

"Ahem, yes," she replied. "This is the case where the chief administration officer died with seemingly normal causes—"

"You, on the other hand, believed his death was within the purview of this department," the captain said. "You convinced me back then. I trusted your analysis that he was murdered. I gave the green light for a full investigation. I had another detective follow up on your case after your attack. I bet you he wished he had your notes to work on this."

"Sorry, but I looked, and I was right, Captain, opening a can of political bribery and corruption; I stumbled on this company. I didn't know at the time how it tied in all together, then again never got the chance to because they attacked me before I could connect the dots."

"Do you guys think he could be behind the *Midtown Murderers*?" agent Henning asked. "The *Sanguine Killer*, the assailants who hit your precinct, and Joy Maxwell kidnapping have to be all connected!"

"Maybe, we are going to have to prove it in the court of law agent Henning. We got to dot all i's, cross all t's, and wrap this case up in a tight little box with a bow on top for DA," the captain replied.

"So, Captain, what do you want the FBI to do? We were sent

down here by the mayor to take the lead, with the recent revelation that you guys couldn't make heads or tails of this case. Let's be honest; that's why you were targeted. So, this goes deeper than politics. It's personal. I am prepared to pull out all the stops with all the bureau's resources."

The captain slapped his hands together and said, "Alright, glad to hear it; let's go out and try to close this case once and for all. Excuse me; I need to make a call to the mayor's office. I imagine the mayor might be thrilled to hear about what we figured out; considering, one of his biggest rivals is the main suspect in this murder investigation. Oh yeah, by the way, agent Henning, you need to talk to your director and call the mayor as well. They've been trying to reach you for updates."

"I'm on it, Captain!" agent Henning replied.

He and Lt. Drakon turned around and opened the door to the captain's office.

The captain snapped his fingers at her and said, "Listen, Lieutenant, stay; I'd like to speak to you for a second."

Agent Henning made his way toward one of his agents. He had a hunch about the attack that day.

Agent Waite leaned back in his chair with his feet up on the desk, playing air drums with two pencils in his hands listening to music in his headphones.

Agent Henning walked up beside him and slapped the desk hard to grab his attention.

"Agent Waite, I need for you to cross-reference agent Gooseburg and any relationship he may have had with this company," agent Henning said, opened the file on his desk, and pointed at the company's name. "And while you're at it, consider the police officers too, okay."

"Why would you want me to consider local law enforcement?" agent Waite replied.

"Just do it, okay. My gut tells me there was something more to it than the hit on the precinct. Some things are starting to make sense, and others simply don't. So, I want to tie up loose ends. Put a rush on things, then shoot me a text with your findings."

Agent Henning stepped away from agent Waite's desk, took out his phone, and saw that he had a dozen missed calls. He scrolled through the call list and thought, "When they captured the suspect for the *Midtown Murders,* that just may have been a diversion to kill the officers involved. My gut says bribery and corruptions were the underline issues; so, we must follow the paper trail. Anywhere there's money, there's greed. These low lives very well may have hatched a plan to clean house all in the name of anonymity."

Agent Henning dialed back the mayor's office number when he spotted the lieutenant coming out of the captain's office. He gestured her to come over while the phone was ringing, "Hey, I have a hunch about something. I don't want you to get mad; once I tell you, don't breathe a word of this to anyone," he said.

"I promise to control my emotions. How can I promise not to get mad for information I haven't heard yet?" Lt. Drakon.

Agent Henning took a deep breath, hung up the phone, and exhaled when the mayor's voicemail answered. He hesitated before explaining to Lt. Drakon what path he was about to take to prove the CEO of SGNN is complicit. When he finished with his hailstorm of ideas, she exhaled heavily through her nostrils. Is she pissed off? I can't tell with her she doesn't ever show any emotions," he thought to himself.

Lt. Drakon couldn't find a good reason not to be angry; she was numb from all the sad songs and tragic stories swirling around this tragic case.

Although, the good officers she knew wouldn't be involved in any criminal activity anyway. But with recent events, especially all that has transpired within the last year, she couldn't put it past anyone.

"Okay fine, it's all good; what about Joy Maxwell?" she asked. "She's still out there somewhere—are we any closer on finding her?"

"No, but let's go down to tech support, and officer Mark Vickers will bring us up to speed. He and agent Waite has been working together around the clock on some leads. He told me to check back with you around this time today."

The two walked down to tech support and found his agent hard at work. "You got something for me, officer Vickers?" agent Henning asked.

"Yes, Sir, I do," agent Vickers replied. "Hey, Lt Drakon, I'm glad to see you're okay." He gave her the once over. His eyes wandered all over her body, looking for bullet wounds. He gave her a half-smile and said, "I heard the worst. I was told that you were riddled with bullets. How are you still standing?"

"Well, agent Waite, believe half of what you hear and none of what you see," she retorts.

A semi-scowl and a partial stamp of confusion paralyzed his face for a moment. "Alright, okay, but they said you were—"

"That's enough agent, how about you give me what you got." agent Henning said.

"Yeah, sure, anything, boss. Here is what I found, since only having a phone number to go off," he replied. "The only other information I had was Ms. Maxwell made the call via an email. So, I had contacted all the popular email providers your Yahoo, MSN, AOL, G-mail. Then I had to request the call logs from the specific providers, narrowing down the search during the specific time the call was made. I also cross-referenced them against the phone—"

"Wait a minute, hold on. How did you swing getting the call logs from these providers without a warrant?" Lt. Drakon asked and put her hand on the huge stack of call logs.

"Good question. Here's the thing because the number is not officially attached to a phone or headset or, for that matter, an individual. A warrant is not needed in this situation."

"Okay, hurry up, what did you find?" agent Henning asked.

"Yes, well, after discovering she used her Gmail account to call you, Lieutenant, everything else was easy."

"So, do you know where she is?"

"Yes," officer Vickers pointed at his monitor. "The call was generated somewhere from the top floors of this building. Once I match the IP address, it was able to pinpoint where the call was generated."

"Perfect, are you able to pinpoint what apartment?" asked Lt. Drakon. "We don't want to go around knocking on doors alerting the wretched kidnappers of our presence."

Officer Vickers faced agent Henning seated in a swivel chair, so he spun his chair around to the computer screen. "No, I was not able to locate the exact floor because two floors seem to be on the same network. So, I need to investigate a little further, Boss."

"That's good investigative work, Agent."

"No problem," I'll have the information you need shortly." officer Vickers said and pointed at blueprints he pulled from the city records.

"Is this who owns the building?" Lt. Drakon asked and pointed at the signature at the bottom of the screen.

"No, she's the architect," he replied. With a couple of clicks on his mouse, they were able to look at the deed. He then zoomed in and magnified the document superimposing the owner's name across the screen. "Hey, isn't that the media mogul who's running for mayor?" he said, but when he looked up, agent Henning and Lt. Drakon were already gone.

Agent Henning took out his phone and said, "Adeline, tell the captain that we've narrowed down Ms. Maxwell's location. I will call the US attorney's office for a warrant to search the place."

Agent Henning and Lt. Drakon walked away from each other as he made a call on his cell phone. She headed towards the captain's office to inform him about the latest development.

Lt. Drakon felt good how she and agent Henning were finally on the right track. The only thing that haunted her was Sgt Mason's involvement in everything. "Mr. Night is free as a bird, out in the world causing havoc, reaping fruit from the evil they planted in the world," she said to herself. "First thing first, the needs of those that I am sworn to serve and protect comes before my own."

Lt. Drakon put her duties as a detective above all else. Despite her growing predatory impetuous instincts to kill, she planned to continue to choose the right side of the line. With her head and heart on the same track, she followed her wilful path to gather the task force together, updating them on the recent developments.

Chapter 12

Frustrated and irritated about being so close to fulfilling his political ambitions by obtaining a seat in office. Bobby Richardson was in pursuit of his demonic plans for the entire world to bear witness. But an obstacle endangered his effort of he and his kind emerging from the shadows into the light.

Alone, high aloft in his cold office, he sometimes referred to it as his "War room." The elder blood demon and CEO of the multimedia conglomerate SGNN (Sera Global News Network) pondered the recent actions to step out of the shadows. He revealed the existence of vampires in the world, then eventually ruling over their food source. "Every other animal in the animal kingdom predominately reign supreme when they're atop the food chain," he thought to himself, scoffed, and turned up his nose while looking out a huge, tinted office window peering over the city.

"We've been forsaken and damned by God throughout the centuries. Hell, we're even shunned by the fallen angel, the morning star–Lucifer himself. We stand alone, condemned to roam the earth until the end of time." He stood there with his hands akimbo, surrounded by banners, buttons, and posters for his mayoral campaign. He sipped on a goblet of warm blood harvested from an unsuspecting streetwalker, which no one will miss.

His cell phone rang and vibrated on his desk. It echoed in the enormous medieval office. Effortlessly he glided toward the telephone like a thief in the night. The stranger's number was displayed across his caller id. He pressed the talk button and said, "Did you get the tape? I don't need to tell you how important this is for the cause."

Joy shuffled and squirmed in the background. "No, father, there were unforeseen circumstances out of my control that I had to contend with," the stranger replied in a tone of despair.

"Why is she still alive?" Mr. Richardson replied. "Kill her! Don't do it in the usual manner. Make it look like an accident this time. I don't want any blowback from this. An investigation is the last thing I need, so close to the election. If you screw this up…" He disconnected the call.

The stranger kept Joy in the penthouse of this luxurious citadel several New York City blocks from SGNN headquarters. A tower in the middle of town stood among the city's high-rises, mixed in New York's skyline.

Mr. Richardson took out the battery then crushed the cell phone in his hands; it crumbled into dust. He dusted his hands off in the wastepaper basket next to his desk. He opened a draw then took out another cell phone.

Shortly after, Lt. Drakon and agent Henning passed the receptionist right into the CEO's office.

"Mr. Bobby Richardson," agent Henning beckoned after both he and Lt. Drakon flashed their badges. "Put your hands behind your back. We have a warrant for your arrest."

Lt. Drakon pulled a shiny pair of handcuffs and walked up to Mr. Richardson.

"You can't believe I had anything to do with whatever it is you're accusing me of," Mr. Richardson replied. "I am a candidate for New York City mayor's office, for God's sake."

"Save it, we have a warrant for your arrest, and we are taking you down to the precinct for questioning," she said.

Lt. Drakon put his right arm behind his back. "I bet you're a strong one."

She put the cuffs on his wrist and pushed his arm up the center of his back.

"Ouch…look, I will cooperate with whatever you need from

me, and I will come down for questioning," he replied and grimaced. "I have nothing to hide."

Lt. Drakon grabbed the other hand and overlapped it with the other behind his back. She clicked the cuffs on tight and read him his Miranda rights: "You have the right to remain silent. Anything you say can and will be used against you in the court of law. You have the right to an attorney. If you can't afford one, the worst lawyer will be appointed to you by the state.

"Do you understand the rights that have read to you?" Agent Henning smiled as she cuffed the CEO of SGNN.

"Are the bracelets necessary?" Mr. Richardson said. "As you can see, I am not resisting. The last thing I want during my campaign is for the city to see me in handcuffs."

Lt. Drakon paused, stepped away, then took off the handcuffs and put them back on her belt–not because she felt sorry for him, but she recognized that he's a powerful elder and a strong vampire.

Although she wanted to bind and haul him into the precinct, she knows two things: One, he would get out if he wanted to. And two, she may not be strong enough to fight him one on one.

"Ok, we'll play along," agent Henning said, "If your try anything funny, I'll make sure that your next meal will be served to you in a mess hall on Pelican Bay."

Overconfident, he was careful with all his discretions. The media mogul willingly followed Lt. Drakon and agent Henning. A bevy of fully charged reporters and cameras gathered downstairs, awaiting their arrival.

Ready for the photo op, he embraced the rush from the propaganda goblins.

"Why are you being arrested?" a female reporter asked from his highest competing station.

"Does it look like I'm in handcuffs?" Mr. Richardson replied and threw his hands in the air and showed his bare wrist to the crowd.

"So, why are you being escorted by the police?" asked a male reporter. "It looks like you're being brought in for questioning."

"Are you a suspect or a witness?" several others shouted questions through the mayhem and chaos.

Mr. Richardson stopped and soaked up the attention from the murder of crows.

"As a mayoral candidate of this great city of ours, whatever the situation, I have no problem lending aid to the law enforcement in any way that I can," he said. "This must doubtingly have to deal with the brutal murders that were committed in this building several weeks ago."

The lieutenant opened the car door and eased the blood demon in the back and drove off.

"Nice play, Detective, well played!" Mr. Richardson exclaimed.

"Excuse me! Are you insinuating that we might have— calling the media is unethical, okay. Maybe one of your employees sold you out," agent Henning replied.

Lt. Drakon kept quiet the whole time because she was the one who alerted the media and tabloids. She retained many reporter's numbers over the years while on the force. A man of his stature wouldn't try anything in front of the cameras. She couldn't take any chances that he wouldn't try something drastic if they went there without the media present and arrested him. He had a reputation to uphold, running for mayor and all.

Several things rested heavily on her mind on her way to the station. "Can I go through with sending a vampire to prison?" she said to herself. "If there are any complications, God only knows what a catastrophe that would be."

The main issue was how Lt. Drakon would handle his arrest. Keeping it a secret was just as important as attaining justice for her fallen comrades. Torn by the duality of her sworn oath as a police officer and her immortal curse, she dreaded the choice.

Silence filled the car as they approached the station. A sea of reporters lined the street. A media circus awaited their arrival outside of the precinct. "Every news media outlet must be camped out there," she thought to herself. "Captain isn't going to be too thrilled about this." The lieutenant immediately regretted her actions. "At least the negative exposure would affect him in the polls."

Agent Henning made a sharp turn around the back of the police department to avoid the media frenzy out in front. He

entered the parking lot adjacent to the station.

"Let's go!" agent Henning demanded after he parked the car. What Lt. Drakon saw and felt was surprising. She didn't have to be a vampire to sense various feelings, good and bad. The powers of a blood demon awarded her with the gifts of detection, enabling the lieutenant to read emotions, something like a mood ring or like a lie detector. She recognized fear, contempt, elation, anger, joy, sadness, relief, etcetera from the other police officer. But for the life of her, she couldn't figure out why she got negative vibes and cold shoulders from her peers. But now, those things don't bother her anymore; more and more, she realized the only thing that mattered was making the right decision.

She embraced her blood demon attributes; they made her hard-edged without being callous. Those characteristics and the experience have given her a new insight into life, and she hopes they will make her a better cop.

The Lt. Drakon went into the captain's office and spoke to

him as soon as she entered. He quickly silenced her and made her aware that he was on the phone with the district attorney.

Agent Henning escorted Bobby Richardson into the interrogation room and left him in there alone. Then he stepped into the observation room. He examined every movement, every tick, and every tell. A technique sometimes used to watch a suspect see any signs of guilt.

The lieutenant, the captain, and the ADA entered the observation room one by one.

"I thought you would be halfway down his throat by now," Lt. Drakon cracked, then closed the door.

"No, not yet. I didn't want to start without you," agent Henning replied.

"What is your impression so far?" the captain inquired.

"So far, nothing, I can't get a good read on him, but I have a plan," agent Henning said. "I have been standing here for a short time, but in that time, I've made a quick assessment. I'm not a professional or anything, but he's overconfident, egotistical, calculated, complex, and a high-risk-taking individual by his demeanor. He's focused on the bottom line; the only thing that motivates him is results. He deems anything less as a complete waste of time. So, he will not be easy to trip up."

"So, what is your plan?" the ADA asked as he tilted his head back and folded his arms with his eyebrows furrowed. Skeptical about the case from the start, he's only interested in a case that he can win for the DA's office. He awaited hearing a terrible plan from the retiring FBI agent. "Before you answer that man is a model citizen, and he couldn't be involved with anything that you're accusing him with," he said and pointed at the two-way mirror and shook his head in disbelief. "I've known the man in there for almost twenty years–I…I can't believe it. He's a pillar of the community, a humanitarian and philanthropist—"

"Listen, you know well as I do that even with many years of thinking that you know someone; you can never truly know a person. So, with all due respect, we have evidence which points to your friend in there. This isn't an open and shut case by any stretch of the imagination, but we've indicted, taken to trial, and had convictions with less," captain Constantine bolstered.

You could've cut the tension in the observation room with a knife; emotions were riding high, and nobody interested in coming off their high horse.

"I need to ask you a question. Are you going to do your job?" agent Henning asked. "Don't answer that; I believe you are too emotionally involved; I think it would be best if you recuse yourself, considering you are incapable of being impartial."

Before the atmosphere got too hot, Lt. Drakon reigned the two bulls and said, "Okay! Okay! We need to focus on the man in the other room. We need to put our heads together before his lawyer comes, then everything stops. A young woman's life may lie in the balance. We have evidence that Joy Maxwell may be held up in a building that this man owns. As of right now, we must put our differences aside for God's sake. Agent Henning, what do you think is the best course of action here?"

"You're right. We need to save Ms. Maxwell, and time is of the essence," agent Henning replied and rubbed his chin. "Ok, follow my lead, he is results orientated, so the best way is to lay all we have on the table." Agent Henning gave the prosecutor a look as he held the door for Lt. Drakon.

Too many variables compound these scenarios swirling around in the lieutenant's head. She's considering committing a drastic act to retrieve information from the CEO of SGNN. He's the key to apprehending the *Sanguine killer*, rescuing Joy Maxwell, and so on.

Upon entering the interrogation room, Lt. Drakon hatched a plan in her head to get the old blood demon alone. The only thing she must figure out now is how.

Mr. Richardson was an elder vampire, so he sensed her metamorphosis when he met her in SGNN headquarters after the cameraman and executive's murder investigation. He knew then that she would soon be part of the vampire world. A blood demon could smell and otherwise sense one of their own like a primal beacon.

"He can't go to jail; the secret is bigger than her professional responsibility," she said to herself.

"I was beginning to think you guys forgot about me," the CEO quipped as they enter the room.

Lt. Drakon slammed the door and stared at Mr. Richardson as she pulled her chair away from the table and sat down. "No, I assure you we did not," she replied.

Agent Henning took a seat positioned on the opposite side of the table, putting himself in front of the monster. He stared intently in the eyes of the CEO of the largest media conglomerate in the world.

Lt. Drakon realized that the man they're looking at was not a man at all; he's a twelve hundred and sixty-three-year-old blood demon. An elder who has lived long enough to outplay a fifty-six-year-old, retiring FBI agent.

His presence didn't matter, which was very apparent from the beginning. The ancient creature didn't pay agent Henning any mind. He stayed fixated on the detective's buxom figure.

"I want to apologize for not cooperating with the police initially, considering we will be working with one another in the future," Mr. Richardson said. "I still don't know why I was brought down here in the first place. Please tell me what you're charging me with, so I can get back to my campaign. I'm a very important businessman, and my time is precious." The astute elitist sat there in a crisp expensive suit; the media billionaire points to an even more pricey timepiece. His outfit cost more than one year salary of Adeline and Henning combined.

"I highly doubt that you will be going anywhere, Mr. Richardson, not before going in front of a judge first," agent Henning replied and opened the case file with the evidence they have compiled against him. He ran off all the proof they had on him, but he might as well have been saying blah blah blah.

Mr. Richardson snickered and said, "You're new, right?"

Lt. Drakon immediately caught the reference and ignored the utterance. She didn't allow him to get into her head or get her off her game. "You know what? I am going to let you in on a little secret while you're busy ignoring agent Henning, thereby being highly disrespectful to my FBI counterpart," she said and slammed her hands on the table. "Have you noticed that you're entangled in the web of the criminal system now, Mr. Richardson?

"So, we are way beyond the time for the usual back forth, where we ask you a series of questions, again and again in different ways, in the hopes of trying to catch you in a lie. Where we are right now, we have you dead to rights. In this file, there is enough evidence here that catalogs your involvement with four counts of criminal activity." Adeline slowly slid the file over to him. "We got you on conspiracy to commit murder, assault a police station, bribery, and kidnapping."

Captain Constantine opened the door and called agent Henning and the ADA to follow him outside. To allow his lieutenant to get a one-on-one with their smug suspect, considering he has only responded to her.

Lt. Drakon figured he would deny every charge against him, which was fine because the first thing on her mind was getting Joy back. She considered that everyone that has been in the path of the "Sanguine Killer" died. The fact that she was still alive gave her hope that they would eventually rescue her.

"Don't you say another word, Mr. Richardson," a short bald man said, barged into the room and closed the door. "May I have a moment with my client, please, Lieutenant?"

"Who are you?" asked Lt. Drakon.

"I'm Bobby Richardson's attorney. So, if you don't mind, I would like to advise my client in private." He was dressed in a tailored Italian suit from head to toe. He stood about five foot six inches tall, medium build. "Mr. Richardson–don't answer any more questions. You have the right to remain silent. So, I'd advise you, as your legal counsel to do so now."

Lt. Drakon closed the file, got up from the table, and sauntered over to the door. "That's alright, counselor, he does have that option," she said as she held open the door.

Using a small amount of her critical thinking skills, the displaced detective decided to play with his fascination with her. She couldn't walk out of the room without anything more than what she currently had, which was circumstantial evidence. So, she asked herself, "If he walks, where would this leave Joy?" All she needed was a bit more time with this sociopath, and she'll find her person of interest. "Once I walk out of this room, Mister Richardson, you won't see me anymore," she insisted. "Do I have to repeat myself!" she exclaimed.

"Excuse me, Lieutenant, he's not going to talk to you," the attorney replied. Of course, his defense attorney was not privy to witnessing his client doting over her, with his tongue hanging out of his mouth, like a dog on a hot summer day.

He can't resist Lt. Drakon as much as a rooster can't resist crowing or as bees can't stop serving their queen. It was more than primitive carnal urges. His infatuation was out of lowliness. He can outlive any mistakes he has made here today. Rising years later as a phoenix from the ashes.

Mr. Richardson's aim was beyond his ambition to become president of the super powerful United States of America. His goal was to find a lifelong companion. So, he reached out for any chance he may have with the fledgling vampire. No matter how irrational his actions may seem right now, there was a logical reason for his madness. Besides, he's a big player in the city.

"Ok, I'll play along, Lieutenant," Mr. Richardson replied.

Lt. Drakon closed the door and sat back down–literally facing her demon. He was the culprit behind the evil that commit heinous crimes against the citizens of this great city. "Ok, what do you have for me?" she asked.

"Ahem, well, let's just say—"

"As your legal counsel, I advise that you not say anything, Mr. Richardson!" his lawyer exclaimed.

"My name is on your check, not the other way around," Mr. Richardson replied.

His lawyer remained quiet for the rest of the conversation Mr. Richardson had with the lieutenant, which didn't stop him from protesting in silence.

"What do you need to know?" he asked with a smug look on his face. "I am an open book Lt. Adeline Drakon."

"I need to know, where's Joy Maxwell, Mr. Richardson?"

"For the sake of argument, what if I knew where she was and I told you, what will I get in return?"

"I can talk to the DA's office and tell them about your cooperation in finding Ms. Maxwell."

"In other words, you can't do anything for me that I couldn't do for myself! Come on, Lieutenant, you are the only one I want to make a deal with–a proposal if you will," he said and deflected her charity. "I am above the law, Lieutenant; I am a billionaire who has been in this city for a very long time. I have been an important contributor in this city longer than most people can fathom. I can tell you that if this pans out for us, it will mean a lot. You can tell your subordinates behind the glass that I'm ready to cooperate."

The men in the surveillance room looked at each other in disbelief.

Adeline sat there expressionless, but a red flag waved high in the back of her mind. "Let's say I "Can" lead you to her, Lieutenant."

"Ok, I'm listening."

"Let's say something happened to come across my desk."

"Mr. Richardson, are you giving me hypothetical information? "If not, tell me directly where Joy Maxwell is located and who kidnapped her, so we can go get her before it is too late!" Lt. Drakon exclaimed. "You do know that withholding information in an ongoing investigation is a crime. Tell me how you obtained this information and why didn't you say something to the authorities."

"I am the CEO and president of the biggest news station in the nation, no scratch that the world," Mr. Richardson replied. "It's my job to obtain information. As for not saying anything, the info just came across my desk, and I think the kidnappers wanted to use my station as a platform to send a message. With that being said, I don't know why he, she, or they didn't just use the internet."

"How recently?"

"That's not important, Lieutenant, and you're not asking the obvious questions. I'm beginning to get offended; you're insulting my intelligence."

"Right, what is it you wanted again?"

"The ball is in your court, Lieutenant; we can move on or remain lost in an arbitrary argument."

"Am I supposed just to trust you?"

"You're not, but "Quid pro quo," Lieutenant; one hand washes the other. I will agree to whatever you want, now just let out!" Mr. Richardson exclaimed.

"Okay, after you get her back, I want the media with you," Lt. Drakon replied.

Mr. Richardson took out a pen from his inside breast pocket and scribbled the location of Joy Maxwell on a piece of paper.

Afterward, he folded the piece of paper and slowly slid it across the table. In a flash, Adeline launched out of her seat like a school kid going out for recess or on the last day of school before summer vacation.

"Are you formally charging my client?" Mr. Richardson's stout and dumpy lawyer attorney asked. "Because all your so-called evidence is purely circumstantial at best."

Annoyed at the sound of his high-priced lawyer's high-pitched screechy voice, Lt. Drakon halted by the doorway. She rolled her eyes, turned around, and snarled at him. She held the door open and spoke through her gritted teeth, "We read him his rights, counselor. It's just a matter of time before these charges stick to your client. I suggest you consider a plea bargain." She scoffed and shook her head before closing the door behind her.

"Make sure Mr. Bobby Richardson doesn't leave this room," Lt. Drakon ordered a uniformed officer to stand guard. "If he gives you any trouble, put him in the cage. I doubt it, though. He's got too much to lose."

Agent Henning flew out of the observation room first, followed by the captain and then the ADA.

"Where is she?" agent Henning asked. "Is she in the penthouse?"

"No, he gave another location," Lt. Drakon replied and gave the paper to the men to look at. "Is that enough to get a conviction?"

"You're good Lieutenant, this is the smoking gun we needed–this is an admission of guilt," the ADA replied.

"The fact that he knew the whereabouts of Ms. Maxwell is too much of a coincidence. For me, it shows some type of involvement. I don't know about you all, but I, for one, don't believe in coincidences."

"You got to admit that if he didn't kidnap Joy Maxwell, he knows something, and it's worth considering," agent Henning points out.

"Recently, we put in a request, and a judge Eilel denied it, citing we did not have definitive evidence for one," Lt. Drakon said. "We're going to need your help to run this past a judge so we can get warrants for both locations."

"What address was that?" the ADA replied.

"It doesn't matter, write it down!" agent Henning exclaimed.

The ADA sighed and flubbered his lips before he took out his fountain pen from his lapel. "This is a long shot. But I'm putting my personal feelings aside to help solve this case even though Mr.

Richardson is innocent," he said. "I don't even know why

I'm getting involved in something like this. If this all blows up your faces and he file a defamation suit against the city for slander– it leaves my name out of it. By the way, what judge did you go to?"

"I went to judge Eilel," captain Constantine replied.

"See, there's your issue, Judge Eilel. Even though he uses computers and such, he's old school. He's wearied about computers. Let me try, and I'll go to another judge," the ADA assured them. "In the meantime, station your men at both locations, and it'll be a good idea to put a B.O.L.O, just in case."

"Give me that address, you two, go to the penthouse," captain Constantine ordered.

"Hope we find her alive," agent Henning said as he and Lt. Drakon walked away.

They went above and beyond the scope of the call of duty in their search for Joy. She became closer to them through the whole murder investigation more than all of them had expected. For Lt. Drakon, Joy Maxwell has grown on her, enough for a budding friendship to grab hold of her dead heart: where the curse of the blood demon has crept in and stopped everything that made her feel alive. At times, she found herself in a pit of desperation, grabbing onto hopeful strands of sound relationships in her life.

When Lt. Drakon strived for anything–she went all-out not only for a small measure of human connection. In some ways, she held their friendship in high reverence because it kept the evil whispers of blood cravings at bay. She dreaded having to down pints of warm blood from an unsuspecting soul, like a morning latte.

Thoughts of this carnal desire sent waves of mixed-up emotions up and down her spine.

Ironically, the same feelings that she tried so desperately to avoid are the same feeling that made her feel alive again. The

317

stranger decided to follow orders and kill Joy Maxwell against his longing for companionship and better judgment. He moved her out of the penthouse, trekking her to a second location. She was still in a daze, controlled by the stranger's hypnotic spell, followed him without resistance.

The stranger told the young reporter, "If I had it my way, my Childe, we would not be taking this trip. We would be leaving, running away together." He displayed a sinister smile and said, "A full contrast, throughout the centuries of fighting and hiding in the shadows, only coming out to hunt, now on the brink of shining light into the shadow."

Survival has deadened the stranger. It's the reason for his crass demeanor. Burdened by the curse of being a vampire has contributed to his hardened exterior. Loneliness seeped through his voice as he expressed himself to her.

Joy sat beside him deep in a trance, a deadpan gaze, looking out into space, oblivious to the happenings of her impending death. They were in the back of his limousine with blacked-out windows, camouflaged from the crowds' peering eyes. Indeed, tucked away from the dragnet of the police, who has eyes out for them.

The stranger ran his long-jagged claws through his captive's hair, strumming the strains with his pale hand like a violinist on the strings of a viola. His nails were as sharp as a warrior's sword, which have seen many battles.

The stranger has disturbingly daunted over Joy like a creepy loner. But as an outcast, he struggled with relating to her humanity because he's a sociopath who covets love and craves attention. He has created a fantasy world for her, where they would live together as one for all eternity. His infatuation for her has laid dormant in is his mind since he learned of her existence. He has coveted the idea of her being in his possession, being careful not to ruin the chance that she'd eventually return the sentiment. He's been watchful over her, treating her like a porcelain doll–mindful that one false move could break her. If that happens then, his fantasy would be lost forever.

While the limo zipped down the highway to Joy Maxwell's last destination, an interesting development has presented itself back at the precinct. The captain waited patiently for agent Henning and Lt. Drakon to return with Joy. He chose to seize the moment and found himself in the interrogation room with Mr. Richardson. "Mr. Richardson, since your lawyer has gone, you and I can have a heart to heart," he said.

The pale vampire elder remained tolerant of this charade; he adjusted in his seat, and the light refracted off his catlike eyes.

"What is it, Captain?" he asked. "I haven't heard from you for a while. I know you didn't have any part in jamming me up like this. I know that you must play "The role" and that's fine. But I must warn you; you don't know who you're dealing with."

The captain loosened his collar, pulled out the chair, and sat down at the other end of the cold metal table. "The only thing I want to talk to you about is your reasons for sending out a hit squad on my precinct: where your creations killed my officers?"

"Captain, am I being recorded?"

"No, this conversation is off the record!"

"You see, therein lies the problem, with all humanity—you're incapable of making real sacrifices. Unlike most vampires, I was born as I am, so I haven't had the pleasure to feel as you do. Maybe that is why you mortals are short-sighted, which results in your conceit."

Captain Constantine let the insults roll off his back like water on a duck. Arguing with Mr. Richardson would be short-sighted, and time was a luxury he couldn't afford.

Both men sat across from each other like two gunslingers dueling at high noon.

The captain's cell phone rang. He took it out of his pocket, and it was from the senator of New York. He turned his body around and answered the call. It was a brief conversation, and his expression told of what had transpired during the call.

Mr. Richardson smirked and said, "I'm going to take a shot in the dark and assume that you were just given direct orders for my release."

The captain sighed and replied, "Ahem, very perceptive. You must have friends in high places."

His cell phone rang again, and the name of the director of the CIA flashed on the screen. He put the phone back in his pocket, got up abruptly, and the chair toppled over. "This isn't over!" he exclaimed and stormed towards the exit.

"Dammit, I wouldn't be surprised if he got a pardon from all charges, as the arrest didn't even happen," the captain thought to himself.

Devoid of fear of any kind, Mr. Richardson said, "It's not what you think it is, Captain. I decided to wipe out all ties when I jumped in the mayoral race, you know. I need to start with a clean slate, so to speak."

The words he spoke made Captain Constantine uneasy.

Bobby Richardson adjusted in his chair and rubbed his hands together. "I can sense the sudden fear rising off you like steam from a pot. Don't tell me, I did not make a mistake leaving you alive, did I! If you don't betray me or cross me, you shouldn't have anything to fret about," he said and displayed his fangs.

The captain couldn't help it, but a terrible fright began

to overtake him. Afraid for his life, he hurried out of the interrogation room. Captain Constantine rushed to his office to grab a drink to calm his nerves. "I hope I am not on the list; I am not willing to sacrifice anything more," he thought to himself.

The captain was a police officer at this department for a long-time. He has sacrificed so much; anymore, and he would have to give up everything he has worked so hard to achieve.

Captain Constantine placed his head firmly into his hands. His mind was heavy with worry, partly because of his guilt. Desperate to be an instrument of something bigger than himself. He allowed his ambitions, selfishness, and chase for immortality, momentarily blind him from what was necessary. Above all else, his essential work as a police officer, brothers, and family came first. "I promised the Lord, I will spend the rest of my life making up for my transgressions," he declared.

His cell phone rang again, and the ADA's name flashed across the screen. He pressed the talk button and put the call on speaker.

"Captain, I just wanted to inform you that we got the warrants," the ADA said. "This is the end we got him."

Captain Constantine sunk in his chair and sighed. Then a sudden burst of energy surge through his body. He perked up in his chair and slammed his hand on the desk. He pressed end on the phone, opened the office door, and announced, "Listen up! We are on the move, people; this is not a drill. I need all available officers to the pier. We have an arrest warrant and, from a very reliable source, a possible location of our suspect.

The captain leaned on the banister overlooking the bay and continued, "Let's go, people. This is not a drill. The S.W.A.T team has already mobilized. This is the golden calf people – if anyone encounters the *Sanguine killer*, approach with extreme caution.

Remember, he has a hostage, Joy Maxwell, in tow, plus he doesn't show any respect for law enforcement. I want everyone to come back in one piece. Move, Move, Move!"

The officers jumped up and rushed to their cars for a showdown. Sirens blared, and tires screeched as they rolled out one by one, weaving through traffic toward the pier.

Captain Constantine mulled over every single standard operation in his head like strategies in a chess game. He anticipated all the complications, possible moves, and different scenarios the standoff could go. While he was on the way to his car, he stopped short while two intimidating figures with muscular builds approached him.

At first glance, he believed the department was under attack again. Until a third less menacing man peered into view behind them. "He looks familiar," the captain thought to himself. "Isn't that the Senator of New York state!"

"Sorry for the intrusion Captain Constantine. You're a smart guy. You can figure out why I'm here," the Senator said.

"No, Senator Cross, I can't say that I can. In my line of work, I learned a long time ago not to assume anything. So, if you'll excuse me, I don't have to play the guessing games," the captain replied.

"I'm here to ensure the release of Mr. Richardson."

The captain's face wrinkled up in complete perplexity. "Senator Cross, I seriously doubt you are aware of what charges we have against Mr. Richardson. I seriously doubt you are aware of what long list of indictments he has racked up here. Or the full extent of what the risks are if I release him."

"I am not warming up to the resistance here, Captain. Let me make things crystal clear, do you think a man like me in my position could afford to be careless and make a miscalculated move? I'm a United States Senator–a position well above your pay grade. If that's not good enough, I have a document for the immediate release of Bobby Richardson, Signed by Judge Eilel himself!"

The seasoned veteran held his tongue as he reached for the release form for the senator. The complex notions of the old blood demon's political or financial influence ran through his mind, like a track star running the fifty-yard dash. He gazed at the document, shook his head, and said to himself, "The CEO is above the law." He gestured, then told the nearest cop to open the door and release the elder vampire.

The elder blood demon strolled past the captain and winked at him. He felt the weight of defeat pressing down on his neck, like a foot crushing a tiny insect, wiping it out of existence. The triviality of his efforts was apparent. In all his years of service, it clicked. He realized that all the gears that churned between the law and the criminals in the city.

He folded the release form and pushed it in his breast pocket. Then the steady commander walked forward to his destiny.

Lt. Drakon and agent Henning arrived at the SGNN luxury high rise with backup. The other team headed down to the pier, per Captain's orders. She jumped out and swung the car door closed behind her. She barked orders, dispatching the reinforcements in place as she stormed the building.

Agent Henning chased closely behind, accompanied by an FBI unit, relinquishing the charge to the hand that initially offended him.

"Secure all the exits, do not let anyone out. I don't want to take any chances to let this monster escape again!" Lt. Drakon exclaimed.

Many officers answered in the affirmative. Some of their

voices trembled. The trepidation embedded in their words was evident. Her subordinates in the department still felt a little shaky about taking orders from the lieutenant.

Lt. Drakon sensed their apprehension, but there wasn't time to reassure anyone. Not because she was a woman, but the lieutenant had a reputation of not keeping partners for a long time. In the years she's been on the force, she has partnered up with eleven other officers. Three out of the eleven officers lost their lives on duty in that span, and somehow, she walked away each time unscathed. Internal affairs cleared the lieutenant in every case.

"What's the matter with everyone?" agent Henning asked after they breached the building.

Lt. Drakon gave a summary describing the reasons why the other officers may have a tiny problem with her.

The security guard that sat behind the desk in the lobby looking at the monitors; protested until one of the officers reassured him of the team's reason for the intrusion. The agent flashed his badge, then gave a little explanation for all the commotion.

As the unit prepared themselves to breach the penthouse doors, they were unaware of what awaited them on the other side.

The officers double-checked their equipment and synchronized their wits and minds in one accord. They were aware that any missteps with this dangerous killer–even suited in full battle gear; could result in dire consequences.

Lieutenant Drakon leads the team, and agent Henning took the rear as the team geared up with the battering ram. She put her hand in the air and counted down: three, two, one. When she held her fist in the air, the tactical team knocked the door off its hinges.

Boom! An explosion blew the men apart; the door disintegrated into pieces. She used her quick supernatural reflexes, grabbed the back of his shirt, and pulled him completely out of harm's way. Dust, smoke, blood spatter, body parts, and pieces of protective gear filled the corridor.

With all the commotion, agent Henning's ears rang, and he coughed insistently. He searched around the hallway for survivors of the blast. He shuttered at the gruesome sight of more fallen comrades at the hand of the *Sanguine killer*. "How the hell did she move so fast," he said. "A normal human being couldn't have done that, especially not a female of her height and build."

While Lt. Drakon tended to the wounded, she made a call over the radio. "10-59, explosion, multiple officers down, buses needed at my location, hurry!"

"How many?" asked dispatch.

"Three, the rest are dead," she screamed in the radio. Quick to her feet, she gently rested the head of one of her comrades on the ground and said, "I need to go and see if Joy is inside. Are you going to be alright here?"

He shook his head and gave the lieutenant the thumbs up.

She gave the signal to agent Henning as he tended to the wounded, and he said in between coughs, "Yeah, go ahead."

Lt. Drakon sprang into action and pulled her weapon as she crept through the gaping hole to the doorway. A familiar voice said, "I hope that bitch was blown to pieces!"

As she crouched up against the wall, she projected her answer in the direction from which it came. "Is that you, Sgt. Mason?" she asked. "Of course, you wouldn't be dead. How about this, put your head out, just your head so that I can lay my sights on you."

Sergeant Mason sat in the back of the magnificent living room, marking the time until he laid his eyes on anyone who entered so that he could blast them to smithereens.

"Where did we go wrong?" Lt. Drakon asked. "What could I have possibly done that was so wrong for you to want to kill me?"

"Nothing, you're just in my way," Sgt. Mason replied. "I can't get what I want until your brains are laid out all over the floor. The problem is you won't flipping die."

"I can assure you that you won't get the chance to hurt me again. The last thing I want is, as you so colorfully put it, my brains splattered all over the floor." Her voice echoed through the immense void.

The heated exchange between the two consisted of harsh words followed by rapid-fire from their police-issue Glock 22 pistol.

Lt. Drakon ceased fire and realized that this might just be a diversion. "She's not here is she!" she exclaimed as she hoped for the best but prepared for the worst.

"Look at you–I guess that's why you made lieutenant," Sgt. Mason replied. He stood up and aimed his gun in the direction of the sound behind the wall.

Lt. Drakon's body pressed up against the wall for protection, with her gun raised, locked, and loaded. She was filled with determination to capture her would-be murderer. So, she chose to talk her former partner down peacefully without adding to the casualties.

"You still haven't told me why you wanted to kill me? You have gone to great lengths to achieve that goal: you transferred to my department, you befriended me, gained my trust, and tried to squirm your way into the private parts of my life, only to stab me in my back. The creepy part is, how the hell did you know so much about me? I'm almost positive that it's no coincidence that you were assigned my partner out of all the detectives in the precinct," she said.

Sgt. Mason smiled and said, "Inquiring minds want to know."

With the arrival of the EMT's agent, Henning crept up behind the lieutenant. "How do you want to approach this," he asked. "Their deeds measure men, but their convictions measure most."

While extraordinary feats of bravery unusually gauge others," Lt. Drakon replied and smiled.

Agent Henning couldn't allow Sgt. Mason to hurt the love of his life again. He raised his weapon in preparation to move on the offensive.

Lt. Drakon gazed into agent Henning's eyes and saw everything that she needed to see. Questions in her head about him, their relationship, and his ability to handle her change diminished to nothing. The only thing left to test was how he would take the news of her being a vampire. This information weighed heavy on the fledgling blood demon's mind.

Agent Henning charged and blasted away at the fugitive Sergeant, hitting him a few times.

Sgt. Mason returned fire, armed with the abilities of a cursed vampire, wounded the agent.

Lt. Drakon ran to his rescue, sacrificing her own body to try and stop the barrage of bullets from hitting their intended target. She wore a bulletproof vest, but the shots were armor-piercing bullets, so they all went through and through. But her efforts at least slowed their speed and weakened their force.

Sgt. Mason reloaded and continued firing nonstop until it dawned on him that he was shooting at a full-fledged blood demon.

"How ironic," he thought to himself. "I killed Adaline Drakon to fulfil my ambitions on becoming a vampire, and she became a blood demon because I killed her." he snickered and turned his head to the side, and warm blood trickled down his neck.

Seconds before his last breath escaped his limp body, Lt. Drakon pounced on Sgt. Mason retracted her fangs, and bit him. She ravaged him, drank her fill to feed her hunger and heal her wounds. The minute she felt whole again, she dropped Sgt. Mason's body and emerged as a fully transformed blood demon.

She glanced out the large windows overlooking the sunset betwixt the skyline. The gruesome scene of everything inside the penthouse mirrored off the tempered glass except for her reflection. Her blood-soaked tattered clothes barely covered the bullet holes in her torso.

Lt. Drakon forgot about agent Henning who laid unconscious on the floor behind her. She licked the blood from the corners of her mouth and wiped what she couldn't reach with her shirt sleeves.

She whirred over to agent Henning and ripped the vest from his torso to check his wounds. "Get in here, officer down!" she yelled. She transformed back into her mortal form and repeated the statement until an EMT, and a Paramedic came rushing inside to help. "Oh my God, he saved my life. Hurry, he's been shot seven times," she said.

"Are you alright?" the medics asked in unison, surprised by the sight of her.

"Yes, this is not my blood, I am ok–help him!" Lt. Drakon exclaimed.

She perked up when she thought about the puncture wounds that the Paramedics would find on the neck of Sgt. Mason. "Dammit,

nice job, Adeline; that will raise a lot of questions," she thought to herself.

"What's the strange puncture wounds on his neck? Detective,

detective!" the Paramedic exclaimed.

His words sounded inaudible to the grief-struck lieutenant; her focus was on agent Henning. "Please, don't leave me! Please don't die on me!" she said.

"Will you be riding with your partner?" the Paramedic asked.

Lt. Drakon wiped away her tears and said, "Yes, I mean no. I can't, and I have to stay here to secure the scene."

"Lieutenant, I think he's going to be fine. The bullets pierced his skin, but not deep enough to be life-threatening," the EMT said as he checked for vital signs. "So, you don't have to worry."

"That's comforting, thank you," Lt. Drakon replied, then she backed away from agent Henning to give the emergency team space to work on him.

As they hoisted the injured agent on the gurney, her father entered the room. He arrived in the nick of time, right into the embodiment of a well of carnage. ME and senior CSI Dr. German captured every aspect of the bloody occurrence. In one quick scan, he chronicled everything that went down, including her fang impressions on the neck of Sgt. Mason.

He rushed to the body, picked up two shell casings, and inserted them into the bite marks. "You got to be more careful," he said.

Lt. Drakon crotched beside her grandfather and whispered, "I wouldn't have to be careful if you didn't make me into this thing," she replied.

Her phone rang as her words shot out of her mouth like poisonous darts. "Where are you?" she asked.

"We are in hot pursuit; we believe the suspect has Ms. Maxwell in a limousine out in front of us!" a voice screamed on the other end.

"Where do you think he's heading?"

"Looks like he's driving southbound on the Henry Hudson."

"I think I know where he's going. Meet me at the North Cove Marina. The *Sanguine Killer* has connections to that slick old goat Bobby Richardson. He's going to the yacht he has on the pier; we have to get him before he gets out in open water." Lt. Drakon hung up the phone and turned to her grandfather. "You can handle this, right?" she asked.

"Yes, but we need to have a serious talk," Dr. German replied, looked up, and she was gone.

"I don't think she'd ever get over this," CSI Madrigal said and shook his head.

Under the clear night sky, the police sirens echoed through the streets. The red and blue lights flashed and bounced off the storefronts and skyrises as they pursued the limousine carrying the blood demon and Joy.

The closer the terrified vampire got to the marina, the more he felt the pressure of disappointing the vampire elder.

The flashing police lights burned like hot oil as they maintained a close distance behind the fleeing vampire and his prized possession. The chances of his freedom looked slim. Now the idea of Joy being by his side under her own volition seemed like a foregone conclusion.

Although a blood demon has little to no conscience, logically speaking, loneliness can affect even the strongest-willed person, intense enough to turn the mind of even a supernatural being insane.

It could render a man helpless, succumbing to his impressions of reality, locked in an impregnable prison.

With his clan scattered, the fear of being captured drove the stranger to willingly convince Joy to run away with him.

Joy put her hand on her temple; her head spun around like it was on a swivel. Fresh out of her trance, she was disoriented and unaware of her surroundings. Her eyes doubled in size as she closed the front of her sheer robe. "Where am I?" she asked. "Why are we in a limousine." She recognized the pale blood demon and said, "I am not sure what's going on here, Stranger—W…what do you want from me?"

The vampire softened his features and reached for Joy's hand.

Joy moved away from him and said, "You couldn't possibly think after you kidnapped me…" her voice cracked under the strain of emotions.

"The only expectations a person can have on another is a decision. You know me–the true me, the one and only me that has feelings for you. I'm fighting against my true nature, my love. You're killing my eternally stunted heartbeat with your indecisiveness. So, as I bare it all to you, all I expect from you is a natural response," the blood demon replied with a raspy voice. "I haven't had the honor of being human, but I do know one thing—"

"Yeah, what's that?"

The limousine sped down the Westside highway zipping through traffic underneath the clear night sky. Joy had a good idea of what the stranger was getting at. She just couldn't bring herself to feel for a man. She was not at all a man. Especially since he caused so much turmoil and strife in her life and took her against her will.

"As crazy as it may sound to you, I am aware of the hell I put you through, my sweet. But all the tall tell signs–whether you realize it or not, you have communicated all you want to say without saying it. In my experience, my understanding of human nature is you care me as much as I do for you," he expressed. "Although what I'm asking of you may be farfetched, a connection such as ours is

331

electric and shouldn't be ignored. Come away with me, and the world would be yours. Whatever you decide, you need to do it now."

"I haven't the slightest idea what you mean. Should I forget about everything you've done to so many innocent people, huh? Am I supposed to fall madly in love with a murderous immortal being, hmm? I don't even know your name; you're a stranger to me–A darn Vampire, for Christ's sake."

Still, like his breath, the stranger considered this moment. When he spoke it, his words danced in the air. First, he reverted to a more natural and a more human-like form. "I haven't been in this form in a very long time," he said. His claws and fangs retracted, his eyes changed to a deep yet golden brown, even the skin tone softened then shifted to a darker hue.

Joy's eyes widened, and she blushed. "He's gorgeous!" she thought to herself. Then the twinkle in her eyes dimmed when she wondered why he hadn't he showed her this form before now.

"I haven't taken this form a while. I experienced my awakening almost 150 years ago, and I know that taking this form leaves me defenseless," he said. "Otherwise, I am immune to pain, both physically and emotionally. I promised myself that I would never be left open to love again. Living with the blood demon curse makes us strong, invincible, and impervious to the cruelty of humankind.

"When I'm like this, I'm susceptible to mortal weaponry as well as human emotions. So, there my precious Childe, I bared my all to you at your behest. Where're my manners? Allow me to introduce myself. My name is Easton Richardson properly."

The stranger took Joy's hand and pressed his lips gently upon her ivory skin.

The limo stopped, the partition lowered, and the driver said in a monotone voice, "We're here, Master." With the police close behind, the driver, a neomort member of his vampire coven, said, "Make haste Master, head to the yacht; I'll hold them off."

"We must go," the stranger turned to Joy, lifted her into arms, and dashed to the luxury watercraft. She felt a wisp of air on her ears and the tip of her nose as they zipped down the boardwalk. It took him all of five seconds to run down the marina. Then he quickly prepared to set sail.

Something didn't sit well with the inquisitive reporter. Joy crossed her arms curled her lips. "Easton Richardson!" she exclaimed.

Her pitch gave the impression that something was wrong.

The stranger stopped, slightly turned his head, and asked, "What's the matter?"

"Are related to my boss, Robert Dasa Richardson III, the CEO of SGNN, the biggest news media conglomerate in the world?"

She looked him right in his brown eyes as the police cars closed in on them.

"Yes, yes I am. He's, my father."

Despair filled the air as the police sirens screamed in the night sky. The red and blue lights danced off the mirrored surfaces illuminating the interior of the yacht.

The cops stopped at the entrance of the pier on the far side of the limousine. They hopped out of their squad cars and aimed at the boat was bobbing up and down in the water.

Flashbacks of Joy's time at SGNN flew throughout her mind. She trained her thoughts on details but couldn't narrow it down to a specific event that was most significant to her during her tenure there. She laid her heavy head into her hands and said, "I can't believe I couldn't see this all along. Mr. Richardson orchestrated this whole thing from the very beginning. He's the mastermind behind the *Midtown Murders*. He created the *Sanguine Killer* and, and—"

"I don't mean to rush you, but we're running out of time. What will you decide? Do you want to go away with me or stay here with the police?"

While they remained on the dock like sitting ducks in a pond, the stranger awaited Joy's decision.

Lt. Drakon sped to Joy and Easton on the pier at breakneck speed. "Let her go. You don't have to kill anymore!" she shouted, with her gun brandished and pointed at the stranger.

Hidden behind baggy clothing and a hoody, The *Sanguine Killer* transformed into his more formidable blood demon form–as easy as turning on a light switch.

The police got into position along the pier; three snipers posted at different sights on the port. One of whom includes sergeant Vickers, head of the S.W.A.T team, had a rifle aimed at its intended target.

Harbour patrol blocked the neck of the marina.

"We're surrounded, Master," the neomort shouted from outside of the limousine.

Every possible scenario flashed through Lt. Drakon's mind as she struggled to choose the right one. An apparent standoff loomed over the fledgling detective's head. She pondered on the events that led up to this point. The pressure built upon her shoulders like steam in a boiler and was ready to spew. She wondered how she would apprehend the suspect and save Joy's life without losing any more of her fellow officer's lives.

The snipers had the suspect in their sights and radioed into the lieutenant. "We have a clear shot, ready to fire on your command."

Joy jumped out in front of the stranger, waved her hands in

the air, and said, "No, don't kill him."

Lt. Drakon removed her finger off the trigger with a puzzling expression all over her face yelled over the radio, "Everyone stands down! I repeat, stand down! We can't risk shooting Ms. Maxwell; if there's an open shot–take him out, stay on track."

Annoyed, the lieutenant walked out in the open with her hands held up in the air and yelled, "Joy, what in God's name are you doing?"

"I'm confused. Why's Joy protecting him?" she said to herself.

Joy stood there with her arms outstretched, and the heavy wind blew her hair and rob to the side. "I know you think I am crazy; I can see it written on all your faces," Joy said.

Captain Constantine has pulled his sidearm and crept up behind the lieutenant.

"I am not crazy; I believe everyone has the right to live!" Joy exclaimed. "Besides, I have questions that nobody has answered. I know that if you kill him, I won't get the answers I seek."

Easton sensed the tension and threw his hands up in the air to quell the situation. He heard everyone's heartbeat slow down a little, except for the S.W.A.T team's leader.

The captain feared that the blood demon would oust him, so he fidgeted as he steadied his firearm. No matter how small or short the time, it's a strike against him. Although he's a small cog in the big machine, a man in his position played a big part in the vampire agenda.

Captain Constantine betrayed his friends, his city, and the people of New York city he swore to protect and serve. He went against his duties to the department he was appointed to lead.

All his years of good service would go down the drain by his misguided decisions. Trapped between the light and the darkness, Captain Constantine chose to side with the blood demons against his better judgment.

Joy turned her back around and faced Easton. "Why me?" she asked. "Weren't you sent to kill me like the others?"

"That doesn't matter, Ms. Maxwell. You're different, I...I love you; at the end of the day, you made me feel whole again."

Calculated and concise with his words, the stranger looked deep into Joy's eyes and caressed her cheek with the back of his hand. He turned around and said, "You are all in danger, each one of you because of what you know." The stranger zeroed in on the captain, and then he smirked when he realized how he knew him.

The captain walked away from Lt. Drakon and radioed the snipers hidden in various locations along the pier to be ready to take the shot.

"Joy, my delicate blooming flower, whether you realize it or not, you know something that can potentially put an end to a plan—a plan that has been into the works for a millennium," the stranger said.

"I haven't the slightest idea what you're getting at," Joy replied.

Lt. Drakon heard the chatter on the radio with her sensitive superior vampire ears.

"What are we waiting for, huh?" asked a uniformed cop.

"We don't need to hear what he has to say!" exclaimed a S.W.A.T team member.

"It burns my bridges that weren't shooting this heartless cop murdering serial killer," a sniper remarked.

Members of the S.W.A.T team and other officers were

getting antsy. The standoff stirred up the anger of all the law enforcement personnel looking on, FBI and police officers alike.

Lt. Drakon thought, "He can't go to jail, at least not a regular one. How can I explain that he is not to have any human contacts, ever?"

"We have a shot, Captain!" the S.W.A.T team leader exclaimed over the radio.

The captain put the walkie-talkie down and took a moment to think before he responded. "I wonder if the other officers heard my secret?" he said to himself, then he said, "Wait for my signal. I don't want anyone of you trigger happy sons of bitches to shoot Ms. Maxwell neither, so be careful!"

The captain put down the walkie-talkie and yelled, "Listen up, come out from behind Ms. Maxwell with your hands up. You're surrounded, son. Surrender now, and I promise to take you downtown safe and sound. We can finish this little talk at the police––"

"You're talking in circles, Captain. You're not saying much of anything," Lt. Drakon said. "What's the meaning of all this? I mean, you murdered people throughout the city in cold blood–for what? You didn't accomplish anything, you lowlife. You're surrounded, and the only thing you can talk about is some old-ass plan of yours. Come on, if you're going to open that mouth of yours, go ahead and say what we all want to know. You said something about the captain––"

"Don't try to rile this creature up, Lieutenant," captain Constantine said.

"You don't understand. Revealing the truth here can get us killed," the stranger said. "There are many among us tonight who are pawns in this big scheme. Much like the Captain, I've moved away from following this evil plot. Redemption was in my heart – but––"

"Good, so you can tell us what's the reason for all this," Joy asked.

Altered by his need for Joy to like him, he continued spilling his guts about Joy and why the tape had to be retrieved. The contents of that video were important enough to kill. "You see, while on the campaign trail, my dad was filmed along with a big powerful vampire ancient when Ms. Maxwell covered the dog show.

"Who is he?" Joy asked.

"A tape! A tape! I can't believe anyone's life was worth losing because of a flipping tape," the captain bellowed. "I witnessed the death of my fellow police officers, and I had to bury one of my dearest friends.

"People died! I died!" Lt. Drakon screamed. "Why me?

"Why sacrifice all those innocent people? What's the meaning of all of this?"

"One day, we all fall into the abyss, and death becomes us all. Seeing we're all doomed to that fate, my ride ends here," the stranger replied. "Fear isn't a human emotion I could relate to; I've been emotionally stunted for centuries. Death is a burden that man alone must bear. There are rules to abide by, and even I understand what lines not to cross and where to stop. And still, there are doors that I dare not open. So, I won't speak the name of the feared one in mixed company. He plans to eradicate this world and harvest humans as the prime food source. Yet I'm torn between his ambitions and the love that has engulfed my soulless body."

The officers all stood around the pier, frozen with their guns by their sides.

The stranger, Easton Richardson, changed form, raised his hand in the air, and pointed in the distance. He set his mouth to say the name of the unmentioned one to rid himself from his burden like a snake shedding skin. But the name remained in his throat like a bone from an oven-baked branzino.

The S.W.A.T sergeant got technical support from a friend in the department to tap into the captain's phone. Sergeant Vickers was appalled overheard him say code "Three six," which was a code for his secret team to go on a secure channel. The captain had made a call and got the green light to shoot to kill. He instructed the team to shoot on his mark, targeting all three people standing on the pier.

Before the stranger could reveal who was behind it all, enlighten Joy and Lt. Drakon of their relevance; the captain's team leader gave the signal to shoot. Without hesitation. The snipers opened fire. The bullets' trajectory surged through the air, bound for its mark.

In a flash, the stranger pulled Joy out of harm's way with him into the water. She never had a chance to decide whether she wanted to go with him and lumber through eternity or stay and face her mortality.

The neomort was riddled with bullets because he moved in the way of the shots to protect his master. "Please forgive me; I tried my best to…"

Lieutenant Drakon shifted to shield the captain, but her efforts were futile. A bullet went through her arm and lodged into captain Constantine's side, piercing his heart. His eyes rolled back in his head and dropped to the ground, and he groaned in pain.

"Hold your fire!" she yelled. "He's hit! The captain's hit!"

Some police officers and FBI agents alike immediately scrambled to their side, instinctively returning cover fire in the direction where the shots were fired. S.W.A.T team members made a search for the *Sanguine Killer*.

"Officer down, bus needed," several officers called over the radio. The rest went directly on the yacht but didn't find any sign of the stranger or Joy.

Harbor patrol searched the harbor with searchlights. Soon after, divers dived in to find their bodies. Three minutes had gone by, and none of the men surfaced yet. Bubbles froth on the surface of the murky Hudson River and swirling lights from the boats focused on the area where the men descended into the deep.

With her mentor dying in her arms, Lt. Drakon watched as the captain gasped for air. She listened to the gurgling as blood filled his lungs. She attempted CPR, but his heartbeat slowed with each compression. "Fight, Captain! Don't you dare give up on me!" she exclaimed.

"It's alright, my dear Adeline," the captain said. "Let me go, and that's an order, Lieutenant. It's my time to..."

Most of the other officers looked away while he took his last few breaths. The otherwise macho men looked away, many couldn't stomach seeing their boss–their leader, and in some cases, good friend, suffer like that. The only one who remained composed was the only female cop.

Lt. Drakon held on to the captain until he was gone. There was not a dry face on any officer or agent except for the blood demon cop herself. She was too numb by all that has happened to her or the vampire blood coursing through her veins. She wouldn't allow herself to break down. She laid Captain Constantine's lifeless body down on the pier and stood up.

Ambulances pulled up on the pier and stopped behind the limousine. EMTs and Paramedics jumped out and ran to aid the fallen officer, but it was seconds too late.

"He's gone," Lt. Drakon said and walked with her head down by the medics on her way to her car.

Lt. Drakon reached for her phone with a bloody hand and called her grandfather. She told him that she forgave him for what he'd done to her. She understood the reasoning behind his decision. She said, "I love you, Grandfather!" Then she ended the call.

She sighed and dropped her hands down to her lap. Her fingers inadvertently pressed agent Henning's contact on the screen.

"Hello! Hello, Adeline?" agent Henning said.

The voice of the man that she'd reluctantly grown to love calmed her nerves. Lt. Drakon fiddled with the phone then said softly, almost like a whisper, "Hello, how are you feeling?" she asked. The beat of his heart, the cadence of his breathing, was music to her ears. It motivated her not to let go. Above all the chaos and loads of crap in her life

"I am alright, just a few bumps and bruises–but I'll live."

"I'm glad to hear that." She smiled and put her hand over her mouth to hold in the laughter.

"What happened? Did we get that bastard or save Ms. Maxwell?"

Lt. Drakon held on to his gruff manly voice. She remained silent before responding. "No, no, we didn't, and Captain Constantine is dead."

"I am sorry, I know how much he meant to you, and Joy was your friend. Do you wanna talk about it?" agent Henning asked.

"Yeah, but not right now; I'll explain everything to you later."

"Okay, great, you could tell me everything over dinner. When was the last time you had a home-cooked meal?"

Lost in her feelings, Lt. Drakon deemed it necessary often to avoid and evade. "Y…yeah, sure, that sounds like a plan–I'm famished. I'll come and pick you up right now."

Agent Henning hopped out of his hospital bed and got ready for Lt. Drakon to come to pick him up. His phone rang, and he answered it.

"Special agent Henning," a man on the other end asked. "Is it done?"

Fear rippled throughout his essence even though he had not heard this voice in ages. He didn't recognize it immediately, but he remembered how his kind was tortured and placed under an oppressive servitude, enslaved, and forcefully bonded for centuries.

Agent Henning stood up straight and cleared his throat. "No, not yet, my Lord,' he replied. A lump filled his throat with despair as he anticipated further instructions.

"When can I expect results?"

"She's like her mother, an iron bird, hard to kill; despite all my efforts, she survived attempts at her life. Against insurmountable odds, she still stands."

"I don't have to tell you how long the plan has taken to reach this point; it has almost come to fruition. Bobby Richardson has failed horribly. As soon as his usefulness comes to an end, so will he. He's on a list that you don't want to be on," the ominous voice said.

"Yes, my lord," he replied.

"Please quit with the formalities."

Agent Henning inhaled deeply until his lungs filled with air. He exhaled, then he said, "Of course, Sir, you have my word, Mr. Drakon."

Made in the USA
Middletown, DE
26 August 2023

37317324R00195